"Am

A new novel of the unbreakable bonds of friendship and the undeniable strength of true love from Nora Roberts.

#1 *New York Times* bestselling author Nora Roberts cordially invites you to meet childhood friends Parker, Emma, Laurel, and Mac—the founders of Vows, one of Connecticut's premier wedding planning companies.

Laurel McBane has always relied on her friends for support, especially when her dream of attending culinary school was almost ruined by her parents' financial problems. Now Laurel is repaying the kindness of her friends by creating extravagantly luscious tiers of cakes and other confectionary delights that add the perfect touch to their clients' weddings.

As for romance, Laurel believes in it—*in theory*. But she's too low-key to appreciate all the luxuries that other women seem to long for. What she does appreciate is a strong, intelligent man, a man just like Parker's older brother, Delaney Brown, on whom Laurel has had a mega crush since childhood.

But some infatuations last longer than others, and Laurel is convinced that the Ivy League lawyer is still out of her reach. Plus, Del is too protective of Laurel to ever cross the line with her, or so she thinks. When Laurel's quicksilver moods get the better of her—leading to an angry, hot, altogether mind-blowing kiss with Del—she'll have to quiet the doubts in her mind to turn a moment of passion into forever . . .

Nora Roberts

HOT ICE	THE REEF
SACRED SINS	RIVER'S END
BRAZEN VIRTUE	CAROLINA MOON
SWEET REVENGE	THE VILLA
PUBLIC SECRETS	MIDNIGHT BAYOU
GENUINE LIES	THREE FATES
CARNAL INNOCENCE	BIRTHRIGHT
DIVINE EVIL	NORTHERN LIGHTS
HONEST ILLUSIONS	BLUE SMOKE
PRIVATE SCANDALS	ANGELS FALL
HIDDEN RICHES	HIGH NOON
TRUE BETRAYALS	TRIBUTE
MONTANA SKY	BLACK HILLS
SANCTUARY	THE SEARCH
HOMEPORT	

Series

Irish Born Trilogy

BORN IN FIRE
BORN IN ICE
BORN IN SHAME

Key Trilogy

KEY OF LIGHT
KEY OF KNOWLEDGE
KEY OF VALOR

Dream Trilogy

DARING TO DREAM
HOLDING THE DREAM
FINDING THE DREAM

In The Garden Trilogy

BLUE DAHLIA
BLACK ROSE
RED LILY

Chesapeake Bay Saga

SEA SWEPT
RISING TIDES
INNER HARBOR
CHESAPEAKE BLUE

Circle Trilogy

MORRIGAN'S CROSS
DANCE OF THE GODS
VALLEY OF SILENCE

Gallaghers of Ardmore Trilogy

JEWELS OF THE SUN
TEARS OF THE MOON
HEART OF THE SEA

Sign of Seven Trilogy

BLOOD BROTHERS
THE HOLLOW
THE PAGAN STONE

Three Sisters Island Trilogy

DANCE UPON THE AIR
HEAVEN AND EARTH
FACE THE FIRE

Bride Quartet

VISION IN WHITE
BED OF ROSES
SAVOR THE MOMENT

Nora Roberts & J. D. Robb

Anthologies

FROM THE HEART
A LITTLE MAGIC
A LITTLE FATE

MOON SHADOWS
(with Jill Gregory, Ruth Ryan Langan, and Marianne Willman)

The Once Upon Series
(with Jill Gregory, Ruth Ryan Langan, and Marianne Willman)
ONCE UPON A CASTLE
ONCE UPON A STAR
ONCE UPON A KISS
ONCE UPON A ROSE
ONCE UPON A DREAM
ONCE UPON A MIDNIGHT

* * *

SILENT NIGHT
(with Susan Plunkett, Dee Holmes, and Claire Cross)

OUT OF THIS WORLD
(with Laurell K. Hamilton, Susan Krinard, and Maggie Shayne)

BUMP IN THE NIGHT
(with Mary Blayney, Ruth Ryan Langan, and Mary Kay McComas)

DEAD OF NIGHT
(with Mary Blayney, Ruth Ryan Langan, and Mary Kay McComas)

THREE IN DEATH

SUITE 606
(with Mary Blayney, Ruth Ryan Langan, and Mary Kay McComas)

THE LOST
(with Patricia Gaffney, Mary Blayney, and Ruth Ryan Langan)

Also available . . .

THE OFFICIAL NORA ROBERTS COMPANION
(edited by Denise Little and Laura Hayden)

NORA ROBERTS

SAVOR *the* MOMENT

JOVE BOOKS, NEW YORK

THE BERKLEY PUBLISHING GROUP
Published by the Penguin Group
Penguin Group (USA) Inc.
375 Hudson Street, New York, New York 10014, USA
Penguin Group (Canada), 90 Eglinton Avenue East, Suite 700, Toronto, Ontario M4P 2Y3, Canada
(a division of Pearson Penguin Canada Inc.)
Penguin Books Ltd., 80 Strand, London WC2R 0RL, England
Penguin Group Ireland, 25 St. Stephen's Green, Dublin 2, Ireland (a division of Penguin Books Ltd.)
Penguin Group (Australia), 250 Camberwell Road, Camberwell, Victoria 3124, Australia
(a division of Pearson Australia Group Pty. Ltd.)
Penguin Books India Pvt. Ltd., 11 Community Centre, Panchsheel Park, New Delhi—110 017, India
Penguin Group (NZ), 67 Apollo Drive, Rosedale, North Shore 0632, New Zealand
(a division of Pearson New Zealand Ltd.)
Penguin Books (South Africa) (Pty.) Ltd., 24 Sturdee Avenue, Rosebank, Johannesburg 2196,
South Africa

Penguin Books Ltd., Registered Offices: 80 Strand, London WC2R 0RL, England

This is a work of fiction. Names, characters, places, and incidents either are the product of the author's imagination or are used fictitiously, and any resemblance to actual persons, living or dead, business establishments, events, or locales is entirely coincidental. The publisher does not have control over and does not have any responsibility for author or third-party websites or their content.

SAVOR THE MOMENT

A Jove Book / published by arrangement with the author

PRINTING HISTORY
Berkley trade edition / May 2010
Jove international edition / October 2010

Copyright © 2010 by Nora Roberts.
Cover photograph of "Bride" by Tereschenko Dmitry / Shutterstock; cover photograph of "Cake" by
Abrahams / Shutterstock.
Cover design by Rita Frangie.
Text design by Kristin del Rosario.

All rights reserved.
No part of this book may be reproduced, scanned, or distributed in any printed or electronic form without
permission. Please do not participate in or encourage piracy of copyrighted materials in violation of the
author's rights. Purchase only authorized editions.
For information, address: The Berkley Publishing Group,
a division of Penguin Group (USA) Inc.,
375 Hudson Street, New York, New York 10014.

ISBN: 978-0-515-14886-2

JOVE®
Jove Books are published by The Berkley Publishing Group,
a division of Penguin Group (USA) Inc.,
375 Hudson Street, New York, New York 10014.
JOVE® is a registered trademark of Penguin Group (USA) Inc.
The "J" design is a trademark of Penguin Group (USA) Inc.

PRINTED IN THE UNITED STATES OF AMERICA

10   9   8   7   6   5   4   3   2

If you purchased this book without a cover, you should be aware that this book is stolen property. It was
reported as "unsold and destroyed" to the publisher, and neither the author nor the publisher has received
any payment for this "stripped book."

For my brother Jim, the family baker

I sing of brooks, of blossoms, birds, and bowers;
Of April, May, of June, and July flowers.
I sing of Maypoles, Hock-carts, wassails, wakes,
Of bridegrooms, brides, and of their bridal cakes.

—ROBERT HERRICK

I wonder by my troth, what thou and I
Did, till we lov'd?

—DONNE

SAVOR *the* MOMENT

PROLOGUE

As THE CLOCK TICKED DOWN ON HER SENIOR YEAR IN high school, Laurel McBane learned one indisputable fact.

Prom was hell.

For weeks all anyone wanted to talk about was who might ask whom, who did ask whom—and who asked some other whom, thereby inciting misery and hysteria.

Girls, to her mind, suffered an agony of suspense and an embarrassing passivity during prom season. The halls, classrooms, and quad throbbed with emotion running the gamut from giddy euphoria because some guy asked them to some overhyped dance, to bitter tears because some guy didn't.

The entire cycle revolved around "some guy," a condition she believed both stupid and demoralizing.

And after that, the hysteria continued, even escalated with the hunt for a dress, for shoes, the intense debate about up-dos versus down-dos. Limos, after-parties, hotel suites—the yes, no, maybe of sex.

She'd have skipped the whole thing if her friends,

especially Parker Right-of-Passage Brown, hadn't ganged up on her.

Now her savings account—all those hard-earned dollars and cents from countless hours waiting tables—reeled in shock at the withdrawals for a dress she'd probably never wear again, the shoes, the bag, and all the rest.

She could lay all that on her friends' heads, too. She'd gotten caught up shopping with Parker, Emmaline, and Mackensie, and spent more than she should have.

The idea, gently broached by Emma, of asking her parents to spring for the dress wasn't an option, not to Laurel's mind. A point of pride, maybe, but money in the McBane household had become a very sore subject since her father's dicey investments fiasco and the little matter of the IRS audit.

No way she'd ask either of them. She earned her own, and had for several years now.

She told herself it didn't matter. She didn't have close to enough saved for the tuition for the Culinary Institute, or the living expenses in New York, despite the hours she'd put in at the restaurant after school and on weekends. The cost of looking great for one night didn't change that one way or the other—and, what the hell, she did look great.

She fixed on her earrings while across the room—Parker's bedroom—Parker and Emma experimented with ways to prom-up the hair Mac had impulsively hacked off to what Laurel thought of as Julius Caesar takes the Rubicon. They tried various pins, sparkle dust, and jeweled clips in what was left of Mac's flame red hair while the three of them talked nonstop, and Aerosmith rocked out of the CD player.

She liked listening to them like this, when she was a little bit apart. Maybe especially now, when she felt a little bit apart. They'd been friends all their lives, and now—rite of passage or not—things were changing. In the fall Parker and Emma would head off to college. Mac would be working, and squeezing in a few courses on photography.

And with the dream of the Culinary Institute poofed due

to finances and her parents' most recent marital implosion, she'd settle for community college part-time. Business courses, she supposed. She'd have to be practical. Realistic.

And she wasn't going to think about it now. She might as well enjoy the moment, and this ritual that Parker, in her Parker way, had arranged.

Parker and Emma might be going to prom at the Academy while she and Mac went to theirs at the public high school, but they had this time together, getting dressed and made up. Downstairs Parker's and Emma's parents hung out, and there'd be dozens of pictures and "oh, look at our girls!" hugs and probably some shiny eyes.

Mac's mother was too self-involved to care about her daughter's senior prom, which, Linda being Linda, could only be a good thing. And Laurel's own parents? Well, they were too steeped in their own lives, their own problems, for it to matter where she was or what she did tonight.

She was used to it. Had even come to prefer it.

"Just the fairy dust sparkles," Mac decided, tipping her head side to side to judge. "It's kind of Tinker Bell-y. In a cool way."

"I think you're right." Parker, her straight-as-rain brown hair a glossy waterfall down her back, nodded. "It's waif with an edge. What do you think, Em?"

"I think we need to play up the eyes more, go drama." Emma's eyes, a deep, dreamy brown, narrowed in thought. "I can do this."

"Have at it." Mac shrugged. "But don't take forever, okay? I still have to set up for our group shot."

"We're on schedule." Parker checked her watch. "We've still got thirty minutes before . . ." She turned, caught sight of Laurel. "Hey. You look awesome!"

"Oh, you really do!" Emma clapped her hands together. "I *knew* that was the dress. The shimmery pink makes your eyes even bluer."

"I guess."

"Need one more thing." Parker hurried to her dresser, opened a drawer on her jewelry box. "This hair clip."

Laurel, a slim girl in shimmery pink, her sun-shot hair done—at Emma's insistence—in long, loose sausage curls, shrugged. "Whatever."

Parker held it against Laurel's hair at different angles. "Cheer up," she ordered. "You're going to have fun."

God, get over yourself, Laurel! "I know. Sorry. It'd be more fun if the four of us were going to the same dance, especially since we all look seriously awesome."

"Yeah, it would." Parker decided to draw some of the curls from the sides to clip them in the back. "But we'll meet up after and party. When we're done we'll come back here and tell each other everything. Here, take a look."

She turned Laurel to the mirror, and the girls studied themselves and each other.

"I do look great," Laurel said and made Parker laugh.

After the most perfunctory of knocks, the door opened. Mrs. Grady, the Browns' longtime housekeeper, put her hands on her hips to take a survey.

"You'll do," she said, "which you should after all this fuss. Finish up with it and get yourselves downstairs for pictures. You." She pointed a finger at Laurel. "I need a word with you, young lady."

"What did I do?" Laurel demanded, looking from friend to friend as Mrs. Grady strode away. "I didn't do anything." But since Mrs. G's word was law, Laurel rushed after her.

In the family sitting room, Mrs. G turned, arms folded. Lecture mode, Laurel thought as her heart tripped. And she cast her mind back, looking for an infraction that might have earned her one from the woman who'd been more of a mother to her than her own through her teenage years.

"So," Mrs. Grady began as Laurel hurried in, "I guess you think you're all grown-up now."

"I—"

"Well, you're not. But you're getting there. The four of you've been running tame around here since you were in diapers. Some of that's going to change, with all of you going your own ways. At least for a time. Birds tell me your way's to New York and that fancy baking school."

Her heart took another trip, then suffered the pinprick of a deflated dream. "No, I'm, ah, keeping my job at the restaurant, and I'm going to try to take some courses at the—"

"No, you're not." Again, Mrs. G pointed a finger. "Now, a girl your age in New York City best be smart and best be careful. And from what I'm told, if you want to make it at that school you have to work hard. It's more than making pretty frostings and cookies."

"It's one of the best, but—"

"Then you'll be one of the best." Mrs. G reached in her pocket. She held out a check to Laurel. "That'll cover the first semester, the tuition, a decent place to live, and enough food to keep body and soul together. You make good use of it, girl, or you'll answer to me. If you do what I expect you're capable of, we'll talk about the next term when the time comes."

Stunned, Laurel stared at the check in her hand. "You can't— I can't—"

"I can and you will. That's that."

"But—"

"Didn't I just say that's that? If you let me down, there'll be hell to pay, I promise you. Parker and Emma are going off to college, and Mackensie's dead set on working full-time with her photography. You've got a different path, so you'll take it. It's what you want, isn't it?"

"More than anything." Tears stung her eyes, burned her throat. "Mrs. G, I don't know what to say. I'll pay you back. I'll—"

"Damn right, you will. You'll pay me back by making something of yourself. It's up to you now."

Laurel threw her arms around Mrs. Grady, clung. "You won't be sorry. I'll make you proud."

"I believe you will. There now. Go finish getting ready."

Laurel held on another moment. "I'll never forget this," she whispered. "Never. Thank you. Thank you, thank you!"

She rushed for the door, anxious to share the news with her friends, then turned, young, radiant. "I can't wait to start."

CHAPTER ONE

ALONE, WITH NORAH JONES WHISPERING THROUGH THE iPod, Laurel transformed a panel of fondant into a swatch of elegant, edible lace. She didn't hear the music, used it more to fill the air than as entertainment while she painstakingly pieced the completed panel onto the second tier of four.

She stepped back to eye the results, to circle, to search for flaws. Vows' clients expected perfect, and that's exactly what she intended to deliver. Satisfied, she nodded, and picked up a bottle of water to sip while she stretched her back.

"Two down, two to go."

She glanced toward the board where she'd pinned various samples of antique lace, and the final sketched design for the cake Friday evening's bride had approved.

She had three more designs to complete: two for Saturday, one for Sunday—but that was nothing new. June at Vows, the wedding and event business she ran with her friends, was prime time.

In a handful of years, they'd turned an idea into a

thriving enterprise. Sometimes just a little too thriving, she mused, which was why she was making fondant lace at nearly one in the morning.

It was a very good thing, she decided. She loved the work.

They all had their passions. Emma had the flowers, Mac the photography, Parker the details. And she had the cakes. And the pastries, she thought, and the chocolates. But the cakes stood as the crowning touch.

She got back to it, began to roll out the next panel. Following habit, she'd clipped her sunny blond hair up and back out of her way. Cornstarch dusted the baker's apron she wore over cotton pants and tee, and the slide-on kitchen shoes kept her feet as comfortable as possible after hours of standing. Her hands, strong from years of kneading, rolling, lifting, were capable and quick. As she began the next pattern, her sharp-featured, angular face set in serious lines.

Perfection wasn't simply a goal when it came to her art. For Icing at Vows it was a necessity. The wedding cake was more than baking and piping, sugar paste and filling. Just as the wedding photos Mac took were more than pictures, and the arrangements and bouquets Emma created more than flowers. The details and schedules and wishes Parker put together were, in the end, bigger than the sum of their parts.

Together, the elements became a once-in-a-lifetime event, and the celebration of the journey two people chose to make together.

Romantic, certainly, and Laurel believed in romance. In theory, anyway. More, she believed in symbols and celebrations. And in a really fabulous cake.

Her expression softened into pleasure as she completed the third tier, and her deep blue eyes warmed as she glanced over to see Parker hovering in the doorway.

"Why aren't you in bed?"

"Details." Parker circled a finger over her own head. "Couldn't settle. How long have you been at this tonight?"

"Awhile. I need to finish it so it can set overnight. Plus I have the two Saturday cakes to assemble and decorate tomorrow."

"Want company?"

They knew each other well enough that it was understood if Laurel said no, there'd be no offense. And often, when deep in work, no was the answer.

"Sure."

"I love the design." Parker, as Laurel had, circled the cake. "The delicacy of the white on white, the interest of the different heights of each tier—and the intricacy of each. They really do look like different panels of lace. Old-fashioned, vintage, that's our bride's theme. You've nailed it with this."

"We're going to do pale blue ribbon around the pedestal," Laurel said as she started on the next panel. "And Emma's going to scatter white rose petals at the base. It's going to be a winner."

"The bride's been good to work with."

Comfortable in her pajamas, her long brown hair loose rather than in its work mode of sleek tail or smooth chignon, Parker put on the kettle for tea. One of the perks of running the business out of her home, and of having Laurel living there—with Emma and Mac right on the estate as well—were these late-night visits.

"She knows her mind," Laurel commented, choosing a tool to scallop the edges of the panel. "But she's open to suggestion, and so far hasn't been insane. If she makes it through the next twenty-four that way, she'll definitely earn Vows' coveted Good Bride status."

"They looked happy and relaxed tonight at rehearsal, and that's a good sign."

"Mmm-hmm." Laurel continued the pattern with precisely placed eyelets and dots. "So, again, why aren't you in bed?"

Parker sighed as she heated a little teapot. "I think I was having a moment. I was unwinding with a glass of wine out on my terrace. I could see Mac's place, and Emma's. The lights were on in both houses, and I could smell the gardens. It was so quiet, so pretty. The lights went off—Emma's first, and a little while after, Mac's. I thought how we're planning Mac's wedding, and that Emma just got engaged. And all the times we played Wedding Day, the four of us, when we were kids. Now it's real. I sat there in the quiet and the dark, and found myself wishing my parents could be here to see it. To see what we've done here, and who we are now. I got stuck." She paused to measure out tea. "Between being sad they're gone and being happy because I know they'd be proud of me. Of us."

"I think about them a lot. We all do." Laurel continued to work. "Because they were such an essential part of our lives, and because there are so many memories of them here. So I know what you mean by being stuck."

"They'd get a kick out of Mac and Carter, out of Emma and Jack, wouldn't they?"

"Yeah, they would. And what we've done here, Parker? It rocks. They'd get a kick out of that, too."

"I'm lucky you were up working." Parker poured hot water into the pot. "You've settled me down."

"Here to serve. I'll tell you who else is lucky, and that's Friday's bride. Because this cake?" She blew stray hair out of her eyes as she nodded smugly. "It kicks major ass. And when I do the crown, angels will weep with joy."

Parker set the pot aside to steep. "Really, Laurel, you need to take more pride in your work."

Laurel grinned. "Screw the tea. I'm nearly done here. Pour me a glass of wine."

*I*N THE MORNING, AFTER A SOLID SIX HOURS' SLEEP, LAUREL got in a quick session at the gym before dressing for the workday. She'd be chained in her kitchen for the bulk of it, but before that routine began, there was the summit meeting that prefaced every event.

Laurel dashed downstairs from her third-floor wing to the main level of the sprawling house, and back to the family kitchen where Mrs. Grady was putting a fruit platter together.

"Morning, Mrs. G."

Mrs. Grady arched her eyebrows. "You look feisty."

"Feel feisty. Feel righteous." Laurel fisted both hands, flexed her muscles. "Want coffee. Much."

"Parker's taken the coffee up already. You can take this fruit, and the pastries. Eat some of that fruit. A day shouldn't start with a Danish."

"Yes, ma'am. Anyone else here yet?"

"Not yet, but I saw Jack's truck leave a bit ago, and I expect Carter will be along giving me the puppy eyes in hopes of a decent breakfast."

"I'll get out of the way." Laurel grabbed the platters, balancing them with the expertise of the waitress she'd been once upon a time.

She carried them up to the library, which now served as Vows' conference room. Parker sat at the big table, with the coffee service on the breakfront. Her BlackBerry, as always, remained at easy reach. The sleek ponytail left her face un-framed, and the crisp white shirt transmitted business mode as she sipped coffee and studied data on her laptop with midnight blue eyes Laurel knew missed nothing.

"Provisions," Laurel announced. She set the trays down, then tucked her chin-length swing of hair behind her ears before she obeyed Mrs. Grady and fixed herself a little bowl of berries. "Missed you in the gym this morning. What time did you get up?"

"Six, which was a good thing, since Saturday afternoon's bride called just after seven. Her father tripped over the cat and may have broken his nose."

"Uh-oh."

"She's worried about him, but nearly equally worried about how he's going to look for the wedding, and in the photographs. I'm going to call the makeup artist to see what she thinks can be done."

"Sorry about the FOB's bad luck, but if that's the biggest problem this weekend, we're in good shape."

Parker shot out a finger. "Don't jinx it."

Mac strolled in, long and lean in jeans and a black T-shirt. "Hello, pals of mine."

Laurel squinted at her friend's easy smile and slumberous green eyes. "You had morning sex."

"I had stupendous morning sex, thank you." Mac poured herself coffee, grabbed a muffin. "And you?"

"Bitch."

With a laugh, Mac dropped down in her chair, stretched out her legs. "I'll take my morning exercise over your tread-mill and Bowflex."

"Mean, nasty bitch," Laurel said and popped a raspberry.

"I love summer when the love of my life doesn't have to get up and out early to enlighten young minds." She opened her own laptop. "Now I'm primed, in all possible ways, for business."

"Saturday afternoon's FOB may have broken his nose," Parker told her.

"Bummer." Mac's brow creased. "I can do a lot with Photoshop if they want me to—but it's kind of a cheat. What is, is—and it makes an amusing memory. In my opinion."

"We'll see what the bride's opinion is once he gets back from the doctor." Parker glanced over as Emma rushed in.

"I'm not late. There are twenty seconds left." Black curls bouncing, she scooted to the coffee station. "I fell back to sleep. After."

"Oh, I hate you, too," Laurel muttered. "We need a new rule. No bragging about sex at business meetings when half of us aren't getting any."

"Seconded," Parker said immediately.

"Aww." Laughing, Emma scooped some fruit into a bowl.

"Saturday afternoon's FOB may have a broken nose."

"Aww," Emma repeated, with genuine concern at Mac's announcement.

"We'll deal with it when we have more details, but however it turns out, it really falls to Mac and me. I'll keep you updated," Parker said to Mac. "Tonight's event. All out-of-town attendants, relatives, and guests have arrived. The bride, the MOB, and the attendants are due here at three for hair and makeup. The MOG has her own salon date and is due by four, with the FOG. FOB will arrive with his daughter. We'll keep him happy and occupied until it's time for the formal shots that include him. Mac?"

"The bride's dress is a beaut. Vintage romance. I'll be playing that up."

As Mac outlined her plans and timetable, Laurel rose for a second cup of coffee. She made notes here and there, continued to do so when Emma took over. As the bulk of Laurel's job was complete, she'd fill in when and where she was needed.

It was a routine they'd perfected since Vows had gone from concept to reality.

"Laurel," Parker said.

"The cake's finished—and a wowzer. It's heavy, so I'll need help from the subs transferring it to reception, but the design doesn't require any on-site assembly. I'll need you to do the ribbon and white rose petals, Emma, once it's transferred, but that's it until it's time to serve. They opted against a groom's cake, and went for a selection of mini pastries and heart-shaped chocolates. They're done, too, and we'll serve them on white china lined with lace doilies to mirror the design of the cake. The cake table linen is pale blue, eyelet lace. Cake knife and server, provided by the B and G. They were her grandmother's so we'll keep our eye on them.

"I'm going to be working on Saturday's cakes most of today, but should be freed up by four if anyone needs me. During the last set, the subs will put leftover cake in the take-away boxes and tie them with blue ribbon we've had engraved with the B and G's names, and the date. Same goes if there are any leftover chocolates or pastries. Mac, I'd like a picture of the cake for my files. I haven't done this design before."

"Check."

"And Emma, I need the flowers for Saturday night's cake. Can you drop them off to me when you come to dress today's event?"

"No problem."

"On the personal front?" Mac lifted a hand for attention. "No one's mentioned that my mother's latest wedding is tomorrow, in Italy. Which is, thankfully, many, many miles away from our happy home here in Greenwich, Connecticut. I got a call from her just after five this morning, as Linda doesn't get the concept of time zones—and, well, let's face it, doesn't give a shit anyway."

"Why didn't you just let it ring?" Laurel demanded, even as Emma reached over to rub Mac's leg in sympathy.

"Because she'd just keep calling back—and I'm trying to deal with her. On my terms for a change." Mac raked her fingers through the bold red of her gamine cap of hair. "There were, as expected, tears and recriminations, as she's decided she wants me there. As opposed to a week ago, when she didn't. Since I have no intention of hopping on a plane, particularly when I have an event tonight, two tomorrow, and another on Sunday, to see her get married for the fourth time, she's not speaking to me."

"If only it would last."

"Laurel," Parker murmured.

"I mean it. You got to give her a piece of your mind," she reminded Parker. "I didn't. I can only let it fester."

"Which I appreciate," Mac said. "Sincerely. But as you can see, I'm not in a funk, I'm not swimming in guilt or even marginally pissed off. I think there's an advantage to finding a guy who's sensible, loving, and just really solid. An advantage over and above really terrific morning sex. Every one of you has been on my side when I've had to deal with Linda, you've tried to help me through her demands and basic insanity. I guess Carter just helped tip the scales, and now I can deal with it. I wanted to tell you."

"I'd have morning sex with him myself, just for that."

"Hands off, McBane. But I appreciate the sentiment. So." She rose. "I want to get some work done before I need to focus on today's event. I'll swing by and get some shots of the cake."

"Hang on, I'll go with you." Emma pushed up. "I'll be back with the team shortly—and I'll drop the flowers off for you, Laurel."

When they'd gone, Laurel sat another moment. "She really meant it."

"Yes, she really did."

"And she's right." Laurel took a last moment to sit back and relax with her coffee. "Carter's the one who turned the key in the lock. I wonder what it's like to have a man who can do that, can help that way without pushing. Who can love you that way. I guess when it comes down to it, I envy her that even more than the sex."

Shrugging, Laurel rose. "I'd better get to work."

𝓛AUREL DIDN'T HAVE TIME TO THINK ABOUT MEN OVER the next couple of days. She didn't have the time or the energy to think about love and romance. She might have been neck-deep in weddings, but that was business—and the business of weddings demanded focus and precision.

Her Antique Lace cake, which had taken her nearly three days to create, had its moment in the spotlight—before being disassembled and devoured. Saturday afternoon featured her whimsical Pastel Petals with its hundreds of embossed, gum-paste rose petals, and Saturday evening her Rose Garden, where tiers of bold red roses layered with tiers of vanilla-bean cake with silky buttercream frosting.

For Sunday afternoon's smaller, more casual event, the bride had chosen Summer Berries. Laurel had done the baking, the filling, the assembly, and the basket-weave frosting. Now, even as the bride and groom exchanged vows on the terrace outside, Laurel completed the project by arranging the fresh fruit and mint leaves on the tiers.

Behind her, the subs completed table decorations for the wedding brunch. She wore a baker's apron over a suit nearly the same color as the raspberries she selected.

Stepping back, she studied the lines and balance, then chose a bunch of champagne grapes to drape over a tier.

"Looks tasty."

Her eyebrows drew together as she grouped stemmed cherries. Interruptions while she worked were common—but that didn't mean she had to like them. Added to it, she hadn't expected Parker's brother to drop by during an event.

Then again, she reminded herself, he came and went as he pleased.

But when she spotted his hand reaching for one of her containers, she slapped it smartly away.

"Hands off."

"Like you're going to miss a couple blackberries."

"I don't know where your hands have been." She set a trio of mint leaves, and didn't bother—yet—to spare him a glance. "What do you want? We're working."

"Me, too. More or less. Lawyer capacity. I had some paperwork to drop off."

He handled all their legal dealings, both individually and as a business. She knew, very well, he put in long hours on their behalf, and often on his own time. But if she didn't jab at him, she'd break long-standing tradition.

"And timed it so you could mooch from catering."

"There ought to be some perks. Brunch deal?"

She gave in and turned. His choice of jeans and a T-shirt didn't make him less of an Ivy League lawyer—not to her mind. Delaney Brown of the Connecticut Browns, she thought. Tall, appealingly rangy, his dense brown hair just a smidgen longer than lawyerly fashion might dictate.

Did he do that on purpose? She imagined so, as he was a man who always had a plan. He shared those deep, mid-night blue eyes with Parker, but though she'd known him all her life, she could rarely read what was behind them.

He was, in her opinion, too handsome for his own good,

too smooth for anyone else's. He was also unflinchingly loyal, quietly generous—and annoyingly overprotective.

He smiled at her now, quick and easy with a disarming flash of humor she imagined served as a lethal weapon in court. Or the bedroom.

"Cold poached salmon, mini chicken Florentine, grilled summer vegetables, potato pancakes, a variety of quiches, caviar with full accompaniment, assorted pastries and breads, along with a fruit and cheese display, followed by the poppy-seed cake with orange marmalade filling and Grand Marnier buttercream frosting, topped with fresh fruit."

"Sign me up."

"I expect you can sweet-talk the caterers," she said. She rolled her shoulders, circled her head on her neck as she chose the next berries.

"Something hurt?"

"The basket weave's a killer on the neck and shoulders."

His hands lifted, then retreated to his pockets. "Are Jack and Carter around?"

"Somewhere. I haven't seen them today."

"Maybe I'll go hunt them down."

"Mmm-hmm."

But he wandered across the room to the windows and looked down at the flower-decked terrace, the white slippered chairs, the pretty bride turned toward the smiling groom.

"They're doing the ring thing," Del called out.

"So Parker just told me." Laurel tapped her headset. "I'm set. Emma, the cake's ready for you."

She balanced the top layer with an offset stem loaded with blackberries. "Five-minute warning," she announced, and began loading her bin with the remaining fruit. "Let's get the champagne poured, the Bloody Marys and mimosas mixed. Light the candles, please." She started to lift the bin, but Del beat her to it.

"I'll carry it."

She shrugged, and moved over to hit the switch for the

background music that would play until the orchestra took over.

They started down the back stairs, passing uniformed waitstaff on their way up with hors d'oeuvres for the brief cocktail mixer designed to keep guests happy while Mac took the formals of the bride and groom, the wedding party and family.

She swung into her kitchen where the caterers ran full steam. Used to the chaos, Laurel slid through, got a small bowl and scooped out fruit. She passed it to Del.

"Thanks."

"Just stay out of the way. Yes, they're ready," she said to Parker through the headset. "Yeah, in thirty. In place." She glanced over at the caterers. "On schedule. Oh, Del's here. Uh-huh."

Leaning on the counter and eating berries, he watched her as she stripped off her apron. "Okay, heading out now."

Del pushed off the counter to follow her as she headed through the mudroom that would soon be transformed into her extra cooler and storage area. She pulled the clip out of her hair, tossed it aside, and shook her hair into place as she stepped outside.

"Where are we going?"

"I'm going to help escort guests inside. You're going away, somewhere."

"I like it here."

It was her turn to smile. "Parker said to get rid of you until it's time to clean up. Go find your little friends, Del, and if you're good boys you'll be fed later."

"Fine, but if I get roped into cleanup, I want some of that cake."

They separated, him strolling toward the remodeled pool house that served as Mac's studio and home, her striding toward the terrace, where the bride and groom exchanged their first married kiss.

Laurel glanced back once—just once. She'd known him all her life—that was fate, she supposed. But it was her own fault, and her own problem, that she'd been in love with him nearly as long.

She allowed herself one sigh before fixing a bright, professional smile on her face to lend a hand herding the celebrants into Reception.

CHAPTER TWO

LONG AFTER THE LAST GUEST DEPARTED AND THE CATER-
ers loaded up, Laurel stretched out on the sofa of the family
parlor with a well-deserved glass of wine.

She wasn't sure where the men might be—back to their
dens with a six-pack maybe—but it was nice, very nice, to
unwind with just the women, and the relative quiet.

"Damn good weekend." Mac lifted her glass in toast.
"Four rehearsals, four events. Not a single hitch in any of
them. Not even a blip of a hitch. That's a record."

"The cake was amazing," Emma added.

"You had a forkful," Laurel pointed out.

"An amazing forkful. Plus it was just sweet today, the
way the groom's little boy stood as best man. He was so
cute. It got me weepy."

"They're going to make a nice family." Parker sat, eyes
closed, BlackBerry on her lap. "You watch some of the
second-time-arounds with kids, and think: Ho boy, rough
sailing coming up. But this? You can just see she and the
kid are nuts for each other. It *was* sweet."

"I got some killer pictures. And the cake was awesome,"

Mac added. "Maybe I should go for the poppy seed for mine."

To ease the cramping, Laurel curled and uncurled her toes. "Last week you wanted the Italian cream."

"Maybe I should have cake samplers. Small versions of several kinds, different designs. It would be a culinary orgy, plus amazing photography."

Laurel cocked a finger. "Die, Mackensie. Die."

"You should stick with the Italian cream. It's your favorite."

Mac pursed her lips as she nodded at Emma. "You're right. And it is all about me. What are you leaning toward, cakewise?"

"I can't even think about it. I'm still getting used to being engaged." Emma studied the diamond on her finger with an undeniably smug smile. "Plus, once I shift into wedding plans and details, I fully expect to succumb to mania. So we should put that off as long as possible."

"Yes, please." Laurel sighed her agreement.

"You need the dress first anyway." Parker kept her eyes closed. "The dress always comes first."

"Now you've done it," Laurel muttered.

"I've barely thought about it. More than a thousand times," Emma added. "I've hardly looked at more than half a million pictures. I'm going for princess. Miles and miles of skirt. Probably an off-the-shoulder bodice, maybe a sweetheart neckline since I do have exceptional breasts."

"It's true, you do," Mac agreed.

"Absolutely nothing simple. Lavish is my byword. I want a tiara—and a train." Dark eyes glowed at the thought. "And since we're squeezing it into next May, I'm going to design myself an incredible, and yes, lavish, bouquet. Pastels, I think. Maybe. Probably. Romantic, heartbreaking pastels."

"But she can't even think about it," Laurel put in.

"All of you in soft colors," Emma went on, unfazed. "A garden of my friends." She let out a sigh of her own, long and dreamy. "And when Jack sees me, he'll lose his breath.

In that one moment, you know, when we look at each other, the world's going to stop for us. Just for a minute, one incredible minute."

From her position on the floor, she rested her head against Parker's leg. "We didn't really know, all those times we played Wedding Day when we were kids. We didn't really know what that one incredible moment meant. We're so lucky we get to see it as often as we do."

"Best job ever," Mac murmured.

"Best job ever because we are." Laurel sat up enough to toast. "We put it together so people can have that one incredible moment. You'll have yours, Em—orchestrated down to the last detail by Parker, surrounded with flowers you've arranged yourself, captured in a photograph by Mac. And celebrated with a cake I'll create just for you. A lavish one. Guaranteed."

"Aww." Emma's dark eyes filled. "As much as I love Jack—and boy, do I ever—I couldn't be as happy as I am now without all of you."

Mac handed Emma a tissue. "I'm still first. I want a cake that's just for me," she said to Laurel. "If she gets one, so do I."

"I can put little cameras and tripods around the tiers."

"And little stacks of books for Carter?" Mac laughed. "Silly, but apt."

"It follows the theme of your engagement shots." Emma dried her eyes. "I love the way you set those up, with you and Carter on the couch, your legs all tangled together, him with a book on his lap, you looking like you've just lowered your camera after taking his picture. Both of you just grinning at each other. Which leads me to ask you about our engagement portrait. When, where, how?"

"Easy. You and Jack in bed, naked."

Emma shot out a foot to give Mac a light kick. "Stop."

"Also apt," was Laurel's opinion.

"We do more than have sex!"

"You certainly do. You think about having sex." Parker opened one eye.

"We have a very layered relationship," Emma insisted. "Which includes lots of sex. But seriously—"

"I've got a few things in mind. We should look at our schedules and set something up."

"Now?"

"Sure. Parks must have both our schedules on her Crack-Berry." Mac reached toward it.

Parker opened both eyes, aimed a smoldering warning stare. "Touch it and die."

"Jesus. Let's go check my book at the studio. We should probably round up the guys anyway—and we'd have to have Jack clear the time."

"Excellent."

"Where are the guys?" Laurel wondered.

"Down with Mrs. G," Emma told her. "Eating pizza and playing poker—or that was the plan."

"Nobody asked us for pizza and poker." Laurel managed a horizontal shrug as eyes turned to her. "Okay, no, I don't want pizza and poker because I like it right here. But still."

"Anyway." Mac pushed to her feet. "Rounding up under the circumstances might take some time. Let's just plant the seed, then go figure the schedule."

"That's a plan. Good job, girls," Emma said as she stood.

As they left, Laurel stretched. "I need a massage. We should have an in-house masseur named Sven. Or Raoul."

"I'll put that on the list. Meanwhile, you could call Serenity and book one."

"But if we had Sven—I think Sven is better than Raoul—I could have one right now, then I'd slide bonelessly into bed and sleep. How many days until vacation?"

"Too many."

"You say that now, but once we're free and get to the Hamptons, you'll still have that BlackBerry attached to your hand."

"I can give it up anytime I want."

Laurel answered Parker's smile. "You'll buy a waterproof bag for it, so you can swim with it."

"They should make them waterproof. We must have the technology."

"Well, I'm going to leave you and your one true love alone, go soak in a hot tub, and dream of Sven." Laurel rolled off the couch. "It's good seeing Emma and Mac so happy, isn't it?"

"Yeah."

"See you in the morning."

THE HOT BATH WORKED WONDERS, BUT LEFT HER WIDE awake instead of relaxed and sleepy. Rather than spending an hour trying to will herself to sleep, Laurel turned on the TV in her sitting room for company, then sat down at her computer to check her week's schedule. She browsed recipes—as much an addiction for her as the BlackBerry was to Parker—and found a couple worth bookmarking to tweak and personalize later.

Still restless, she settled down in her favorite chair with her sketch pad. The chair had been Parker's mother's, and always made Laurel feel cozy and safe. She sat cross-legged on the deep cushion, the pad across her lap, and thought of Mac. Of Mac and Carter. Of Mac in the fabulous wedding dress she'd chosen—or that Parker had found for her.

Clean, sleek lines, she mused, that so suited Mac's long, lean body. Not a lot of fuss, and just a touch of flirt. She sketched a cake that mirrored the idea—classic and simple. And immediately rejected it.

Clean lines for the gown, yes, but Mac was also about color and flash, about the unique and the bold. And that, she realized, was one of the reasons Carter adored her.

So bold. Colorful fall wedding. Square tiers rather than the more traditional round, with the buttercream frosting Mac favored. Tinted. Yes, yes. Dusky gold then covered with fall flowers she'd make them oversized with wide, detailed petals—in russet and burnt orange, loden.

Color, texture, shape, to appeal to the photographer's eye, and romantic enough for any bride. Crowned with a bouquet, trailing ribbons in dark gold. Touches of white in some piping, to bring out all the color.

Mac's Fall, she thought, smiling as she added details. The perfect name for it—for the season, and for the way her friend had tripped into love.

Laurel held the sketch out to arm's length, then grinned in satisfaction.

"I am damn good. And now I'm hungry."

She rose to prop the open sketchbook against a lamp. First chance, she decided, she'd show it to Mac for the bride's opinion. But if she knew Mac—and she did—this was going to get a big, happy *woo!*

She deserved a snack—maybe a slice of cold pizza if there was any left. Which she'd regret in the morning, she told herself as she started out, but it couldn't be helped.

She was awake and she was hungry. One of the perks of running your own business and your own life was being able to indulge yourself from time to time.

She moved through the dark and the quiet, guided by her knowledge of the house and the stream of moonlight through the windows. She crossed out of her wing, started down the stairs as she talked herself out of cold pizza and into a healthier choice of fresh fruit and herbal tea.

She needed to be up early to fit in a workout before Monday morning baking. Then she had three couples coming in that afternoon for tastings, so she'd need to prep for that, and get cleaned up.

An evening meeting, full staff, with a client to determine basic details of a winter wedding, then she had the rest of the night free to do what needed to be done—or what suited her fancy.

Thank God she'd initiated a dating moratorium so there was no worry about getting dressed to go out—and what to wear when she did—making conversation, and deciding whether or not she was inclined to have sex.

Life was easier, she thought as she turned at the base of the stairs. It was easier, simpler, and just less *fraught* when you took dating and sex off the menu.

She rammed straight into a solid object—male-shaped—then tumbled backward. Cursing, she flailed out to save herself. The back of her hand smacked sharply against flesh—causing another curse that wasn't hers. As she went down, she grabbed a fistful of material. She heard it rip as the male-shaped solid object fell on top of her.

Winded, her head ringing where it thudded against the stair tread, she lay limp as a rag. Even dazed in the dark, she recognized Del by his shape, his scent.

"Jesus. Laurel? Damn it. Are you hurt?"

She drew in a breath, constricted by his weight—and maybe by the fact that a certain area of that weight was pressed very intimately between her legs. Why the hell had she been thinking about sex? Or the lack thereof?

"Get off me," she managed.

"Working on it. Are you okay? I didn't see you." He pushed up partway so their eyes met in that blue dust moonlight. "Ouch."

Because his movement increased the pressure—center to center—something besides her head began to throb. "Off. Me. Now."

"Okay, okay. I lost my balance—plus you grabbed my shirt and took me down with you. I tried to catch you. Hold on, let me get the light."

She stayed just where she was, waiting to get her breath back, waiting for things to stop throbbing. When he flicked on the foyer light, she shut her eyes against the glare.

"Ah," he said and cleared his throat.

She lay sprawled on the steps, legs spread, wearing a thin white tank and a pair of red boxers. Her toenails were sizzling pink. He decided concentrating on her toes was a better idea than her legs, or the way the tank fit, or . . . anything else.

"Let me help you up." And into a really long, thick robe.

She waved him off, half sat up to rub at the back of her head. "Damn it, Del, what are you doing sneaking around the house?"

"I wasn't sneaking. I was walking. Why were you sneaking?"

"I wasn't— Jesus. I live here."

"I used to," he muttered. "You tore my shirt."

"You fractured my skull."

Annoyance dissolved instantly into concern. "Did I really hurt you? Let me see."

Before she could move, he crouched and reached around to feel the back of her head. "You went down pretty hard. It's not bleeding."

"Ouch!" At least the fresh ringing took her mind off the torn shirt, and the muscle beneath it. "Stop poking."

"We should get you some ice."

"It's fine. I'm *fine*." Stirred up, no question, she thought, and wishing he didn't look so tousled, roughed-up, and ridiculously sexy. "What the hell are you doing here? It's the middle of the night."

"It's barely midnight, which, despite the term, isn't the middle of the night."

He stared straight into her eyes, looking, she imagined, for signs of shock or trauma. Any second he'd take her damn pulse.

"That doesn't answer the question."

"Mrs. G and I were hanging out. There was beer involved. Enough beer I decided I'd just . . ." He pointed up. "I was going to crash in one of the guest rooms rather than drive home with a buzz on."

She couldn't argue with him for being sensible— particularly since he was always sensible. "Then . . ." She mimicked him, and pointed up.

"Stand up so I can make sure you're okay."

"I'm not the one with a buzz on."

"No, you're the one with a fractured skull. Come on." He solved the matter by hooking his hands under her arms and lifting her so she stood on the step above him with their faces nearly level.

"I don't see any X's in your eyes, no birds circling over your head."

"Funny."

He gave her that smile. "I heard a couple birds chirping when you backhanded me."

She couldn't stop her lips from twitching even as she scowled. "If I'd known it was you, I'd've put more behind it."

"There's my girl."

And wasn't that exactly how he thought of her? she thought with a slippery mix of temper and disappointment. Just one of his girls.

"Go, sleep off your buzz, and no more sneaking around."

"Where are you going?" he asked as she walked away.

"Where I please."

She usually did, he mused, and it was one of the most appealing things about her. Unless you considered how her ass looked in short red boxers.

Which he wasn't. Exactly. He was just making sure she was steady on her feet. And on her really excellent legs.

Deliberately, he turned away and walked up the stairs to the third floor. He turned toward Parker's wing, and opened the door to the room that had been his as a child, a boy, a young man.

It wasn't the same. He didn't expect it to be or want it to be. If things didn't change, they became stagnant and stale. The walls, a soft, foggy green now, displayed clever paintings in simple frames rather than the sports posters of his youth. The bed, a gorgeous old four-poster, had been his grandmother's. Continuity, he thought, wasn't the same as stagnation.

He pulled change and keys out of his pocket to toss them on the dish set on the bureau, then caught sight of himself in the mirror.

His shirt was ripped at the shoulder, his hair disordered, and if he wasn't mistaken, he could see the faint mark where Laurel's knuckles had connected with his cheekbone.

She'd always been tough, he thought as he toed off his shoes. Tough, strong, and damn near fearless. Most women would've screamed, wouldn't they? But not Laurel—she fought. Push her, she pushed back. Harder.

He had to admire that.

Her body had surprised him. He could admit it, he told himself as he stripped off the torn T-shirt. Not that he didn't know her body. He'd hugged her countless times over the years. But hugging a female friend was an entirely different matter than lying on top of a woman in the dark.

Entirely different.

And something it was best not to dwell on.

He stripped off the rest of his clothes, then folded down the quilt—the work of his great-grandmother in this case. He set the old-fashioned wind-up alarm clock beside the bed, then switched off the light.

When he closed his eyes, the image of Laurel lying on the stairs popped into his head—lodged there. He rolled over, thought about the appointments he had the next day. And saw her walking away in those brief red boxers.

"Screw it."

A man was entitled to dwell on whatever he wanted to dwell on when he was alone in the dark.

In their Monday morning habit, Laurel and Parker hit their home gym at nearly the same moment. Parker went for yoga, Laurel for cardio. Since both took the routine seriously, there was little conversation.

As Laurel approached her third mile, Parker switched to Pilates—and Mac trudged in to give the Bowflex her usual sneer.

Amused, Laurel throttled back to cool down. Mac's conversion to regular workouts stemmed from her determination to have happening arms and shoulders in her strapless wedding dress.

"Looking good, Elliot," she called out as she grabbed a towel. Mac just curled her lip.

Laurel unrolled a mat to stretch while Parker gave

Mac some tips on form. By the time she moved on to free weights, Parker was shoving Mac to the elliptical.

"I don't wanna."

"Woman does not rule by resistance training alone. Fifteen cardio, fifteen stretching. Laurel, where did you get that bruise?"

"What bruise?"

"On your shoulder." Crossing over, Parker fluttered her finger on the bruise exposed by Laurel's racer-back tank.

"Oh, I tripped under your brother."

"Huh?"

"He was wandering around in the dark when I went down for some tea—which ended up being cold pizza and a soda. He ran into me and knocked me down."

"Why was he wandering around in the dark?"

"My question exactly. Beers and Mrs. G. He crashed in one of the guest rooms."

"I didn't know he was here."

"Still here," Mac said. "His car's out front."

"I'll see if he's up. Fifteen minutes, Mac."

"Nag. When do I get my endorphins?" Mac demanded of Laurel. "How will I know when I do?"

"How do you know when you orgasm?"

"Yeah?" Mac brightened. "It's like that?"

"Sadly no, but the principle of 'you know when you get there' is the same. Are you eating breakfast here?"

"I'm thinking about it. I think I'll have earned it. Plus, if I call Carter to come over, he can talk Mrs. G into French toast."

"Do that then. I've got something I want to show you."

"What?"

"Just an idea."

It was just after seven when Laurel, dressed for the day, sketchbook in hand, stepped into the family kitchen.

She'd assumed Del would be gone, but there he was, leaning against the counter with a steaming mug of coffee. In a near mirror image of the posture, Carter Maguire leaned on the opposite counter.

Still, they were so different. Del, even in the torn shirt and jeans, projected a kind of masculine elegance, while Carter exuded a disarming sweetness. Not sugary, she thought. She'd have hated that—but an innate sort of *niceness*.

And despite Del's fumble in the night, he was agile, athletic, while Carter tended toward the klutzy.

Still, they were both so damn cute.

Obviously, the sturdy Mrs. Grady wasn't immune. She worked at the stove—French toast winning the day—her eyes bright, her cheeks a little flushed. Happy to have the boys around, Laurel thought.

Parker came in from the terrace, slipping her BlackBerry into her pocket. She caught sight of Laurel. "Saturday evening's bride. Basic nerves. All smooth. Emma and Jack are heading over, Mrs. G."

"Well, if I'm cooking for an army, some of the troops had better sit. Keep your fingers off that bacon, boy," she warned Del, "until you're at the table like the civilized."

"Just trying to get a head start. I'll take it over. Hey, Laurel, how's the head?"

"Still on my shoulders." She set down the sketchbook, picked up the pitcher of juice.

"Morning." Carter smiled at her. "What happened to your head?"

"Del beat it against the stairs."

"After she hit me and ripped my shirt."

"Because you were drunk and knocked me down."

"I wasn't drunk, and you fell."

"That's his story."

"Sit down and behave," Mrs. G ordered. She turned as Jack and Emma came in. "Are your hands clean?" she demanded of Jack.

"Yes, ma'am."

"Then take this and go sit."

He accepted the platter of French toast, sniffed deeply. "What did you make for everybody else?"

She laughed and swatted at him.

"Hey," he said to Del.

They'd been friends since college, and as tight as brothers since Jack had relocated to Greenwich to open his architectural firm. He took his place at the breakfast nook, movie-star handsome with his wavy, dark blond hair, smoky eyes, quick grin.

The fact that he was dressed in a suit told Laurel he had a client meeting in his office rather than an appointment on a construction site.

"Shirt's ripped," Jack said to Del as he nabbed a slice of bacon.

"Laurel did it."

Jack wiggled his eyebrows at her. "Feisty."

"Idiot."

They grinned at each other as Mac came in. "God! This better be worth it. Come here." She grabbed Carter, yanked him against her for a noisy kiss. "I earned that."

"You're all . . . rosy," he murmured and bent his head to kiss her again.

"Stop that nonsense and sit down before the food gets cold." Mrs. G gave him a flick on the arm as she carried the coffeepot to the table to fill mugs.

Mrs. G was in her element, Laurel knew. She had a full brood to fuss over and order around. She'd revel in the number and the noise of them, and when she'd had enough of both, she'd kick them all out of her kitchen. Or retreat to her rooms for some peace and quiet.

But for now, with the scents of coffee and bacon and cinnamon, with platters being emptied and plates filled, Mrs. G had things just as she wanted.

Laurel understood the need to feed, the desire—even the passion—to put food in front of someone and urge them to eat. It was life and comfort, authority and satisfaction. And if you'd prepared that food with your own hands, your own skill, it was, in a very real way, love.

She supposed she'd learned some of that right here when Mrs. G had taught her how to roll out a pastry shell or mix batter or test a loaf of bread for doneness. More than the basics of baking, she'd learned if you put some love and pride into the mix, the dough rose truer.

"Head okay?" Del asked her.

"Yes, no thanks to you. Why?"

"Because you're quiet."

"Who can get a word in?" she asked as conversations crisscrossed the table.

"How about a professional query?"

She eyed him warily over a bite of French toast. "Such as?"

"I need a cake."

"Everyone needs cake, Del."

"That should be your slogan. Dara's coming back from maternity leave. I thought we'd do a little office welcome back, happy baby and all that."

It was a nice thing to do for his paralegal, and very like him. "When?"

"Ah, Thursday."

"As in this Thursday?" Also just like him, she thought. "What kind of cake?"

"A good one."

"That's the only kind I make. Give me a clue here. How many people?"

"Maybe twenty."

"Sheet or layered?"

He sent her a pleading look. "Help me, Laurel. You know Dara. Just whatever you figure."

"Is she allergic to anything?"

"No. I don't think." He topped off her coffee an instant before she thought to do so herself. "It doesn't have to be spectacular. Just a nice cake for an office deal. I could go to the market and pick one up but . . . that's what I'd get," he said, pointing at the scowl on her face. "I can pick it up Wednesday after work if you can squeeze it in."

"I'll squeeze it in because I like Dara."

"Thanks." He reached over to give her hand a pat. "Gotta run. I'll pick up that paperwork Wednesday," he told Parker.

"Let me know about the other stuff when you figure it out."

He stood, then walked to Mrs. G. "Thanks."

He gave her a quick, casual kiss on the cheek first. Then came the hug, and it was the hug that always made Laurel's heart mush. Serious grip, cheek to the hair, eyes closed, just a little sway. Del's hugs *mattered*, she thought, and made him impossible to resist.

"Pretend to behave yourself," Mrs. Grady ordered.

"That I can do. See you." He gave a wave to the rest of the group, then went out the back.

"I'd better get moving, too. Mrs. G." Jack said, "you are the goddess of the kitchen. The empress of epicure."

She gave her big laugh at that. "Go to work."

"Going."

"I'd better get started, too. I'll walk out with you," Emma said.

"Actually, I've got something I'd like your take on," Laurel said to Emma before she could rise.

"Then I get to have more coffee." She shifted to fuss with the knot of Jack's tie, then tugged it until their lips met. "Bye."

"See you tonight. I'll drop those revised plans by, Parker."

"Anytime."

"Should I get out of the way?" Carter asked when Jack left.

"You're allowed to stay, and even comment." Laurel scooted out for her sketchbook. "I had a brainstorm last night, so I worked up an idea for the wedding cake."

"My cake? Our cake," Mac corrected quickly with a grin for Carter. "I wanna see, I wanna see!"

"Presentation," Laurel said sternly, "is a watchword of Icing at Vows. So, while the inspiration for this design primarily stems from the bride—"

"Me!"

"It also factors in what the designer sees as qualities that attract the groom to said bride, and vice versa. So we have,

I think, a blending of the traditional and nontraditional in both form and flavor. Added to this, the designer has known the bride for more than two decades, and has developed a deep and sincere attachment to the groom—all of which play into the concept—but will ensure that any critiques of said concept will be gracefully accepted."

"That's bull." Parker rolled her eyes. "You'll be pissed off if she doesn't like it."

"That's only true because if she doesn't like it, she's an idiot. Which means I've been friends with an idiot for over two decades."

"Just let me see the damn design."

"I can adjust the size once you've nailed down your guest list. The current concept's good for two hundred." Laurel flipped open the book, held up the sketch.

She didn't have to hear Mac's breath catch to know. She saw it in the stunned delight on her face.

"The colors are pretty true to what I'd do, and you can see I'd want to do a variety of cakes and fillings. Your Italian cream, and the chocolate with raspberry Carter favors, the yellow, maybe with pastry cream. It's just one way to do your cake sampler fantasy."

"If Mac doesn't like it, I'll take it," Emma announced.

"It doesn't suit you. It's Mac's if she wants it. The flowers can be changed," Laurel added, "to whatever ones you and Emma decide on for your bouquets and arrangements—but I'd stick with the color palette. You're not white icing, Mac. You're color."

"Please don't hate it," Mac murmured to Carter.

"How could I? It's stunning." He glanced over at Laurel, gave her a slow, sweet smile. "Plus, I heard chocolate with raspberry. If we're voting, it gets mine."

"Mine, too," Emma said.

"I'm thinking you'd better hide that sketch." Parker nodded at Laurel. "If our clients get a look at it, we're going to have brides fighting for that cake. Nailed it in one, Laurel."

Mac stood to step closer, to take the pad and study. "The

shape, the textures, not to mention the colors. Oh, oh, the photographs we'll get! Which you considered," she added, shifting her gaze to Laurel's.

"It's hard to think about you without thinking photography."

"I love it. You know I love it. You knew I'd love it. You know me." She put her arms around Laurel, squeezed hard, then did a little dance. "Thank you, thank you, thank you."

"Let me have a look at that." Mrs. Grady took the book out of Mac's hand and studied the sketch with narrowed eyes and pursed lips.

Then she nodded, looked at Laurel. "Good girl. And now, all of you, out of my kitchen."

CHAPTER THREE

By WEDNESDAY, LAUREL JUGGLED BAKING, TASTINGS, MEET-ings, and design sessions. Her cooler and freezer bulged with a variety of fillings, frostings, and layers, precisely la-beled, that she'd use to create the cakes and desserts for the weekend events. And she still had more to go.

With her kitchen TV tuned to *The Philadelphia Story* for the buzz and pop of the dialogue, she added egg yolks, one at a time, to the fluff of butter and sugar in her mixing bowl. Her board held sketches or photos of this week's designs, and a printed schedule of tasks to be done.

Once each yolk was fully incorporated, she added the mixture of flour and baking powder she'd already sifted together three times, alternating it with the milk she'd mea-sured out.

She was whisking egg whites and salt in a separate bowl when Mac came in.

"Working."

"Sorry. I need cookies. Please, can I have cookies?"

"Doesn't Mrs. G have any?"

"They're not to eat. I mean not for *me* to eat. Although,

cookies. I need some for a shoot I have in a couple hours. I got this idea, and cookies would work. Emma let me have flowers."

Laurel arched her eyebrows at Mac's pleading smile as she added a quarter of the stiffened egg whites to the batter. "What kind of cookies?"

"I won't know until I see what you've got. You always have cookies."

Resigned, Laurel gestured with her head. "In the cooler. Write down what you take on the inventory board."

"There's another board? A cookie board?"

Laurel began folding in the remaining whites. "We now have two men in our world. They're known for mooching cookies."

Mac angled her head, pouted a little. "You give Carter cookies?"

"I'd give Carter my love and devotion if you hadn't gotten there first, sister. So I give him cookies instead. He's over here nearly every day since school let out, working on his book."

"And eating cookies without bringing home any to share, apparently. Ah, the chocolate chunk," Mac announced with her head and shoulders in the cooler. "Big as my hand, traditional, and will photograph nicely. I'm taking half a dozen, well, seven, because I'm eating one now."

She took one of the small bakery boxes for transport while Laurel poured batter into prepared pans.

"Do you want one?" At Laurel's head shake, Mac shrugged. "I've never known how you resist. My shoot's your tasting today."

"Right. I've got them on the list."

"I love this movie." Mac crunched into a cookie, then glanced away from the TV toward the display. "What's this design? It's not in my book."

Laurel tapped the pans on the counter to break up any air bubbles. "It's off book." She transferred pans to the oven, set the timer. "For Del's paralegal. She's coming back from maternity leave, and he's having a little cake and coffee thing for her."

"That's nice."

"I'm the one who made the cake."

"Which is nice, too, Miss Crankypants."

Laurel started to snarl, then stopped herself. "Shit. I am Miss Crankypants. Maybe it's the sex moratorium. It has its upside, but there is the inevitable down."

"Maybe you need a booty buddy." Sagely, Mac pointed with the remainder of the cookie. "Somebody who can just pop the cork every couple weeks."

"That's an idea." Laurel tried a bright, eager smile. "Can I please have Carter?"

"No. Not even for cookies."

"Selfish, that's what you are." She got to work cleaning up the baking area. Next on the list, she noted, were the crystallized flowers for Friday's cake.

"We should go shopping," Mac decided. "We should all go buy shoes."

Laurel considered. "Yes. Shoes are a viable substitute for sex. Let's schedule that. Soon. Ah, here's just the woman who can schedule anything," she said as Parker strode in. "But she's got that work look on her face."

"Good, Mac's here, too. I'm going to make some tea."

Laurel and Mac exchanged looks. "Uh-oh," Mac murmured.

"It's not uh-oh. Very much," Parker qualified.

"I don't have time for not very much. I have to make a zillion crystallized baby roses and Johnny-jump-ups."

"You can get it set up while I'm dealing with the tea."

Useless to protest, Laurel thought and got out her wire racks and baking pans, her bowls, her ingredients.

"Mia Stowe, January bride?" Parker began.

"Big, fat Greek wedding," Mac commented. "The MOB's Greek, and her parents still live there. They're after a big, wild, traditional Greek deal."

"Right, exactly. Good. It seems the grandparents have

decided—impulsively—to visit. Grandmother wants to check on some of the wedding plans, since apparently she's never completely forgiven her son-in-law for taking her daughter to the U.S., and lacks confidence that we—or anyone—can pull off the kind of wedding she wants."

"The grandmother wants," Laurel said as she got the edible flowers Emma had provided out of the cooler.

"Again, exactly. MOB is in a panic. Bride is scrambling. Grandmother is demanding an engagement party—and yes, they've been engaged for six months, but this doesn't deter Grandmother."

"So let them have a party." Laurel shrugged and began trimming stems.

"She wants it here, so she can check us out, approve the location, our services, and so on. And she wants it here next week."

"Next week?" Mac and Laurel sputtered in unison.

"We're booked. Full slate," Laurel pointed out.

"Not on Tuesday night. I know." Parker held up both hands for peace. "Believe me, I know. I've just spent most of an hour on the phone between a hysterical MOB and a bride who feels caught in the middle. We can do this. I've checked with the caterer, managed to book a band. I called Emma and she'll handle the flowers. They want some formal family portraits, and some candids. But the formals are the key," she said to Mac. "And some traditional Greek desserts, along with a weddingish cake."

"Weddingish?"

Parker merely spread her hands at the wasp on Laurel's tone. "The bride is firmly against a reproduction of the design she's picked for the actual event. And it's a much smaller deal. About seventy-five people, but I'd plan for a hundred. She said she'd leave the design, the flavor completely up to you."

"That's considerate of her."

"She's really stuck, Laurel. I feel for her. I'll handle the rest, but I need the two of you on board." She set a cup of tea on the counter while Laurel dipped a flower into beaten egg whites and water. "I said I'd call her back one way or the other after I'd checked with my partners."

Laurel shook off the excess egg wash, blotted the rosebud with a paper towel before sprinkling it with superfine sugar. "You booked the band."

"I can unbook the band. All for one."

Laurel laid the first flower on the wire rack. "I guess I'm making baklava." She glanced at Mac. "You in?"

"We'll make it work. I know all about crazy mothers. How much different is a crazy grandmother? I'll go add it to my schedule, and talk to Emma about the flowers. Let me know the cake design when you decide on it."

"Thanks, Mac."

"It's what we do," she said to Parker. "I've got a shoot," she added, and ducked out again.

Parker picked up her own cup of tea. "I'll get someone in to help you if you need it. And I know you hate that, but if you need it."

Laurel drizzled the next flower. "I can put something together. I've got emergency layers and fillings in the freezer for just such occasions. I think I'll work up something to kick Greek Grandma's ass—and shut her up. Maybe Primrose Waltz."

"Oh, I love that one. But it's a lot of work, as I remember."

"It'll be worth it. I've got the fondant, and I can make the primulas ahead of time. Mia's got a couple younger sisters, right?"

"Two sisters and a brother." Parker's smile bloomed. "And, yes, we're both thinking we're planting fertile seeds for future business. If you make up a list, I'll take care of the marketing."

"That's a deal. Go call the MOB and earn her grateful tears."

"I will. Hey, how about pajama and movie night?"

"Best offer I've had all day. See you there."

Laurel continued to coat the flowers, thinking the only dating she was doing these days was with her best pal Parker.

* * *

WITH THE LAYERS BAKED, WRAPPED, AND IN THE FREEZER
to set the crumb, the crystallized flowers drying on the rack,
Laurel prepped for her tasting. In the lounge off her kitchen,
she set out the albums of designs along with the flowers
Emma had arranged for her. She fanned cocktail napkins
with the Vows logo, stacked spreading knives, spoons, tea-
cups, wineglasses, and champagne glasses.

Back in the kitchen she sliced a variety of cakes into
slim rectangles and arranged them on a glass platter. In
small glass dishes, she placed generous dollops of different
frostings and fillings.

She slipped into the bathroom to freshen her makeup
and hair, then buttoned on a cropped jacket, and changed
out of her kitchen shoes into heels.

When her clients rang the buzzer, she was ready for
them.

"Steph, Chuck, it's good to see you again. How was the
shoot?" she asked as she gestured them in.

"It was fun." Stephanie, a cheerful brunette, hooked her
arm with her fiancé's. "Wasn't it fun?"

"It was. After I stopped being nervous."

"He hates getting his picture taken."

"I always feel goofy." Chuck, sandy-haired and shy,
ducked his head as he grinned. "I usually am."

"Mac had me feed him a cookie because I'd told her
we'd had cookies on our first date. When we were eight."

"Only I didn't know we were dating."

"I did. Now, eighteen years later, I've got you."

"Well, I hope you left room for cake. How about some
champagne, or wine?"

"I'd love some champagne. God, I love this place," Steph
enthused. "I love everything about it. Oh, is this your kitchen?
Where you bake?"

She made a point of bringing clients through her kitchen,
so they could get a feel for it—and see it sparkle. "It is. It

was originally used as a secondary or caterer's kitchen. Now it's all mine."

"It really is beautiful. I like to cook, and I'm pretty good at it. But baking . . ." Steph fluttered her hand side to side.

"It takes practice, and patience."

"What are these? Oh, they're so pretty!"

"Crystallized flowers. I just made them. They have to set several hours at room temperature." Please don't touch them, Laurel thought.

"You can eat them?"

"You sure can. It's best not to use any flower or garnish on a cake, I think, unless it's edible."

"Maybe we should do something like that, Chuck. Real flowers."

"I have a lot of designs that incorporate them. And I can customize for you. Why don't you come in and sit? I'll get you that champagne, and we'll get started."

It was easy when the clients were inclined to be pleased, as these were, Laurel decided. They seemed to love everything, including each other. Her hardest job, she realized after the first ten minutes, would be to steer them toward what made them the happiest.

"They're all delicious." Steph spread a bit of white chocolate mousse on vanilla bean. "How does anyone ever pick?"

"The best part is there's no wrong choice. You like the mocha spice," Laurel said to Chuck.

"What's not to like?"

"It's a good choice for a groom's cake, and it's fabulous with the chocolate ganache. Manly," she said with a wink. "And in this design, it resembles a heart carved into a tree, with your names and the dates piped on."

"Oh, I love it. Do you love it?" Steph asked him.

"It's pretty cool." Chuck angled the photo for a better look. "I didn't know I got a cake."

"It's up to you. No wrong choices."

"Let's do it, Chuck. He can have the manly, and then I can go completely girly on the wedding cake."

"That's a deal. This is the ganache, right?" He sampled, grinned. "Oh yeah. Sold."

"Yay! This is fun, too. People keep telling us planning a wedding is a huge headache, and how we'll fight and get edgy. But we're having such a good time."

"It's our job to have the headaches and fight and get edgy."

Steph laughed, then lifted her hands. "Tell me what you think. You hit it dead-on with Chuck."

"Okay. Valentine's Day wedding. Why not go full-out romance? Now, you liked the idea of crystallized flowers, but this design uses sugar paste. Still, I think it's romantic and fun and really, really girly."

Laurel found the photograph in the album, turned it.

Steph slapped her hands over her mouth. "Oh, oh, wow!"

It was, Laurel thought, definitely a wow. "Five graduated tiers, separated by dowels to give it that open, airy look. And the dowels are covered with sugar paste petals, more petals and blossoms overlaying the top of the tiers and spilling over for abundance. These are hydrangea blossoms," Laurel went on, "but I can do any kind. Rose petals, cherry blossoms, name it. Any colors or tones. I use royal icing on this, generally, piping it out on each tier to form the crown. But again, I can customize. Using fondant for a sleeker look, doing ribbons or pearls, in the white, or in the color of the flowers."

"It's my colors, the blue and that lavendery pink. You knew that. You knew that and showed me the perfect cake." Steph let out a reverent sigh. "It's so beautiful."

"It is," Chuck agreed. "But you know what else? It's really charming. Like Steph."

"Oh. Chuck."

"I have to agree. If you like this direction, you could go with more than one flavor and filling."

"I don't like this direction. I love this cake. This is my cake. Can we still do a topper? The bride and groom topper."

"Absolutely."

"Perfect. Because I want us to be on top. Can I have another glass of champagne?"

"You bet." Laurel rose to pour.

"Can't you have one, too? Are you not allowed?"

Glancing back, Laurel smiled. "I'm the boss, and I'd love to have one."

The champagne and the clients left her in an excellent mood. And since she was done for the day, she decided to pour herself a second glass and make herself a little fruit and cheese platter to go with it. Relaxed, she sat at her counter sipping, nibbling, and making a list of supplies for Parker to pick up.

Greek meant butter, butter, butter, and lots of nuts. She'd have to make phyllo sheets—a pain in the ass, but the job was the job. Honey, almonds, pistachios, walnuts, bread flour.

While she was at it, it wouldn't hurt to list her staple bulk items, then the supplies she'd need to order soon from her wholesaler.

"Now this is the kind of work I want."

She glanced up to see Del in the doorway. Full lawyer mode, she thought, with the tailored suit—charcoal with subtle pinstripes—the elegant tie in a precise Windsor knot, the serious leather briefcase.

"You can have it after you've been on your feet for ten hours."

"Might be worth it. Is that coffee fresh?"

"Enough."

He helped himself. "Parker said you should think sexy, weepy, or silly. Whatever that means."

Movie night, Laurel concluded. "Okay. You want your cake?"

"No rush." He stepped over, used her knife to spread some Camembert on a rosemary cracker. "Good. What's for dinner?"

"You're eating it."

The faintest of disapproving frowns clouded his eyes. "You have to do better than this, especially after a ten-hour day."

"Yes, Daddy."

Impervious to the sarcasm, he tried a slice of apple. "I could've brought you something since part of the ten's on me."

"It's not a big deal, and if I wanted something, I could make it, or tug on Mrs. G."

Just one of his girls, she thought as frustration simmered. "Somehow we grown women get through the day without you fussing over our nutritional choices."

"Champagne ought to put you in a better mood." He cocked his head to scan her lists. "Why don't you do that on the computer?"

"Because I'm doing it by hand, because I don't have a printer down here, and because I didn't feel like it. What's it to you?"

Obviously amused, he leaned on the counter, bracing on his forearms. "You need a nap."

"You need a dog."

"I need a dog?"

"Yes, so you'd have someone to worry about, fuss over, and order around."

"I like dogs, but I have you." He stopped, laughed. "And that really came out wrong. Besides, 'fuss over' is what grandmothers do, so it's an inaccurate term. Worrying about you is my job, not only as your lawyer and a silent partner in your business, but because you're my girls. As for ordering you around, that only works about half the time, but five hundred's a damn good batting average."

"You're a smug bastard, Delaney."

"Can be," he agreed and tried the Gouda. "You're a moody woman, Laurel, but I don't hold it against you."

"You know your problem?"

"No."

"Exactly." She jabbed a finger at him as she hopped off the stool. "I'll get your cake."

"Why are you mad at me?" he demanded and trailed behind her to the walk-in refrigerator.

"I'm not mad, I'm irritated." She picked up the cake

she'd already boxed for travel. She might have turned and shoved it into his hands, but even irritated she took care with her work.

"Okay, why are you irritated?"

"Because you're in my way."

He held up his hands for peace, stepped aside so she could walk by him and set the cake on the counter. She flipped up the lid, flicked her hand toward it.

Cautious, because he was getting fairly irritated himself, he eased over and looked inside. And couldn't help but smile.

The two round layers—tiers, he corrected—were glossy white, and decorated with colorful symbols of Dara's current life. Briefcases, baby strollers, law books, rattles, rocking chairs, and laptops. In the center, a clever cartoon depiction of the new mother held a briefcase in one hand and a baby bottle in the other.

"It's great. It's perfect. She's going to love it."

"Bottom layer is yellow, buttercream filling. Top's devil's food with Swiss meringue. Make sure you keep it level."

"Okay. I really appreciate it."

When he reached for his wallet, she actually hissed. "You are not paying me. What the hell is *wrong* with you?"

"I just wanted to . . . What the hell's wrong with *you*?"

"What the hell's wrong with me? I'll tell you what the hell's wrong with me." She planted a hand on his chest to push him back a step. "You're irritating and overbearing and self-righteous and patronizing."

"Whoa. All this because I wanted to pay you for a cake I asked you to make? It's your business, for Christ's sake. You make cakes, people pay you."

"One minute you're fussing—and yes, the word *is* fussing—because I'm not eating the kind of dinner you approve of, and the next you're pulling out your wallet like I'm the hired help."

"That's not what— Goddamn it, Laurel."

"How can anybody keep up?" She threw her arms in the

air. "Big brother, legal advisor, business associate, mother-fucking hen. Why don't you just *pick* one?"

"Because more than one applies." He didn't shout as she did, but his tone boiled just as hot. "And I'm nobody's motherfucking hen."

"Then stop trying to manage everyone's lives."

"I don't hear anyone else complaining, and helping you manage is part of my job."

"On the legal end, the business end, not on the personal end. Let me tell you something, and try to get this through that thick skull once and for all. I'm not your pet, I'm not your responsibility, I'm not your sister, I'm not your girl. I'm an adult, and I'm free to do what I want, when I want, without asking your permission or courting your approval."

"And I'm not your whipping boy," he shot back. "I don't know what's gotten into you, but you can either tell me or take it out on somebody else."

"You want to know what's gotten into me?"

"Yes, I do."

"I'll show you."

Maybe it was the champagne. Maybe it was just the mad. Or maybe it was the look of baffled annoyance on his face. But she went with the impulse that had been bubbling inside her for years.

She grabbed him by the perfect knot of his elegant tie, jerked him down even as she gripped a handful of his hair, and yanked him forward. And she fixed her mouth to his in a hot, sizzling, frustrated kiss, one that gave her heart a jolt even as her mind purred: *I knew it!*

She threw him off balance—she meant to—so his hands came to her hips, and his fingers dug in for one gloriously heady moment.

She threw herself into that moment, to exploit, to savor, to absorb. Tastes and textures, heat and hunger, all there for the taking. She took exactly what she wanted, then shoved him away.

"There." She tossed her hair back while he stared at her. "The sky did not fall, the world did not end, neither of us was struck by lightning or beamed straight to hell. I'm not your damn sister, Delaney. That ought to make it clear."

She strode out of the kitchen without a backward glance.

Aroused, astonished, and still considerably annoyed, he stood exactly where he was. "What was that? What the hell was that?"

He started to go after her, then stopped himself. That wouldn't end well, or it would end . . . He'd better not think of that until he could think, period.

He frowned at the half glass of champagne. How much had she had before he'd come in? he wondered. Then, because his throat was uncommonly dry, he picked up the flute and downed the rest of the contents.

He should go, just go home, and set the whole thing aside. Chalk the whole incident up to . . . something. He'd figure out what to chalk it up to when his brain regained full function.

He'd just come for the cake, that's all, he reminded himself as he carefully closed and secured the lid on the bakery box. She'd picked a fight, then she'd kissed him to prove some sort of point. That's all there was to it.

He'd just go home and let her stew over whatever she was stewing over.

He picked up the box. He'd just go home, he admitted, and take a really long, cold shower.

CHAPTER FOUR

𝒮HE TRIED NOT TO DWELL ON IT. A PUNISHING SCHEDULE
of summer weddings helped keep her from thinking about
what she'd done, at least for four out of every five minutes.
Then again, so much of her work was solitary, and gave her
entirely too much time to think and to ask herself how she
could have done something so incredibly stupid.

He'd deserved it, of course. And it had been a long time
coming. But when she came right down to the nitty, just
who had she punished with that kiss except herself?

Because now it wasn't merely theory or speculation.
Now she knew how it would feel, how she would feel, if she
let herself go—just for a minute—with Del. She'd never be
able to convince herself again that kissing him in reality
would fall far short of kissing him in her imagination.

She'd bought the ticket, and she'd rung the bell. No way
to ask for a refund.

If he hadn't made her so mad, she thought as she scurried to help with the turnover in the brief window between
the two Saturday events. Del being infuriatingly Del with
his "Why don't you do it this way," "Why aren't you eating

a real meal"—then, *then* reaching for his big, fat wallet as if . . .

And that wasn't fair; she had to admit it. She'd poked, pushed, prodded. She'd been primed for a fight.

She assembled the centerpiece on the graceful top tier of the white and gold cake she called Gilded Dreams. She considered it one of her more fanciful cakes with its silklike layered overskirt and coiled rosettes.

Not her particular taste either, she mused, and arranged some of the extra rosettes around the base, scattered over the sparkling gold tablecloth. Probably because she wasn't a dreamer or especially fanciful.

A pragmatist was what she was, she thought. Reality-steeped. She wasn't a romantic like Emma, or as free-flowing as Mac, or as optimistic as Parker.

At the bottom of it, she dealt in formulas, didn't she? She could experiment with amounts and ingredients, but at the end of it she had to accept that certain components simply didn't mix. Insisting on stirring the incompatible together ended up making an unpalatable mess. When that happened, the only thing to do was chalk it up to a mistake and move on.

"Gorgeous." Taking a quick and approving survey of the cake, Emma set her hamper down. "I've got the candles and the table flowers." She tipped her wrist to angle her watch before letting out a brief *whew*. "We're right on schedule. Everything's dressed, in and out, and Mac's about done with the preceremony shots."

Laurel turned to look at the Ballroom, surprised so much had been done while she'd brooded. More flowers, more candles yet to be lit, a scattering of tables draped in the shimmery gold and summer blue the bride had chosen.

"How about the Great Hall?"

"The caterers are finishing up, but my team's done." Emma arranged the tapers, tea lights, blossoms with her clever florist's hands. "Jack's keeping the groomsmen entertained. It's nice, having him pitch in."

"Yeah. Does it ever strike you as weird?"

"What?"

"You and Jack. Does it ever sneak up and strike you as weird, the way you knew each other for years, and hung out as friends, then took that one-eighty?"

Emma stepped back, then forward again to slide a rose over a quarter of an inch. "It strikes me as surprising sometimes, but more, scary when I think what wouldn't have happened if we'd kept going straight ahead instead of taking that turn." She shoved at one of the pins trying to keep her mass of curls restrained. "It's not weird to you, is it?"

"No. I sort of wonder if it's weird that it's not weird." Laurel stopped, shook her head. "Ignore me. My head's in a strange place." With some relief, she heard Parker's signal in her earbud. "Two-minute warning. If you're good here, I'll go down and help with the lineup."

"I'm good. I'll be right behind you."

Shedding her apron, unclipping her hair as she went, Laurel hurried down and arrived at the checkpoint with thirty seconds to spare. Not her taste, she thought again, but she had to admit the bride knew what she was doing. A half dozen attendants lined up under Parker's orders, glittering in their bell-skirted gold gowns with the striking bouquets Emma had created of blue dahlias offset with white roses. The bride herself, a regal vision in lustrous silk, pearls gleaming, sequins sparkling on her formal train, stood radiant beside her father—and he was damn dashing in white tie and tails.

"MOG's in place," Parker murmured to Laurel. "MOB's being escorted now. Ladies! Remember to smile. Caroline, you look spectacular."

"I feel spectacular. This is it, Daddy," she said.

"Don't get me started." He took his daughter's hand, pressed it to his lips.

Parker cued the music change so the string orchestra the bride had chosen segued into the entrance music. "Number one, go. Head up! Smile! You're gorgeous. And . . . number two. Heads up, ladies."

Laurel smoothed skirts, adjusted headpieces, and finally

stood with Parker to watch the bride take her walk on the flower-strewn path.

"*Spectacular*'s the word," Laurel decided. "I thought it might be too much, just tipping over into gaudy. But it stops just an elegant inch short."

"Yeah, but I can tell you I'll be happy not to see gold or gilt for a month. We've got twenty minutes before we need to move the guests into the Great Hall."

"I'm stealing ten and taking a walk. I need a break."

Instantly Parker turned. "Are you okay?"

"Yeah, just need a break."

Head-clearing time, Laurel thought as she circled around. Away-from-people time. The valet team would be in the kitchen now, getting fed before they went back on duty, so she took the long way around, past the side terraces and gardens to where she could enjoy the quiet, and the abundance of summer flowers.

Emma had set urns and pots here and there to add to that abundance, with wildly blue lobelia spilling or sweetly pink impatiens dancing. The beautiful old Victorian stood dressed for the wedding with the bride's favored blue dahlias and white roses rioting around the entrance portico, swags of tulle and lace adding romance.

Even without them, the house was romantic, to her mind. The soft, quiet blue trimmed with cream and pale gold. All the rooflines, the pretty bits of gingerbread brought that romance, and a touch of fancy, to dignity. It had been a second home to her as long as she could remember. Now, of course, it was home. And that lovely house stood only a quick call from the pool house and guest house where her friends lived and worked.

She couldn't imagine it any differently, even with Carter and Jack now in residence, even with the addition nearly complete on Mac's studio to make it a home for two.

No, she couldn't imagine her life without the estate, the house, the business she'd built with her friends and, well, the community they'd made here among them.

She had to think about that, Laurel admitted, about why she had what she had.

Her own hard work, certainly, and the hard work of her friends. Parker's vision. The check Mrs. G had handed her that day, so many years ago—and the faith that had been as valued as the money—had thrown open the door.

But that wasn't all.

The house, the estate, everything on and in it had gone to Parker and Del when their parents died. Del had taken a leap of faith, too, every bit as vital and essential as Mrs. G had when she'd written that check.

This was his home, Laurel mused, standing back, studying the lines, the grace, the beauty of it. But he'd signed it over to Parker. There were legal ins and outs, business models, projections, percentages, contracts—but the bottom line remained.

His sister—no, all four of them, what he liked to call the Quartet—had wanted something, had asked, and he'd given. He'd believed in them, and he'd helped them make a dream a reality. It hadn't been for percentages or with projections in mind. He'd done it because he loved them.

"Damn it." Irritated with herself, she dragged a hand through her hair. She hated knowing she'd been unfair and bitchy and just plain stupid.

Del hadn't deserved the things she said to him—and she'd said them because it was easier to be pissed at him than attracted to him. And finally, kissing him? Stupid wasn't even close.

Now she had to make amends, cover her ass, and save face. That sort of hat trick wouldn't be a snap.

But she was the one who'd crossed the line, and she was the one with feelings that had to be resolved. So she was the one who had to fix it.

She heard Parker cue the lighting of the unity candle and the vocal solo. Time's up, she told herself. She'd figure out how to work the fix later.

* * *

$\mathscr{S}$INCE SHE DIDN'T TRUST ANYONE ELSE TO PROPERLY CUT the complicated design, Laurel stationed herself by the cake table. She waited while the bride and groom made the ceremonial first slice—where she'd instructed—and fed each other while Mac memorialized the moment. Then, while the music and dancing continued, she took over.

With a chef's knife, she broke away the side decorations.

"Damn, that seems wrong."

She glanced at Jack as she began to slice and transfer cake to serving plates. "It's meant to be eaten."

"I look at something like this and think, if I'd built it, I'd have to be far away when it was demolished. And I might still have to dab at a few tears."

"It hurts the first few times, but then it's not like building a house. You don't do that knowing a wrecking ball's going to swing into it eventually. Want a piece?"

"Damn right."

"Hang on until we get the first couple of server trays filled." Which, she concluded, would give her an opening to pump him for information. "So, Del's not coming over to play with you tonight?"

"I think he's got something going."

Something female, she supposed. But that was none of her business, and not to the point.

"I guess you're both too busy to hang out much these days."

"Actually, we caught dinner Thursday night."

After "The Kiss," she thought. "So, what's the news, what's the gossip?" She slanted up a quick smile, trying to read his face.

"The Yankees are having a good month," he said, and smiled back.

No awkwardness, she concluded, no smirkiness. She couldn't decide whether to be insulted or relieved that Del hadn't mentioned the incident to his closest friend.

"Here." She handed him a generous slice of cake.

"Thanks." He sampled. "You're a genius."

"Too true." Satisfied she'd cut enough servings for now, she wound through wedding guests to check the dessert table and groom's cake.

Music pumped, packed the dance floor. With the terrace doors wide open to the balmy night, guests danced or gathered outside as well.

Parker sidled up beside her. "The cake's an enormous hit, FYI."

"Good to know." Laurel scanned the nearest dessert table and judged that supplies would probably last through the final dance. "Hey, is that the MOB?" She nodded toward the dance floor. "Girl's got some moves."

"She was a professional. Danced on Broadway."

"I can see it."

"That's how she and the FOB met. He was a backer, came in to watch a rehearsal, and—he says—fell for her on the spot. She danced until after their second child was born, and a few years later started giving private lessons."

"Sweet. But seriously, how do you remember all that?"

Parker continued to scan the room, eagle-eyed, for any problem. "The same way you remember all the ingredients in that cake over there. The B and G requested an extra hour."

"Ouch."

"I know, but everyone's having a great time. The band's okay with it. We'll transfer the gifts as scheduled, so that'll be done. Then, hell, let them dance."

"It's going to be a long night." She reassessed the desserts. "I'll go get some more pastries."

"Need help?"

"Probably."

"I'll beep Emma. She and Carter should be free. I'll send them down."

⁂T NEARLY ONE IN THE MORNING, WHILE THE CLEANING crew massed over the Ballroom, Laurel completed her check of the Bride's Suite. She gathered forgotten hair clips, a stray shoe, a pink leather makeup bag, and a lacy bra. The bra might be evidence of a quickie during the reception, or an attendant's need to free her girls.

The items would go into Parker's Lost and Found bin until claimed—with no questions asked.

As she carried them out, Parker swung by. "Looks like we're clear. I'll take those. Quick staff meeting."

Every muscle in Laurel's body whined in protest. "Tonight?"

"Quick one—I've got most of an open bottle of champagne to kill the pain."

"Fine, fine."

"Our parlor. Couple minutes."

No use complaining, Laurel thought, and made her way down to the parlor to claim the sofa.

She stretched out. Groaned.

"I knew you'd get here first." Since she couldn't claim the sofa, Mac lay down on the floor. "The BM hit on me. Carter thought it was funny."

"The sign of a confident man."

"I guess. But the thing is, I hardly ever got hit on at events before Carter. It doesn't seem right. I'm not available."

"Hence the hitting on." With a sigh instead of a groan, Laurel toed off her shoes. "I think men have built-in radar for that. Unavailable is sexier."

"Because they're dogs."

"Yes, of course."

"I heard that," Emma said as she came in. "And I think that's cynical and untrue. You got hit on because you're gorgeous—and because now that you have Carter, you're happier and more open—therefore only more appealing." She dropped into a chair, curled up her legs. "I want to go to bed."

"Join the crowd. We have to meet tomorrow for the Sunday run-through. Why can't whatever it is wait?"

"Because." Parker stepped in, pointed at Laurel. "I have something that'll make everyone go to sleep just a little

happier." She took an envelope out of her pocket. "The
FOB gave us a bonus. Though, I, of course, politely and del-
icately demurred, he wouldn't take no for an answer. Ahh,"
she added when she stepped out of her shoes. "We gave his
little girl the wedding of her dreams, gave him and his wife
an extraordinary night, and he wanted to show his appreciation over and above."

"Nice." Mac yawned. "Really."

"It's five thousand dollars." Parker smiled as Laurel
reared up on the sofa. "Cash," she added, pulling out the
bills to fan them.

"That's really nice appreciation. So very, very green,"
Laurel commented.

"Can I touch it before you put it away?" Mac asked.
"Before you roll it back into the business?"

"My vote is take the money. Maybe I'm just really tired,
but that's my vote. A thousand for each of us, and a thousand
for Carter and Jack to split." Parker waved the bills. "Up to
you."

"Aye." Emma shot up a hand. "Wedding fund for me!"

"Seconded. Or thirded. Hand it over," Mac ordered.

"No argument from me." Laurel wagged her fingers. "I
can use a grand."

"Okay then." Parker handed Laurel the open champagne.
"Pour and I'll count it out." She knelt on the floor.

"This is very, very sweet. Champagne and cash money
at the end of a really long day." Mac took a flute, passed it
to Emma. "Remember our first official event? After, we
popped a bottle, ate leftover cake, and danced. The four of
us and Del."

"I kissed Del."

"We all kissed Del," Emma pointed out and tapped her
glass to Mac's.

"No, I mean the other day I did." Laurel heard herself
say it with some shock, then considerable relief. "I'm incredibly stupid."

"Why? It's just . . ." Mac blinked, clued in. "Oh. *Kissed*
Del. Well. Huh."

"I was mad, and out of sorts, and he came for the cake. He was just so *Del*," she said with rancor she thought she'd walked off.

"I've been mad at Del," Emma commented. "It didn't lead me to kissing him."

"It's not a big deal. Not to him. He didn't even bother to tell Jack. Which means it didn't mean anything. Don't tell Jack," she ordered Emma. "Because he should have, and he didn't, so it meant nothing. Less than."

"You didn't tell us until now."

Laurel frowned at Mac. "Because I . . . had to think about it."

"But it meant something to you," Parker murmured.

"I don't know. It was an impulse, a moment of insanity. I was pissed off. It's not like I have a thing for him, really. Oh shit," she muttered and dropped her head in her hands.

"Did he kiss you back? Well?" Mac demanded when Emma kicked her. "It's a question."

"He didn't not. But he wasn't expecting it. I wasn't expecting it. It was mostly temper."

"What did he say? Don't kick me again," Mac warned Emma.

"Nothing. I didn't give him a chance. I'm going to fix it," she promised Parker. "It was my fault, even though he was being irritating and patronizing. Don't be upset."

"I'm not upset, not about that. I'm wondering how I could be so oblivious. I know you as well as I know anyone, so how could I not sense or see or know that you have feelings for Del?"

"I don't. Okay, I do, but it's not like I pine for him day and night. It comes and goes. Like an allergy. Only instead of making me sneeze, it makes me feel like an idiot." Distress rolled up from her belly and into her voice. "I know how tight you are. It's great how tight you are, but please don't tell him I said any of this. I wasn't going to say anything, but it just spilled out. Apparently I have an impulse-control problem."

"I won't say anything to him."

"Good. Good. It was nothing, really. It was just lips."

"No tongues?" Mac scooted out of Emma's reach, then hunched down as she got hit with scowls instead. "What? I'm interested. We're all interested or we wouldn't be here at one in the morning, with five thousand in cash on the table, talking about it."

"You're right," Laurel decided. "We shouldn't be talking about it. I only brought it up in the interest of full disclosure. Now, we can all just put it aside, take our bonus money, and go to bed. In fact, now that I've disclosed, I don't know why I was so twisted up about it. It was nothing."

She gestured broadly—too broadly, she realized, and dropped her hands again. "Obviously it was nothing, and Del's certainly not losing any sleep over it. He didn't say anything to Jack or you. Right?" she asked Parker.

"I haven't talked to him since early in the week, but no. No, he hasn't said anything to me."

"Listen to me." She managed a weak laugh. "I'm making it like high school. I didn't make it like high school when it *was* high school. Stopping now. I'm taking my money and going to bed."

She scooped up one of the piles Parker had counted out. "So, let's not think about this anymore, okay? Let's just . . . be normal. Everything's . . . normal. So, good night."

At her hasty retreat, her three friends looked at one another.

"It's so not normal," Mac said.

"It's not *ab*normal. It's just different." Emma put down her glass, picked up her money. "And she's embarrassed. We should leave it alone so she isn't embarrassed. Can we leave it alone?"

"It's more a question of whether she can," Parker said. "I guess we'll find out."

PARKER LET IT GO—FOR THE MOMENT. SHE LET IT RIDE through the Sunday event, and gave her friend space on Sunday evening. But Monday, she carved out an hour from her own schedule when she knew Laurel would be trapped in her kitchen preparing for the last-minute weekday party.

When she walked in to find Laurel rolling out phyllo dough, she knew she'd timed it perfectly.

"I brought you an extra pair of hands."

"I've got it under control."

"The bulk of this Greek extravaganza got dumped on you. Hands." She held hers up. "They can clean up behind you." She walked over to gather empty bowls. "We could get you a kitchen assistant."

"I don't want a kitchen assistant. Assistants get under-foot. Which is exactly why you don't have one."

"I'm toying with the idea." Parker started loading the dishwasher. "Maybe finding someone to train, to take care of some of the legwork."

"That'll be the day."

"We have to decide whether we want to go as we are, or consider expanding. Expanding means we'll need assis-tants. We could offer more weekday events if we brought in more staff."

Laurel paused. "Is that what you want?"

"I don't know. It's just something I think about now and then. Sometimes I think absolutely not. Others I think maybe. It'd be a big change, a shift. We'd have employees rather than just subs. We're good as we are. In fact, we're great. But sometimes a shift opens up other avenues."

"I don't know if we're . . . Wait a minute." Laurel's eyes narrowed on Parker's back. "You're using this as a meta-phor, or a segue—or both—for the Del thing."

They knew each other too well, Parker thought. "Maybe. I had to take time to think about it, then to obsess about what would happen if you and Del worked this out—then obsess about what would happen if you didn't."

"And?"

"Inconclusive." Parker turned back. "I love you both, and that's not changing. And, as much as I am the center of the universe, this isn't—or wouldn't be—about me. But it would be a shift."

"I'm not shifting. See, I'm standing right in one place. Steady, no shifts."

"Already done, Laurel."

"And I shifted back," Laurel insisted. "Right back to where I started. Jesus, Parks, it was only a kiss."

"If it was only a kiss you'd have told me about it right away, and you'd have made a joke out of it." She paused, just a beat, giving Laurel a chance to argue. Knowing she couldn't. "It worried you, so that means it was more. Or you're wondering if it was more. You care about him."

"Of course I care about him." Flustered, Laurel lifted the rolling pin, waved it. "We all care about Del. And okay, that's part of the problem. Or the thing. It's more a thing than a problem." She continued to roll out the dough until it was thin as paper. "We all care about Del, Del cares about all of us. Sometimes he cares to the point I want to give him a shot right in the eye, particularly when he lumps us all together. Like we're one body with four heads."

"Sometimes . . ."

"Yeah, I know, sometimes we are. But it's frustrating to be part of the lump, and to know he thinks of me as some-body he has to look after. I don't want to be looked after."

"He can't help that."

"I know that, too." She looked over, met Parker's eyes. "Adds to the frustration. He's wired, I'm wired, and the problem—the *thing* . . . I prefer *thing* to *problem*."

"Thing it is."

"The thing is my deal entirely. And it has to be strange for you to have me talk like this."

"A little bit. I'm working on it."

"It's not like I'm lovesick or have this major crush or anything mortifying like that. It's just a . . ."

"Thing."

"Yes, it's that. And since I did what I did, I'm already smoothing out about it."

"He's that bad a kisser?"

Laurel spared a bland glance as she reached for her bowl of filling. "I made the move, and now that I'm over being embarrassed, I feel better. It was just part of the argument really, which was my fault. Mostly my fault. He shouldn't have tried to pay me for the cake. It was the red flag when I was already pawing the ground. You wouldn't try to pay for a damn cake."

"No." Still Parker held up a finger. "So, let me see if I understand. You don't want him to lump you in the pile, so to speak, but you don't want him to offer to pay you for your work, because that's insulting."

"You had to be there."

"Can we forget he's my brother for a minute?"

"I'm not sure."

"Let's give it a shot." To keep it casual, Parker leaned back against the counter. "You're attracted. You're both interesting, unattached, attractive people. Why wouldn't you be?"

"Because it's Del."

"What's wrong with Del?"

"Nothing. See, this is weird." She grabbed her bottle of water, then set it down again without drinking. "It's not logical, Parker, and not something you can work out for me. We're going to be fine—Del and me, I mean. I'm already over it, and I doubt he gave it a minute's thought after the fact. Now, go away, so I can concentrate on this baklava."

"All right. But you'll tell me if there's anything to tell."

"Don't I always?"

Up till now, Parker thought, but left it at that.

CHAPTER FIVE

$\mathcal{G}$ROWING UP IN A FEMALE–DOMINATED HOUSEHOLD PRO-
vided Del with certain basics to live by. One, which he
thought applied at the moment, decreed if a man didn't understand what was going on, and the lack of understanding
meant trouble, a certain distance was recommended.

The same rule, he felt, applied in more . . . personal
male/female relationships—which was also oddly apt under
the circumstances.

He'd kept his distance from Laurel, and while it hadn't
led him to a brainstorm of understanding, he could only
hope the space had given her room to simmer down.

He didn't mind a fight. They kept things lively, for one
thing, and often cleared the air, for another. But he liked to
know the rules of the bout. In this case, he didn't have a
clue.

He was used to her temper, what he thought of as her
quicksilver moods. And having her take a few swipes at
him was nothing new.

Kissing him brainless? Brand-spanking-new. He couldn't

stop thinking about it, and thinking about it hadn't helped him reach any conclusions.

Which just pissed him off.

Conclusions, solutions, alternatives, compromises—they served as his stock-in-trade. And with this very personal puzzle, he just couldn't find the key pieces.

Regardless, he could hardly stay away indefinitely. He not only liked dropping in when he had the time, but the steady stream of business flowing between him and Parker and their business demanded attention.

A week was long enough for space and cooling off, he determined. They'd just have to deal with each other. One way or another. Which they would, of course. It was no big deal. No deal at all, he told himself as he turned into the long drive on the estate. They'd just had an argument—with unusual elements. She'd been trying to prove a point. On some level, he got the point. He tended to think of her—of all of them—as his responsibility, and it annoyed her.

She'd have to be annoyed because they damn well were his responsibility. He was Parker's brother, he was their lawyer. And through circumstances none of them could control or change, he was head of the family.

But he could try to be more subtle about shouldering responsibility.

Although it wasn't like he pushed his nose in her business every five minutes.

Still . . . Still, he told himself, he could try to back off a little. He couldn't argue the fact she'd made her point. She wasn't his sister. But that didn't mean she wasn't part of his family, and damn it, he had every right to . . .

Stop, he ordered himself. They'd get nowhere if he approached her already spoiling for trouble. Best to gauge the ground and let her take the lead.

Then he could haul her back where they belonged. Subtlety, he reminded himself.

Where the hell had all these cars come from? he wondered. It was Tuesday night, and he couldn't remember anything on Vows' slate. He swung off to park by Mac's studio, got out, frowned at the house. No question an event was in progress. He could see Emma's handiwork in lavish displays around the portico, and hear—even from the distance—the clatter and voices of a party going on.

For a moment, he simply stood where he was, watching. Lights glowed in the windows, turning the house into a welcoming celebration. Hospitality, with an elegant flair. It had always been. His parents had loved to entertain—small intimate gatherings, big flashy parties. He supposed Parker came by her skills there naturally. Yet when he came home unexpectedly—and it was still home—he'd feel that quick tug, that poignant sorrow for what he'd lost. For what they'd all lost.

He took the path, wound his way home, choosing the side door with its easy access to the family kitchen.

He'd hoped to find Mrs. Grady there, fussing at the stove, but a single light burned in the empty kitchen. He wandered to the window, watched some of the guests who'd gathered on the terrace, strolled the gardens.

Relaxed, at home, impressed, he judged. Infusing an event with those qualities was another Parker skill, or the blend the Quartet combined.

He caught sight of Emma and a few of the catering staff he recognized carrying linens, flowers. A last-minute adjustment, he assumed, then watched as they set up a table. Quick, efficient, he noted, with Emma chatting with some of the guests. All smiles and warmth—that was Emma. No one would know her mind was scrambling toward the next duty.

Emma and Jack, he mused. Now that was a last-minute adjustment for him. His closest friend and one of his girls. Even as he considered it, Jack came out carrying a tray of tea lights. Pitching in, Del thought, as they all pitched in from time to time. But it was different, he thought. And it occurred to him that this was the first time since Emma and Jack became "Emma and Jack" that he'd observed them when they weren't aware of him.

The look that passed between them, yes, that was different. The way Jack brushed a hand down her arm, casual and intimate, the way a man did when he simply needed to touch what he loved.

A good thing, he decided, what was between them. And he'd get used to it—eventually.

Meanwhile, he was here, there was a party. He might as well head up to the Ballroom and pitch in, too.

SHE'D BAKED LIKE A MANIAC, LAUREL THOUGHT, AND there was little more satisfying than seeing that work devoured. Now that the cake had been cut, dessert plates arranged, she left the serving to the caterers and took a minute to catch her breath. Music rolled, and those not swarming the dessert tables took advantage. Dozens more gathered at tables, most still tossing back ouzo.

Opa!

Happy, happy, she thought, everything under control. And the perfect time to slip away for five minutes and take off her shoes. She scanned for any potential problems as she moved to the door.

"Ms. McBane?"

Just this close, she thought, but turned and put on her professional smile. "Yes, what can I do for you?"

"Nick Pelacinos." He offered a hand. "Cousin of the bride-to-be."

And fairly gorgeous, she thought, shaking his hand. All bronzed Greek godlike with molten amber eyes and cleft chin. "It's nice to meet you. I hope you're enjoying yourself."

"I'd be a fool not to. You throw a hell of a party. I know you must be busy, but my grandmother would like a word with you. She's holding court over there."

He gestured to the head table, crowded with people, drinks, food, flowers—and unquestionably ruled over by the steel-haired, laser-eyed matriarch. The grandmother, Laurel thought.

"Sure." She walked with him, wondering if she should signal Parker for backup.

"She and my grandfather only come to the States every year or two normally," Nick told her. "Usually we're required to go to them, so this trip is a major event for the family."

"So I understand."

"And I understand you and your partners managed to put all this together in under a week. Kudos—seriously. I help manage the family restaurants in New York, so I have a good idea what went into this."

She flipped back mentally to Parker's rundown of the family. "Papa's. I've eaten at the one on the West Side."

"You'll have to come in again, and let me know. Dinner's on me. Yaya, I've brought you Ms. McBane."

The woman inclined her head with the slightest of regal tilts. "I see."

"Ms. McBane, my grandmother, Maria Pelacinos."

"Stephanos." Maria tapped her hand on the arm of the man seated beside her. "Let the girl sit."

"Please, don't trouble—" Laurel began.

"Up, up." She waved the man away, pointed to the chair. "Here, by me."

Never argue with a client, Laurel reminded herself, and took the vacated seat.

"Ouzo," the woman demanded, and almost instantly a glass was put in her hand. She set it down in front of Laurel.

"We toast to your baklava." Lifting her own glass, she arched an imperial eyebrow at Laurel. With little choice, Laurel took up her own glass, braced herself, and drank. Then, knowing the routine, slapped the glass down again. "Opa."

She got a round of applause and an approving nod from Maria. "You have a gift. It takes more than hands and ingredients to make food that matters. It takes a good head, and an open heart. Your family is Greek?"

"No, ma'am."

"Ah." She flicked that away. "Everyone's family is Greek. I'm going to give you my own recipe for lathopita, and you'll make it for my granddaughter's wedding."

"I'd love to have it, thank you."

"I think you're a good girl. So, dance with my grandson. Nick, dance with the girl."

"Actually, I need to—"

"It's a party. Dance! This is a good boy, handsome. He has a good job and no wife."

"Well, in that case," Laurel said and made Maria laugh.

"Dance, dance. Life is shorter than you think."

"She won't take no." Nick held out a hand again.

One dance, Laurel thought. Her aching feet could handle one dance. And she really wanted that recipe.

She let Nick lead her to the dance floor as the band switched to slow and smooth.

"It may not seem like it," he began as he took her into his arms, "but my grandmother paid you a very high compliment. She sampled a bit of everything you made, and she's convinced you're Greek. You couldn't have made traditional Greek desserts with such skill otherwise. And . . ." He twirled her stylishly. "You and your partners have saved the family an enormous argument. Getting her approval for this venue wasn't easy."

"And if Yaya isn't happy . . ."

"Exactly. Do you get into New York often?"

"Now and then . . ." Her heels lifted her to nearly his height. A nice balance for dancing, she decided. "The business keeps us pretty close to home. It must be the same for you. I worked restaurants while I was studying, and before we got the business off the ground. It's a demanding field."

"Crises followed by drama followed by chaos. Still, Yaya's right. Life's shorter than you think. If I called you sometime, maybe we could both get away from the job."

Dating moratorium, she reminded herself. But . . . It might be a good idea to end it so she'd stop obsessing about Del. "Maybe we could."

The dance ended, and with fanfare and cheers, the band moved into the traditional Greek circle dance. Laurel started to back away, but Nick kept her hand in his.

"You can't miss this."

"I really shouldn't. Plus I've only watched it at events, never done it."

"Don't worry, I'll guide you through."

Before she could come up with another excuse, someone else gripped her free hand, and she was linked in the circle.

What the hell, she decided. It was a party.

Del came in during the slow dance, and automatically looked around for Parker. Or so he told himself. Almost instantly he saw Laurel.

Dancing. Who was she dancing with? She wasn't supposed to be dancing with some guy he didn't know . . . She was supposed to be working.

Had she brought a date? They looked as if they knew each other when he considered how they moved together— and the way she smiled at whoever the hell he was.

"Del, I wasn't expecting you tonight." Parker strode over, kissed his cheek.

"I just dropped by to . . . Who is that?"

"Who?"

"With Laurel. Dancing."

Bemused, Parker glanced over, picked Laurel out of the crowd. "I'm not sure."

"She didn't bring him?"

"No. He's one of the guests. We're doing a kind of after-engagement, prewedding reception. Long story."

"Since when do you dance at your events?"

"It depends on the circumstances." She slid her eyes toward Del, said, "Hmm," quietly under the sway of music and chattering voices. "They look good together."

He only shrugged, slipped his hands into his pockets. "It's not smart for you to encourage guests to hit on you."

"*Encourage* is a debatable word. In any case, Laurel can

handle herself. Oh, I love when they do the traditional dance," she added when the music changed. "It's so happy. Look at Laurel! She's got it."

"She's always been good on her feet," Del muttered.

She was laughing, and apparently having no problem with the footwork or rhythm. She looked different, he thought. *How* he couldn't exactly say. No, that wasn't it; he was looking at her differently. He was looking at her through that kiss. It changed things—and the change made him uneasy.

"I should do another walk-through."

"What?"

"I need to do another walk-through," Parker repeated, tilting her head to study him closely.

His brows drew together. "What? Why are you looking at me like that?"

"Nothing. You can mix and mingle if you want. Nobody in this crowd will care. Or if you want something to eat besides dessert, you can go down to the kitchen."

He started to say he didn't want anything, but realized it wasn't quite true. He didn't know what he wanted. "Maybe. I just dropped by. I didn't know you were all working tonight. Or most of you," he corrected as Laurel circled by.

"Last-minute thing. We've got about another hour. You can go to the parlor if you want, and wait for me."

"I'll probably head on."

"Well, if you change your mind, I'll see you later."

He decided he wanted a beer, and if he wanted one without the obligation of helping out, he'd need to get one out of the family kitchen rather than one of the event bars.

He should just go home and have a beer, he told himself as he started downstairs. But he didn't want to go home, not when he was thinking about Laurel dancing as if she'd been born on Corfu. He'd just get a beer, then find Jack, hang out for an hour. Carter was bound to be around somewhere, too. He'd have a beer and find both of them, have some hangout time with friends.

Men.

The best way to take your mind off women was to sit down and have a beer with men.

He backtracked to the family kitchen, and found a cold Sam Adams in the fridge. Just what the doctor ordered, he decided. After opening it, he looked out the window again to see if he could spot either of his friends. But on the terrace, lit by candles and colored lights now, strangers gathered.

He sipped the beer and brooded. Why the hell was he so restless? There were a dozen things he could be doing other than standing here in an empty kitchen, drinking a beer and looking out the window at strangers.

He should go home, catch up on some work. Or screw the work and watch some ESPN. He'd left it too late to call anyone for a date, for dinner or drinks—and the damn thing was, he just didn't feel like being alone.

Carrying her shoes, her tired feet soundless, Laurel walked into the kitchen. Alone was exactly what she was after. Instead, she saw Del, standing at the window looking, to her mind, like the loneliest man in the world.

Which didn't fit, she knew. She never thought of Del as lonely. He knew everyone, and had a life so full of people she often wondered why he didn't run off somewhere just for a breath of solitude.

But now, he seemed entirely alone, completely separate, and quietly sad.

Part of her wanted to go to him, put her arms around him, and comfort away whatever put that look on his face. Instead, she went into survival mode and started to back out of the room.

He turned, saw her.

"Sorry. I didn't know you were here. Do you need Parker?"

"No. I saw Parker upstairs." He lifted his eyebrows at her bare feet. "I guess all that dancing's hard on the feet."

"Hmm? Oh . . . Not that much dancing, but when it comes at the end of a day like this, it's cumulative." Since he was here, and so was she, Laurel decided to get it over with and apologize. "I've only got a few, but since you're here I want to say I was over the line the other night. I shouldn't have jumped all over you like that."

Bad choice of words, she thought. "I understand you feel a certain sense of . . . duty," she decided, though the word wanted to stick in her throat. "I wish you wouldn't, and I can't help being irritated by it any more than you can help feeling it. So it's pointless to fight about it."

"Uh-huh."

"If that's the best you can do, I'm just going to consider it bygones."

He lifted a finger as he took another sip of beer. And watched her. "Not quite. I'm wondering why your irritation took the particular form it did."

"Look, you were being you, and it got under my skin, so I said some things I shouldn't have said. The way people do when they're irritated."

"I'm not talking about what you said so much as what you did."

"It's all of a piece. I was mad; I'm sorry. Take it or leave it."

Now he smiled, and she felt the low burn of temper in her belly.

"You've been mad at me before. You've never kissed me like that."

"It's like my feet."

"Sorry?"

"It's cumulative. It's annoying when you put on the 'Del knows best' act, and since that's been going on for years, the annoyance built up and so . . . It was to prove a point."

"What was the point? I think I missed it."

"I don't know why you're making such a big deal out of it." She felt the temper rising, just like the heat of embarrassment in her cheeks. "We're adults. It was just a kiss, and a nonviolent alternative to punching you in the mouth. Which I wish I'd done instead."

"Okay. To be clear. You were irritated with me. Said irritation having built up over the course of years. And your actions were an alternative to punching me in the face. Does that sum it up?"

"Yes, Counselor, that's close enough. Do you want me to get a Bible and swear on it? Jesus, Del."

She walked to the fridge, yanked it open to grab a bottle of water. She could probably think of a man who pissed her off more, but right at the moment, Delaney Brown headed the list. With an angry twist of the wrist she unscrewed the cap on the bottle as she turned. And bumped right into him.

"Cut it out." She wouldn't have called it panic, but her temper took on a different edge.

"You opened the door. The metaphorical one as well as." He gestured to the open refrigerator. "I bet you're irritated now, too."

"Yes, I'm irritated now."

"Good. Since we're on the same page, and I know how it works. . . ."

He gripped her by the shoulders and hauled her up to the toes of her bare feet. "Don't even th—"

It was as far as she got before her brain fizzled.

The heat, mouth to mouth, opposed the cold air blasting at her back. She felt trapped between the ice and the fire, helpless to move in either direction as he kept her poised on that thin, shaky line.

Then his hands slid down, found her waist, and the kiss softened into slow, melting lust. Her body went pliant, her mind drowsy as he drew her just a little closer.

The sound he heard, a soft, low purr in her throat, didn't signal anger but surrender. The surprise of her, like a gift held for years, opened. He wanted to carefully, painstakingly fold aside those layers and find more.

She shifted, reached—and the icy water in the bottle splashed them both. He eased back, glanced down at his wet shirt, and hers. "Oops."

Her eyes, dazed and dark, blinked. Even as he grinned, she scrambled away. She gestured with the bottle, the movement jerky enough that more water sloshed out. "Okay.

Okay. So . . . we're even. I have to get back. I have to." She wiped at her wet shirt. "Crap."

She turned, fled.

"Hey. You forgot your shoes. Oh well." He shut the refrigerator, then picked up the beer he'd set on the counter.

Funny, he thought as he leaned back against the counter in the quiet kitchen. He felt better. In fact, he felt pretty damn good.

He studied the shoes she'd left on the floor. Sexy, he mused, especially when paired with the professional suit she'd worn. He wondered if it had been a deliberate combination or an impulse.

And wasn't it a little strange to be thinking about her shoes? But since he was . . . Amused at himself, he opened the drawer for a notepad.

They were even? he thought, as he scribbled a note. He wasn't interested in even.

𝒥N THE MORNING, LAUREL OPTED FOR A SWIM INSTEAD OF a workout. She told herself she just wanted a change, but had to admit the change made it possible to avoid Parker until she'd figured out what to say. Or if she should say anything.

Probably best to leave it alone, she told herself as she kicked off the side for another lap. Nothing to tell, really. Del's competitive streak was a mile wide. She'd kissed him, so he'd kissed her back. Double. That was his way. He'd decided to put her in her place—it was just like him.

And that grin? She kicked off harder for another lap. That stupid, smug, superior grin? *That* was just like him, too. Idiot *man*. It was ridiculous to believe she had feelings for him. She'd just lost her mind for a minute. Or a decade or so. But who's counting? she demanded. She was back. She was fine. Situation normal.

When she hit the side again, she closed her eyes and let herself sink. After the punishing laps the sensation of weightlessness felt perfect. Just drifting, she thought, just as she was in her personal life. And that was fine, that was good, really. She didn't need form and function and structure in every area of her life.

It was good to be free to do what she wanted when the workday was done, or like this, before it began. No one to answer to but herself. She didn't need everything set and settled. She didn't even want it to be. Del—or the thing with Del—was just a bump on the road. All smoothed out now, she thought. All better.

She skimmed back her hair as she reached for the ladder—then yelped as Parker stepped forward with a towel.

"God, you scared me. I didn't know you were out here."

"That makes two of us on the scared me. For a minute I wondered if I'd have to jump in and pull you out."

She took the towel. "I was just drifting. Change of pace from running at full speed the last few days. We don't drift enough, that's what I think."

"Okay, I'll put drifting on the list."

Laughing, Laurel wrapped the towel around her waist. "You would. You're dressed. What time is it?"

"About eight. I take it you were drifting for a while."

"I guess. Busy night."

"It was. Did you see Del?"

"Why? Yes, but why?"

"Because he was here, and for a while you were AWOL."

"I wasn't AWOL, Captain. I just took a break."

"And changed your shirt."

Something like guilt began to inch up her spine. "I spilled something on it. What is this?"

"Curiosity." Parker held out an envelope. "This was on the kitchen counter. Mrs. G gave it to me to give to you."

"Well, why didn't she just . . . Oh." Laurel stopped when she recognized Del's handwriting.

"Don't you want to know what it says? I do." Parker stood, blocking the way and smiling brightly. "The polite thing would be for me to go back inside, give you privacy when you read it. But, I'm just not that mature."

"It's nothing. Fine." Feeling foolish, Laurel opened the envelope.

You might think this is over, but you'd be wrong. I've taken your shoes hostage. Contact me within forty-eight hours, or the Pradas get it.

Laurel made a sound caught between a laugh and a curse as Parker read over her shoulder.

"He took your shoes?"

"Apparently. What am I supposed to do about this?" Laurel waved the note. "I'm drifting. I decided I wanted to drift, and now he's playing games. I just bought those shoes."

"How did he get your shoes?"

"It was nothing like that. I took them off, and then he was there, and I left them after . . . Nothing. It was sort of tit for tat."

Parker nodded. "Your tit or his tat?"

"Neither of those, gutter-brain. I apologized for going off on him, but that's not enough for Del and he started cross-examining me. One thing led to another in the refrigerator. It's hard to explain."

"Obviously."

"He's just being a smart-ass. He can keep the damn shoes."

"Really?" Eyes placid, Parker smiled. "Because that would say to me—and probably him—that you're afraid to deal with it. Him. Any of it."

"I'm not afraid—and don't play that card with me." Laurel yanked off the towel to rub it furiously over her hair. "I just don't want to stir anything up."

"Because it's hard to drift when things are stirred up."

"Yes. Anyway, I have other shoes. I have better shoes. I'm not going to give him the satisfaction of drawing me into his silly game."

Parker smiled again. "Boys are so lame."

Laurel rolled her eyes. "He's your brother," she muttered and strode back toward the house.

"Yes, he is." And she wondered how long it would take her best friend to crack. "More than twenty-four," Parker decided, "less than forty-eight."

The BlackBerry in her pocket rang. She glanced at the display as she strolled across the lawn. "Good morning, Sybil. What can I do for you?"

CHAPTER SIX

$\mathcal{T}$HERE WAS ALWAYS A WAY TO GATHER INFORMATION. To
Parker's mind, information wasn't just power; it led the
way to efficiency—and in her world, efficiency ruled them
all. To get anything done well, and yes, efficiently, you first
lined up the details and facts.

And whenever possible, multitasked.

The first order of business roughly twenty-four hours
into the hostage situation was to tap Del for a ride. It was a
simple matter to arrange, particularly since she'd opted to
use his mechanic for the regular maintenance check on her
car. Malcolm Kavanaugh might have been rough around the
edges with a hefty dose of cocky, but he excelled at his
work—and that mattered most. It didn't hurt that he was a
friend of Del's.

With a weekend packed with events, starting with a rehearsal that evening, she could honestly tell Del she needed
the lift, as none of her partners could spare the time.

It didn't matter that she could have called half a dozen
other people—or a cab for that matter, she thought as she
freshened her lipstick. The favor would make Del feel like

big brother—a role he enjoyed—and would give her the
opportunity to pump him for information since Laurel had
clammed up.

She checked the contents of her bag, then the schedule
on her BlackBerry.

Talk to Del. Pick up car. Meet clients for lunch, pick up
dry cleaning, go to market, return by four thirty to prep for
rehearsal. The sub lists for the meeting, the items to be picked
up at the cleaners and the market ranged under each entry.

She did a quick turn in the mirror. The clients were major,
and as they'd booked lunch at their country club, presenting
the correct appearance mattered.

The summer dress in soft yellow struck a nice balance,
she thought, between casual and professional. Understated
jewelry, but the client's hawkeyed mother would recognize
the real deal, which would carry some weight. She'd left her
hair down and loose for a change—girl lunch, friendly.
Nothing flashy, nothing too eye-catching. The wedding plan-
ner never, never outshone the bride. Satisfied, she added a
tissue-thin white sweater to combat the air-conditioning if
the clients chose to eat inside the club.

A full ten minutes before her brother's scheduled arrival
time, she walked downstairs. The house she loved seemed
so quiet, so big in the middle of the morning with no clients
scheduled, no events demanding her time and attention.
Emma's flowers perfumed the air in massive arrangements
or pretty little displays, and some of Mac's photos mixed
with the art on the walls.

Still, she'd changed little here, moving only the most personal items to her private quarters or into Laurel's. But it
remained very much a home, and a happy place, one that
had witnessed hundreds of celebrations. And arguments, she
thought as she adjusted the placement of a bowl. Laughter,
tears, drama, and foolishness.

She couldn't remember ever being lonely in this house,
or wishing to be somewhere else.

She checked her watch, gauged her time, and decided to
drop in on Laurel.

At the counter, Laurel kneaded a round of fondant. Nearby, six baked tiers sat waiting on their racks. Since she'd chosen a morning talk show instead of music, Parker understood Laurel was willing to be distracted.

"I'm heading out," Parker announced. "Need anything?"

Laurel glanced over. "Great color on you."

"Thanks. It makes me feel sunny."

"And look the same. I could use about five pounds of strawberries," she added. "Really fresh. I don't want all of them completely red and ripe. Mix it up. It'll save me from running out this afternoon."

"No problem." Parker took out her BlackBerry to key it into her list. "I'm going to the market anyway, after the lunch meeting. Jessica Seaman and her mother."

"Right." Laurel stopped kneading to cross the fingers of both hands.

"MOB wants to discuss menu and music. That one's for tomorrow night?" she asked as Laurel dusted her work surface with cornstarch.

"Yeah. Six layers, fondant with a pleated skirt and gum paste orchids to match the bride's signature flower." She rolled out the first sheet of fondant. "Wait, I thought your car was in the shop."

"It is, and it's ready. Del's going to drop me off at the mechanic's."

"Oh." Frowning, either over Del or the air bubbles she spotted, Laurel pricked the tiny bubbles with a straight pin.

"Any message—for him or your shoes?"

"Funny." Working quickly, Laurel lifted the fondant with both hands and laid it over the first tier. "You could tell him to stop being so asinine and give them back."

"Okay."

"No, don't say anything." She shrugged then smoothed the top and sides, pushing out more air bubbles as she worked. "I don't need the shoes. I've already forgotten them."

"Sure."

Laurel picked up a pizza cutter, shook it at Parker. "I

know your games, Brown. You're trying to get me worked up so I'll call him about it. It won't work."

"Okay." Parker smiled easily while Laurel ran the cutter around the base of the cake to cut away the excess fondant. "He'll be here in a minute. I'll come back with strawberries."

"Different sizes, different shades," Laurel called out.

"Got it." She strolled back to the front of the house, pleased to know she'd done just what she'd set out to do. Laurel would work the rest of the day with Del and the shoes on her mind.

She stepped outside, slipped on her sunglasses, and walked down the path just as Del pulled up.

"Right on time," he said.

"You, too."

"We're Browns. We're obsessed with punctuality."

"I consider it a virtue, and a skill. Thanks for doing this, Del."

"Easy enough. I'm going to swing by and meet with a client, then hook up with Jack for lunch. Worked out."

"Multitasking. The key to all. New shoes?" she asked.

"No." He glanced over at her as he made the turn out of the drive. "Why?"

"Oh, I heard you recently acquired some fabulous new shoes."

"Right." The corner of his mouth twitched in amusement. "They're not the right size. Plus walking around in heels makes my toes cramp."

She poked him in the arm with her finger. "Taking Laurel's shoes. When are you going to stop being twelve?"

"Never." He laid a hand over his heart as if to swear it. "Is she pissed or amused?"

"Both, and neither. I'd say she's confused."

"Then mission accomplished."

"That's so typical. Why do you want to confuse her?"

"She started it."

She tipped down her sunglasses to peer at him over the

tops. "I think you just regressed to the age of eight. Started what?"

He shot her another look. "I may be eight, but I know you and your pack. You know what she started, and now you're trying to wheedle out my side of it."

"I don't have to wheedle, and you don't have to tell me. Sorry," she added when her phone rang. "Shawna, hi! I just left Laurel in the kitchen where she was finishing your cake. It's going to be gorgeous. All right. Uh-huh. No, no, don't worry. I'll call my travel agent and . . . That was resourceful. Do you have his new flight number? Yes."

As she spoke she took out a pad and pen, and repeated the information as she noted it down. "I'll check shortly, just to make sure it's on schedule, and I'll arrange for a car to pick him up and bring him to rehearsal. No, it won't be a problem. You just leave it to me, and we'll see you tonight. Relax, everything's under control. Go, get your nails done and don't worry about a thing. Yes, me, too. Bye.

"BM's flight canceled. He's rerouted," she said as she put the pad away. "He'll be a little late tonight."

"I was worried for a minute."

"Laurel's right. You are a smart-ass."

"Is that what she said?"

With a careless shrug, Parker tucked her BlackBerry away.

"Okay, okay, your torture methods are efficient and cruel. She changed the playing field so I'm trying to figure out if I should suit up. I'm not sure it's a good idea, but . . . well, it's an idea. Comments?"

"I think you're both going to try to be in charge so you'll either fight like rabid dogs or fall wildly in love. Possibly both, as you're each starting out with strong and long-term feelings for and about each other. And those feelings will shift and change if you . . . suit up."

"I'm not looking to fight or fall wildly. I'm just exploring a potential new dynamic. Is it weird for you?"

Interesting, she thought, they'd both asked her the same

question. "I don't know yet. When she gets in touch with you about the shoes, which she will even though she thinks she won't, don't gloat."

"Only on the inside." He turned into the parking lot of the garage. "She's going to get in touch?"

"She really likes those shoes. Plus, she'll decide not getting in touch is letting you win." She leaned over, kissed his cheek. "Thanks for the lift."

"I can wait for you. Mal's around somewhere, so I can hang out with him until you're set."

"That's okay." If Del talked to Malcolm, then Malcolm would know she was there, and he'd certainly have something to say. She'd prefer to avoid it, and him. "I called ahead so they know I'm coming."

"Of course you did. Well, tell Mal I'll see him at poker night."

"Hmm. Come to dinner next week." She stepped out of the car. "We'll do a big family dinner. I'll check everyone's schedule and let you know what night's best if you're open."

"I can be open. Hey, Parker. You look pretty."

She smiled. "Just keep your eyes off my shoes." She shut the door on his laugh and walked into the office.

The frazzled woman with the orange hair and green-framed cheaters sat behind the counter and gave Parker a little come-ahead as she talked on the phone. A few discreet inquiries had given Parker the info that the woman was Malcolm's mother.

Not that it mattered, particularly. She just liked to know who she was dealing with.

"That's right, tomorrow afternoon. After two. Look, buddy, the part just got here, and the boy's only got two hands." She rolled sharp green eyes—the same shade as her son's—at Parker while she chugged from a bottle of Dr Pepper. "Do you want it fast or do you want it right? He told you it'd take a day once the part showed up. I heard him myself. Maybe you oughta buy American. If it's ready sooner, I'll call you. Best I can do. Yeah, you have a real good day. Dickhead," she added when she'd hung up.

"Everybody thinks the world revolves around them," she said to Parker. "Everybody's the center of the freaking universe."

Then she sighed, then she smiled—a singularly sweet smile. "You look real fresh and pretty."

"Thank you. I'm meeting a client."

"I got your bill right here. Got it together and printed it out after you called. I'm getting the hang of this damn computer."

Parker remembered their first meeting and Mrs. Kavanaugh's frustration. "They do save time once you figure out the program."

"Well, it's only taking me half again as long as it would to just write it out rather than three times that like it used to. Here you go."

"Great." Parker stepped up to look it over.

"I knew your ma a little."

"Oh?"

"You got the look of her some, now that I put it together. She was a real lady. The kind that doesn't have to act snooty to be one."

"She'd have appreciated that exact description." Satisfied with the bill, Parker took out her credit card. "I think you know Maureen Grady, too. She's run the house, and us, as long as I remember."

"Yeah, I know her some. I guess if you're around Greenwich long enough, you know most everybody. My boy plays poker with your brother."

"He does," Parker agreed, and signed the credit slip. "In fact, Del dropped me off. He said to tell Malcolm he'd see him on poker night." There, she thought, duty discharged.

"You can tell him yourself," she said as Malcolm walked in from the side garage door, wiping his hands on a red bandanna.

"Ma, I need you to . . ." He paused, slowly smiled. "Hey. Nice."

"Ms. Brown here's just picking up her car." His mother took the keys, and to Parker's dismay tossed them to Malcolm, who caught them one-handed. "Walk her on out there."

"It's not necessary. I just—"

"Part of the service." Mal walked to the front door of the office, held it open.

"Thanks, Mrs. Kavanaugh. It was nice to see you again."

"Come back anytime."

"Really," Parker began once they were outside, "I'm in kind of a hurry, so—"

"Got a date?"

"A meeting."

"Shame to waste that dress on business, but we'll get you there."

He smelled of his work, which wasn't nearly as unpleasant as she'd assumed it would be. His jeans had a hole in the knee and grease stains on the thigh. She wondered if he wore a black T-shirt because it wouldn't show the stains.

His hair was nearly as dark and left to fall any way it chose around his sharply defined face. He hadn't shaved, she noted, but the result made him look more dangerous than scruffy.

"You've got a nice ride." He jingled her keys in his hand, his eyes on her face when they reached her car. "And you take care of it. We detailed it on us since it's your first service, but I couldn't've charged you anyway. You keep your baby clean and polished."

"Tools work better when they're taken care of."

"Words to live by. Most people don't. So, what's after the meeting?"

"Sorry? Oh . . . errands, and work."

"You ever not have meetings, errands, and work?"

"Rarely." She knew when a man was hitting on her, but couldn't remember the last time it had flustered her. "I really need those keys. The car won't start without them."

He dropped them into her open palm. "If you hit one of those rare times, give me a call. I'll take you out in my ride."

While she tried to think of a response, he jerked a thumb. She followed the direction to a big, burly, gleaming motorcycle.

"I don't think so. I really don't think so."

He only smiled. "If you change your mind, you know how to reach me." He waited a beat while she got into the car. "It's the first time I've seen you with your hair down. It goes with the dress."

"Um." Jesus, Parker, she thought, what has tied your tongue into a knot? "Thanks for the work."

"Back at you."

She shut the door, turned the key, and with a genuine sense of relief drove away. The man, she decided, just threw her off balance.

It was silly, Laurel told herself, and had to be handled. Ignoring Del and his childish game had seemed like a good idea initially, but the more she chewed on it, the more it seemed ignoring it could be construed as avoidance. That gave him the upper hand, which would never do.

She kept her plan—such as it was—to herself. Since she wasn't needed at rehearsal, it limited contact with her friends, and the temptation to share. She kept to her kitchen, making the cream filling and buttercream frosting for Saturday afternoon's Summer Strawberry cake. She checked her board and her timing, and tried not to feel guilty about sneaking out of her own house.

She pulled off her apron, then cursed. She wasn't going over to Del's to face this situation all sweaty and mussed. Cleaning up didn't equal fussing.

She took the back stairs, slipped into her own wing to shower off the day. Putting makeup on wasn't fussing either. It was just basic grooming. And she liked wearing earrings. She was entitled to wear earrings and a nice top, wasn't she? It wasn't a crime to want to look her best, whatever the circumstances.

Refusing to argue with herself any longer, she took the back steps again with the idea of getting out without being seen. She'd be home, she assured herself, before anyone noticed she was gone.

"Where are you off to?"

Busted. "Ah." She turned to see Mrs. Grady in the kitchen garden. "I just have something to do. A little something to do."

"Well, I guess you'd better go do it. That's a new shirt isn't it?"

"No. Yes. Sort of." She *hated* feeling the heat of guilt creeping up the back of her neck. "There's no point in buying a shirt and not wearing it."

"None at all," Mrs. Grady said placidly. "Run along then, and have fun."

"I'm not going to . . . Never mind. I won't be long." She circled around the house toward her car. An hour, tops, then she'd—

"Hi. Heading out?"

Oh, for Christ's sake, it was like having a community of parents. She worked up a smile for Carter. "Yeah. I just have a thing. I'm coming right back."

"Okay. I'm going to beg a casserole from Mrs. G. We'll be defrosting later, if you're interested."

"Thanks, but I grabbed a salad before. Enjoy."

"We will. You look nice."

"So what?" She shook her head. "Sorry, sorry. Distracted. Gotta go." She jumped in the car before she ran into anyone else.

As she sped away, it occurred to her she should've gone to Del's during the day, when he'd be gone. She knew where the spare key was hidden, and had his alarm code. Except he probably changed it regularly, as that was the safe thing to do. Still, she could've risked it, and gotten inside, found her shoes. Left *him* a note, she thought. Now *that* would've been clever.

Too late now. But he might not be home, she considered.

He had an active social life—friends, clients, dates. Seven thirty on a pretty summer evening? Yes, he probably had a hot date—drinks, dinner, debauchery. She could get in, find the shoes, leave him a funny note.

> *Dear shoenapper: We escaped and have informed the FBI. A tactical team is on the way. The Pradas.*

He'd laugh, she decided. He didn't like to lose—who did?—but he'd laugh. And that would be the end of that.

As long as she didn't set off the alarm and end up calling him to be her attorney of record. Think positive, she advised herself and warmed up to the new plan as she drove.

And imagined it falling like a bad soufflé when she spotted his car in the drive.

Oh well, back to Plan A.

He had a great house, one she'd admired since he'd had it built. Probably too big for one man, but she understood the need for space. She knew Jack had designed it with very specific requirements from Del. Not too traditional, but not too modern, lots of light, lots of room. And the sprawl of river stone, the pitch of the triple roofs had a kind of casual elegance that suited the owner.

And she was stalling, she admitted.

She got out of the car, walked straight to the front door, and rang the bell.

She shifted from one foot to the other, tapped her hand on her knee. Nerves, she realized. For God's sake she was nervous about seeing a man she'd known her entire life. One she'd fought with and played with. They'd even been married a couple of times—when Parker had nagged, bribed, or blackmailed him into playing Groom in their Wedding Day games as kids. Now she had the jitters.

That made her a wuss, she decided. She hated being a wuss.

She punched the bell again, harder.

"Sorry, you were so quick, and I was just . . ." Del, shirt

open over a chest where a few drops of water glimmered, hair dark with damp, stopped, cocked his head. "And you're not the delivery guy from the China Palace."

"No, and I came for . . . You can't get delivery out here from the China Palace."

"You can if you defended the owners' son on possession and got him into a program instead of a cell." He smiled, hooked a thumb in the pocket of the jeans he'd zipped but had yet to button. "Hi, Laurel. Come on in."

"I'm not here to visit. I'm here for my shoes. Just get them, and I'll be gone before your shrimp fried rice gets here."

"I went for the sweet-and-sour pork."

"Good choice. My shoes."

"Come on in. We'll discuss terms."

"Del, this is just absurd."

"I like some absurd now and again." To settle the matter, he grabbed her hand, pulled her inside. "So, want a beer? I picked up some Tsingtao for the Chinese."

"No, I don't want a Chinese beer. I want my shoes."

"Sorry, they're in an undisclosed location until the ransom terms are determined and met. Did you know they let out this thin, high-pitched scream when you twist those skinny heels?" He fisted his hands, twisted to demonstrate. "It's a little eerie."

"I know you think you're being funny, and okay, you're not entirely wrong. But I've put in a really long day. I just want my shoes."

"You deserve a Tsingtao after a really long day. And look, here's dinner. Why don't you go out back on the deck? It's nice out. Oh, grab a couple of beers out of the fridge on your way. Hey, Danny, how's it going?"

She could argue, Laurel thought. She could even make a scene. But neither would get her the shoes until Del was good and ready. Keeping her cool, that was the ticket, she decided and, grinding her teeth only a little, started toward the kitchen. She heard Del and the delivery guy talking baseball as she walked away. Apparently somebody somewhere had pitched a no-hitter the night before.

She turned into his spacious kitchen, washed now in the softening evening light. She knew he used the space for more than beer and take-out Chinese. He had a couple of specialties down cold—fancy little meals designed for seducing women—and had a hand with omelettes for the morning after.

So she'd been told.

She opened the fridge and took out a beer, and since it was there, took out one for herself. Knowing the setup here nearly as well as in her own kitchen, she opened the freezer, got out a couple of chilled pilsners. And noted a handy selection of Mrs. G's casseroles and soups in labeled containers.

The woman fed the world.

She was pouring the second beer when Del came in with take-out bags.

"See, I'm having a beer. I consider that terms met. When I finish the beer, I get my shoes."

His look transmitted mild pity. "I don't think you understand the situation clearly. I've got something you want, so I set the terms." He stacked a couple of plates, napkins, then took two sets of chopsticks from a drawer.

"I said I didn't want dinner."

"Pot stickers." He shook one of the bags. "You know you have a weakness."

He was right about that, plus anxiety combined with the scent of food stirred up her appetite. "Fine. A beer and a pot sticker." She carried the beers out to the deck and to the table overlooking the lawn and gardens.

The water in his pool sparkled. On the edge of its skirt stood a charming gazebo that housed a massive grill. He was known for manning it territorially when he threw a summer party where people played cutthroat boccie on the lawn and splashed in the pool.

He entertained well, she mused. It must be in the genes.

He came out with a tray loaded with cartons and plates. At least he'd buttoned his shirt, she noted. She wished she didn't like his looks quite so much. She'd be able to get a handle on her emotional response if she didn't find him so physically attractive.

Or vice versa.

"I figured I'd eat this with ESPN and some paperwork. This is better." He put a place setting in front of her, opened cartons. "Rehearsal tonight, right?" He sat and began to take samples from every carton. "How'd it go?"

"Fine, I imagine. They didn't need me, so I did some prep for the weekend."

"I'll be at the commitment ceremony Sunday," he told her. "I went to college with Mitchell, and I wrote up their partnership contract." He ate while she sat, sipping her beer. "So what's the cake?"

"Chocolate butter cake, with white chocolate mousse filling, frosted in broad strokes with fudge frosting."

"Triple threat."

"They like chocolate. All that's offset with alternate layers of red geranium blossoms on flower foam trays. Emma's making interlocking geranium hearts for the topper. Now should I ask about your day?"

"No need to be bitchy."

She sighed because he was right. "You stole my shoes," she pointed out, and gave in to the scent of the food.

"*Stole* is a strong word."

"They're mine, you took them without permission." She bit into a pot sticker. God, she did have a weakness.

"How much are they worth to you?"

"They're just shoes, Del."

"Please." He made a dismissive noise as he waved one hand. "I have a sister. I know the value you people put on footwear."

"Okay, okay, what do you want? Money? Baked goods? Household chores?"

"All viable options. But this is nice for a start. You should try the sweet-and-sour."

"What, this is nice? This?" She nearly choked on the beer. "Like this is some kind of a date?"

"Two people, food, drink, pretty evening. It has datelike elements."

"It's a drop-in. It's a ransom drop. It's . . ." She stopped herself because the jitters were back. "All right, let's clear the air. I feel I started something. Something or . . ."

"Other?" he suggested.

"Okay, something or other. Because I was in a mood, and I acted impulsively, which caused you to reciprocate the impulse. And I see now, I certainly see knowing you, that the 'we're even' remark was a gauntlet thrown. You couldn't leave that alone, so you took my damn shoes. And now there's Chinese and beer and the whole dusk falling light show, when we both know perfectly well you've never thought about me this way."

He considered for a moment. "That's not accurate. An accurate statement would be I've tried not to think about you this way."

More than a little stunned she sat back. "How'd you do with that?"

"Hmm." He lifted a hand, turned it side to side.

She stared at him. "Damn you, Del."

CHAPTER SEVEN

$\mathcal{H}$E COULDN'T SAY IT WAS THE REACTION HE'D EXPECTED, but with Laurel that was often the case.

"Damn me for what, exactly?"

"Because it's exactly the right thing to say. You're good at saying exactly the right thing, except when you say the completely wrong thing. But it's usually the right thing anyway, just that I didn't want to hear it."

"You should've been a lawyer."

"I'm eating another pot sticker," she muttered.

She'd always delighted him, he thought, except when she'd irritated him. It was probably the same thing.

"Do you remember when we were all over at Emma's parents' for Cinco de Mayo?"

"Of course I remember." She scowled at her beer. "I had too much tequila, which is only natural under the circumstances because, hello, Cinco de Mayo."

"I think that's *hola*."

"Har-har. You played big brother and sat with me on the front porch steps."

"It's not playing big brother to have some mild concern

for a friend in a tequila haze. But anyway." He scooped some sweet-and-sour onto her plate with his chopsticks. "Earlier Jack and I were standing around, and I was scoping the crowd, the way you do."

"The way *you* do."

"Okay. I spot this blue dress with a great pair of legs and . . ." He made a vague gesture that gave her a clear picture of the *and*. "I thought, nice, very nice indeed, and made some mention of same to Jack. He pointed out that the legs and the rest I happened to be scoping were yours. It gave me a hell of a jolt, I admit." He gauged her reaction, judged surprise led the way. "In the interest of full disclosure, I also admit it wasn't the first time. So whether or not it was the right thing to say, it was accurate."

"I'm not a pair of legs, or an *and*."

"No, but they're still very nice. You're a beautiful woman. That's also accurate. Some have a weakness for pot stickers, some for beautiful women."

She looked past him, toward the deepening shadows. "That should piss me off."

"You're also one of my oldest and most important friends." Teasing no longer colored his tone. "That matters, a lot."

"It does." She pushed her plate away before she made herself sick.

"I think it's also accurate to say something unexpected, or at least surprising, hit when you acted on impulse the other night."

As dusk thickened, his garden and patio lights sent out a soft glow, and in the distance a loon's eerie wail echoed. It struck him as oddly romantic, and somehow suitable.

"You're being awfully delicate about it."

"Well, it's a first date," he said and made her laugh.

"I just came for the shoes."

"No, you didn't."

She let out a breath. "Maybe not, but I had this plan, banking on you being out on an actual date where I'd sneak in, take back my shoes, and leave you a clever note."

"Then you'd have missed all this. So would I."

"There you go again," she murmured. "I think part of my thing here is a direct result of my sexual moratorium."

Amused, he tipped up his beer. "How's that going for you?"

"All too well. I'm probably a little more—what's the delicate term? Itchy, more itchy than usual these days."

"In the spirit of friendship I could take you upstairs and help you scratch that itch. But that doesn't really work for me."

She started to say she could scratch her own itch, thanks all the same, but decided that was too much information, even between friends. So she shrugged instead.

"It's not like Jack and Emma," he said.

"Jack and Emma aren't scratching an itch. They're—"

"Simmer down, Quickdraw," he said mildly. "That's not what I meant. They were friends—are friends—but they became friends, what, ten or twelve years ago? That's a long time, but you and I? It's basically our whole lives. We're not just friends, we're family. Not in an illegal and incestuous way that makes this conversation creepy, but family. Tribal," he decided. "We're from the same tribe, you could say."

"Tribal." She tried it out. "You have been thinking about this. And I can't disagree with you about any of that."

"Which is a nice change. We're talking about changes, and not just for us, but for, well, the tribe."

"I bet you get to be chief." With her elbow on the table, she propped her chin on her hand. "You always get to be chief."

"You can be chief if you can beat me arm-wrestling."

She was strong—she prided herself on it. But she also knew her limits. "And being tribal chief you've already decided how this should go."

"I have what you could call an outline. What would be a draft of an outline."

"You're so like Parker. Maybe that's part of it. If Parker were a guy, or we were both gay, we'd be married. Which would mean I'd never have to date again. My annoyance thereof the key cause for the sexual moratorium. And very likely this conversation."

"Do you want to hear the outline?"

"Yes, but I'm passing on the quiz that follows."

"We give it a month."

"Give what a month?"

"The adjustment. Seeing each other this way. We go out, stay in, have conversations, socialize, engage in recreational activities. We date, like people do when they're easing into a different dynamic. And, given the tribal connection, and given what I assume is a mutual desire to limit potential damage to our current connection—"

"Now who's the lawyer?"

"Given that," he went on, "though it gives me no pleasure, literally, we continue the sexual moratorium."

"You'd also be in a sexual moratorium?"

"Fair's fair."

"Hmm." She switched from beer to water. "We do all the stuff normal, consenting, unattached adults do with each other, but no sex, with each other or anyone else?"

"That's the idea."

"For thirty days."

"Don't remind me."

"Why the thirty?"

"It's a reasonable time line for both of us to determine if we want to take it to the next step. It's a big step, Laurel. You matter too much to me to rush it."

"Dating's harder than sex."

He laughed. "Who the hell have you been dating? I'll try to make it easy for you. How about we catch a movie after the event on Sunday? Just a movie."

She angled her head. "Who picks the flick?"

"We'll negotiate. No tearjerker."

"No horror."

"Agreed."

"Maybe you should draw up a contract."

He took the dig with a shrug. "If you've got a better idea, I'm open."

"I don't have any idea. I never thought we'd get to a point where I would need an idea. How about we just sleep together and call it even?"

"Okay." When her mouth dropped open, he grinned. "I not only know you, but I know a bluff when I hear one."

"You don't know everything."

"No, I don't. I think that's part of it, and I guess we'd better take some time and find out. I'm in if you are."

She studied the attractive and familiar face, the calm eyes, the easy posture. "We'll probably want to murder each other half the time."

"That won't be anything new. In or out, Laurel?"

"In." She offered a hand to close the deal.

"I think this calls for more than a handshake." But he took her hand, used it to draw her to her feet along with him. "Plus we should see what it's like when neither of us is irritated."

A little frisson, as much anticipation as nerves, jittered up her spine. "Maybe I am."

"No. No little crease here." He skimmed a fingertip between her eyebrows. "Dead giveaway."

"Wait," she said when he ran his hands down her arms. "Now I'm self-conscious. It's no good if I'm thinking too much and—"

He shut her up, drawing her in and up to brush his lips over hers in slow, soft sweeps.

"Or," she murmured, and let her hands glide up from his shoulders until her arms could link around his neck.

More surprises, he thought, when there was warmth and exploration instead of just heat and impulse. Sweet and easy wrapped in layers of the familiar and the new. He knew her scent, her shape, but the taste of her, ripe and seductive, merged what was into what might be.

He took his time, drawing it out, drawing her in, to savor the new mix of sensations.

She poured herself into it, taking every ounce of the moment she'd imagined dozens of times. A dying day, soft lights, the quiet sigh of a summer breeze. Foolish fancies of a young girl's crush, longings transformed over time into a woman's need.

Now the fancies were real, the longings met. And in the kiss she felt his need rise with hers. Whatever happened, this moment, this dying day, would always be hers.

When their lips parted, he stayed close. "How long do you think that's been in there?" he wondered.

"Hard to say." Impossible to tell him.

"Yeah."

He touched his lips to hers again, testing, stirring, then deepening until they were both breathless.

"I'd better go get your shoes."

"Okay." But she pulled him back, racheting up the heat, groaning with it when his hands stroked down her sides to grip her hips.

He teetered on the edge, but made himself pull back. "Shoes," he managed. "Free the hostages. You really need to go. Home."

Stirred and shaken, she leaned back against the deck rail. "I told you dating's harder than sex."

"We don't shirk from challenges. You've got some lips. I've always liked the look of them. I like them even better now."

They curved. "Come over here and say that."

"Better not. I'll be back in a minute with the shoes."

She watched him go and thought it was going to be a really long month.

$\mathscr{S}$NEAKING BACK INTO THE HOUSE SHOULD BE, BY ALL THE odds, simpler than sneaking out. Carter and Mac would be tucked into their place, Emma and Jack in theirs. Mrs. G would either be watching TV in her cozy apartment with her feet up and a pot of her evening tea, or out with some cronies. Parker? Probably still working, but in her own suite and in comfortable clothes.

Laurel parked, reassured by the lights in the studio and guesthouse. She just wanted to get into her own space, alone, and think about everything that happened, everything that had changed or started to change tonight.

Her lips still tingled from his; her skin still hummed. She could all but dance to the tune. If she'd kept a diary, she'd cover today's page with little hearts and flowers.

Then rip it out and tear it up because that was embarrassing. But still, she'd do it.

Smiling at the idea, she let herself into the house, carefully and quietly locked up behind her. She didn't exactly tiptoe up the stairs, but it was close.

"Are you just getting in?"

She didn't scream, but that was close, too. Whirling, Laurel gaped at Parker, then sat down hard on the steps before she tumbled.

"Jesus Christ! Jesus! You're scarier than a Rottweiler. What are you doing?"

"What am I doing?" Parker waved the carton in her hand. "I went down for a yogurt and I'm going up to my room. What are you doing sneaking up the steps?"

"I wasn't sneaking. I was walking. Quietly. You have yogurt in the little fridge upstairs."

"I'm out of blueberry. I wanted blueberry. Do you mind?"

"No, no. God." Laurel took a ragged breath, patted her heart. "You just scared the crap out of me."

This time Parker pointed with her spoon. "You have guilty face."

"I do not."

"I'm looking at it. I know guilty face when I'm looking at it."

"I'm not guilty. Why should I be guilty? I don't have a curfew, do I, Mom?"

"See, guilty."

"Okay, okay, put away the rubber hose." Laurel threw up her arms in surrender. "I just went to Del's to get my shoes."

"Laurel, I can see that. You're holding them in your hand."

"Right. Right. Well, they're great shoes and I wanted

them back." She stroked one affectionately. "He'd ordered Chinese. There were pot stickers."

"Ah." Nodding, Parker walked up to sit beside Laurel.

"I wasn't going to stay, but I did, so we sat out on the deck and talked about me kissing him, then him kissing me. Which I didn't actually mention to you. It feels weirder talking to you about it than it does talking to him."

"Get over it."

"I'm working on it, aren't I? Anyway, we had to get to what do we do about it, if anything. He had an outline."

"Of course." Parker smiled as she spooned up yogurt.

"You'd expect that because the two of you are from the same mold. I told him if you and I were gay we'd be married."

Parker nodded again as she ate her yogurt. "I could see that."

"We talked it over and we agreed we'd see each other and do stuff that people do, except no sex."

Brows lifting, Parker licked her spoon. "You're going to date but not have sex?"

"For thirty days. The theory being we'd know by then if we really wanted to have sex, or if it's just . . . hmm. I know it's reasonable and adult, but we know we want to have sex now."

"You take a little time first to make sure you'll still like each other if and when you do."

"Yeah, that's the sticker. There was more in there. Tribes and my legs, but the upshot was we're going to see how it goes. You're really okay with it?"

Parker rapped her knuckles lightly on Laurel's head. "Of course I'm okay with it, and if I wasn't okay with it, you should tell me to go to hell and mind my own business. Want some of this yogurt?"

"No, thanks. Pot stickers." But she leaned her head on Parker's shoulder. "I'm glad I didn't manage to sneak in."

"Be gladder I've decided to be magnanimous and not be insulted you tried to."

"Best friend ever."

"It's so true. I am. He's a good man. I know he can be bossy because, same mold. And I know he has flaws, but he's such a good man." She laid her hand over Laurel's briefly. "He deserves you. You and I have to make a pact right now, that when you need to bitch about him—or he needs to bitch about you to me—that you and I handle it the way we handle any other bitching about guys. You don't feel hamstrung because he's my brother, and I don't take offense because he's my brother."

"All right."

They hooked pinkies on the swear.

"Now I'm going up, finishing up a couple things." Parker rose. "You know if you don't fill in Emma and Mac, their feelings are going to be hurt."

"I'll update them." She pushed to her feet to walk to the third level with Parker.

*F*ULL DISCLOSURE, DEL DECIDED, AND MADE ARRANGEMENTS to meet Jack for a morning workout. Since the word was *full*, he told Jack to drag Carter along. He started off with cardio while Carter approached a treadmill with obvious trepidation.

"I try to avoid doing this sort of thing in public. People could get hurt."

"Start off slow, then kick it up every couple minutes."

"Easy for you to say."

"I've missed this place." In solidarity, Jack took the machine on the other side of Del. "Having the home gym right there's convenient, but you miss the group buzz. Plus the many athletic females in skimpy outfits. I'm engaged, but still breathing," he said at Del's look.

"I don't understand walking on an electric belt when there are sidewalks right outside." Gripping the bar with one hand—just in case—Carter gestured vaguely. "And they don't move under your feet."

"Kick it up, Carter. Snails are passing you. How's my Macadamia?"

"She's good." Brow furrowed, Carter increased the speed slightly. "Staff meeting this morning, and a studio shoot. It's probably good I'm out of the way for a couple hours."

"You'll have your professor room before long," Jack told him. "Then we'll move on to Emma's new space, and Laurel's."

"Speaking of Laurel, we're dating." He heard the *oof* from the left and glanced over. "You okay, Carter?"

"Just missed my footing. Um, by dating, you mean each other?"

"That would be my definition."

"This would be my cue to jump down your throat and demand to know what you mean by taking advantage of one of my girls?"

Del shifted his gaze toward Jack as he punched up his speed. "Unlike you, I'm not sneaking around and hiding it."

"I wasn't sneaking and hiding, I just hadn't figured out how to explain about Emma, for a short period of time. And since I'm marrying into the Quartet, I have certain privileges and duties. If you're sleeping with Laurel—"

"I'm not sleeping with Laurel. We're dating."

"Right, and the two of you are just going to hold hands, admire the moon, and sing camp songs."

"For a while. Minus the singing. No comments from you?" he asked Carter.

"I'm kind of busy trying to stay on my feet." To ensure he did, Carter gripped the bar one-handed again. "I guess, off the top of my head, I'd say this is a quick situational change."

"I thought so at first, now I'm not so sure. It feels like it's been brewing awhile."

"Could've fooled me," Jack said, punching up his speed to match Del's pace. "How did this brewing situational change happen?"

"We had a fight, culminating in her telling me, and demonstrating that, I wasn't her brother. Which I'm not. So we're dating, and I'm just letting you know."

"Okay. Three miles?"

"You're on. Kick it up, Carter," Del told him.

Carter said, "Oh God."

SUNDAY MORNING LAUREL LEFT HER KITCHEN WORK TO
dash upstairs for the pre-event briefing. When she found her
three partners already in place, she held up a hand. "I'm not
late." And since she'd already had two cups of coffee that
morning, grabbed a bottle of water. "Just FYI, it's raining."

"The forecast calls for it to stop midmorning," Parker
stated. "But we're prepared to move everything inside if it
doesn't."

"The arrangements are pretty simple," Emma put in. "If
it clears by noon, we can have everything dressed outside
by one. Otherwise, we can shift it all to the Great Hall, do
a big fireplace arrangement pretty quickly, add candles.
We're set either way. We'll have both suites finished by
ten."

"The grooms are due to arrive at eleven."

"I'll shift back and forth for formals." Mac nodded at
Parker. "Both grooms have sisters standing up for them,
which makes it nice. I can get some good shots with that
dynamic. Doing guys means less hair and makeup time, and
each has just the one attendant, so I should be done with the
formals by twelve, twelve fifteen."

"Guests arriving twelve thirty, short cocktail mixer."
Parker read off her schedule. "For the outside ceremony, we
line up at one, attendants will walk down the aisle together,
then grooms will approach from either side. Ceremony time,
twenty minutes. Mac takes post-pictures, caterers pass
finger food."

"Again, it'll be pretty quick. Fifteen minutes should
do it."

"Figure one forty-five for the grooms to be announced,
buffet brunch, toasts. DJ announces first dance at two thirty.
Cake cutting three thirty."

"All the pastries are done for the dessert table. I'll finish the cake by ten, and we'll move it into the Ballroom. We're providing the knife and server. The happy couple has requested the top layer be removed and boxed for them to take home."

"Okay. Dancing continues at three forty until four fifteen. We'll transfer the gifts, announce the last dance. We're clear at four thirty. Any concerns? Potential disasters?"

"Not on my end. They're both really cute and should photograph well."

"They went with big, happy geranium boutonnieres to match the cake," Emma added. "Pretty adorable."

"They wrote the script for the ceremony themselves." Parker tapped her file. "It's incredibly sweet. We're going to have a lot of crying. Laurel, anything on your end?"

"I just need the cake topper from Emma, and I'm good."

"It's done, and in the cooler. I'll get it to you."

"Then, we're all good."

"Not so fast." Mac shot out a finger as Laurel started to rise. "Business completed, now let's get personal. What's the latest with Del?"

"There is no latest. I just saw you eight hours ago."

"He didn't call?" Emma wondered. "Leave you a message or anything?"

"He sent an e-mail with a list of potential movies for tonight."

"Oh." Emma struggled not to look deflated. "That's considerate."

"It's practical," Laurel corrected. "And it's Del. It's me. I'm not looking for charming little notes and sexy little messages."

"They're fun though," Emma murmured. "Jack and I sent each other lots of sexy little e-mails. We still do."

"What're you wearing?" Mac demanded.

"I don't know. It's the movies. Something movieish."

"But he'll be dressed for the wedding," Emma pointed out, "so you can't be too casual. You should wear the blue top. The one with the scoop-neck that ties in the back. It looks great on you. With the white capris I wish I could wear but would make my legs look stumpy. And the kitten-heel slides."

"Okay, thanks for dressing me."

"Happy to help," Emma said with a bright smile that acknowledged the sarcasm.

"We have a betting pool going," Mac informed her. "Nobody figures you'll last the full thirty before you get naked. Carter gives your willpower the most credit with twenty-four days."

"You're betting on when I'm going to have sex with Del?"

"Damn right. You're disqualified," she said when Laurel started to speak again. "Conflict of interest. I give you sixteen days, not because of willpower but stubbornness—in case that might influence you to help me add to my wedding fund."

"Unfair, unfair," Emma caroled.

"How much is in the pool?"

"We kicked in a hundred each."

"Five hundred? Seriously?"

"Six, counting Mrs. G."

"Man."

"We started at ten dollars each." Emma shrugged and chose a strawberry to nibble on. "But then Mac and Jack kept challenging each other. I had to make them stop when we hit a hundred. Parker's keeping the bank."

Laurel cocked a challenging eyebrow. "What if we have sex and don't tell anyone?"

"Please." Mac just rolled her eyes. "First, you'd never be able to keep it to yourself, and second, even if you did, we'd know."

"I hate when you're right. And nobody gave us the full thirty?"

"No one."

"Okay, here's the deal—and I should get some say since it's my sex, potentially. I will not be disqualified. I put in a hundred, and if we get to the thirty, pot's mine."

Objections broke out, but Parker waved them off. "You know, that's fair."

"You know how competitive she is," Mac complained. "She'll hold out just to win the bet."

"Then she'd have earned it. Get me the hundred, and I'll add your bet."

"You're on." Gleefully Laurel rubbed her hands together. "At long, long last, the sexual moratorium pays off. I've got a cake to frost." She did a quick boogie at the door. "See you later, suckers."

"We'll see who's the sucker," Parker said after Laurel danced out. "Okay, ladies, let's get to work."

CHAPTER EIGHT

$\mathscr{I}$T WAS STRANGE AND INTERESTING TO GO OUT WITH DEL as a date rather than one of the group. Comfortable on many levels, Laurel discovered, which was probably good. Neither of them had to listen to the other's life story, because they already knew each other's life story.

Not the whole cake, she thought, but most of the layers. Which made it all the more fun to take samples of the filling.

She knew he'd served on the *Law Review* at Yale, and played baseball as an undergraduate, just as she knew that law and sports were two of his passions. But she hadn't known he'd made a deliberate choice over which to pursue as a career.

"I didn't know you were serious about professional baseball." The things you learned, Laurel reflected, on a third date.

"Deadly. And serious enough I kept it to myself, mostly."

They strolled the park eating ice cream cones while the summer moonlight silvered the pond—an activity she believed to be the perfect cap to a casual dinner date.

"What was the tipping point?" she asked him.

"I wasn't good enough."

"How do you know? I saw you in action when you played at the Academy, and a couple times at Yale—and since at softball games." With the faintest of frowns she studied his profile as they walked. "I may not consider baseball my religion like *some* people, but I get the game. You knew what you were doing."

"Sure. And I was pretty good. Pretty good isn't good enough. Maybe I could've been if I'd put everything into it. I talked to some scouts from the Yankees' farm team."

"Get out." She shoved his arm. "Seriously? I never knew that. The Yankees scouted you? Why didn't I know that?"

"I never told anybody. I had to decide. I could either be a really good lawyer or a decent ballplayer."

She remembered watching him play since . . . always, she realized. Without much effort, she pulled out a mental picture of him as a boy playing Little League.

God, he was cute.

"You loved baseball."

"I still do. I just realized I didn't love it enough to give it everything I had, and to give up everything else for it. So I wasn't good enough."

She understood that, yes, understood that very well. She wondered if she could've made the same sensible, rational choice to give up something she loved and wanted.

"Do you ever regret it?"

"Every summer. For about five minutes." He draped an arm over her shoulders. "But you know, when I'm old and sitting on the rocker on the front porch, I get to tell my great-grandchildren how back in the day, the Yankees scouted me."

She couldn't quite build that image in her mind, but the idea of it made her smile. "They won't believe you."

"Sure they will. They'll love me. And my pocketful of candy. What about you? One regret."

"I probably have a lot more of them than you."

"Why?"

"Because you—and Parker—always seem to know what

direction you need and want to take. So let's see." She crunched into the sugar cone as she considered. "Okay. Sometimes I wonder how it would've been if I'd gone to France, stayed there. Run my own exclusive patisserie—while having many passionate affairs."

"Naturally."

"I'd design and bake for royalty and stars, and run my staff like dogs. *Allez, allez! Imbeciles! Merde!*"

He laughed at her broad, undeniably Gallic gestures, and dodged her cone.

"I'd be a terror, and a genius, world-renowned, jetting off to exciting places to make birthday cakes for little princesses."

"You'd hate that. Except for the cursing in French."

More than full, she tossed what was left of her cone in the trash. "Probably, but it's something I think about sometimes. Still, I'd be doing what I'm doing now at the core of it. I didn't have to choose."

"Sure you did. Solo or partnership, home or European adventure. That's a big choice, too. You know, if you'd gone to France, you'd have pined away for us."

God, that was so absolutely true. But keeping to her theme, she shook her head. "I'd have been too busy with my wild affairs and towering ego ride to pine. I'd have thought of you fondly from time to time, and swirled in occasionally from a trip to New York to dazzle you all with my European panache."

"You have European panache."

"Is that so?"

"Sometimes you mutter or swear in French when you're working."

She stopped, frowned. "I do?"

"Now and then, and with a perfect accent. It's entertaining."

"Why hasn't anyone told me this before?"

He took her hand, linked fingers while they angled away from the pond. "Maybe because they figured you knew, since you were the one muttering and swearing."

"That could be it."

"And if you'd gone, you'd have thought about this, what you're doing here now."

"Yeah, I would. Still, other times I imagine I have a pretty bake shop in a small village in Tuscany, where it only rains at night and charming little children come in to beg for treats. It's a pretty good deal."

"And here we both are, still in Greenwich."

"All in all, it's a good place to be."

"Right now?" He tipped her face up to kiss her. "It's close to perfect."

"This seems almost too easy," she said as they walked back to the car.

"Why should it be hard?"

"I don't know. I'm just naturally suspicious of too easy." At the car she turned, leaned back against the door to look up at him. "When it's going easy I know there's a disaster waiting to fall on my head. It's just around the corner, a piano being lowered out the window."

"So you walk around it."

"What if you're not looking up until—*snap*—the cable breaks, then you're splatted under the Steinway."

"Most of the time the cable doesn't break."

"Most of the time," she agreed, tapping a finger on his chest. "It only takes once. So it's better to keep looking up, just in case."

Lifting a hand, he tucked her swing of hair behind her ear. "Then you can trip over the curb and break your neck."

"That's true. Disasters are everywhere."

"Would you feel better if I started a fight?" He laid his hands on the car on either side of her, leaned in to brush his lips against hers. "Rough you up a little so it's not so easy."

"Depends on the roughing up." She drew him down for a deeper kiss. "Twenty-four more days," she murmured. "Maybe it's not so easy after all."

"Almost a week down." He opened the door for her. "And an eight-hundred-dollar pool on the line."

There was that, she thought as he walked around the car

to get behind the wheel. He'd insisted on tossing a hundred of his in on the kitty. "Some would say our tribe's a little too intimate when they start a pool on when we'll have sex."

"Those *some* aren't our tribe. And thinking of tribes, why don't we gather ours for the Fourth?"

"Fourth of what—oh. July. God, it's nearly here."

"We could play some ball, eat some hot dogs, watch the fireworks in the park. You don't have an event that day."

"No events on the Fourth, no matter how much they beg or bribe. A Vows tradition. We have a day off." She sighed it. "An entire day off, away from the kitchen. I can get behind that."

"Good, because I already said something to Parker about the gathering of the tribe."

"What if I'd said no?"

He flashed her a grin. "Then we'd have missed you."

She narrowed her eyes at him, but her lips twitched. "I suppose I already have an assignment."

"There might have been some mention of a suitably patriotic cake. And we thought we'd go over to Gantry's after, for some music."

"I'm not designated driver. If I bake, I get to drink."

"Reasonable. We'll make Carter do it," he decided and made her laugh. "We can all fit in Emma's van."

"That works for me." It was all working for her, she thought as he turned in the drive.

She was going to have to keep a careful eye out for pianos.

$\mathscr{S}$HE DECIDED TO GO WITH A FIREWORKS THEME, WHICH meant working with a lot of spun sugar. Probably silly to go to so much trouble for a park picnic with friends, she thought as she threw heated strands from her whisk to the wooden rack, but also fun.

She'd use the strands to form exploding fountains on the

cake she'd already piped out in red, white, and blue. Some gum paste flags around the border, and you had a winner.

Enjoying herself, she began to form the fireworks with the sugar strands made pliable with just a touch of beeswax.

She stepped back to check the first formation, and nearly yelped when she saw a man in her doorway.

"Sorry. Sorry. I didn't want to say anything when you were working. Afraid I'd screw you up. Nick Pelacinos, from the last-minute engagement party?"

"Sure." He had a summer bouquet in his hand that made her think: uh-oh. "How are you?"

"Good. Your partner said I could come back, that you weren't working, but . . ."

"This isn't for a job."

"It ought to be." He stepped closer. "Fun."

"Yeah, it is. Spun sugar's like a toy."

"And your hands are full with it, so why don't I just put these over here." He crossed over to set the flowers out of the way.

"They're beautiful." Had she flirted with him? Yes. Sort of. "Thank you."

"I have my grandmother's recipe for the lathopita."

"Oh, that's great."

"She gave me orders to deliver it in person." He took a recipe card out of his pocket, laid it beside the bouquet. "And to bring you the flowers."

"That's awfully sweet of her."

"She liked you."

"I liked her, too. How about some coffee?"

"No, I'm fine. Her third order was for me to ask you out to dinner—which I'd intended to do anyway, but she likes to take credit."

"Oh. And that's sweet of both of you. But I've actually started seeing someone recently. Well, the seeing part is recent. Sort of."

"My grandmother and I are disappointed."

She smiled a little. "Can I still keep the recipe?"

"On the condition I can tell her you only turned me down because you're madly in love with someone else."

"That's a deal."

"And . . ." He took out a pen, turned the recipe card over, and wrote something down. "My number. You'll call me if things change."

"You'll be the first." She took a strand of sugar from her rack, offered it. "Have a taste."

"Nice. As consolation prizes go."

They grinned at each other as Del walked in.

"Hi. Sorry, I didn't know you were with a client."

Awkward, Laurel thought. "Ah, Delaney Brown, Nick—"

"Pelacinos," Del said. "It took me a minute."

"Del, sure." Nick held out a hand for a shake. "It's been a while. How are you?"

Or not awkward at all, Laurel decided as the two men settled in.

"I talked to Terri and Mike just a couple weeks ago. Are you in the market for a wedding cake?"

"Me? No. I have a cousin getting married here in a few months."

"Nick's grandmother's visiting from Greece," Laurel put in, in case they'd forgotten she was there. "We had a pre-event event so she could see the setup."

"Right. I was by that night."

"You should've joined the party. It was a good one."

"I glanced in for a minute. You got Laurel on the dance floor." Del glanced at her, deliberately. "Big night."

She went back to her spun sugar. "I got a recipe from the matriarch out of it," she said with a smile as sweet as her sugar. "That's a major night for me."

"I'd better get going. I'll let my grandmother know I made the delivery."

"Tell her how much I appreciate it, and I'll try to do her proud at the wedding."

"I will. Good to see you again, Laurel. Del."

"I'll walk you out. What's your handicap now?" Del asked as they left the kitchen.

Laurel frowned after them until she realized Del was talking golf. With a shake of her head, she tossed more sugar. It wasn't as if she'd wanted the moment to be awkward or tense. Jealousy was weak and self-absorbed and irritating.

But a little hint of it—like beeswax in spun sugar—couldn't hurt.

Nick had asked her out, after all. He'd even left his number where she'd see it every time she took out the recipe for lathopita. Which had been very clever of him, now that she thought of it.

Of course, Del didn't know that, but he could *infer* it, couldn't he? And so inferring be just a little irked or something instead of all "how's it going, how's the golf game?"

Men, she thought—or rather, men like Del—just didn't get the subtle nuances of a relationship.

He came back in a few moments later. "That's great," he said nodding toward the cake as he opened a cupboard. "Want a glass of wine? I want a glass of wine."

When she shrugged, he opened a bottle of pinot and poured two.

"I didn't know you were coming by." She ignored the wine for now as she added the dazzle of sugar fireworks to her cake.

"I'm staying over, since we're all leaving from here tomorrow. Mrs. G's going with some of her friends, but she'll see us there. She's bringing enough food to feed the village."

"Yes, I know."

He sipped his wine and watched her. "Flowers, huh?"

She shrugged and kept working.

Casually, and in long-standing habit, Del opened a canister for a cookie. "He's not your type."

She stopped long enough to arch her eyebrows. "Really? Attractive, considerate men who work in the food industry and love their grandmothers aren't my type? I'm glad you let me know."

Del crunched into the cookie. "He plays golf."

"Good God! That was a lucky escape."

"Twice a week. Every week."

"Stop it. You're scaring me."

He pointed with the cookie, then took another bite. "And he likes art films. You know, the kind with subtitles and symbolism."

She paused to take a sip of her wine. "Did you date him? Bad breakup?"

"Funny. I happen to know someone who did."

"Is there anyone you don't know?"

"I'm his cousin Theresa's lawyer—and her husband's. Anyway, Nick's more Parker's type, except his schedule's nearly as insane as hers and they'd never manage to get together anyway."

"Parker doesn't like art films, especially."

"No, but she gets them."

"And I don't because, what, I didn't go to Yale?"

"No, because they'd annoy you."

They did annoy her, but still. "There's more to types than cinema choices and golf. He's a good dancer," she shot out, and hated the defensive tone in her voice. "I like to dance."

"Okay." He stepped over, put his arms around her.

"Cut it out. I'm not finished with the cake."

"It looks good. You look better, and smell really good, too." He sniffed at her neck. "Sugar and vanilla. I didn't recognize Nick when you were dancing with him." He turned her smoothly, right, then left. "It was crowded. And I was looking at you. Really, I was just looking at you."

"That's pretty good," she murmured.

"It's pretty true." He dipped his head to brush her lips with his. "Hi, Laurel."

"Hi, Del."

"If you give Parker those flowers, I'll buy you some more."

It was, she thought, the perfect amount of beeswax in the sugar. "Okay."

HOLIDAYS, THE REAL DEAL WITH NO WORK ON THE SLATE, were so rare Laurel's internal clock woke her at six sharp. She started to roll out of bed when she remembered she didn't have to roll out. She snuggled back in with the same sort of giddy wonder she'd felt as a child with an unexpected snow day.

Even as she sighed and closed her eyes again, she thought of Del in another bed, conveniently close by.

She could get up after all, sneak into his room, into his bed. All bets off.

It was Independence Day, after all. Why not be independent? He wasn't likely to complain or yell for help. She could change into something sexier than her tank and boxers. She had the equipment. The blue teddy would do the job. Or maybe the silk chemise with the pastel flower pattern, or . . .

Thinking about it, she fell back to sleep.

Opportunity missed, she thought as she wandered down to the family kitchen nearly three hours later. Probably for the best as the others would surely gloat about her and Del losing the bet. This was the best way, the way to show they both were adults with willpower and sense. Just a couple more weeks, really, so no big deal.

Breakfast scents and voices filled the kitchen. And there he was, looking all gorgeous and relaxed, drinking coffee and flirting with Mrs. G. She could only wish she'd followed through on that early-morning thought.

"And she's up," Mac announced. "Just in time. We're having the ginormous holiday breakfast, which, thanks to Del's persuasive powers, includes Belgian waffles."

"Yum."

"I'll say. We're going to do nothing but eat and fat-ass all day, until we go to the park and eat and fat-ass there. Including you." Mac pointed at Parker.

"Not all fat asses are created equal. I'm going to do a little reorganizing in my office. It relaxes me."

"Your office is already organized to Obsessiveville," Emma pointed out.

"It's where I live, where I make my home."

"Nag the girl while you finish setting the table," Mrs. Grady ordered. "I haven't got all day."

"We're eating on the terrace because, holiday." Mac picked up a stack of plates, shaking her head when Carter started to take them from her. "Uh-uh, cutie. Grab something unbreakable."

"Good thought."

"We're having mimosas, like grown-ups." Emma handed Carter the bread basket. "What this is, is a prelude for our vacation next month, where every day's a holiday."

"I'll tend bar." Jack hefted the champagne and a pitcher of orange juice.

"Someone should've woken me up. I'd have given you a hand with this, Mrs. G."

"Under control." Mrs. Grady flicked her spatula. "Get the rest out there. We'll be ready in two minutes."

"Nice start to the day." Laurel glanced at Del as they carried platters outside. "Your idea?"

"Who wants to be inside on a day like this?"

Laurel remembered how often there'd been fun summer meals on the terrace when she'd visited as a child. Flowers, good dishes, and easy company on lovely, lazy mornings.

They'd already put tables together to accommodate the whole group, draped them in pretty cloths, and, yes, there were flowers and good dishes, and the sparkle of crystal in the morning sunlight.

She'd forgotten what it was to indulge like this with nothing more pressing on the day than enjoyment.

She took the glass Jack offered her. "Thanks." Took a sip. "You could have a career."

He gave her hair a friendly tug. "A fallback's always good."

When Mrs. G came out with the last platter, Del took it from her. "Head of the table for you, Waffle Queen."

Of course she loved him, Laurel thought, watching as he fussed over Mrs. Grady until she was settled with a mimosa in her hand. How could she help it?

She stepped up, kissed his cheek. "Good job."

It would be like this from now on, she realized. Oh, not Belgian waffles and mimosas on the terrace. But this group, this family. These voices, these faces, on holidays and impromptu family meals.

Voices crisscrossed the table along with the food. A sliver of waffle for Emma, fruit for Parker while she talked to Carter about a book they'd both read recently. Heaps of whipped cream for Mac, and Del arguing with Jack about a call on a baseball game.

"What's on your mind, girl?" Mrs. Grady asked her.

"Hardly anything. It's a nice change."

Mrs. Grady leaned over, lowered her voice. "Are you going to show them the design you just worked up?"

"Should I?"

"Eat first."

Mac tapped her spoon on her glass. "I want to announce we're holding tours after breakfast for the new Carter Maguire Library. Carter and I hauled half a million books up there last night, so we expect lavish praise, with some left over for the architect." She lifted her glass to Jack.

"It wasn't more than a quarter million books," Carter corrected. "But it's great. Really great, Jack."

"Nothing I like more than satisfied clients." He aimed a look at Emma. "Well, almost nothing."

"And no more hammering, sawing, painting. Not that we're complaining," Mac said. "But, oh boy."

"Hammering and so forth starts next door next week," Jack warned her.

"Earplugs," Mac said to Emma. "Highly recommended."

"I can take it. For a new cooler and work space, I can take it."

"We'll be doing some work on your space in tandem, Laurel."

"She'll bitch." Mac waved her fork. "Me? I'm a saint, but she'll bitch and complain."

"Probably." Laurel shrugged and finished her waffle.

"We'll block off the work area from your kitchen," Jack told her. "Keep out of your space as much as possible."

"She'll still bitch. It's her nature."

Laurel gave Mac a cool stare, then rose and walked inside.

"What? What? I was kidding. Mostly."

"She's not mad. If she was mad she'd have snapped your head off." Parker glanced toward the house. "She'll be back."

"True. You're not mad, right?" Mac wagged her fork at Del. "If she's mad you'd be mad on her behalf since you're hooked up."

"If that's a rule, it's a girl rule."

"It's not a girl rule. It's a couple rule." Mac looked to Emma for verification.

"Yes, it is. If you know what's good for you."

"I'm not mad, so if she's mad she's going to have to get over it."

"You really don't get how this works," Mac decided. "Parker, you should write some of this stuff down for him. Rules are the thread that knits the fabric. He's got holes in his fabric."

"Are these girl rules, couple rules, or Quartet rules?"

"It's really all the same," Parker told him. "I'll get you a memo." She glanced over as Laurel came back out with her sketchbook. "But the point's moot at the moment."

"What's the point?" Laurel asked.

"Anger and insult rule."

"Oh. I'm not angry or insulted, I'm just ignoring her." She walked around the table to Carter. "This is for you, not for her. Just for you."

"Okay." He glanced at Mac. "Is that allowed?"

"Depends."

"She has nothing to say about it. For you, if you like it. The groom's cake." Laurel angled the pad so Mac's view was blocked, and opened it for Carter.

She watched his face and saw exactly what she'd hoped to see. The quicksilver flash of pure delight. "It's amazing. It couldn't be more perfect, and I'd never have thought of it."

"What is it?"

Even as Mac asked, shifted, Laurel snapped the book shut.

That brought a few hoots of laughter from around the table as Mac cursed. Then she shifted tactics with a sad, pitiful expression.

"Please? Pretty, pretty please?"

Laurel opened the book a fraction. "I'm only showing you for Carter. Not for you."

"Okay."

Laurel opened the book, heard Mac's breath catch before she managed a shaky, *"Oh."*

Jack craned his head to get a look. "It's a book. It's nice. Fits."

"It's not just a book. It's *As You Like It*. It's kind of our book, isn't it, Carter?"

"I was teaching it when we started seeing each other. It's even open to Rosalind's speech. See down here." He ran his finger down the open page. "'No sooner looked but they loved.'"

"Oh, big *awww*." Emma leaned over for a better look. "I love the bookmark ribbon with their names on it."

"I think I'm taking Mac's off. I'll just have Carter's." Laurel considered. "Yeah, just his. Carter Maguire, PhD."

"You won't take me off the cake. You love me."

Laurel made a *pfft* sound.

"You love me," Mac said again, scooting up. "You designed the perfect cake for my guy. You love me." She grabbed Laurel in a hug, did a little dance.

"Maybe I love Carter."

"Of course you do. Who wouldn't? Thank you, thank you," she whispered in Laurel's ear. "It's the best."

"You almost deserve it," she whispered back, then laughed and hugged hard.

"I'll have a look at that while the lot of you deal with the dishes." Mrs. Grady curled a finger. "Food's ready to be packed up for the park when you are. You'll need to get the hampers out."

"Packing, family kitchen at three thirty," Parker announced. "I'll hand out specific assignments after kitchen duty. Loading up the van at four, which includes food, folding chairs, blankets, any sports equipment, and people. I have your assigned seats for transportation," she added and only inclined her head at the groans. "It'll save arguing. I'm driving." This time she held up a hand. "I alone among us am dateless, and as such am to be pitied, indulged, and obeyed."

"You could've had a date," Emma objected. "I can get you a date in five seconds."

"That's really sweet, but no. Big no." Parker rose and began to stack dishes. "Let's get this done because I have some relaxing and satisfying file purging to do."

"That's just really sad." With a shake of her head, Mac grabbed a tray.

"Who could you get in five seconds?" Jack wondered. Emma shot him a laughing look over her shoulder as she carried in dishes.

"I'll be right in," Del told Laurel. "I just need to take care of something first."

"If you're more than five minutes, I'm sticking you with the pans."

When Del pulled out his phone, Mrs. Grady looked up from Laurel's sketchbook. "What are you up to?"

"Just looking out for my sister." He wandered off to make a call.

$\mathscr{I}$T WASN'T EXACTLY LIKE HERDING CATS, LAUREL supposed, but it was pretty damn close. Here were people who successfully ran their own businesses, who taught the youth of the country, who represented citizens in the court of law—and none of them could get to one place at one time.

A dozen essential items were remembered at the last minute, then retrieved. Debates broke out on the system of loading the van, then on Parker's seat assignments.

Laurel dug a soft drink out of one of the coolers and, popping it open, walked over to sit on one of the low garden walls while chaos reigned.

"Why aren't you over there fixing this?" she asked Parker when her friend sat down beside her.

"They're having fun." She held out a hand for the drink. "And I built an extra twenty minutes into the load time."

"Naturally. Did you really purge files all afternoon?"

"Some people do crossword puzzles."

"How many calls did you get?"

"Five."

"Some holiday."

"It works for me. Things seem to be working for you, too."

Laurel followed Parker's gaze and watched Del rearrange the placement of a hamper and a pair of folding chairs. "We haven't had a fight. It's kind of nerve-racking."

"Oh, you'll get back to that." Parker patted Laurel's knee, then rose. "All right, people, this bus is leaving the station. Everyone into their assigned seats."

Del shut the back door of the van then walked over to take Laurel's hand. "You get to sit beside me. My sister fixed it."

"It's going to be pretty crowded. I might have to sit on your lap."

He grinned as she climbed in. "We can hope."

CHAPTER NINE

Thanks to Parker's schedule they arrived early enough to claim a good location for what Laurel thought of as their camp. Folding chairs were unfolded, blankets spread, hampers and coolers hauled.

Del tossed a ball glove into Laurel's lap. "Right field."

"I always get stuck back in right field," she complained. "I want to play first base."

Dating status notwithstanding, he looked at her with pity. "Face it, McBane, you field like a girl. Most of the shots are going to stay in the infield, so I need Parker on first."

"Parker's a girl."

"But she doesn't field like one. Jack's got Emma and Mac, Carter's going to ump so nobody gets hurt. Plus he'll be fair. We're filling in the rest with pickups, and some are unknown quantities, so until . . . And here comes my ringer."

Laurel looked over. "You drafted Malcolm Kavanaugh?"

The light of competition sparked in Del's eyes. "He's got serious skills, plus it evens things out."

"The lineups?"

"No. You know, with Parker."

"Parker?" Shock, then amusement, then her own dose of pity ran over her face. "You got Parker a date? Jesus, Del, she's going to kill you."

"Why?" Absently, he tossed a ball from hand to glove, hand to glove. "I'm not asking her to marry him. We're just hanging out."

"It's your funeral."

"Why?" he asked again. "Does she have some sort of problem with . . . Hey, Mal."

"Hey." He caught the ball Del tossed him, winged it back. "How's it going?" he said to Laurel.

"We're going to find out."

"Ball game, free food." Mal, in worn jeans, a white tee, and dark sunglasses used the bat he'd brought with him to pop up a fungo. "Good deal. My mother's hooked up with your Mrs. Grady and some of them." He laid the bat on his shoulder. "So, what's the lineup?"

"I've got you on third, batting cleanup."

"That'll work."

"Laurel's in right field, leading off. Her fielding's crap, but she's got a good bat."

"My fielding is not crap." She hit Del with the glove. "Keep it up and you're not going to have any problem winning that bet, Brown."

When she stalked off, Mal took an easy, testing swing. "What bet?"

Laurel strode straight up to Mac. "I want to switch with you. I want to play on Jack's team."

"Baseball slut. Okay by me, but you'd better tell Jack."

She walked over to where Jack sat on the ground writing his lineup. "I switched with Mac. I'm on your team."

"Trading the redhead for the blonde. Okay, let me figure . . . You're right field, leading off."

Son of a bitch. Did he and Del have telepathy? Laurel narrowed her eyes. "Why right field?"

He flicked her a glance, and she *saw* him reconsider his response. "You've got a strong arm."

She pointed at him. "Good answer."

"How come you . . . ? Hey. Hey, is that Mal? Del hooked Mal?" Jack bared his teeth. "So that's the way he wants to play the game."

"Let's kick his ass."

Jack rose to slap palms with Laurel. "I won the flip. We're home team. Let's take the field."

She did just fine at right field. And not just because no one hit a ball in her direction, but because she was *prepared*.

Once they'd bagged three outs, she switched her glove for a bat and faced down Del on the mound.

He winked at her. She snarled back. Then swung hard at thin air as she mistimed the ball. He tried to fool her with a pitch that hung low and outside, but she held her ground. She caught the third with enough meat on the bat for a solid base hit. When she held up at first, she tossed her batting helmet aside.

"Del called Mal in to balance things out for you."

"What?" Beside the bag, Parker straightened out of her waiting crouch. "Are you kidding me? Like some sort of pity date?"

"That, and Mal's good at the game. I thought you'd want to know."

"Damn right." Parker sent a scorching look toward the mound as Del wound up for the pitch. "He's so going to pay."

By the fourth inning Del had them five to three. He'd been right about Malcolm, Laurel had to admit. Serious skills. He held second now on a strong leadoff double, and the strikeout behind him brought Del to the plate. Cheers and calls went up from teammates and the audience that had gathered. Laurel watched Del set, and Jack shake off the first suggestion from the twelve-year-old catcher.

He went with a fastball. Or she thought it was, as it looked fast to her. It looked even faster when Del's bat smacked it and the ball winged into the air. In her direction.

"Shit. Oh, shit."

She heard someone yelling—maybe it was her—as she raced back to meet the path of the ball, but her heart pounded so hard in her ears she couldn't tell.

She lifted her glove and prayed.

When the ball slapped into it, no one was more surprised than she was. She shot up ball and glove to acknowledge the cheers from the crowd. And saw Mal had already tagged up and was charging third. She threw the ball to Emma's waving hands. Her throw, while hard and fairly true, hit Emma's glove one wild slide too late.

Jubilation to disgust, she thought, in less than five seconds.

Baseball sucked.

"Good catch, Laurel."

"Don't patronize me, Jack," she muttered when they got out of the inning with Mal stranded on third.

"Who's patronizing? Del creamed that ball. If you hadn't caught it, we'd be behind a couple more runs. We held them off." He gave her a brotherly punch on the shoulder.

"It was a good catch." She nodded in satisfaction. Maybe baseball didn't suck after all.

It sucked again when they lost seven to four, but she had the satisfaction of knowing her fielding hadn't been crap.

"You did good out there." Del tossed her a canned soft drink. "Two singles and an RBI. Plus you robbed me of a potential two-run homer."

"You shouldn't have said my fielding was crap."

"It usually is." He flicked the bill of her cap, in the same sort of brotherly gesture as Jack's arm punch. Laurel tossed the cap aside, grabbed a handful of Del's shirt.

"I think you're forgetting something."

She yanked him down for a good strong kiss, amused when the gesture brought on a smattering of applause by those who'd dropped down on the blanket or chairs.

"No, I remembered that." Del linked his arms casually around her waist. "But thanks for the heads-up."

"Well, well, isn't *this* a surprise." Hillary Babcock, one

of Mrs. Grady's friends, beamed at Del and Laurel. "I had no idea this was going on! Maureen, you don't tell me anything!"

"What I don't tell you, you find out."

"But this is *big*. I've always thought of the two of you as the next thing to brother and sister, and here you are, getting all romantic."

"Laurel fielded a long fly." Del shifted to drape his arm around Laurel's shoulders. His hand rubbed lightly at her biceps as if to soothe away a mild irritation. "She gets a reward."

Hillary laughed. "Next time, sign me up! But really, how long has this been going on? Look at all of you." She beamed the smile again, and her eyes got a little teary. "It seems like five minutes ago you four girls and Del were all running around this park with the rest of the kids, now you're all grown-up. All paired up, too! Oh, Maureen, you should talk these girls into a triple wedding. Wouldn't that be something special?"

"Hilly, the boy just kissed the girl. That doesn't mean they're picking out the china pattern. Why don't you get the potato salad out of the cooler over there."

"Why, sure. Kay, this must be your boy Malcolm. All grown-up, too! And you're with Parker. Isn't that nice?"

Mal watched Parker's face as he answered. "She pulled her weight on line drives and pop flies, but I haven't even kissed the girl. Yet."

"Mal's not actually with—"

One searing stare from his sister in Del's direction stopped his explanation. Deliberately, Parker stepped forward. Aware they were directly in Del's eyeline, she pressed her body to Mal's, linked her arms behind his neck, and fixed her mouth to his in a long, slow, sumptuous kiss.

She pulled back, rubbed her lips together. "That ought to do it."

Mal caged her hips in his hands. "I think we should play a doubleheader."

She spared Mal the slightest smile, flicked a cool glance at Del, then stepped over to help unpack a hamper.

"What was that?" Del demanded as he crouched down beside her. "What the hell was that?"

"What? Oh, that? Just trying to keep things nice and *balanced*. Wasn't that the idea, big brother?"

"For God's sake, Parker, I just . . . He's a friend of mine, so why not ask him along? Plus you said how you were the only one without a date."

"And it was so nice of you to arrange one for me, without even asking if I'd like you to." She jabbed him with her finger as he started to speak. "You'd better back out of my personal business, or I'll sleep with him just to make your life hell."

He paled, visibly. "You would not."

"Don't test me, Delaney." She jabbed him again. "Don't test me."

"Time for a walk." Laurel reached down to tug on Del's arm. "No. Really time for a walk. Some things even you can't talk your way out of," she muttered to him as she dragged him away.

"What's wrong with her?"

"She's pissed at you, of course. I told you she would be."

He skirted the path of a flying Frisbee, then stopped. "She wouldn't be if you hadn't told her. Why did you do that?"

"Because she's my friend, and I was pissed at you before she was. I'd have told her even if I hadn't been pissed at you, but that was a secondary factor. You can't pull a date for her out of your hat without telling her, Del, or I have to."

"Another rule. Maybe she should send me a damn memo."

She gave the hand she held an impatient shake. "You should know better."

"I should know better? She's the one who grabbed him and kissed him like that, in front of everybody."

"Yes, she should've dragged him off to the bushes and done it in private, but you know Parker. She's brazen."

"You think it's funny?" He stopped, stared her down. "She made a move on him in public, she's really steamed at me, plus now I have to talk to Mal. It's not funny."

"No. No, you don't have to talk to Mal. Leave it alone, Mr. Fix-It. They're grown-ups."

"You have your rules, I have mine."

"Sometimes I could just . . ." She turned away, turned back. "How many guys did you 'talk to' and/or warn off when it was me?"

He slid his hands into his pockets. "The past is the past."

"You should probably have a talk with yourself."

"Believe me, I have been. It doesn't seem to do any good. I've got a taste for you now."

"A taste for me?"

"Yeah. You know about tastes, and how some of them are just irresistible. That's you."

She let out a half sigh, then framed his face with her hands. "Semi-redeemed. Let's walk the long way around. We'll work up an appetite."

WITHIN FIFTEEN MINUTES, LAUREL DECIDED THAT BE-tween the two of them they knew too many people. A simple walk around the park became a meet-and-greet, with the added slightly sticky layer of curiosity from those seeing them as a couple for the first time. She felt the speculation buzzing around her ears like mosquitoes.

"At least Mrs. Babcock came right out and asked."

Del glanced over as they wound their way back. "Asked what?"

"'What's going on with them? Are they dating? Are they sleeping together? What's Delaney Brown doing with Laurel McBane? When did that happen? What's going on with them?' I feel like I should've written up a mission statement."

"People like to know what's going on with other people, especially if there's any hint or possibility of sex or scandal."

"I can feel the eyebrows wiggling behind my back." As

if to dislodge them, she rolled her shoulders. "That doesn't bother you at all?"

"Why would it? In fact, let's give them something to wiggle about."

He spun her around, locked her into a just-short-of-steamy kiss. "There. Questions answered. Let's get some of that potato salad."

It was easier for him, she decided, because he was easier with people. Added to it, he was Delaney Brown of the Connecticut Browns, and that meant something in Greenwich. She didn't think of him that way—often—and she suspected he only thought of himself that way when it was useful. But others did.

He had the name, the position, the wealth. Their first real public outing as a couple served to remind her he was more than her childhood friend and her potential lover.

Sex and scandal, she thought. Well, there had been both in her family, hadn't there? She supposed some people would remember and have that to chew over, and the same ones would speculate over cocktails and country club tennis if she set her sights on Del for that name, position, and wealth.

It didn't bother her overmuch, and she wouldn't let it bother her, she thought. Unless it reflected on him or Parker.

"Long thoughts." Mac came over and gave her an elbow nudge. "Long thoughts aren't allowed on national holidays."

"Not all that long." But since she wondered . . . "Do you ever wonder what you and I are doing here?"

Mac licked icing off her fingers. "In a Zen way?"

"No, that's entirely too long a thought. You and me in particular. The public school kids with crappy families and a bumpy childhood."

"Mine was bumpier."

"Yes, you win that prize."

"Yay." For a moment, Mac studied her plastic cup of lemonade. "Speaking of bumps, Linda got back yesterday."

"You didn't say anything."

Mac shrugged. "It's not such a deal for me anymore.

Plus, she's living in New York with the new husband, and still currently pissed at me. It's a nice distance."

"May it continue."

"Doesn't matter so much, because I really did win the prize." She looked over at Carter while he talked to a couple of his students who'd found him in the crowd.

"He is pretty great," Laurel agreed. "Did we ever have any teachers that cute?"

"Mr. Zimmerman, U.S. History. He was cute."

"Oh yeah, the Zim Man. Very cute, but gay."

Green eyes wide, Mac lowered her cup. "He was gay?"

"Definitely. You must've been doing one of your stints at the Academy when that hit."

"I missed a lot of the good stuff bouncing back and forth. Well, gay or straight, he starred in several of my adolescent dreams. Here's to the Zim Man."

"To the Zim Man," Laurel echoed and tapped her can to Mac's cup.

"Anyway," Mac continued, "you and me."

"There's Emma. Solid family. They're legion, but rock solid. Certainly privileged. Then Parker. The Browns *are* Greenwich. Then there's you. Crazy mother, feckless father. Never knowing if you're going to be up or down. Then there's me, with my father and his little problem with the IRS and his mistress. Oops, we're very nearly broke and nobody's talking to anybody. We barely kept the house, and my mother's more pissed about having to let the staff go than the mistress. Strange times."

Mac nudged Laurel's arm with hers, in solidarity. "We got through them."

"We did. And we're still here. I guess I didn't think I would be, not when I look back. I was embarrassed and confused and angry, and imagined I'd take off as soon as I turned eighteen."

"You did, in a way. Going to school in New York, getting your own place. Man, that was fun—for me for sure. Having a pal with an apartment in New York. Young, single, and

not completely broke in New York City. We had some interesting times. When we weren't working our asses off."

Laurel drew her knees up, rested her cheek on them to
keep her eyes on Mac. "We always worked, you and me. I
don't mean Emma and Parker sat on their ass, but . . ."

"They had a cushion," Mac put in with a nod. "We didn't.
Except, we had them, so we did."

"Yeah, you're right. We did."

"So I guess I don't wonder about it too much. We got
here, and that's what counts. And look, you've got a very
nice prize there, too."

Laurel lifted her head and studied Del. "I haven't claimed
him yet."

"I know I've got money riding on it, but I've got to say,
McBane, why the hell haven't you?"

"You know, I'm asking myself the same question."

LATER, WHEN THE FIRST SHOWER OF LIGHT FOUNTAINED
in the sky, Del sat behind her, drawing her back so she
could rest against him. It was all color and sound and spec-
tacle, with his arms loose around her.

However she got here, Laurel thought, it was exactly
where she wanted to be.

LOADING BACK UP WAS NEARLY AS FRAUGHT AS THE INI-
tial chore, but once done, Parker piloted them to a local
club. At the door she passed Carter the keys. "Del's buying
the first round," she announced.

"I am?"

"You are, and our designated driver's money is no good
here." She glanced over as Mal came in behind them. "We'd
better grab a couple tables."

They pushed a couple together, claimed their spots. Once
the round was ordered, the women moved off en masse to
the ladies room.

"What do you figure they do in there, as a pack?" Mal wondered.

"Talk about us," Jack said, "and plot strategy."

"Since we have a minute, I figured I should tell you Parker just made that move earlier because she was mad at me."

Mal smiled easily at Del. "Okay. Maybe you could piss her off again."

"Ha. See, I didn't tell her I'd called you, and she got the wrong idea."

At ease, Mal kicked back and looped an arm over the back of his chair. "Yeah? What idea's that?"

"That I was setting the two of you up."

"Does your sister have trouble getting dates?"

"No. Of course not."

"Then I wouldn't worry about it."

The band started up as their drinks arrived—and the women came right behind them. "Dance! Come on, Jack." Emma grabbed his hand, tugged.

"There's beer."

"Dance, then beer."

"A plan." Del got up and claimed Laurel. "It's been a while for you and me."

"So, let's see what you've got."

"Okay, Carter."

"I'm a terrible dancer," he reminded Mac.

"You'll have to dance at the wedding, so it's time to practice."

"Oh well."

Mal gave it a moment, then stood and held out a hand to Parker.

"Really, you don't have to—"

"You can dance, can't you?"

"Of course, I can dance, but—"

"Not afraid to dance with me, are you?"

"That's ridiculous." Obviously annoyed, she rose. "This isn't a date, and I'll apologize for before, but I was—"

"Pissed at Del. I get it. So, we'll have a drink, we'll dance. No big deal."

The music was hot and fast, but he gave her an unexpected little spin, then twirled her in close. And began to move.

He had the beat, and still it took her a minute to match his steps and rhythm. She had to admit, he'd thrown her off guard again.

"Somebody's had lessons," she said.

"No, somebody just figured out dancing's a solid way to pick up women." He spun her out again, then in so their bodies meshed. "And jobs. Fight scenes are choreography. I did a lot of stunt work in fight scenes."

"Jobs and women."

"Yeah. Life's better with both."

Nearby, Laurel snapped her fingers in front of Del's face. "Stop. You're staring at them."

"I was just . . . checking."

"Look at me." She forked her fingers in front of her eyes, then pointed them at his.

He took her by the hips to tug her closer. "You were too far away."

"Okay." She linked her hands behind his neck, and used her hips. "How's that?"

"A lot better." His mouth found hers. "Better yet, even though it's killing me."

"You can take it." She ran her teeth over his bottom lip. "Or me."

"Definitely killing me. Come on, let's sit down."

She thought about the last time she and her three friends had gone to a club. Just the four of them, she recalled, to a trendy place in the city. All of them unattached, and just out for an evening of dancing. A lot could change in a few months, she mused.

Now there were eight of them squeezed together, yelling at one another over the music. Every now and again, Del would brush a hand over her hair, or down her back. He couldn't know, couldn't possibly know what that absent touch did inside her body.

It made her want to curl up and purr—or drag him out to the van where they could be alone. It was pitiful how much she yearned, how much he could do to her with so little.

If he had any idea how desperately in love with him she was . . . He'd be kind, she thought. And that would destroy her.

Better, much better they take it slow and easy, just as he'd said at the beginning. Maybe some of these feelings would settle. Maybe they'd be able to meet somewhere in the middle so she wouldn't feel so outweighed by her own heart.

He glanced her way and smiled, and that heart stuttered.

So much could change, she thought. And yet, if she counted the longing, so much could stay the same.

Just after midnight they piled back into the van with Carter behind the wheel. She listened to the muted voices around her, the winding down of the day. But there was still a moon, still stars, still a long night ahead.

"I've got a client dinner tomorrow," Del told her, "then poker night. Why don't you think about what you'd like to do, where you'd like to go when we go out next time."

"Sure."

"You could miss me in the meantime."

"I might."

As Carter turned toward his house, Del tipped her face up for a kiss. "Why don't you make a point of it?"

He shifted to get out, nudged Parker on the shoulder. "You're not still mad."

She gave him a long look. "I'm only not still mad because we won the ball game and he's a good dancer. Try that again, and I'll make you hurt."

"You had fun." He kissed her cheek. "Thanks for the lift. See you all later. You men, sooner. Poker night."

He stepped out, gave a wave, then headed up the walk to his door.

Laurel argued with herself for nearly a quarter mile.

"Stop! Stop! Pull over."

"Oh, honey, are you sick?" Emma straightened in her seat, swiveled around.

"No, no, just . . . This is stupid. It's all just stupid." She wrenched the door open. "Screw the bet. I'm going to Del's. Go home."

She ignored the cheers and slammed the door.

"Wait." Carter stuck his head out. "I'll drive you back. Just—"

"No. Thanks. Go."

And turning, she began to run.

CHAPTER TEN

$\mathscr{A}$s HE TOSSED HIS KEYS IN THE LITTLE BOWL ON HIS dresser, plugged his cell phone into its charger, Del considered a quick swim before he turned in. Something physical, he thought, to take the edge off the sexual frustration and help him sleep. He pulled off his shirt, his shoes, and headed down to the kitchen to grab a bottle of water.

It was the right thing to do, this waiting. Laurel held too important a place in his life—played too intricate a part—to rush this change between them.

She wasn't just an interesting, attractive woman. She was Laurel. Tough and funny, smart and resilient Laurel McBane. She had so many of the qualities he admired in a woman—and all in one sexy package.

All these years, he mused, he'd considered that package off-limits. Now that she—he—they, he decided, had torn down the restrictions, he wanted her more than he'd anticipated.

It added another reason for the wait.

Impulse was great; he was a fan of acting on impulse. But not when it came to someone who mattered as much as she did, and on so many complicated levels. Slow and sensible, he reminded himself. It was working, wasn't it? In a short amount of time they'd learned things about each other neither of them had explored in all the years they'd known each other.

They'd spent the holiday together as they'd spent countless others—but in a whole new light, with an entirely different approach. That was the sort of thing they needed to do more of before they took the next step.

He was fine with it; he was good with it.

He wondered if the month would ever end.

Swim, he ordered himself an instant before the banging on his front door, the insistent buzzing of his bell, had him rushing back through the house.

Sharp claws of panic ripped viciously through his gut at his first glimpse of Laurel, winded, wide-eyed, and flushed.

"Was there an accident? Parker." He grabbed her, checking for injuries even as his mind jumped forward. "Call nine-one-one, and I'll go—"

"No. No accident. It's fine. Everyone's fine." She waved him back, sucking in a breath. "Here's the thing. You can't count today, and it's actually tomorrow, so you can't count that. Or the first day, because it's the first."

"What? Are you okay? Where's everyone? What happened?"

"Nothing happened; I came back." She held up one hand as if to calm him and shoved the other through her hair. "It's just all about the math, really, and today being tomorrow because it's after midnight. So there's that. Plus you don't count weekends. Who counts weekends? Nobody does. Five business days, that's what they all say."

Panic throttled down to bafflement. "About what?"

"Everything. Pay attention." She jabbed a finger at him. "Keep up."

"Well, I would—could—if I knew what the hell you're talking about."

"Listen, okay?" She started to slip out of the sandals

she'd changed into after the ball game, but stopped. "This is how it works. You take off the first day and today, and the weekends. That's like ten days, which is actually two weeks by most definitions." As the words tumbled out, she gestured, one hand, then the other. "Plus, I don't think thirty days works when you really meant a month. That's four weeks. Twenty-eight days—seven times four. It's just basic math. Then if you take off the two weeks that don't count due to weekends and whatever, we're actually behind."

"Behind wh— Oh." Understanding brought relief, amusement, and gratitude in one big rush. "Uh-uh. I'm not sure I got all of that. Can you run it by me again?"

"No. I figured it out. Take my word. So I came back because we're falling behind."

"Can't have that, can we?"

"That's the math. Now we have the multiple choice portion. A, you take me home; B, I call a cab; or C, I stay."

"Let me think it over. Done." He grabbed her again, took her mouth with his.

"Correct answer." She boosted herself up to wrap her legs around his waist. "Definitely the correct answer. You can thank me later for figuring it out." Her mouth found his again in a hot, urgent kiss. "But now, I'm going crazy. You'd better be going crazy, too."

"I was thinking about you, and wanting you." He started up the stairs. "It's all I could think about. Thank God for the five-business-days rule."

"It's industry standard," she managed as her heart began to pound in her ears again. "We made it too big a deal. The sex. I can't think straight when I'm obsessing, and I can't think about anything else but wanting to be with you. I keep thinking about how it'll be, but I don't want to think. I just want it to be. I'm talking too much. See? Crazy."

"Then let's be."

When he lowered to the bed with her, her legs tightened around his waist, her hands skimmed down his back and up again. She felt the first twinges of desperation even as their mouths met again. Heat washed over her, spilled into her—so fast, so intense she lost her breath. Too long the waiting, she thought, and the wondering and the wanting.

She gripped his hips, arching up as his teeth scraped lightly down her throat and awoke dozens of nerve endings. She tried to get her hands on the button of his jeans, but he took her wrists, brushed his thumbs over her drumming pulse.

"Too fast."

"It's already been forever."

"What's a little longer?" He eased back and in the swatch of moonlight began to unbutton her shirt. "I've spent a lot of time not looking at you in a certain way. I want to enjoy the looking. And the touching. The tasting." As he spread her shirt open, his fingers trailed down her skin.

Touching her was like finally understanding a puzzle, seeing for the first time the beauty and complexity of it. The angles of her face, the curves of her body, his now to explore.

When she reached for him, he drew her up so he could slip the shirt aside, taste the smooth skin of strong shoulders. He flicked open the catch of her bra, heard her little gasp before he smoothed the straps off her shoulders. More silky skin pressed to his as she tipped her head back to invite his kiss.

Slow, smoldering, deep with tongues sliding as he lowered her down again to look into those bold blue eyes, as he feathered his fingers over her breasts. She quivered, and her reaction coiled need, hot and hard, in his belly.

"Let me," he murmured, and closed his mouth over her breast.

Pleasure seared over her skin and flashed through her body as she gave herself over to his hands, his mouth. He wanted; he took, but inch by scorching, torturous inch, exploiting her vulnerabilities, her longings, as if he knew every secret she held.

"I've wanted this. Wanted you," she murmured.

"Now we have this. Have each other."

He slid her jeans down her legs, his mouth gliding over

her belly, her thigh. Time, an eternity of time spun out, and stopped.

Just now, she thought. This moment.

It seemed everything in her opened for him, and everything in her was warm and willing. Slow, he ordered himself, though his need had begun to buck at the end of its tether, and he used his hands to guide her over the peak.

He watched pleasure turn her eyes to blue crystals, tasted her moan as he crushed his mouth to hers.

Finally, when their eyes met again, he slipped out of his clothes and into her, held himself there while they both trembled.

She said his name, a single, catchy sigh, then rose in welcome.

No more wondering, but only wonder as they moved together. At last, she thought, at last. And broke apart.

She lay under him, weak and wildly happy, with her lips curved against his shoulder because his heart pounded against hers.

She'd let him lead this time, she thought, but he'd ended up as wrecked and satisfied as she had. She stroked a hand down his back, and over his very fine ass, because she could.

"My idea."

He managed a weak laugh. "A good one." He shifted to draw her against his side. "Yeah, this is good."

"If we use my math and formula, we didn't actually lose the bet."

"I think, under the circumstances, we can forfeit the bet. We still won."

She decided if she were any happier, little pink hearts and singing bluebirds would shoot out her fingertips. "I guess you're right." She let out one contented sigh. "I have to get up really early."

"Okay." But his arms came around her, signaling she wasn't going anywhere yet.

She angled her face up for one last kiss. "Worth waiting for?"

"Definitely."

She closed her eyes and slept in his arms.

ℒAUREL WISHED SHE HAD A PENLIGHT. AND A TOOTHBRUSH. Fumbling around in the dark the morning after never got any easier, she decided. At least she'd found her bra and one shoe. She let out a grunt of satisfaction when her seeking fingers hooked on the elastic of her panties.

A shirt, a shoe, and her pants to go, she thought, and her purse was downstairs where she'd dumped it. There she'd find mints and cab fare.

She'd have killed for coffee. She'd have maimed for even the scent of coffee.

On her hands and knees she continued to search the floor, then awarded herself a mental *aha* when she came across the other shoe.

"What are you doing down there?"

"Sorry." She sat back on her heels. "I'm looking for the rest of my clothes. I told you I had to get up early."

"How early is early? Jesus, it's barely five."

"Welcome to bakers' hours. Listen, if I could just have the light for thirty seconds, I could find the rest and get out of your way so you can go back to sleep."

"You don't have a car."

"I'll call a cab from downstairs. I've got everything but my—" The light flashed on, causing her to squint before she covered her eyes with one hand. "You could've warned me. Just a second."

"You look . . . interesting."

"I bet." She could imagine it well enough. Naked, her hair looking like a couple of cats had wrestled in it, squatting on the floor holding underwear and shoes.

Why couldn't he be a heavier sleeper?

"Two seconds." She spotted her shirt and debated which was less dignified. Crawling over to get it or standing up and walking over to get it. Crawling, she concluded, was never dignified.

Naked didn't matter. He'd seen her naked. But he hadn't seen her naked in the morning when she wasn't even close to the low end of her best.

And damn it, she wished he'd stop smiling at her that way.

"Go back to sleep."

She stood, stepped over for the shirt. Her shoes went flying when he grabbed her and pulled her down on the bed.

"Del, I have to go."

"This probably won't take long." He rolled on top of her, making it absolutely clear her bed hair didn't put him off in the least.

When he lifted her hips, eased inside her, she decided there were some things even better than coffee in the morning.

"I've probably got a couple minutes."

He laughed, nuzzling his face in the curve of her shoulder.

She let it build in her, slow, soft, sweet, the rising up with quickening pulse and sighing release. Everything in her went warm and loose with him filling her, heart and body.

The fall, as gentle as the rise, made her wish she could just curl up with him and sleep all over again.

"Morning," he murmured.

"Mmm. I was going to say sorry for waking you up, but it turns out I'm not."

"Me, either. I guess we'd better find the clothes so I can drive you home."

"I'll take a cab."

"No, you won't."

"Don't be silly. There's no reason for you to get up and dressed and drive there and back when all I have to do is call a cab."

"The reason is you spent the night in my bed."

"Welcome to the twenty-first century, Sir Galahad. I got myself here, so I can—"

"You know, you're in a very strange position to start an argument." He braced on his elbows to look down at her. "If you keep it up for about ten more minutes, I should be able to give you one more reason you're not taking a cab."

"That's a pretty optimistic recovery time."

"Want to see who's right?"

"Let me up. And since you're going all gallant, how about scoring me an extra toothbrush?"

"I can do that. I can even get some coffee into a couple of travel cups."

"For coffee, you can drive me anywhere."

𝒥N UNDER FIFTEEN MINUTES, AND ARMED WITH A TALL coffee, Laurel stepped outside. "It's raining. Pouring," she corrected. How had she missed that? "Del, don't—"

"Stop arguing." He just grabbed her hand and pulled her into a dash for the car. Drenched, she climbed in, then shook her head at him when he got behind the wheel.

"It's not an argument."

"Okay. How about a discussion?"

"Better," she allowed. "I just wanted to avoid setting a precedent where you'd feel obligated to drive me home, or that sort of thing. If I follow an impulse I should handle what's connected to it. Like transportation."

"I really enjoyed the impulse, but regardless, when I'm with a woman, I take her home. Consider it a Brown Rule of Thumb."

She did consider while tapping her fingers on her knee. "So, if you followed an impulse, I'd be obligated to drive you home."

"No. And no, I don't consider that sexist, I consider it elemental." He glanced over, all sleepy midnight eyes as he drove through the rainy morning. "Equal rights, equal pay, choice, opportunities, and so on. I'm for them. But when I'm with a woman I take her home. And when I'm with a woman, I don't like the idea of her driving around in the middle of the night, or alone at five-thirty-whatever in the morning if there's a way around it."

"Because you have the penis."

"Yes, I do. And I'm keeping it."

"And the penis shields against accidents, breakdowns, and flat tires?"

"You know what's always been interesting, and occasionally frustrating, about you? You're able to turn the simple into the complicated."

It was true, but it didn't change the point. "What if I'd had my car?"

"You didn't."

"But what if I did?"

"I guess we'll find out when you do." He turned into the drive.

"That's evasive."

"It is, isn't it? How about I give you a point back? I won't walk you to the door."

She cocked her head. "But you're going to sit here until you know I'm inside?"

"Yes, I am." He leaned over, cupped her chin, kissed her. "Go bake a cake."

She started to get out, then shifted back and gave him a longer, much more satisfying kiss. "Bye."

She dashed to the door, then turned, dripping, to wave as she let herself in.

Then, alone in the quiet, she leaned back on the door and indulged herself. She'd made love with Del. She'd slept in his bed, awakened beside him. A lifetime of dreams had come true in one night, so she was allowed to indulge herself in private, to grin like a maniac, hug herself, and feel utterly, foolishly wonderful.

Nothing she'd imagined had come close to those moments, and here alone in the quiet she could revel in them. She could remember each one and savor it.

What happened next was anyone's guess, but now, right this minute, she had what she'd always wanted.

She almost floated up the stairs and into her room. Full day ahead of her, she thought, but God, she wanted to chuck it all and just flop down on the bed, kick her heels at the ceiling, and wallow.

Couldn't be done, but she could wallow in a long, long hot shower. She stripped off her damp clothes, hung them over a towel bar, pulled out the hair clip she'd dug out of her purse to handle the mess of it. Still grinning, she stepped under the hot spray.

She was basking in the steam and the scent when she caught a movement outside the glass door. It amazed her the scream she ripped out didn't crack the glass.

"Jesus, Laurel, it's just me." Mac opened the door a crack. "I knocked, then I shouted, but you were too busy singing to hear me."

"A lot of people sing in the shower. What the hell do you want?"

"Not a lot of people who are us sing 'I've Got Rhythm' in the shower."

"I wasn't singing that." Was she? And now it would be stuck in her head all day. "You're letting out the heat. Go away."

"What's taking you so long?" Emma demanded as she came in.

"Parker?"

"Gym," Emma answered Mac. "But I told her what's up."

"For God's sake, has it escaped the notice of you morons that I'm taking a shower?"

"Smells good," Mac commented. "You're clean. Get out. We're having pancakes in honor of the anticipated sexy breakfast story."

"I don't have time for pancakes."

"Mrs. G will make them."

"We just had waffles."

"Oh, you're right. Omelettes. We'll have sexy breakfast story omelettes. Ten minutes," Emma ordered. "The men are banned from breakfast."

"I don't want to—"

But Mac shut the shower door. Laurel pushed dripping hair out of her eyes. She could sneak down to her own kitchen, but they'd just come in and nag her. Resigned, she got out and grabbed a towel.

When she walked into the kitchen twenty minutes later, she found Mac and Emma already there, the table set, and Mrs. Grady at the stove.

"Listen, I have a really full day, so—"

"Breakfast is the most important meal of the day," Mac said piously.

"So speaks the Pop-Tart Princess. I really need to get started."

"You can't hold back." Emma wagged a finger. "We shared ours, and Mrs. G's already making sexy breakfast story omelettes. Right, Mrs. G?"

"I am. Might as well sit down," she told Laurel. "They'll nag your ears off otherwise. And since I'm told you didn't get home until about thirty minutes ago, I've a mind to hear about it myself."

As she gulped down juice, Laurel tracked her gaze from one face to another. "Do you all have some sort of radar?"

"Yes," Parker said as she came in. "And if I'm getting called down before I've had *my* shower, this better be good." In sweat shorts and a loose T-shirt, she went over to pour herself coffee. "I take it Del didn't bolt the door and turn you away."

"This is just bizarre." Laurel took Parker's coffee. "You know this is bizarre."

"Traditions are traditions, even when they're bizarre." Cheerfully, Parker got another cup. "So, what happened?"

Laurel sat, shrugged. "I lost the bet."

"Yay!" Emma scooted in beside her. "I lost it, too, but some things are more important than money."

"Who won, Parker?" Mac wanted to know.

Parker sat, frowned into her coffee. "Malcolm Kavanaugh."

"Kavanaugh?" Since it was there, Laurel took a piece of toast out of the rack. "How did he get in on it?"

"Somebody told him, and he cornered me at the ball game. I said no, bets were closed, but he's pushy and persistent. Plus he said he'd put two hundred in as a late fee, and he'd pick July fifth."

"You mean he nailed it on the button?" Mac demanded. "Lucky guy."

"Yeah, lucky guy. I figured he didn't have a chance anyway, as we were all going out, all going together. I didn't expect Laurel to jump out of the van and make a run for it."

"It was romantic." Emma smiled. "All rushed and flushed and urgent. What happened when you got there?"

"He opened the door."

"Spill," Mac insisted and pointed a finger.

"You can't be uncomfortable because he's my brother. You and I have been friends nearly as long as Del's been my brother. So it's a wash."

"Eat," Mrs. Grady ordered and served the omelettes.

Laurel obediently took a bite. "I'd worked out the math."

"What math?" Emma asked.

"About what days didn't count in the given thirty. It's complicated. It's a formula, but I'd worked it out. Once he caught up with me, logistically, he agreed it made sense, but thought we should just forfeit the bet. So we did."

"Weekends, right?" Mac shoveled in some eggs. "I thought about that. Weekends don't count."

"Exactly. And the first and last days don't count. It gets more complicated, but that's the gist. But in all fairness, since we didn't set those terms, we went with the forfeit. Then we . . ."

Bizarre or not, these four women were her women. "It was wonderful. I had this place in my head that worried I'd be nervous, that we'd be awkward. But I wasn't, and we weren't. He wouldn't rush, and wouldn't let me rush, so it was slow and sweet. He was . . ."

When she trailed off, Parker sighed. "If you think I'd squirm because you'd say my brother is a good lover, a considerate one, you're wrong. It's not just skill, you know. It's also a sign of respect and affection for his partner."

"He made me feel that there was nothing else that mattered but the two of us, then and there. That's all there was. And after, I could sleep with him, feeling absolutely safe, absolutely natural. That's always the hardest part for me. Trusting enough, I guess, to sleep."

Emma rubbed Laurel's thigh under the table. "That's a really good sexy breakfast story."

"We had a little tangle this morning."

"A sexy tangle?"

"That, too, One-Track Mind," she said to Mac. "I needed to find my clothes in the dark so I could call a cab and get back. Full day. But he woke up, which led to a sexy tangle even though I had bed hair."

"I hate that," Emma muttered. "There should be an instant cure for bed hair."

"Then he insisted on driving me home."

"Of course."

Laurel rolled her eyes at Parker. "The two of you have this unshakable code of conduct. Why should he have to get up, dressed, drive me when I can get myself home?"

"Because you were in his home, that's number one. Second, you were in his bed. Good manners are just that, and don't threaten your independence."

"Brown Rule of Thumb?"

Parker smiled a little. "I guess you could call it that."

"He did. Well, that's going to have to hold you, because I have to get to work."

"Don't we all? I have half a million lilies coming in this morning to be processed. And the crew's starting today."

"Here, too?" Laurel asked.

"Here, too, according to Jack." Emma glanced at her watch. "Any minute."

"You will now live in interesting times," Mac told her. "And noisy ones."

"It'll be worth it. I'm going to keep telling myself it'll be worth it. Thanks for breakfast, Mrs. G."

"It was a good story, so paid in full."

"If things get too crazy in my space, can I shift some of the work in here?"

"You can. Emmaline and Mackensie, you called for the story. You're on dishes. I'm going to take a walk around the garden before the hammering starts."

Parker walked out with Laurel. "Happy's what counts. Remember I like seeing you and Del happy when you feel weird about it again."

"I'm working on it. Tell me if I start screwing this up, okay?"

"Absolutely." Her phone rang. "And there we have the opening bell. I'll see you later. Good morning, Sarah. How's the bride today?"

CHAPTER ELEVEN

Emma's lilies scented the air and bloomed in summer colors of brilliant scarlet and buttery yellow, bright, hard-candy pink and blinding white. The bride, who'd considered a mis-scheduled manicure a disaster on the morning of July fifth, posed radiantly for Mac while Parker dealt with a groomsman's misplaced vest and tie.

After checking to see no emergencies required her attention or assistance, Laurel carried the cake's centerpiece—a sugar vase she'd molded from a hexagon bowl and filled with miniature lilies.

Emma's lilies had nothing on hers, Laurel thought—in execution or time spent. She'd embossed gum paste with a rolling pin covered with textured grosgrain ribbon, then meticulously cut out each individual petal. The result, once the stems had been wired and dipped in thinned royal icing, was both charming and elegant.

In the Ballroom, she ignored the buzz and hum of setup and studied the cake. More textured petals adorned each tier—a circular dance of those strong colors. More scattered over the cake board in what she considered a pretty and organic touch.

As she lifted the topper out of the box, someone knocked over a chair with a crash. She never blinked.

That's what Del noticed. The noise, the shouts, the movement might not have existed. He watched her center the bowl of flowers on the top tier, step back to check the positioning, then take one of her tools out of the box to run a line—no, pipe, he corrected. He knew that much. She piped a couple of perfect lines, like a base on the bowl, around it with hands steady as a surgeon's.

She circled the table again, nodded.

"Looks great."

"Oh." She took a step back. "I didn't know you were here. Or going to be here."

"It was the only way I could figure out how to have a Saturday night date with you."

"That's nice."

He brushed his thumb over her cheek.

"Do I have icing on my face?"

"No. It's just your face. How many flowers on that?"

"About fifty."

He glanced around at the arrangements. "It looks like you and Em matched petal for petal."

"We worked at it. Well, so far everything's going smooth, so I might be able to—"

"Code Red!" Emma shouted in her earbud.

"Crap. Where?"

"Great Hall. We need everybody."

"I'm on my way. Code Red," she told Del as she rushed for the stairs. "My own fault. I said everything was going smooth. I *know* better than to say that."

"What's the problem?"

"I don't know yet." She hit the second-floor landing from one wing as Parker charged in from the other.

"SMOB and MOB altercation. Mac and Carter have the bride occupied and unaware."

Laurel whipped the clip out of her hair, shoved it in her suit jacket pocket. "I thought we had detente there."

"Apparently that's over. Del, good you're here. We might need you."

As they approached, the sound of shouting pumped out of the Great Hall. And something crashed. Then someone screamed.

"You might need the cops," Del commented.

They burst in to see Emma, her hair tumbling from its pins, trying desperately to separate the two snarling, elegantly dressed women. The bride's stepmother's hair and face dripped with the champagne tossed from the flute still in the mother of the bride's hand.

"You bitch! You're going down!"

Shoving, flailing arms sent Emma skidding on her heels then onto her ass as the women flew at each other.

Game, and with a hot beam in her eye, Emma scrambled up as Parker and Laurel sprang forward. Grabbing the closest body, Laurel hauled while curses spewed like grapeshot.

"Cut it out! Stop it now!" Laurel dodged a fist, then blocked an elbow with her forearm. The force of the contact sang straight up to her shoulder. "I said *stop*! For God's sake, it's your daughter's wedding."

"It's *my* daughter's wedding," the woman Parker and Emma struggled to control shouted. "*My* daughter. *Mine!* Not this home-wrecking bimbo bitch's."

"Bimbo? Bimbo? You tight-assed lunatic, it's your last face-lift I'm going to wreck."

Emma solved the mother of the bride problem by sitting on her while Laurel grappled with her opponent.

As Del risked his skin by stepping between the two women, Laurel spotted reinforcements coming. Jack, and oddly Malcolm Kavanaugh, rushed into the melee.

Kneeling on the floor, Parker spoke quietly and steadily to the MOB whose temper was already giving way to wild tears. Laurel put her mouth close to the stepmother's ear. "This isn't solving anything, and if you care about Sarah, you'll put it away, you'll suck it up for the day. Are you listening? If you want to fight, you'll do it another time, another place."

"I didn't do *anything*, and she threw champagne in my face. Look at my hair, my makeup. My *dress*."

"We'll take care of it." She glanced at Parker, got a nod. "Del, I need you to bring a couple glasses of champagne up to my room, then you can take— I'm sorry, I've forgotten your name."

"I'm Bibi," the SMOB said in something close to a wail. "It's all ruined. Everything's ruined."

"No, we'll fix it. Del, you can take Bibi's dress down to Mrs. G. She'll fix it up. Come on with me, Bibi. We're going to take care of everything."

As she steered Bibi away, Parker repeated the routine on the MOB. "Emma's going to take you somewhere to freshen up. I'll be there in just a few minutes."

"Don't tell Sarah," the MOB sobbed. "I don't want to upset her."

"Of course not. Go on with Emma. Don't want to upset her," Parker muttered when the woman was out of earshot.

"Hell of a party so far," Mal commented.

Parker tugged down her suit jacket, smoothed her skirt. "What are you doing here?"

"Just dropped by to collect my winnings."

"I don't have time for that now." She dismissed him by turning to one of the subs. "Make sure all the glass is cleaned up, and any spilled champagne. If anything else is broken or damaged, tell one of Emma's team so they can deal with it. Jack, track down the FOB, will you? I'll need to speak with him in my office. Immediately."

"Sure. Sorry it took me so long. I was outside when I got the alert."

"I moonlighted as a bouncer in L.A.," Mal told her. "In case you want anybody tossed."

"Funny, and not completely out of the question. FOB, Jack, thanks. Mac," she said into her headpiece as she hurried away.

"She sure moves." Mal watched her zip across the room and out the door.

"You haven't seen anything yet," Jack said. "Let's go find the FOB."

"Jack? What the hell is an FOB?"

In HER ROOM LAUREL EXAMINED THE APRICOT SILK DRESS she'd ordered Bibi to strip off. She could hear both the shower and the sobs through the bathroom door.

A few spots, a torn seam—could've been worse, she decided. Mrs. G would deal with it. And according to the emergency plan for just such situations, she knew Parker would have a hair and makeup team en route very shortly.

Her mission, and she had no choice but to accept it, was to keep Bibi calm, help put her back together, listen to her whine, bitch, and/or complain. And to get her to promise— with a blood oath if necessary—to behave herself through the rest of the event.

Smoothing her own disordered hair, she answered the knock on the door.

"Two glasses, as ordered." Del eased in to set them on a table, and glanced toward the bathroom. "How's it going?"

"Well, she's down from sobs to whimpers. Here's the dress. It's not too bad. Parker would've given Mrs. G a heads-up, so she'll be ready for it."

"Okay." He reached out to straighten her left earring. "Anything else I can do?"

"You could check with Mac, just to make sure the bride's insulated from all this. Parker would've come up with a reason for a slight delay." Calculating, Laurel rubbed at the tension in the back of her neck. "We're twenty minutes out, so I figure ten or fifteen for the delay. We're good. She turned off the shower," Laurel noted. "You'd better go."

"I'm gone. By the way? Nice block," he added, lifting his arm to demonstrate.

She gave him a laughing shove, then closed the door.

Taking a deep, bracing breath, she walked over to the bathroom, knocked. "Okay in there?"

Bibi opened the door. She wore Laurel's best robe with her hair in dark blond dripping ropes over the shoulders. Her red, puffy eyes shimmered with the threat of more tears.

"Look at me. I'm a mess."

"This should help."

"Is it a gun?"

"Champagne. Have a seat, take a breath. We're having your dress fixed, and we'll have someone in to do your hair and makeup in a few minutes."

"Oh, thank God." Bibi took a deep gulp of the champagne. "Thank God, and thank you. I feel horrible. Sick. Stupid. Twelve years. I've been married to Sam for twelve years. Doesn't that count for something?"

"Of course." Soothe, Laurel thought, remembering the Vows directive. Soothe, stroke, smooth over.

"I didn't wreck anybody's home. They were separated when we met. Well, okay, not technically, not officially, but practically. She hates me because I'm younger. She's the starter wife; I'm the trophy wife. She's the one who throws those labels around. And twelve years, I mean, well, *shit*."

"It's never easy to handle those kinds of relationships and connections."

"I've tried." Bibi's red-rimmed eyes pleaded for understanding. "I really have. And they were divorced before we got engaged. Almost. And I love Sarah. I really do. And Brad's great. They're great together. I want them to be happy."

"That's what counts most."

"Yeah." She sighed, took a slower sip. "I signed a prenup. I even asked for it. It wasn't about the money, even though she's always saying it was. Is. We just fell in love. You can't help that, right? You can't help who you fall in love with, or when or how? It just happens. She's pissed, that's all, because her second marriage hit the skids and we're still going. I'm sorry for all the trouble. Sarah doesn't have to know, does she?"

"No. At least not today."

"They weren't even sleeping together anymore. When I met Sam they had separate bedrooms, separate lives. That's like being separated, isn't it?"

Laurel thought of her own parents. "I guess it is."

"Maybe I was the reason Sam finally took the step and asked for a divorce, but I wasn't the reason they weren't happy together. It's got to be better to take that step than to keep being unhappy together, don't you think?"

"Yes, I do." Twelve years, Laurel thought. Yes, that did have to count for something. "Bibi, you have a good marriage, and a good relationship with your stepdaughter. You can afford to take the high road on this."

"She screamed at me. She threw champagne in my face. She tore my dress."

"I know. I know." Soothe, soothe, Laurel thought again. "Now, you can be the one to step back, to let it all go today, and focus on Sarah. To help make it the happiest day of her life."

"Yeah. Yeah, you're right." Bibi knuckled her eyes like a child. "I'm really sorry about what happened."

"Don't worry about it." Laurel rose at the knock on the door. "And in about fifteen minutes, you're going to look perfect."

"I—I never even asked your name."

"It's Laurel."

"Laurel." Bibi's lips trembled up into a shaky smile. "Thanks for listening."

"No problem. Now, let's get you ready again." She opened the door to the hairdresser.

THE BRIDE, BLISSFULLY UNAWARE OF THE BACKSTAGE drama, stood with her father while her attendants walked toward the flower-drenched pergola. Some brides glowed, Laurel thought, and this one certainly did while the pretty, playful breeze fluttered the gauzy layers of her veil.

Mac changed angles, and Laurel imagined caught that shimmer of joy and anticipation as Sarah turned her head to grin at her father.

"Oh boy! Here we go."

The music changed for the bride. Laurel saw Sam glance toward Parker, give the faintest of nods. Appreciation or acknowledgment—maybe both. Then he walked his radiant daughter toward the waiting groom.

"So far, so good," Del murmured beside Laurel.

"It's going to be fine. Probably better they had their battle before it started. Got it out of their system."

"There won't be any more trouble." Parker's tone was cold as January ice. "At least not from that source."

"What did you say to the father?" Del wondered.

Parker's smile would have frozen flame. "Let's just say I'm confident the MOB and SMOB will behave in a civil manner, that Vows will be compensated for the additional hair and makeup fees, the gown repairs, and all damages." She patted Del's chest. "And we won't need your services to collect."

"I need to go finish the setup." Laurel checked her watch. "Not that far off time, considering."

"Do you want some help?" Del asked her.

"No. Go . . . get a beer or whatever."

She went back to her kitchen, where it was quiet and cool. Where she could sit for just a couple of minutes. Listening to Bibi had depressed her, and she needed to shake it off.

Loveless marriages, unhappy homes, the X factor of another woman. She knew exactly the sort of miserable brew those ingredients created—and how long the bitter aftertaste could linger.

Surely Sarah had tasted some of that brew, and likely more than once. Yet she'd stood beaming joy on her father's arm. The father who'd been unfaithful to her mother, the father who'd broken the very vows she herself was about to make.

Yes, she understood unhappy marriages, but she didn't understand and couldn't accept using that unhappiness as an excuse or rationale for being unfaithful.

Why didn't people just end it? If they wanted someone else, or something else, why not break it off clean first instead of cheating, lying, tolerating, just existing?

Divorce couldn't be more painful for a couple, or the child or children stirred up in that brew with them, than the deceit, the pretense, that smoldering anger. Wasn't that why, even after all these years, a part of her wished her parents would walk away from each other instead of pretending to be married?

"Well, and here I've come in to see if I can help since you had all that trouble." Mrs. Grady fisted her hands on her hips. "And here you are loafing."

"I'm about to get to it."

Lips pursed, Mrs. Grady walked over to tap Laurel's chin up so their eyes met. "And what's wrong with you?"

"Nothing. Nothing really."

Mrs. Grady had a way of using her eyebrows in certain expressions that had very clear nonverbal meanings. At the moment, they said *bullshit*.

"It's just that whole business before got under my skin. It's nothing."

"It's not the first time you've had donnybrooks at one of these dos. Won't be the last either."

"No. It's not really the fight. That—after the fact—was pretty entertaining. Parker won't think so for a couple of days, but really, it had shining moments."

"You're circling around it."

"It's stupid. I ended up with the stepmother. Luck of the draw. I guess she felt sad and embarrassed, so she had to explain to me how she'd gotten involved with the FOB when he was sort of, but not really, separated, and how he and his first wife weren't together so much as just occupying the same house."

"Most of the men who want a taste of something fresh say something like that."

"Yeah, which is lame and it's false. But I think I believe her—the stepmother. But why does it matter? Why is it supposed to be okay if you get involved with someone who might be on the way out of a marriage? They're still in it, aren't they?"

"That's true," Mrs. Grady agreed. "But life's rarely a matter of truth and lies, without the gray in between."

"Then why the hell don't they get out of it if they're going to hook up with someone else?"

In a gesture more practical than comforting, Mrs. Grady smoothed down Laurel's hair. "People have their reasons for the damnedest things in my experience."

"She's okay with it. The bride. I remember the consults, and the tastings, the rehearsal. She loves her parents, that's clear. And she loves her stepmother. How do people manage that?"

"It's not always about taking sides, Laurel."

"No, it's not. But you know, I never had a chance to take sides, or not, because they were both so wrong." She didn't have to explain she'd shifted to her own parents. "And even now, if I think about it, if I think about sides? It's them on one, me on the other. It's stupid, but part of me is still pissed off that they're both so . . . careless."

"You're angry with them when you should feel sorry for them. They're the ones who are missing out."

"They like their life—lives—arrangement." She shrugged. "At this point it's really none of my business anyway."

"Laurel Anne." Mrs. G cupped Laurel's face in her hands, using a name and a gesture rarely employed. "They'll always be your parents, so it'll always be your business."

"Will I always be disappointed in them?"

"That's up to you, isn't it?"

"I guess it is." She sighed, hugely. "Okay. Brooding time's up. I need to get the groom's cake and the rest of the desserts dealt with."

"I'm here, so I'll give you a hand with it."

Together they carried boxes of pastries to the Ballroom. "I'm always dazzled by the flowers," Mrs. Grady said as she looked around the room. "Our Emma has a magic touch. I like the colors for this one. Nothing pale about it, all bright and bold. Well, would you look at that." She stepped over to study the wedding cake. "Talk about the magic touch. You've outdone yourself here, Laurel."

"I think it's my new favorite summer cake. I'll save you a piece."

"I'll let you. Wedding cake's lucky cake."

"So I hear. Mrs. G? Did you ever think about getting married again, or . . ."

Mrs. Grady let out a delighted laugh. "Oh, there's been some *or* from time to time. I'm not doddering. But marriage?" She walked back to help Laurel with the desserts. "I had mine. I had my Charlie. My one."

"Do you believe that?" Laurel asked. "That there's one person? One?"

"I do, for some of us. For others, if things don't work, or you lose someone, there's another. But for some there's the one, beginning to end. No one else can fit. No one else gets into the heart the same way, and lives there."

"Yeah. No one else. But you're not always the one back." She thought of Del, then made herself shake it off. "Do you miss him, still? Your Charlie?"

"Every day. Thirty-three years this November. I miss him every day. But I had him, didn't I? I had my one. Not everyone can say that. You can."

Slowly, Laurel shifted her gaze over.

"He's been your one from the start. Took you long enough to go after him."

Why deny it? Laurel thought. Why pretend otherwise with someone who understood so well? "It's scary."

Mrs. Grady let out a laugh. "Sure it is. You want safe? Find a nice puppy you can train to come to heel. Love's supposed to be scary."

"Why?"

"Because if there's no fear there's no thrill."

"If that's true, then I'm thrilled half to death." Laurel

cocked her head. "That's Parker's signal. Cocktail and din-ner hour."

"Go on and give her a hand. I can finish this."

"Are you sure?"

"I like to get my hand in now and then. Go on."

"Thanks. Thanks," she repeated, laying a hand over Mrs. Grady's. "I'll make sure you get that cake."

Alone, Mrs. Grady shook her head and sighed. Her girls, she thought, knew all there was to know about weddings. But love turned them upside down.

Then again, she supposed love was meant to do just that.

$\mathcal{W}$HEN THE HOUSE CLEARED, LAUREL JOINED THE OTHERS for a little unwinding on the terrace. Del put a glass of champagne in her hand.

"You earned it."

"Damn well did. Thanks. Where's Parker?"

"Something to do." Mac stretched out her legs, curled her tired toes. "She'll be right down. Sorry I missed the Battle of the Mothers. I heard it was worth the price of ad-mission."

"Brief but brutal." Laurel yawned and thought of fluffy pillows and cool, cool sheets.

"Do you have many wrestling matches?" Mal wondered.

"I got punched in the face once." Carter wiggled his jaw.

"It adds an element," Mal decided. "Good food. Great cake." He lifted his beer in toast to Laurel, then watched Parker come out looking as if she'd spent the day sipping tea rather than riding herd on a couple hundred people.

"Your winnings," she said and handed him an envelope.

"Thanks." He hiked up a hip to stuff it in his pocket. "So you do all this again tomorrow?"

"Hugely." Emma groaned. "We usually have smaller events on Sundays, but this time of year we have plenty of big ones. And with that in mind, I'm going to bed."

"Better walk my girl home." Jack stood to take Emma's hand. "I'll drop the truck off on Monday, Mal."

"Got it. Better get going myself."

"Thanks for pitching in." Mac stretched. "Come on, Professor. Let's go home and kick the cat out of bed."

"Can't move yet." Pleased it was close, Laurel dropped her head on Del's shoulder. "Need a minute. Bye, Mal," she added. And closed her eyes.

"I'll walk you out. See the rest of you tomorrow," Parker added as she turned to lead Mal around the house.

With her head still on Del's shoulder Laurel opened her eyes. "I knew breeding would do it."

"Hmm?"

"Parker'd be obliged to walk Malcolm out if I stuck here with you. They look good together."

"What? Come on."

She made an effort to clear her fuzzy brain, then gave up and closed her eyes again. "Sorry. I forgot who I was talking to. Of course there are no sexual sparks there, nothing smoldering beneath the surface. Nope, nothing there at all."

"He's not her type."

"Exactly. No obsessing unless it's about me. Haul me up, will you?"

"If he's not her type, why the talk about sparking and smoldering?"

"It was probably me." She laughed as he pulled her to her feet. "I get sparky and smoldery when you're around."

"Good one. Excellent way to shift my attention."

"And true." She felt wobbly, and half drunk with fatigue. "Are you staying the night?"

"That was the plan."

He glanced toward the door as they approached the stairs, and Laurel knew damn well he considered strolling out just to . . . be Del, she decided, when it came to Parker.

"See, I'm sparking and smoldering again." She nudged ahead of him, stepped up to bring their mouths on level for a kiss.

"Sweetie, you're all but asleep on your feet."

"True, which makes me a lousy Saturday night date."

"I like to look ahead, to Sunday morning."

"A Sunday morning date sounds perfect," she said as they walked upstairs. "Especially since it's an evening event, and I don't have to be up at dawn. How about eight o'clock?"

"Eight works."

"How about meeting me in the shower?"

"A Sunday morning shower date? Even better."

She drew him into the bedroom, then remembered to shut the door—something she rarely if ever did. Something she rarely had reason to do. She walked over to the terrace doors. "I like these open on summer nights. Does that bother you?"

"No. I didn't hear Parker come in yet. Is she still out there?"

Laurel rolled her eyes, considered the options. Turning she shed her suit jacket, slowly unzipped her skirt. "Maybe I'm not so tired after all." She stepped out of the skirt so she wore only a chemise, panties and heels. "Unless you are."

"I'm getting an unexpected second wind."

"Must be the fresh air." And moving to him she put a great deal of effort into distracting him. It was the least she could do, she thought as his hands went to work. For friendship.

CHAPTER TWELVE

𝒫ARKER POKED HER HEAD INTO LAUREL'S KITCHEN. "GOT a minute?"

"Yeah. I thought you had a consult and a tour."

"Had both, did both."

Laurel scraped vanilla beans into the mixture of milk and sugar in her saucepan, added the pods. "How'd we do?"

"The consult nailed down several details, and added more. The tour booked the last Sunday we had available next May." She glanced toward the mudroom, and the sheet of plywood blocking it off from the space and the banging and buzzing beyond it. "It's not as noisy as I thought it might be."

"Not if I keep the TV or radio on, and pretend it's background noise at an event. Could be worse. Well, it was worse during the demo, so this is almost tranquil."

"And it'll be worth it, right? With all the extra space."

"So I keep telling myself."

"What are you making?"

"Pastry cream."

"Want something cold?"

"Wouldn't mind." Laurel prepared an ice water bath for the last stage as Parker fixed two glasses of lemonade.

"No date tonight, right?"

"No date. The guys are off to cheer the Yankees and eat hot dogs." Laurel glanced up, arched her eyebrows. "Girl Night?"

"I'm thinking. Especially as I think I found Emma's wedding dress."

Laurel paused. "Seriously?"

"Well, I know what she's after, and it feels like I started a tradition with Mac's. I'd like us to surprise her tonight, so she can try it on, see if it works."

"I'm in."

"There's something else I'd like to talk about."

"Talk." Laurel gave the mixture a stir as it came to a boil.

"I'm told Jack asked Malcolm Kavanaugh to join us at the beach house in August."

"Oh?" While she turned that over in her head, Laurel removed the saucepan from heat, covered it. In one of the bowls on her counter she broke four eggs, then broke another four, separating them and adding the egg yolks to the bowl. "I guess they've gotten to be pretty good friends. Plus, there's plenty of room, right? I can't wait to see the place myself. To wallow in the place," she continued as she began to whisk. "To bury myself in the glory of vacation until I— Sorry," she said when Parker held up a hand. "I get carried away with the idea of doing whatever the hell I want to do for days and nights at a time."

"To continue. I just got off the phone with Del, who called to swear to me on his life that he had nothing to do with the invite."

"Well, you punished him over the Fourth of July deal."

"I did. I may have to punish Jack."

"Aww." Amused at the thought, Laurel added the sugar and cornstarch she'd already mixed together to the eggs, kept whisking.

"Doesn't your arm get tired?"

"Yes."

"Jack's fate hangs— Damn it." She broke off as her phone rang. "Give me a minute."

Used to interrupted conversations, Laurel judged the egg and sugar mixture ready, so took the vanilla pod out of the milk, and put it back on the stove. While she waited for it to return to a boil, she drank some lemonade and listened to Parker solve a problem for an upcoming bride.

Several problems, she decided as her milk had time to boil. She ladled half of it into the egg-yolk mix and went back to whisking.

"You just leave that to me," Parker said. "Absolutely. Consider it done. I'll see you and your mother on the twenty-first. Two o'clock. No problem at all. Bye." She finished the call. "Don't ask," she told Laurel.

"Wasn't going to." Laurel poured the mixture from the bowl to the saucepan. Whisked, whisked, whisked. "Can't stop now. Critical, but I'm listening."

"Where was I?"

"Jack's fate."

"Right. Whether or not I have to hurt our beloved Jack depends on if this is a setup."

"Do you really believe our beloved Jack would even think about setting you up with Malcolm?"

"No, but Emma might."

"If she did, she'd tell me." Laurel thought about it for a moment. "Yes, she'd tell me. She couldn't help herself. She'd probably swear me to secrecy, which I'd honor. But there'd be the lie escape clause. I'd have to tell you the truth if you asked."

"I'm asking."

"Then no. Emma hasn't said anything to me, so I therefore declare both her and Jack innocent of all charges. You don't have a problem with Mal, do you?"

"Not especially. I just don't like setups."

"None of us does, which is why none of us ever attempts one for any of the rest of us. You know that, Parker."

Parker's fingers tapped the glass as she rose and wandered to the window and back again to sit. "There are always exceptions, especially when some of us are blinded by love and wedding plans."

Fidgeting, Laurel thought. Parker rarely if ever fidgeted. "This isn't one, to the best of my knowledge. You'll have to imagine me lifting my hand to cross my heart because I can't stop whisking yet."

"All right. Jack's spared. And I suppose there's even more room since you and Del will be sharing a bedroom."

She frowned into her lemonade as Laurel finally stopped whisking and took the pan off the burner. "Next problem?" Laurel asked.

"I have to decide whether to make sure Malcolm doesn't have or get the wrong impression about this, or wait to make that clear if and when he does."

Laurel strained the cream through a sieve over the bowl she'd set on the ice water bath. "Do you want my take?"

"I do."

"It seems to me if you said anything about wrong impressions ahead of time, you'd invite them and/or irritate him into making a move anyway. He strikes me as the type who takes a darc. I'd leave it alone."

"Sensible."

"I can be." Laurel took the small pieces of butter she'd already set out, and whisking yet again, added them one at a time to the cream.

"All right. I'll just consider Malcolm a playmate for the other boys, and let it go."

"Wise." At last, Laurel put down her whisk and rubbed her arm. "I like him. Mal. I know I don't know him all that well, but I like him."

"He seems likeable enough."

"Plus sexy."

"Excuse me, aren't you currently sleeping with my brother?"

"I am, and really hope to continue that. But one must

notice sexy men. And if you tell me you haven't noticed, I'm going to have to use this ice bath to put out the fire in your pants."

"He's not my type. And what are you grinning about?"

"Del said the same thing."

Challenge and irritation ran over Parker's face. "Oh, really?"

"Just the way Del does—because really, nobody's his sister's type in Del's overprotective mind. But when he said it, I thought, yeah, exactly. Which is why I like him."

Parker took a slow sip of lemonade. "You don't like my type?"

"Don't be dense, Parker. He's sexy, interesting, and different from your usual—and that could be fun for you. Maybe you should let him get the wrong impression."

"Blinded by love."

"I guess I am."

"And why does that worry you?"

Laurel stopped massaging her fingers to point one at Parker. "You're changing the subject."

"I am, but it's still a good question."

"I guess it is," Laurel admitted. "I've never loved anyone but him. Knowing I've got all this in me for him, and only being sure he cares. Cares a lot, but there's such a big difference between cares a lot and loves. It's scary, which is the way I'm told it's supposed to be, but that doesn't make it less scary."

"He'd never hurt you. And that's the wrong thing to say," Parker realized immediately. "Don't you want him to know you've got all that in you for him?"

"Can't. Because he'd never hurt me, and he'd try so hard not to."

"Which would hurt more."

"Oh, yeah. I'm doing my best to just stay in the moment. I think it's working. Most of the time. Still, I can't help looking for the trapdoors and trip wires." And pianos over my head, she thought.

"Sensible advice back at you. Sometimes you look for the trapdoor and run into a wall instead."

"I wish I didn't know you were right. Okay." Laurel waved her hands as if clearing a board. "I'm in the moment. I'm practically Zen."

"Stay that way. I'm going to call Mac and get things set up for later. Six okay?"

"Six is perfect."

Parker stood up, then blew out a breath. "Give me just a taste of that, will you? It's cruelty otherwise."

Laurel got a spoon, dipped it into the warm cream, then offered.

"Oh God." Parker closed her eyes. "It was worth every whisk. Shit!" she muttered as her phone rang.

"Do you ever think about just not answering?"

"Yes, but I'm not a coward." She checked the readout as she walked out of the kitchen. "This is Parker at Vows. How are you, Mrs. Winthrop?"

Parker's voice had barely faded away when Del came in from the other direction.

"Well, this is a popular spot today."

"Why have I never noticed how sexy you look in an apron?" He leaned down to kiss her—but she saw his move toward the bowl of cream and slapped his hand away.

"Do you want to get me in trouble with the board of health?"

"I don't see any agents around here."

She got out a spoon, gave him the same taste as she'd given Parker.

"Good. Really good. You taste better."

"Very smooth, but that's all you get." She moved the bowl out of reach. "I thought you were going to the game with your little pals."

"I am. I'm meeting up with Jack and Carter here, then we're swinging by to pick up Mal."

"You're taking a limo to the ball game again." It was, she thought, so absolutely Del.

"What's wrong with taking a limo to the game? That way you can have beer, not worry about parking or the frustration of traffic. It's a pure win."

"I should've made this a silver spoon," she said, and took the spoon from him to put it in the sink.

"Just for that I might not give you your present."

Both intrigued and suspicious, she turned. "What present?"

He opened his briefcase, took out a box. "This present. But you may be too much of a smart-ass to deserve it."

"Smart-asses need presents, too. Why did you get me a present?"

"Because you need it, smart-ass." He handed it to her. "Open it."

She admired the Wonder Woman wrapping and big red bow before ruthlessly tearing them off. Then she frowned at the picture on the box. It looked like some sort of hand-held computer or oversized recorder. "What is it?"

"A time-saver. Here. I set it up already." He opened the box, took out the device with a gleam in his eye that told her the gift was something he wanted for himself.

"Instead of writing out lists," he told her, "you do this. Push Record." He did so, then said *eggs*. "See?" He turned it around to show her the word *eggs* on a little display screen. "Then you push the Select button, and it's on the list."

Okay, she thought, he'd caught her interest. "What list?"

"The list you'll have when you're finished and push this." He tapped another button. "It prints it out, and better yet, arranges the items in categories. Like, you know, dairy or condiments, whatever."

Her serious interest. "Get out. How?"

"I don't know how. Maybe there's someone in there arranging. And it has this library feature, so you can add specialized items it wouldn't have in there already. You use a lot of unusual ingredients."

"Let me try it." She took it, pressed Record. "Vanilla

beans." Her lips pursed as she read the display. "It says vanilla pudding."

"It probably doesn't have vanilla beans in the library because most people just buy the bottled stuff."

"True. But I can put it in?"

"Yeah, then it'll get it next time. And you can put in the quantities. Like three dozen eggs, or however many vanilla beans you'd buy. Are they actual beans?"

"They come in a pod," she murmured, studying her gift. "You bought me a kitchen recorder lister thing."

"I did. It's magnetic, so you can put it up on the side of one of your coolers, or wherever it works for you."

"Most guys go with flowers."

She clearly saw the hitch that put in his stride.

"Do you want flowers?"

"No. I want this. A whole bunch. It's a really great present." She looked up at him. "It's a really great present, Del."

"Good. Don't be jealous, but I bought one for Mrs. G, too."

"That slut."

He grinned, kissed her again. "I need to run over and give it to her, then get going or I'm going to be late."

"Del," she said before he got to the door. He'd bought her a kitchen gadget, one both practical and fun. All that was in her for him wanted to say it, just tell him. *I love you.* Only three words, she thought, all just one syllable. But she couldn't.

"Have a good time at the game."

"Planning on it. Talk to you later."

Sighing a little, she sat down to wait for the cream to cool, and played with her present.

$\mathscr{G}$IRL NIGHT WAS A FAVORITE EVENT. IT OFTEN INVOLVED dinner and DVDs, popcorn, gossip, and always just the ease and comfort of friends in a tradition that went back to childhood. The addition of Emma's possible wedding dress was, well, the icing on the cake. Anticipating an indulgent evening, Laurel ended the workday by setting her kitchen to rights as Emma came in.

"I thought I might catch you here."

"Just finishing up," Laurel told her.

"I have a request for cupcakes, two dozen. Two weeks," Emma added quickly. "So at least the client didn't squeeze it too close. It's my cousin. Coworker's office baby shower. The only directive was cute."

"Boy or girl?"

"Surprise, so not gender specific. Really whatever you want."

"Okay. Put it on the board."

"I appreciate it." Emma added the order and date to Laurel's task board. "What's this?" She tapped the electronic list maker.

"Del gave me a present."

"Oh, that's so nice. What did he give you?"

"That. It's so cool. Watch this." She walked over, pushed Record. "Unsalted butter. I programmed that in. See, there it is. I push this, and it's on the list."

Emma just stared. "This is a present?"

"Yes. I know to your way of thinking a present from a guy isn't a present unless it's shiny. But I can hot glue some sequins on it if it makes you feel better."

"It doesn't have to be shiny. It can also smell good. Well, it's thoughtful, and you like it, so it's a nice gift. What's the occasion?"

"No occasion."

"Oh, just a gimme? That definitely bumps up the ranking."

"It's going to fall on your scoreboard when I tell you he got Mrs. G one, too."

"Well, *jeez*!" Firm on this, Emma fisted her hands on her hips. "I'm sorry, it falls to the token category. A present has to be a one-on-one under these circumstances. It's a thoughtful token. This, my friend, is a present." She lifted her arm to dangle the bracelet Jack had given her. "The earrings Carter gave Mac for Valentine's Day? That's a present. I fear Del requires some training."

"He would if he were your boyfriend."

"Del's your boyfriend!" With a laugh, Emma grabbed Laurel to dance her in a circle.

"That sounds so high school. There has to be another term."

"Why are we dancing?" Parker wondered as she stepped in.

"Del is Laurel's boyfriend, and he gave her a token. I'm sorry, it's just not present-worthy. Look."

Parker went over. "Oh! I've seen these. I want one."

"Of course you do," Emma said with a sigh. "You're his sister. But would you consider it a gift, especially if he gave one to Mrs. G, too?"

"Hmm. It does fall in the murky area. But it's thoughtful, and very appropriate for Laurel."

"There." Emma lifted a finger in triumph. "That's what I said. Here's Mac. Mac, we need a tiebreaker."

"For what? And what are we doing in here? This is Girl Night."

"We need to clear this up first. Is this a gift or a token?" Emma gestured.

"What the hell is it?"

"See, token. You never have to ask what a present is. Parker, tell Del to buy Laurel something pretty."

"No. Stop it." Laurel gave Emma a shove, but she had to laugh. "I *like* it. If you like it, all rules are off, and it's a present."

"What the hell is it?" Mac asked again.

"It's an electronic organizer for marketing and errands," Parker explained. "I want one, too. Why didn't Del buy me one? I like presents."

"Token," Emma insisted.

"You don't need another organizer," Laurel told Parker.

Mac continued to frown at it. "For God's sake don't show it to Carter. He'll want one, then he'll want me to use it."

"Del bought one for Mrs. G, too, so Carter's bound to see it," Emma commented.

"Damn it."

"This is entirely too much controversy over my new toy. I'm going upstairs."

"Is Mrs. G making pizza?" Emma wondered. "I've been thinking all day about Mrs. G's pizza and a large quantity of wine."

"We'll get to it, but we've got something to do first."

"Not work." Emma grabbed Parker's arm. "I'm so ready for carbs and alcohol and girls."

"Not work, exactly. I happened to pick something up today for approval. You'll need to see it."

"What did you . . . Oh! Oh!" Now Emma spun Parker in a dance. "My wedding dress? Did you find my dress?"

"Maybe. And to follow a recent tradition, we're in the Bride's Suite."

"This is the best surprise. The best."

"If it doesn't work for you . . ." Parker began as Emma pulled her up the stairs.

"It'll still be the best surprise. Oh, I'm nervous." She stopped outside the door of the Bride's Suite. "I'm really nervous. Okay, here we go." She reached for the door, pulled her hand back. "I can't open it. Somebody else open it."

Laurel pushed open the door. "In you go," she said, then gave Emma a shove.

Emma gasped, then pressed a hand to her lips.

Parker never missed, Laurel thought. The dress *was* Emma. Romantic and fanciful with its acres of frothy skirts, with just a hint of sexy in the sparkle of the deeply off-the-shoulder bodice. A garden of fabric roses bloomed on the warm white of the elaborate pick-up skirt and along the sweeping train fit for a princess.

"It's a fairy tale," Emma managed. "Oh, Parker, it's a fairy tale."

"Have some of this." Mrs. Grady, who'd been waiting with champagne, handed a flute to Emma. "No crying with champagne. You'll water it down."

"It's the most beautiful dress in the world."

"You have to try it on. Strip it off, Em," Laurel ordered. "Parker and I will help you. Mac's documenting."

"The skirt." Reverently, Emma brushed her fingertips over the fabric. "It's like clouds. It'll billow. Oh, look at the back!" Tiny white rosebuds trailed down to hide the zipper. "Could there be a more perfect dress for a florist?"

"It kept saying 'take me to Emma,'" Parker told her as she and Laurel helped her into it.

"No peeking!" Laurel ordered as Emma started to turn her head to look in the mirror. "Not until we're done."

"Needs a couple of tucks." Mrs. Grady stepped over with her pins as Mac circled with her camera.

"Laurel, the train needs a little . . . Yeah, that's it," Mac said. "Oh, Em. Just wow."

"I have to see."

"Hold your horses," Mrs. Grady muttered, and finished her pinning. She stepped back out of the way, gave the nod.

"Ready?" Emma held her breath, turned.

Mac caught it, Laurel thought, caught that moment of wonder, the sheen of tears that was joy.

"All my life," Emma murmured. "Ever since we were little girls, I dreamed of this. And here I am, in my wedding dress. And it feels exactly as I hoped it would."

"You look like a princess," Laurel told her. "Honestly, Emma, you're just staggering."

Emma reached out, touching fingertips to the mirror. "It's me. I'm going to wear this dress to marry the man I love. Isn't that amazing?"

"Good work." Laurel put an arm around Parker. "Damn good work." She took the tissue Parker offered, dabbed her eyes. "Let's toast the bride."

"Give me the camera, Mackensie," Mrs. Grady ordered, "so I can get one of the four of you. There you are, and aren't you a picture?" she added, and captured it.

Later, over pizza and champagne, they dived into wedding plans. "I'll have my mother, and maybe my sister, come into the bridal shop to see it when I do the first fitting. I'll cry again. We'll all cry."

"They're holding two headpieces. One if you wear your hair up, the other if you wear it down. Your mom can help you decide."

"Parker. You think of everything." Emma blinked, sniffled. "No, I don't want to start that again. Oh, the bouquet I'm going to design for that dress! And my three maids of honor—or hey, by then two maids and one matron."

"I can't imagine being a matron," Mac said over a bite of pizza.

"I think lavender. Different styles, but the same color tones. I'm leaning toward whites and lavenders for the flowers. Soft, soft, soft, and romantic. White candles everywhere."

"A mix of real, silk, and sugar paste flowers for the cake," Laurel mused.

"Yes! Look, Parker's taking notes. Parker's taking notes on my wedding."

"Of course I am."

"I want to schedule the engagement shoot for an evening next week," Mac told her. "I want a night shot—sexy and atmospheric. In the gardens here."

"The gardens. That's perfect. I have the best pals in the universe."

"I'd like to tag along for the fitting," Mac added. "Get some shots of you and your mom."

"You should do it here." Laurel sipped champagne. "We can arrange the first fitting here—and bring the headpieces, right, Parker?"

"We could." Parker's face lit up as she warmed to the idea. "Sure we could."

"Then Mac could get her shots, and your mom could sit down for a first official consult, go over things you've decided, or where you're leaning."

"That's a really good idea," Parker decided.

"I have one now and then."

"We could really do it up for her," Mac added. "Your mom. The Vows VIP client treatment."

"She'd love that. I'd love that. There I go again."

Laurel passed Emma another tissue. "Think about shoes."

"Shoes?"

"Shoes for that dress."

"Oh. Shoes."

"See, nobody cries over shoes. I'd go for something with just a touch of sparkle, just a hint of sexy and all-out fabulous."

"We need to go shopping. You don't have your wedding shoes yet, do you, Mac?"

"Not yet."

"Wedding shoe safari!" Emma cried. "God, this is fun."

"Wait until you start trying to pick out invitations, place cards, and all that, and start obsessing over fonts. I never thought I'd obsess over fonts." Mac shook her head. "But I am. It's like a drug. I see that look, McBane." Mac wagged a finger. "That amused superiority. Like you believe you'll never sink as I have sunk. But you will. Mark my words. One day, fonts will haunt your sleep."

"I just don't think so. Anyway, I'm not getting married."

"But don't you think you and Del . . . at some point," Emma began.

"We've only been dating since last month."

"Evasive," Mac said. "You've known each other forever."

"And you're in love with him," Emma finished.

"I'm not thinking about that."

"About being in love with him," Parker asked, "or spending the rest of your life with him?"

"It's not—I'm not projecting that far ahead."

"Stop it," Parker ordered.

"It's really hard."

"Stop what?" Emma looked from one to the other. "What's hard?"

"Laurel saying what she'd say to us if the man wasn't my brother. You're insulting me."

"No! Damn it, Parker, that's just cheating."

"No, it's just making the point. Should I just leave?"

"Now you stop it." Scowling, Laurel tossed back more

champagne. "You always did fight dirty. Okay, fine. Fine. Yes, I'm in love with him. I've always been in love with him, which makes it unsteady because maybe *that's* projecting. But it doesn't feel like it, especially since I've spent a good part of my life trying not to be in love with him. And I couldn't pull it off. So yes, if we ever got to the point where we talked about the rest of our lives, I'd dive headfirst, jump in with both feet, name your cliché. The thing is, it takes two people to get to that point."

"Why wouldn't he love you?" Emma demanded.

"Of course he loves me. He loves all of us. It's different with me now, but it's not . . ." God, it was lowering, she realized, even among her closest friends. "It's hard loving someone more than they love you, and it's something I have to deal with. My feelings, my responsibility."

"I understand that." Mac reached over, squeezed Laurel's hand. "I let Carter feel that way. I didn't want to be in love, I didn't want to take that dive, that jump, so I kept holding back. I know it hurt him."

"I'm not hurting. Or maybe a little, but that could just be pride. I'm happy where we are. I know I may not be happy later, but this is more than I expected to have."

"I'm surprised your expectations would be so low," Parker commented. "You've always aimed high."

"When it's something I can work for or compete at. But you can't win love, can you? Not like an award or a game. We played at Wedding Day. Now we work at it. But when it comes to our own, it's not a game or a job. I don't need the dress or the ring, or the fonts," she added with a smile for Mac. "But I guess I need to know I'm the one. I can't work my way into being the one for him. I just have to be the one."

"That's really smart," Emma murmured.

"No one else has been the one for him," Parker told her. "I'd know."

"Not even Cherise McConnelly?"

"Oh God." Parker gave a mock shudder. "What was he

thinking? Besides that," she added at Laurel's cocked brow.

"Considering Cherise, I'd say his taste has improved considerably with me." Laurel took another slice. "So, there's hope for the man."

CHAPTER THIRTEEN

$\mathscr{E}$VEN AS JACK AND DEL SETTLED ON STOOLS AT THE BAR AT the Willows, the bartender stepped over. "Looks like I hit the daily double."

"How's it going, Angie?"

"No complaints, which is more than I can say for half the people who plop down on those stools. What can I get you?"

"Pellegrino," Del ordered.

"I'll have a Sam Adams."

"Gotcha covered. Just in for a drink?" she asked while she put a pint glass under the tap and added ice to a water goblet.

"I am," Jack told him. "This one's got a date."

"Yeah? Who's the lucky lady tonight?"

"I'm having dinner with Laurel."

"McBane?" Mild surprise showed in Angie's eyes. "A date-date?"

"Yeah."

"That's a switch." Knowing Del's preferences, she added a slice of lime to the sparkling water, then put both glasses on the bar. "I heard some speculation about that, but I just put it down to talk."

"Oh, why?"

"Because you've known Laurel for a couple of decades, and never dated her before. I haven't seen her in here for a while, but I hear business is booming on her front."

"Booming's the word."

"I've been to a couple of weddings there. First class. But that's your sister, isn't it?" Angie added as she wiped the bar with her white cloth. "First class all the way. We still miss Laurel around here. Best damn pastry chef we've ever had. So, Jack, how's Emma—and the wedding plans?"

"She's great. Found her dress, which is apparently the key to the kingdom."

"You can take that to the bank. Maybe something's in the water over there. First Mac, then Emma." She winked at Del, tapped the side of his glass with a finger. "Be careful what you drink." She moved down the bar to wait on another customer as Jack laughed.

"Don't look so surprised, bro." Jack tipped his glass in Del's direction. "It's a pretty natural progression."

"We've been dating what, a month, and wedding plans are a natural progression?"

Jack shrugged. "Mac to Emma to Laurel. It's like a marriage triple play."

"Laurel doesn't think that way." Hadn't it been pointed out he'd known her for a couple decades? "Weddings are a business. She's a businesswoman. A serious, ambitious businesswoman."

"So are the rest of them. Serious, ambitious people get married all the time." He studied Del over the rim of his glass. "This really never occurred to you?"

"*Occurred* is a wide word," Del evaded. "We're still adjusting to the change in our relationship. I'm not opposed to marriage. In fact, a big fan of the institution here. I just haven't given it any serious personal thought."

"Maybe it's time for a little role reversal with you and me, considering the blast I got from you when Emma and I

got together. Just what are your intentions toward my sur-
rogate sister?"

"I intend to have dinner with her."

"And do you intend to get lucky later?"

"I'd be a fool not to. We're enjoying this new phase.
It's . . . new," he decided. "For both of us. She matters, always
has. You know that. She just matters differently now. But I'm
not thinking of hiring my sister to plan the wedding."

"Ever, or yet?"

"Jesus, Jack." Because his throat was suddenly dry, Del
took a long drink of water.

"It's a fair question."

"You've got weddings on the brain," Del muttered.
"Maybe there is something in the water over there. Anyway,
I don't know. I haven't thought about it, really. And now I
can't think about anything else. Look, I know Laurel. She's
not thinking about getting married, and certainly not just
because Mac and Emma are. This is the girl who went off
to New York and Paris on her own to study. Hell, she seriously considered moving to Paris, was working here to save
up the money for it when . . ."

"Yeah, I know." The teasing light winked out of Jack's
eyes. "All that changed when your parents died."

"She put her Paris plans on hold then." He hadn't forgotten that; would never forget that. "She wouldn't have left
Parker. And I guess, now that I think about it, she stayed for
me, too. Then Parker's brainstorm took all of them over."

"Plans change."

"Yeah, plans change. But my point is that Laurel's always had her own direction, always followed her instincts
rather than the trend. If things had been different, she'd be
living in some stylishly bohemian Paris flat, running her
own upscale bakery."

"I don't think so." Jack shook his head. "I think when it
comes down to the sticking point, those four are too solidly
linked. New York maybe, but not Europe. The pull from the
other three's just too strong."

"I said almost the same to her not long ago, only half-kidding."

Jack ate one of the almonds from the dish Angie set on the bar. "I thought I got it before, before Emma and I changed direction. But living there, being in the mix the way I am now? It's the next thing to a psychic connection there. A little spooky sometimes, to tell the truth." He lifted his beer, a half toast. "That's love, man, wide and deep as it gets."

"Always has been." Del considered for a moment. "I still say this isn't something Laurel's got on the brain, but if there's anything there, the other three would know. You could feel out Emma about it."

"No way. Not even for you. If I start that, it'll lead to a whole discussion on what I think about you guys, how I might feel *you* out about it." Jack popped another almond. "The end is madness."

"You've got a point. Besides, that would only launch the idea balloon on it anyway. We're fine. We'll leave it alone. We're on a smooth road for the moment, so why test the detours?"

Jack grinned. "That's what I thought about Emma and me."

"You've got to stop that."

"I have to admit, it's fun poking at the vulnerable spots. But speaking of Emma and me, you'll do the best man thing, right?"

"Sure. Wouldn't have it any other way."

"Good. That's about the only thing I have to do. Mostly, I just have to smile and say that's great when she tells me what they've come up with for the wedding. Parker told me my deal's the honeymoon, then gave me the contact for a travel agent she says is the best—and an entire packet on Bora-Bora because she says it's somewhere Emma's always wanted to go, plus it's exotic and romantic. So I guess that's where we're going."

Intrigued, Del studied Jack over his sparkling water. "Do you want to go to Bora-Bora?"

"You know, I do. As soon as I looked at the packet, I thought, hey, this is it. Your sister's a little scary, Del."

"She can be."

"Carter got a packet on Tuscany, which included those 'Learn Italian' discs for both of them."

He had to laugh. "I guess that's taken care of."

"Apparently. Hey, I've got to run. I got an e-mail before I left the office. Emma's in a cooking mood."

"I'll get your beer."

"Thanks."

"Jack? The getting married suit? It looks good on you."

"Feels good. Who knew? See you later."

It wasn't just the getting married that looked good on him, Del mused. It was the whole life with Emma, the foundation he could so easily see—now—Jack building on. Home and family, dinner together at the end of a long day. They'd need more room eventually in the pretty little guest house. Knowing Jack, he'd come up with something.

The estate was turning into a kind of commune. When he considered it, Del decided it was something that would have pleased and amused his parents.

"Your table's ready, Mr. Brown." The maitre d' stepped up to the bar. "Would you like to be seated, or would you prefer to wait for your party here at the bar?"

He glanced at his watch. Laurel was running late—or Mac who was dropping her off on the way to a shoot was running late.

"She should be here any minute. I'll take the table."

He decided to go ahead and order a bottle of wine, and had barely made his selection when he heard his name.

"Hello, stranger!"

"Deborah." He rose to greet her, and exchanged a light, friendly kiss with the woman he'd known for years. "You look great. How are you?"

"Fabulous." She tossed back her lush mane of red hair. "Just back from two months in Spain—with the last two weeks in Barcelona."

"Business or pleasure?"

"Both, a lot of both. I'm meeting my mother and sister for a little catch-up girl time. I'm early, as usual; they're late, as usual."

"Sit down, wait with me."

"I'd love to, Delaney." She gave him a sparkling smile as he pulled out a chair. "I haven't seen you since . . . when? I think it's since the Spring Ball. What have you been up to?"

"Nothing as interesting as Barcelona." As the wine steward offered the bottle for approval, Del glanced at the label, nodded.

"Well, catch me up. Who's doing what, and who are they doing it with? What's the latest hot gossip?"

Del smiled as he sampled the taste the steward poured in his glass. "I think you'll need your mother and sister for that. It's perfect," he told the steward, and gestured toward the glass in front of Deborah.

"You're too discreet. Always were." She sipped the wine. "And you still have excellent taste in wines. Come on, spill something. I heard a rumor that Jack Cooke's engaged. Confirm or deny."

"That I can confirm. He and Emmaline Grant set the date for next spring."

"Emma? Really? Well, here's to them." She lifted her glass. "Though scores of single females may mourn. Obviously I've been out of the loop. I didn't even know they were an item."

"I guess it moved pretty quickly once it started."

"I'm happy for them. Is it odd for you? I mean, Emma's the next thing to a sister, and Jack's your closest friend."

"I had a moment or two," he admitted. "But they're good together. Tell me about Barcelona. I've never been there."

"You need to go. The beaches, the food, the wine. The romance." She smiled at him. "It's in the air."

They were laughing, leaning across the table toward each other when Laurel came in. It stopped her dead in her tracks, as if she'd walked into a glass wall—and she stood on the wrong side of it.

He looked so relaxed, she thought. No, *they* looked so relaxed, and gorgeous—both of them. If Mac had come in with her, she could have snapped a photo, captured that moment, that image of two beautiful people sharing wine and laughter over candlelight.

Anyone would think they were a couple, perfectly suited, absolutely in tune.

"Laurel, hi."

"Hi, Maxie." Laurel worked up a smile for the waitress who paused. "Busy night."

"Tell me." Maxie rolled her eyes. "I didn't know you were coming in. We'll fix you up."

"Actually I'm meeting someone."

"Oh, okay. Don't let Julio see you." She winked as she talked of the chef. "He'd be tempted to drag you back into the kitchen on a night like this. We miss you around here."

"Thanks."

"Gotta keep it moving. I'll talk to you later."

She nodded, then slipped into the restroom to give herself a minute. Stupid, she told herself, stupid to lose her balance because Del was having a drink with a friend. Stupid to feel somehow *less* because a handful of years before she'd have been back in the kitchen hustling instead of sitting at a table. She'd have created some lovely dessert for a couple like Delaney Brown and Deborah Manning.

"Nothing wrong with that," she muttered, and dug out her lip gloss as she scolded herself in the mirror. She was proud of the job she'd done here—and the money she'd earned to help launch Vows. She was proud of her talent, and proud that talent enabled her to have a business, earn her living, create something that made people happy.

She took care of herself, made her own way, and God, nothing was more important to her than that.

But it stung, she couldn't help it, to remember that she'd always be, in some sense, on the wrong side of that glass wall.

"It doesn't matter." She replaced the lip gloss, took a breath. "It just doesn't matter."

Confidence, she reminded herself, was like lip gloss—
all you had to do was put it on.

She stepped out of the restroom, turned toward the dining room, and started toward the table.

Okay, she mused, it helped considerably to see the way
Del's eyes warmed when he spotted her. He rose, held out
a hand for hers as Deborah shifted and glanced up.

Laurel saw the momentary struggle to place the face
with a name. She and Deborah didn't run in the same cir-
cles, after all.

"Laurel, you remember Deborah Manning, don't you?"

"Sure. Hello, Deborah."

"Laurel. It's good to see you again. Del just told me
about Emma and Jack. You must be planning a spectacular
cake."

"I have some ideas."

"I'd love to hear them. Weddings are so much fun. Can
you sit down? Del, we need another glass."

To her credit, Deborah caught on quickly, and her flaw-
less redhead's skin flushed at her bungle. "I'm an idiot."
She laughed as she got to her feet. "Del's been waiting for
you. He was sweet enough to keep me company."

"That's fine." Look how mature I am, Laurel thought. "You
should stay, finish your wine. We can get another chair."

"No, no. I've been waiting for my mother and sister. I'm
going to step out and give them a call, make sure I haven't
been stood up. Thanks for the wine, Del."

"It was good seeing you, Deborah."

"You, too. Enjoy your dinner."

She strolled off, but not before Laurel caught the look of
baffled speculation.

"I'm late," Laurel said brightly. "Completely Mac's fault."

"It was worth the wait." He held her chair. "You look
beautiful."

"I was thinking the same thing about you."

With the smooth efficiency the restaurant was known
for, a waiter removed Deborah's glass, replaced it, and
poured Laurel's wine. She sipped, nodded. "Very nice."

She took the menu the waiter offered, but didn't open it. "Hi, Ben."

"Hi, Laurel. I heard you were here."

"What's good tonight?"

"The red snapper, topped with crab, sautéed in a white wine reduction, and served with jasmine rice and asparagus."

"Sold. And a small side salad with the house to start."

"I'll play," Del said. "What else is good?"

"You might like the pork tenderloin with honey-ginger sauce. We're serving it with fingerling potatoes and roasted vegetables nicoise."

"Sounds perfect. I'll have the salad as well."

"Excellent choices."

He'd barely stepped away when another server placed the restaurant's signature olive bread and dipping sauce on the table.

"You know, the service is always good here," Del commented. "It's better with you."

"We like to take care of our own." She nibbled on some bread.

"I'd forgotten you used to work here—or didn't think of it when I suggested we have dinner here. We'll have to have dessert, so you can check out your replacement."

"I think it's my replacement's replacement now."

"Once you've had the best, it's hard to settle for less. Do you miss it at all? Working with a team, I mean, the energy, the controlled chaos."

"Not always so controlled. And not really. I like having my own space, and restaurant hours are brutal."

"And you have so much time on your hands now."

"Well, it's *my* time, and that makes a difference. Ah, looks like Deborah's mother and sister showed up." She lifted her glass toward a nearby table, and Del glanced over to see the three women being seated.

"They probably weren't late, or not by much. She tends to be early."

"That's right." Casually, easy, *mature*, Laurel congratulated herself. "You dated her."

"Briefly, and long ago. Before she was married."

"I hope you didn't date her while she was married. After her divorce?"

He shook his head. "I represented her in the divorce. No dating clients, and I have a policy about dating former clients in divorce cases. Just a bad idea."

"Penny Whistledown." Laurel pointed at him. "I remember you handled her divorce, *and* you dated her a couple years after."

"Which is why I know it's a bad idea."

"She was so needy. If she couldn't get you at home or the office, she'd call the house nagging Parker about where you were." She sipped her wine again. "That, Counselor, was a serious error in judgment on your part."

"Guilty as charged. You've had a couple."

"Uh-uh. I steer clear of needy men."

"Errors in judgment. Drake, no, Deke something. How many tattoos did he have?"

"Eight, I think. Maybe nine. But he doesn't count. I was sixteen and hoping to piss off my parents."

"It pissed me off."

Her eyebrows winged up. "Really?"

"Really. He hung around most of that summer, in his torn-off-sleeve T-shirts and motorcycle boots. He had an earring, and I think he practiced his smirk in the mirror."

"You remember him better than I do."

She paused while Ben served the salads, topped off their wine.

"We know too much about each other's dating past. Could be dangerous."

"I won't hold yours against you, if you don't hold mine against me."

"Fair and reasonable," she concluded. "You know, people are wondering what we're doing, what's going on with us."

"What people?"

"Here, tonight. People who know you." She inclined her head slightly toward the table where the three women were pretending not to be talking about them. "And people who know me."

"Does that bother you?"

"No. Not really. Maybe a little." She shrugged and gave her salad her attention. "It's natural enough, especially when one of us is a Brown of the Connecticut Browns."

"I'd say it's natural enough because I'm sitting here with the most beautiful woman in the room."

"Good. That's very good. A popular standard for a reason."

He laid his hand on hers on the table. "I know who I'm looking at."

Undone, she turned her hand over to link her fingers with his. "Thanks."

Let them wonder, she thought. Let them talk. She had what she'd always wanted right in her hand.

They ate, sampling each other's choices, sipping good wine, talking about whatever came to mind. They'd always been able to talk, Laurel mused, about anything and everything. She found herself able to put that glass wall around them, close everyone else out on the other side and savor the interlude as much as the meal.

Ben set a trio of mini soufflés on the table. "Compliments of Charles, the dessert chef. He heard you were here and wanted to do something special for you. He's a little nervous," Ben added, lowering his voice as he leaned down.

"Seriously?"

"You're a tough act, Laurel. If you'd rather have something else—"

"No, this is great. They're beautiful." She sampled the chocolate first, with a dollop of whipped cream. And closing her eyes, smiled. "Gorgeous. Try it," she told Del, then took a taste of the vanilla. "Really wonderful."

"He'd love to come out and meet you."

"Why don't I go back? After we do justice to these."

"You'd make his day. Thanks, Laurel."

She tried the last while Ben walked away. "Mmm, the lemon's exquisite. Just the right blend of tart and sweet."

"A Brown of the Connecticut Browns. That's what you said before." He shared the soufflés with Laurel. "But I'm with the Diva of Desserts."

"Diva of Desserts." A laugh bubbled out, then she paused and just grinned. "I like it. I may get a sign. God, I'm going to have to work out like a maniac tomorrow, but I don't want to hurt his feelings," she added and took another bite. "Listen, I'll only be a few minutes in the back."

"I'm coming with you."

"Are you sure?"

"Wouldn't miss it," he said, and rose to take her hand.

"It'll have calmed down by now," she told him. "The dinner rush is well over. But don't touch anything. Julio can be fairly insane. If he threatens to fillet you like a trout, don't take it personally."

"I know Julio. I've met him several times when he's come out to the table."

Laurel spared Del a glance as they approached the kitchen. "Then you don't know Julio."

She pushed open the door.

Calm, she'd said. They obviously had different definitions of the term. People moved everywhere at once, it seemed to Del, and the noise level—raised voices, the clatter of dishes, the hum of vents, the thwack of knives, and sizzle from the grill—was simply huge.

Steam rose in air thick with heat and tension.

At a section of the enormous stove, Julio stood in his apron and short chef's hat, cursing steadily in several languages.

"Can't decide?" he boomed. "Need more time?" He erupted with a stream of gutter Spanish that singed the already simmering air. "Don't want mushrooms, want extra carrots. Assholes! Where's my fucking plate, goddamn it."

"Nothing changes," Laurel said just loud enough for him to hear.

He turned, a scrawny man with beetled black brows over molten brown eyes. "You, don't talk to me."

"I'm not here to talk to you." She turned away to

approach the younger man who'd stopped drizzling raspberry sauce around a slice of chocolate cake on a dessert plate. "You must be Charles."

"Don't talk to him until he gets that done. You think this is a social club?"

Charles's eyes rolled in a handsome face the color of freshly ground coffee. "Please. Just one minute."

He completed the plate with a scattering of berries, added thin cookies around a bowl of trifle. As if by secret signal, a waitress scooped them up and out the door.

"I'm so pleased to meet you. So pleased."

"Your soufflés were wonderful—the lemon one in particular. Thank you."

His face simply lit up, Del thought, as if Laurel had switched on electricity. "You liked them? When I heard you were here I wanted to do something for you. The lemon. You liked the lemon?"

"Especially the lemon. Rich and fresh at the same time."

"We don't serve it yet. It's new. I've been working on it."

"I think you've perfected it. I don't suppose you'd share the recipe."

"You . . ." His voice went breathless. "You want my recipe? I'll write it down. Right now. I'll write it down for you, Ms. McBane."

"Laurel."

"Laurel."

Del swore her name came from the man's lips like a prayer. When he scurried away to get the recipe, she turned to Del.

"I'll be right back."

When she walked off with Charles, Del slipped his hands in his pockets and glanced around. Julio guzzled from a water bottle and eyed him.

"Pork medallions."

"That's right. They were excellent."

"Mr. Brown." Julio acknowledged his due, then shifted his gaze to Laurel, back to Del. He said, "Hmm."

He capped his water before striding over to where Laurel huddled with Charles. "I'm still mad at you."

She shrugged.

"You left my kitchen."

"With plenty of notice, *and* I came in on my own time to help train my replacement."

"Your replacement." He cursed and sliced a hand through the air. "Useless. He cried."

"Some of them do once you've chewed on them awhile."

"I don't need crybabies in my kitchen."

"You're lucky to have Charles. Luckier if he stays and puts up with your crap."

"He does okay. He doesn't cry. He doesn't talk back."

"Give him time. I'll get you that recipe, Charles. I think it's a good trade." She tucked the one Charles gave her in her bag.

"Thank you for coming back. It means so much to me."

"I'll see you again." She shook his hand, then turned back to Julio. "The snapper was fabulous." She kissed his cheek. "You bastard."

He let out a laugh that boomed as effectively as his curses. "Maybe I'll forgive you."

"Maybe I'll let you. 'Night."

Del ran a hand down her back as they walked outside. "That was a very nice thing you did, on both counts."

"I can be nice."

"You're like a lemon soufflé, Laurel. Just the right blend of tart and sweet." As he brought her hand to his lips to kiss, she blinked at him.

"Well. Somebody's going to get lucky tonight."

"I was hoping."

CHAPTER FOURTEEN

MOVING AS QUIETLY AS POSSIBLE IN THE DARK, LAUREL crept to the bathroom to change into a sports bra and bike shorts. She had to start remembering to get her workout gear together the night before when Del stayed over.

That's what Parker would've done, she thought as she wiggled into the shorts.

She clipped up her hair, pulled on her socks, then decided to carry her shoes. As she eased the door open she let out a strangled gasp. Del sat on the side of the bed, illuminated by the bedside lamp.

"What, do you have superhearing? I was quiet."

"Reasonably. Working out? Good idea. I'll dig up some gear and join you."

Since he was awake anyway, she sat to put on her shoes. "You can leave some stuff in here next time."

He smiled a little. "Some of our tribe are sensitive about such matters."

"I'm not."

"Good. Neither am I. Makes it easier all around." He glanced at the clock, winced. "Mostly."

"You can go back to sleep. I won't hold it against you, or think you're a wimp. Or soft. Or lazy."

He squinted at her. "I'll meet you in the gym."

"Okay."

She strolled out thinking it was a good way to start the day. Teasing Del, getting in an hour's gym time followed by a hot shower, hot coffee, and a solid day's work.

In fact, it was pretty damn perfect.

In the gym she found Parker already doing cardio to CNN.

"Morning," she called out.

"Good morning. You look awfully damn chipper."

"Feeling awfully damn chipper." Laurel got a mat from the rack, unrolled it on the floor for warm-up stretches. "Del's coming in to work out."

"Which explains the awfully damn chipper. How was dinner?"

"It was good. Really good. Except . . ."

"What?"

Laurel glanced toward the door. "I don't know how quick he'll be. Later." Stretching, she studied Parker's exercise tank and capris. The chocolate brown pants and floral top managed to be serviceable and feminine. "I should probably get some new exercise outfits. I think most of mine are getting tatty."

She walked over to take the second elliptical. "How long have you got in?"

"Just passing thirty."

"I'd better catch up."

"No chance, I'm coming up on mile three then switching to Pilates."

"I can do three, then I'll see your Pilates with some yoga. Maybe I'll do four. I had soufflé last night."

"Worth the extra mile?"

"And then some. They've got a solid dessert chef at the Willows."

"Charles Barker."

"Do you know every damn thing?"

"Yes," Parker said with satisfaction. "And there's my three."

Parker wiped down the machine, switched off the news, switched on music.

"Morning, ladies." In ancient sweat shorts and a faded T-shirt, Del grabbed a bottle of water out of the case, took out another for Laurel, then headed for Parker's machine.

"Thanks," she said when he tucked her water in the holder.

"Gotta stay hydrated. What did she do?"

"Parker? Three. I'm going for four."

He stepped on, set a program. "I'm up for five, but I won't hold four against you. Or think you're a wimp."

"Five?" She nodded. "I'm in."

Competitive, Parker thought as she stretched out on her mat to start her ab work. Well, she couldn't fault either of them for that. She was competitive herself—and was already wishing she'd done an extra couple of miles just because they were.

They looked so good together. Did they realize it? Not just the physical looks, she mused as she switched to leg scissors. But the way they moved, the way they connected.

She wanted them to be good together. More, she wanted them to be *right* together so much it was nearly painful.

She'd wanted that rightness for Mac and Emma, too, but this was more. This was her brother, and her sister in everything but blood. These were two of the most important people in her life, and she wanted, so much, for them to be happy. To be happy together would be like a gift for her nearly as much as it would be for them.

She believed, absolutely, that each person, each heart, had a counterpart—had a mate. A rightness. She'd always believed it, and understood that unshakable belief was a reason she was good at what she did.

"One down!" Laurel announced.

"You started before I did."

"Not my problem."

"Fine." Parker watched Del dig in. "No more nice guy."

Shaking her head, Parker started another set of crunches.

They'd passed mile three with Del taking the lead when Mac dragged herself in.

"There it is." She bared her teeth at the Bowflex. "The enemy." She scowled at Parker, who finished up her session with basic yoga poses to stretch out. "You're already finished, aren't you? I can tell by that smug look on your face."

Parker put her palms together in prayer position. "My face reflects the centered peace of my mind and body."

"Up yours, Parks. Hey, don't look now but there's a man in here."

"They're in a five-mile competition."

"Jesus, why? Why would anyone want to puff on that monster for five miles? So, hey, what do you think?" She did a turn to show off her sports tank and cropped yoga pants. "I broke down and bought some buff-yourself-up outfits. To inspire myself."

"Pretty and functional. Good for you." Parker ended with a handstand that had Mac craning her head.

"Now that I have the outfit, do you think I can do that?"

"I'll spot you if you want to try."

"No, better not. I'll hurt myself and I'm supposed to call Carter for a swim when I finish my self-imposed torture. Have you seen him swim?"

"Mmm." Parker did an upside down split, then righted herself. "I might have caught a glimpse while stepping out on the terrace. Not that I was ogling, of course."

"He's worth an ogle. He's pretty cute in his trunks. But the thing is, he gets in the water and suddenly he's Mister Grace instead of Professor Klutz." After setting the machine, she started with biceps curls. "Why is that?"

"Maybe because there's nothing solid to run into or trip over in the water."

"Hmm, that could be it. Anyway, when I finish abusing myself here, Carter and I are taking a morning swim.

Swimming's a civilized exercise. It's probably the only one. Speaking of pretty cute," she added, lowering her voice as she jerked her chin at the elliptical machines. "They are."

Parker nodded as she hooked the towel around her neck, then gulped down water. "I was thinking the same thing earlier." She checked her watch. "You know, I've got just enough time to sneak in a quick swim myself before I start the day. Ten o'clock consult, full staff."

"I've got it."

"See you then. Oh, Mac? Your shoulders look awesome."

"Seriously?" Mac's face brightened with pleasure and hope. "You're not just saying that because you love me and I'm suffering?"

"Awesome," Parker repeated, then walked out to get her swimsuit.

"Awesome," Mac muttered and switched to her triceps.

"Mile four." Del grabbed his water and drank deep. "Oh, look, you're behind."

"I'm saving myself for the kick." Laurel swiped sweat from her face. No way she'd catch him, she thought, but she could make him work for it.

She glanced over. He'd sweated through the T-shirt in a dark vee that had lust curling in her belly. She used it to push herself a little harder.

His hair had darkened at the temples, and the damp brought out those sexy curls. His arms gleamed; muscles bunched.

He'd taste salty, she thought. He'd be slippery under her hands. That energy, that strength and endurance would be over her, under her, all around her. In her.

Her breath began to quicken from more than the exertion, and she hit mile four.

He looked at her, and she saw in his eyes what was quivering inside her. That drumming, primal need. Her pulse pounded along with the music, her skin hummed along with the machines. Beat slapped into quick beat.

She smiled slowly, spoke breathlessly. "I'm coming up on you."

"You don't have enough left to take me."

"I've got plenty left."

"You're winded."

"You, too. I can finish strong. Can you?"

"Watch me."

Across the room, Mac rolled her eyes, and deciding there were some things even the closest of friends shouldn't be part of, slipped out of the room.

Neither Laurel nor Del noticed, or gave her a single thought.

He slowed, just a little, and she understood the competition was over, and the sexual dance—hot and primitive—had begun.

They'd finish together.

"Let's see your kick," he demanded.

"You want it?"

"Yeah, I want it."

"Then come get it." She bore down, hard, driving herself until she was both thrilled and astonished to feel that dark pleasure build inside her. When he once more matched his pace to hers, she heard herself moan.

Closing her eyes she let it come, let it ride through her, all the hot and grinding need, all the aching anticipation.

They hit the finish together.

Breath fast and ragged, she opened her eyes to look at him. Her throat burned with a thirst water wouldn't quench. She stepped off on unsteady legs.

"I'm going to skip the yoga," she said.

"You're damn right." He hooked his fingers in her sports bra, yanked her against him.

His mouth was a fever on hers, burning reason, spiking delirium. Need and hunger—his ran as deep and desperate as hers, and that alone was a thrill. Heat, another wild surge of it, crashed through her so she wondered how either of them could stand against it.

"We have to hurry. We have to hurry." She broke away from him, fighting for air. For one humming moment, they just stared at each other. "Catch me!" She sprinted to the door, heard her next gasping breath come out in a half-crazed laugh as she raced toward her room.

He caught her, swung her through the door.

Still laughing, she pivoted, slammed him back against the door to shut it, then devoured his mouth with hers.

"God. Oh God," she managed, and yanked his shirt up, tossed it aside. Then ran her hands over his chest. "You're all sweaty and slippery, and . . ." She ran her tongue over him. "Salty. It makes me crazy. Quick," she demanded and started to drag down his shorts.

"Not that quick." He reversed, pushed her back against the door. He pulled off her sports bra, tossed it over his shoulder, then filled his hands with her breasts.

Her head fell back as his thumbs stroked her nipples. "I can't."

"Yes, you can. The race isn't over. You don't know what you do to me. I don't know what you do to me. But I want more. I want you. I want more of you."

She took his face in her hands to bring his mouth back to hers. "You can have all you want. All you want. Just don't stop touching me. Don't stop."

He couldn't. How could he keep his hands, his mouth, off that tight, taut body, that soft, hot skin? She pressed against him, murmuring against his lips, urging him to do what he wanted, take what he needed.

He'd never had another woman excite him like this, not like this until he could all but feel the blood pulsing, pounding, under his skin. Desire was too simple, too quiet a name for what she stirred in him. Passion too easy.

He dragged her arms over her head, pinned them against the door while he ravaged her mouth, her neck. Then he moved down her body, feasting. But the hunger only grew.

The bike pants fit her like a second skin, molding her hips, her thighs. He peeled them from her as he journeyed down. Until it was his hands molding her. Until there was no barrier between that wet heat and his lips, his tongue.

The orgasm tore through her, shocking her senses, blurring her vision. Her legs buckled, but he tightened his grip.

He did what he wanted. Took what he needed.

She couldn't find air through the torrent of pleasure, couldn't find balance in the thick, sultry dark. She could only feel the mad barrage of sensations that left her body quaking for the next assault.

Once again, he pulled her hands over her head, cuffed them. And with his eyes on hers, drove into her.

She came again, one long, shocking tear of control. When she shuddered, he thrust. When she shuddered, he plunged until it began to build again, impossibly.

Her wrists slipped from his hands so she gripped his shoulders, held fast as she felt his control begin to fray. She watched him watch her as they started the sprint, found the speed, matched their pace.

And hit the finish together.

They sprawled on the floor, both too weak, too sated to move. When the power of speech returned, Laurel sighed. "We're going to be rich."

"Huh?"

"Forgot. You're already rich. *I'm* going to be rich, and you'll be richer."

"Okay."

"I'm serious. We've just discovered a no-fail motivation for exercise. Hot jungle sex. We'll be Bill Gates rich. We'll write a book. There'll be DVDs and infomercials. America, then the world, will become buff and sexually satisfied. And they'll have us to thank."

"Will the DVDs and infomercial have demonstrations of the hot jungle sex?"

"On the Adult Only versions—and we can use a lot of mist and clever lighting and camera angles to keep it classy."

"Honey, one of the perks of hot jungle sex is it's not classy."

"For production purposes it will be. We're not making porn here. Think of the millions, Delaney." She rolled onto her stomach so she could see his face. "The millions of unfit bodies who will read our book, see our DVD or info-mercial, and think: holy shit, I can get me some of that if I work out? We'll need to build the McBane-Brown Motivational Health Club so we can offer a safe, clean place for membership. We'll franchise. They will pay, Del. Oh yes, they will pay big for this."

"How come your name goes first on the Motivational Health Club?"

"My idea."

"That's true, but you wouldn't have had the idea if I hadn't just rocked your world."

"Rocked yours right back."

"Damn right, you did. Come here." He pulled her over until she splayed across his chest. "Your name can go first."

"Good. That's settled. Of course we'll have to have various DVDs for levels. Like Yoga for Beginners, and that sort of thing. Beginners, Intermediate, and Advanced. We don't want anyone getting hurt."

"I'll start the paperwork."

"Do that. God, five miles and hot jungle sex. I should be exhausted, but I feel like I could do it all again and then . . . Oh shit."

"What?"

"The time! Five miles and HJS take longer than three miles and yoga. I've got to get in the shower."

"Me, too."

She gave his shoulder a light pinch. "It has to be just a shower. I'm off schedule."

"Laurel, every man has his limits. I think I've reached mine for this morning."

She got up, pushed back her hair. "Wimp," she said, then dashed for the shower.

* * *

$\mathscr{B}$Y THE TIME SHE'D FINISHED HER MORNING BAKING, Laurel was back on schedule. She'd opted for a DVD of *The Thin Man*, and arranged pastries for the ten o'clock on a pretty dish while Nick and Nora's dialogue zinged from the kitchen set.

The air smelled indulgently of sugar and rich coffee, and held the cheer of some of Emma's Shasta daisies.

She reached back to untie her apron as Parker walked in.

"Oh, you're finished. I was coming in to help you with the setup."

"With five minutes to spare? That's not Parker time."

"The clients called to reschedule for ten thirty."

Laurel shut her eyes. "I killed myself to stay on schedule. You could've told me."

"They just called . . . okay, twenty minutes ago. But this way, nobody's late."

"You didn't tell anyone."

"I love that top," Parker said brightly. "It's almost a shame to cover most of it with a suit jacket."

"That kind of thing only works on distracted clients." But with a shrug, Laurel reached for the jacket she'd hung up before baking. "But it is a great top."

"We're not late!" Mac and Emma rushed in together.

"No, but the client's going to be," Laurel told them. "Sneaky Brown kept that to herself."

"Only for twenty minutes."

"Jeez. I don't know whether to be annoyed or relieved. I need a hit." Mac opened the refrigerator for a Diet Pepsi. "So . . ." Mac uncapped the top, took a long sip as she studied Laurel. "I bet you're feeling all loose and relaxed."

"I'm fine. Why?"

"Oh, I bet a whole buncha lots better than fine. I bet hanging off a lamppost belting out a show tune in the rain kind of fine after that workout. Wait, let me put air quotes around 'workout.'" She set down her drink and did just that.

"What, did you set up a hidden camera in my room?"

"I would never be so crude—unless I'd thought of it

first. Besides, who needs a hidden camera? The two of you were sending off such wild sex vibes in there I had to leave before they caught me and I jumped both of you and had a threesome."

"Really?" Parker asked, drawing out both syllables.

"Well, not about the threesome probably. Laurel's not my type. I'd go for you, hot stuff." She gave Parker a lewd wink.

"I thought I was your type," Emma said.

"I'm such a slut. Anyway, the two of them are on those elliptical bastards, and the steam's rising. Then they're using workout code for sex talk."

"We were not."

"Oh, I broke your code." Mac pointed a finger. "'I'm coming up on you. I can finish strong.' I'm getting hot just thinking about it."

"You are a slut," Laurel decided.

"I'm an engaged slut, and don't you forget it. But I should thank you, as I took my unexpected sexual frustration out on Carter after our swim. And he thanks you, too."

"Anytime."

"This is all very interesting, and I mean that sincerely. But—" Parker tapped her watch. "We need to set up in the parlor."

"Wait." Emma tossed up a traffic cop hand. "Just one question, because I have to get the flowers out of the van. Do you really have energy for sex after your workout?"

"Read the book. Watch the infomercial."

"What book?" Emma demanded as Laurel carried the pastries out of the kitchen. "What infomercial?"

"Flowers," Parker said, then carted off the coffee setup.

"Damn it. Don't talk about anything good until I get back. In fact, you have to help me haul in the flowers."

"But I want to—"

Emma just made a cut-off sound, held up a finger at Mac.

"Okay, okay."

In the parlor, Laurel and Parker set up the refreshments. "So, is it later?"

"Later than what?" Laurel responded.

"Later than it was earlier when you said later."

"Yeah, it's later." Laurel fussed with the fan of napkins. "How many clients?"

"Bride, MOB, FOB, Groom, SMOG. Five."

"Right. FOG was a widower. He's not coming?"

"Out of town. You don't have to tell me. It's okay. Of course, it's not okay. I'm saying that because you're my friend, and I don't want you to feel bad."

"You're such a bitch." Laurel had to laugh. "It's not that I don't want to tell you. It's just that I feel stupid about it. Especially now, after the hot jungle sex."

"It was hot jungle sex?" Emma demanded as she came in with a box exploded with star lilies. "What kind of workout was it? How long? Be specific. Parker, take notes."

"Five miles on the elliptical."

"Well, God." Heaving a sigh, Emma began taking out the vases, placing them. "Forget it. I'd be dead after five miles of anything, then Jack would have hot jungle sex with someone else. It'd just piss me off. There are easier ways to HJS."

"I wonder," Parker began, "is it possible, is it perhaps conceivable, we're all a little obsessed with sex at the moment?"

"It's her fault." Mac helped Emma with the flowers. "You'd understand if you'd been in the gym with all those sex vibes dancing around."

"We're not talking about sex," Laurel said.

"When did we stop?" Emma wondered.

"Before you came in. We're talking about something else."

"Just as well since I'm not doing five miles on some machine. What something else?"

"It's about dinner last night. Or before dinner. I was late. It's your fault." She pointed at Mac.

"What? I couldn't help it. The studio shoot ran over, and I couldn't find my shoes. The ones I needed. Besides, you were hardly late. Maybe ten or fifteen minutes."

"Long enough for Deborah Manning to sit down with Del at our table and have a glass of our wine."

"I thought Deborah Manning was in Spain."

"So you don't know everything." Laurel smiled thinly at Parker. "She's obviously not in Spain as she was drinking wine with Del."

"He's not interested in Deborah."

"He used to be."

"That was years ago, and they only dated a couple of times."

"I know." Laurel held up her hands before Parker continued. "I know, which is one of the reasons I feel stupid. I wasn't jealous—I'm not jealous—of her, that way. If I was, I'd feel even more stupid because he was so obviously not interested in her that way. I don't think she was either. In him."

"Then what's the problem?" Emma asked her.

"It was just . . . when I came in and saw them, sharing wine, laughing. They looked so right together."

"No, they don't." Parker shook her head.

"You didn't see them. They looked beautiful and smooth and perfect."

"No. Beautiful and smooth, okay. Perfect and right, no. They'd look attractive together because they're both attractive. That's not the same thing as right."

"That's profound. That's actually profound," Mac decided. "And I know exactly what you mean. Sometimes I'll do photographs of couples and I'll think this is a pretty shot, they look great together. But I know they don't look *right*. I can't change that, fix it, arrange it. Because they're not, and that's all."

"Exactly."

"Okay, they looked beautiful. We'll stick with that. And for just a minute, I felt stuck, separate. It's stupid." Laurel pushed at her hair. "It was like looking through a glass wall, and that I was on my side, they were on theirs."

"That's insulting, to all three of you." Emma stopped placing flowers to poke Laurel in the shoulder. "And none of you deserve it. Deborah's a nice woman."

"Who is Deborah?"

"You don't really know her," Emma told Mac. "But she's a perfectly nice woman."

"I didn't say she wasn't. I don't really know her either. I'm just saying I don't think she's ever waited tables or sweated it out in a restaurant kitchen."

"That's reverse snobbery."

Laurel shrugged at Parker. "Sure it is. I told you I felt stupid about it. And I got over it. I did. I know it's my problem, and I don't like it. But it's what I felt for that moment. And I felt it when she realized he was having dinner with me, that we were together, and I could see that flicker of what-the-fuck? on her face before she got rid of it. She was perfectly nice," she said to Emma. "It wasn't her fault I felt that way, which makes it worse. It snuck up on me. It does sometimes. Then we had a lovely dinner. Really lovely. So there was this part of me under the part having that really lovely dinner that felt even more stupid for the reaction. I hate feeling stupid."

"Good." Parker nodded. "Because when you hate something, you stop doing it."

"Working on it."

"Then— That must be the clients," Parker said as the bell rang. "Crap, I lost track. Emma, get rid of those boxes. Laurel, you're wearing your kitchen shoes."

"Damn it. Be right back." She sprinted out of the parlor, with Emma behind her with the empty boxes.

Parker tugged down her suit jacket. "You didn't say much."

"Because I've been behind that glass wall," Mac told her. "I know how she felt. It takes some time and effort to smash it down, but she will."

"I don't want there to be any sort of wall between us."

"Never between us, Parks. Not the four of us. It's different for her with Del, but she'll crack it."

"All right. You'll tell me if you think she's feeling that way."

"Promise."

"All right," she said again. "Show time." She hurried out to answer the door.

CHAPTER FIFTEEN

$\mathscr{L}$ATER IN THE WEEK, AND WITH CONSIDERABLE PLEASURE, Laurel sat down with Carter's sister and her fiancé. Sherry Maguire bubbled like the champagne Laurel kept chilled, and was just as delightful.

From their first event meeting—the day Carter had filled in for Nick, and reconnected with Mac—the key word for the fall wedding had been *fun*.

Laurel planned to make sure the fun extended to the cake.

"I'm so excited." Sherry danced in her seat. "Everything's just coming together so well. I don't know what I'd do without Parker. Well, without all of you. Probably drive Nick crazy."

"Er," he said and grinned at her. "Craz*ier*."

She laughed and poked him. "I don't talk about the wedding more than a hundred times a day. Oh, my mom got her dress. It's so pretty! I pooh-poohed every boring mother-of-the-bride type suit she tried on until she finally gave up." Sherry let out her infectious laugh again. "It's red. I mean serious, kick-your-ass red with glittery shoulder straps and a swingy skirt that'll look great on the dance floor. Because, baby, my mom can dance. I'm going with Nick's mom tomorrow to find hers. And she will *not* settle for fade-into-the-background matronly. I can't wait to bend her to my will."

Charmed, Laurel shook her head. "And some brides worry about being upstaged."

Sherry dismissed the idea with a flick of her hand. "Everybody at our wedding's going to look awesome. I'll just make sure I look the most awesome."

"No chance of otherwise."

Sherry turned to Nick. "Any wonder I'm nuts about him?"

"None. How about a glass of champagne?" Laurel offered.

"Can't, but thanks," Nick said. "I'm working tonight."

"The ER frowns on doctors with a champagne buzz." But Sherry wiggled in anticipation. "But I'm not working tonight, or driving, since Nick's dropping me off on his way to the hospital."

Laurel poured a glass. "Coffee?" she asked Nick.

"Perfect."

She poured, then sat back. "I just have to say working with the two of you and your families has been so much fun for all of us. I really think we're looking forward to September as much as you are."

"Then you're looking forward a lot. And then, you've got the next Maguire wedding in December." Sherry did another quick chair dance. "Carter's getting married! He and Mac are . . . Well, they're just exact, aren't they?"

"I've known her all my life and can honestly say, she's never been happier. I'd love him for that alone, but just being Carter is plenty of reason on its own."

"He's really the best of us." Sherry's eyes filled, and she blinked quickly. "Wow, one sip of champagne and I'm all sentimental."

"Then let's talk cake." Laurel tucked her hair behind her ears before she poured herself a cup of tea. "What I've got here are various samples for you to taste. Cake, fillings, frostings. From the size of your guest list, I'd recommend five tiers, graduated sizes. We can mix cakes, fillings for the tiers, or go with one for all. Whatever you want."

"This is where I'm terrible, because I can never make up my mind. By the time we're done here," Sherry warned, "you'll have stopped looking forward to the wedding."

"I don't think so. Why don't I show you the design I have in mind? If you don't like it, we'll try some more until we come up with what works for you."

Laurel didn't sketch a design for every client, but Sherry was family now. She opened her sketchbook, offered it.

"Oh gosh." Sherry stared and blinked again. "The layers—tiers—aren't round. They're—what is it?"

"Hexagons," Nick supplied. "Very cool."

"They're like hat boxes! Like fancy hat boxes with all those flowers between, and all different colors. Like the attendants' dresses. Not white and formal. I figured you'd do white and formal, and it would be beautiful but it wouldn't be . . ."

"Fun?" Laurel prompted.

"Yes! Yes. This is *fun*, but beautiful, too. Special, beautiful fun. You designed this just for us?"

"Only if you like it."

"I *love* it. You love it, right?" Sherry said to Nick.

"I think it's great. And, man, this is a whole lot easier than I expected."

"It's a fondant frosting. I initially thought that might be too formal, but when I thought about tinting each tier to play along with the colors your attendants picked, it felt as if it showed off better, and suited your style."

As Sherry simply beamed over the sketch, Laurel sat back, crossed her legs.

Nick had it right. This was a whole lot easier than expected.

"The flowers push more color so it's bold and cheerful and anything but formal. Emma will work with me so we have the flowers keyed into what she does for you, and we'll arrange more on the cake table. I did the piping in gold—and can change that if you'd like something else. I like the way it played off the colors, and thought we'd use a gold cloth for the cake table—set it all off. But—"

"Stop!" Sherry shot up a hand. "Don't give me more choices. I love this, I love everything about it. It's so us. I mean, you just nailed us with this. Look at our awesome cake." Sherry tapped her flute to Nick's cup.

"Okay, please avert your eyes while I indulge in unprofessional behavior." With a grin, Laurel lifted fisted hands in the air. "Yes!"

Sherry bubbled out another laugh. "Wow, you really get into your work."

"I do. But I have to tell you, I really wanted this design for you—and me. I'm excited about making it. Oh boy." She rubbed her hands together. "All right, done. Now back to professional mode."

"I really like you," Sherry said suddenly. "What I mean to say is I didn't—really don't—know you as well as I do Emma or Parker, and since Mac and Carter got together, I've gotten to know her really well. But the more I get to know you, the more I like you."

"Thanks." Laurel smiled at her. "It's completely mutual. Now let's eat some cake."

"This is going to be my favorite part," Nick said and reached for a sample.

It took a lot longer and entailed a great deal more discussion and deliberation to choose the inside of the cake than it had the outside. Laurel steered them, just a little, and in the end they went for a variety as delightful as the design.

"How will we know which is which?" Sherry asked as they started out. "Like which is the apple cake with the caramel filling or the mocha spice with the apricot or the—"

"I'll take care of that, and the servers will offer a full complement as they pass or serve at the tables. If you want any changes, you only have to let me know."

"Don't say that," Nick warned, and Sherry laughed again.

"He's right. I hate that, but he's right. I'm better off

thinking it's carved in stone. Wait until Mom and Dad get samples." She shook the box Laurel had given her. "Thanks, Laurel, for everything." She grabbed Laurel in a hard hug. "We should run over real quick and say hi to Carter and Mac."

"I don't think they're home." Laurel checked her watch. "She had an outside shoot, and she was going to drop him off at Coffee Talk. He's meeting his friend. Bob?"

"Oh. Well. Next time."

Laurel walked outside to wave them off, and decided it had been one of her most satisfying consults. Not only would she enjoy creating that cake, but they were so happy with it—and each other, she thought, catching the way they leaned into each other for a kiss as they approached their car.

In tune, she thought. That's what they were, even though Sherry's beat was often blindingly quick, and Nick's more deliberate and thoughtful. They complemented each other, *got* each other, and best of all so obviously enjoyed each other.

Love was lovely, she thought, but being in tune? That spoke of the long haul.

She wondered if she and Del were in tune. Maybe you couldn't tell, not for certain, when you were inside the dance. They got each other, she mused, and certainly they enjoyed each other. But did they, could they, find a way to match their different beats?

"I missed them." Parker hurried outside in time to see Nick's car make the turn from top of the drive to road. "Damn it. I got stuck on the phone and—"

"Shock! Disbelief!"

"Oh, shut up. Friday night's bride just found out she doesn't have a bad case of the nerves or a stomach bug."

"Pregnant."

"Yeah, you bet. She's a little panicked, a little thrilled, a little stupefied. They'd planned to start a family within the year, but this is a lot closer to the beginning of their time frame than the end of it."

"How's he feel about it?" Laurel asked, knowing the bride would have told Parker everything.

"He had a moment of speechless *huh?* and now he's excited. And apparently very attentive when she's dealing with morning sickness."

"It says a lot about a guy if he can stick when you're puking."

"He gets the gold star there. She's told her parents, and he's told his, but that's it. She wanted my advice on if she should tell her MOH, the BM, anyone else. And so on. Anyway, I was hoping to get down before Sherry and Nick left. How did it go?"

"I can't think of a single way it could've gone better. It was one of those times when you're done, you just can't imagine being in another business. Or why anyone else would be. In fact, we should go in, pour ourselves a glass from the bottle of champagne I opened for Sherry, and toast ourselves for being so damn good."

"Wish I could, so save me a glass. I've got a meeting in Greenwich. I'll be back in a couple of hours."

"Okay. I'm done for the day. Maybe I'll take a swim, then have a glass of champagne."

"Now you're just trying to make me jealous. It worked."

"Another layer of success to my day."

"Such a bitch."

Amused, Laurel watched Parker walk to her car in her pretty buttercream summer suit and hot pink heels.

She wondered idly if Emma was done for the day. They could take a swim together, laze around with a glass of champagne before Jack got home. She was in entirely too good a mood to be alone.

She considered her own heels—donned for the consult—and the walk down to the guest house. She could go inside and call, but if Emma wasn't ready to quit, she'd have a better time convincing her face-to-face. Better to go in, change her shoes, and wander down to Emma's and seduce her with pool time and champagne.

She went back in, changed to her kitchen shoes, then headed out from the back of the house.

The hot, close summer evening absolutely demanded a swim, she decided. She listened to the hum of bees busy in the garden, took in the scent of grass mown early that morning, of flowers drowsing in the heat. It all felt so lazy and endless.

Tomorrow, she thought, they'd be set up for rehearsal for Friday night's event by this time. And there would be no lazy moments for days.

So she'd savor it now. The blues and greens of summer, the scents and sounds of it, and that feeling that it would go on forever. Maybe she should call Del, she thought, see if he wanted to come over. They could all have a cookout. Fire up the grill, sit outside, and enjoy the summer night and the company of friends.

Later they could make love with the terrace doors open to the sultry air. She still had time to toss a strawberry short-cake together.

Warming to the plan, she came around the house. Mac's studio came into view first—and the hot little sports car parked in front of it. And, an instant later, the hot blonde preparing to open the door Mac wouldn't have bothered to lock.

"Linda!" She called out the name sharply, pleased when the woman jolted. Linda, dressed in a breezy summer sundress and mile high strappy sandals, whirled.

The brief flicker of guilt on Linda's face brought Laurel another shot of dark pleasure.

"Laurel. You scared the *life* out of me." Linda gave her golden, windblown hair a shake so it settled to frame her inarguably lovely face.

Too bad the inside didn't match the packaging, Laurel thought and strode toward her.

"I drove in from New York earlier to meet some friends, and was just popping in to see Mac. It's been *ages*."

She sported a delicate, glowing tan—likely nurtured on

some Italian beach or her new husband's yacht. Her makeup was perfect, which told Laurel she'd taken the time to stop and freshen it up before the "popping in."

"Mac's not home."

"Oh, well, I'll just say hi to Carter." She waved a hand in a practiced way that had the sun exploding off the substantial diamonds in her wedding and engagement rings. "See what my future son-in-law's been up to."

"He's with Mac. There's nobody to pop in on, Linda. You should get back to New York."

"I can spare a few minutes. Don't you look . . . professional," Linda said with a quick eye flick up and down Laurel's suit. "Interesting shoes."

"Parker made it very clear to you, Linda, that you're not welcome here."

"Just a moment's pique." Linda dismissed it with a shrug, but temper sharpened her eyes. "This is my daughter's home."

"That's right, and the last time you were in it, she told you to get out. I haven't heard she's changed her mind on that. I know Parker hasn't."

Linda sniffed. "I'll just wait inside."

"Try to open that door, Linda, and I'll put you on your ass. Guaranteed."

"Who the hell do you think you are? You're nothing. Do you really think you can stand there in your off-the-discount-rack suit and ugly shoes and *threaten* me?"

"I think I just did."

"You're only here because Parker feels obliged to put a roof over your head. You don't have any right to tell me to stay or go."

"Rights won't much enter into it when you're picking yourself up off the ground. Go back to New York and your latest husband. I'll tell Mac you were here. If she wants to see you, she'll let you know."

"You always were cold and hateful, even as a child."

"Okay."

"Small wonder with that tight-assed mother of yours.

She liked to pretend she was better than anyone else, even when your father tried to screw the IRS, and any woman who *wasn't* your mother." Linda smiled. "At least he had some heat in him."

"Do you think it bothers me that you and my father had sex in some sleazy motel room?" But it did, Laurel thought as her stomach muscles squeezed. It did.

"A suite at the Palace," Linda countered. "Before his accounts were frozen, of course."

"Sleazy's sleazy, whatever the venue. You don't matter to me, Linda. You never did. The three of us tolerated you because of Mac. Now we don't have to. So, do you need me to help you to your car, or would you rather get there without limping?"

"Do you think because you've managed to get Delaney Brown into bed it makes you one of them?" This time Linda laughed, a bright trill on the summer air. "Oh, I've heard all about it. Plenty have, and they *love* to talk."

"God, you must be really bored with the new fish already if you're spending any time talking about my sex life."

"You?" Linda's eyes widened in humor, and just enough pity to draw blood. "Nobody's interested in you. Everyone's interested in a Brown, especially when he decides to play with the help. Actually, I admire you for the attempt. Those of us who don't have the name or the finances have to use whatever we can to get them."

"Do we?" Laurel said coolly.

"But a man like Del? Sure he'll sleep with you. Men will sleep with any woman who knows how to play the game— that's something you should've learned from your father. But if you think he'll stick, or actually marry you, that's just sad. A Brown isn't going to marry out of his class, sweetie. And you? You've got no class at all."

"Well, on the last part, I'd say that makes us sisters under the skin, except . . . eww." Her knees shook. She had to lock them to stay steady. "I'm going to ask you one more time to leave, then I'm going to make you. So I really hope you don't listen."

"There's nothing here that interests me." With another toss of her head, Linda strode to her car, then slid behind the wheel. "People are laughing at you." She turned the key, fired the engine. "They'll laugh harder when he's finished with you." She gunned the engine, then drove off with her blond hair flying.

Laurel no longer felt like a swim, or a glass of champagne. She no longer felt like a summer cookout with friends. She stood where she was, making sure Linda kept going, turned onto the road, and sped off in her flashy car.

Her head ached now, and in her belly swam a vague sickness. She'd lie down, sleep it off, she told herself. Nothing that woman said meant anything.

Goddamn it.

Realizing she was very close to tears, she struggled to bear down and started back to the house. She had gone no more than a dozen steps when Emma hailed her. And Laurel squeezed her eyes tight, made herself breathe in hopes that the threat of tears wouldn't show.

"God, it's hot! I love it." Emma threw out her arms. "Summer is my friend. I thought I'd never get done so I could take a break out— What's wrong?" The minute she saw Laurel's face, Emma's smile faded. She quickened her pace, and reached out to take Laurel's hand. "What's the matter?"

"Nothing. Just a headache. I was just going in to take something and lie down until it's gone."

"Uh-uh." Eyes dark with concern, Emma took a long study. "I know that face. Not just a headache. You're upset."

"I'm upset I have a headache."

Emma merely shifted until her arm looped around Laurel's waist. "Then we'll walk over to the house together, and I'll badger you until you tell me what happened to give you a headache."

"For God's sake, Emma, everybody gets headaches. That's why they make headache pills. Go fuss over your flowers instead of me. It's irritating."

"As if that's going to work." Ignoring Laurel's bad-tempered shrug, Emma kept her arm in place and matched Laurel's pace. "Did you have a fight with Del?"

"No. And my moods, aches, days, nights, my *life* doesn't revolve exclusively around Delaney Brown."

"Um-hmm, something or someone else then. You might as well tell me. You know I won't leave you alone until you do. Don't make me have to rough you up to get it out of you."

Laurel nearly laughed, but sighed instead. When Emma thought a friend was hurting, she'd stick like glue. "I just had a run-in with Scary Linda, that's all. She'd give anyone a headache."

"She was here?" Emma stopped in her tracks, looked over toward Mac's studio. "Mac and Carter are gone, right?"

"Yeah. When I spotted Linda it didn't look like that was going to stop her from walking right in."

"It wouldn't. She actually had the nerve to come here after Parker told her, flat-out, not to? Did Parker—?"

"Parker's at a meeting."

"Oh. So just you. I wish I'd come out before, then she'd know the true wrath of Emmaline."

Which, when roused, Laurel thought, was considerable— if only because it was rare. "I got rid of her."

"Yeah, but it obviously upset you. You're going to sit out on the terrace in the shade while I get you some aspirin and a cold drink. Then you're going to tell me exactly what happened."

She could argue, but not only would it be useless, it would make the entire business more important than it was. Or should be.

"I want the sun."

"Fine, you'll sit in the sun. Crap, is the crew still here?"

"No, they left a while ago."

"Good, then it'll be quiet. I didn't appreciate enough how Mac and Carter dealt with the whole 'life in a construction zone' thing until they started work on my place, and your mudroom. Former mudroom. Here, sit down."

Laurel did what she was told as Emma hurried into the

house. At least letting Emma fuss with aspirin and drinks would give Laurel time to smooth herself out. She told herself to consider the source, reminded herself that Linda loved creating upheaval and was particularly skilled at creating it when thwarted.

It didn't help.

She sat and brooded until Emma came out with a pretty tray of iced tea and cookies.

"I raided your supply," Emma said. "Cookies are called for." She passed Laurel the bottle of aspirin. "Take two, then spill it."

"I had a really good consult. Sherry and Nick."

"They're so cute together."

"And so damn happy. They really put me in a terrific mood. I was actually walking down to your place, to see if you wanted to take a swim and tap into the champagne I'd opened for the consult when I saw Linda about to walk into Mac's."

"There goes the terrific mood—and my champagne."

"Yeah. She started off the way she usually does. Big smile, all innocence. Just popping in since she'd come in to see some friends." Laurel picked up a cookie, nibbling a little as she continued the story.

"You told her you'd knock her on her ass?" Emma interrupted, with relish. "Oh, I wish I'd been there. I really do. What did she say?"

"Basically, that I had no say around here, how I'm here on Parker's sufferance—"

"What bullshit."

"She jabbed me about my parents. I'm hard and cold like my mother, and that's why my cheating father slept with her—among others."

"Oh, honey."

"I always figured he'd probably had a spin with Linda— basically every cheating husband in the county has— but . . ."

"It hurts," Emma murmured.

"I don't know. I don't know if it hurts. I think it just

pisses me off, and disappoints me. Which is stupid, considering."

"But it's Linda."

"Yeah." There was nothing more precious than a friend who understood exactly. "I shrugged it off. No way was she going to get a rise out of me on that score. So, I had to give it back to her, and told her to get gone again, or I'd make her."

"Good for you."

"Then she hit me with Del."

"What do you mean?"

"How everyone's talking about me and Del, how they're laughing at me, how he'd never be serious about someone like me. I'm not in his class—the Brown class."

"Vicious bitch." Emma's hand fisted. "I'd like to punch her. You are *not* going to tell me you bought one word of that, or I'll have to punch *you*."

"Now I'm terrified." Laurel sighed again. "It's not a matter of buying it, Emma. I know the kind of person she is, and it's just how she thinks. And I know even if she didn't think it, she'd say it to slap at me. But the fact is . . . The fact is, he's Delaney Brown, so people are talking, and speculating, and some of them probably are getting a laugh out of it."

"So what if they are?"

"I know, and I tell myself the same." She hated, *hated* that the tears burned again, and this time filled, this time spilled. "Most of the time I feel just that way. So what? But other times . . ."

"It's insulting to Del as much as you."

"Maybe. We've never really talked about if we're serious, or if we're looking to make what we have long-term. It's really just about the moment. Most of the time I'm good with that, fine with it, because the moments are really good. But other times . . ."

"Do you think he's with you just because you're available?"

"No." She brushed impatiently at the tears. "No, of course I don't."

"Do you think it's just about the sex for him?"

"No."

"Or that he's given a single thought to the fact that your last name doesn't have the same cachet as his?"

Laurel shook her head. "Emma, I know when I'm being stupid, but even knowing it doesn't always stop someone from being stupid. I wish I didn't have this vulnerable spot, and God knows I wish I hadn't let Linda poke her sharp stick right into it. But it's there."

"We've all got them." Emma covered Laurel's hand with hers. "Especially when we love somebody. That's why we need girlfriends."

"She made me cry. How weak is that? I would've gone up to my room and blubbered over it if you hadn't stopped me. When I think of how frustrated I'd get with Mac when she'd let Linda push her around emotionally." She blew out a breath.

"The woman's poison."

"Damn right, she is. Well, at least I kicked her off the estate."

"It's my turn next time. You, Parker, and Mac have all had yours. I want a shot."

"Only fair. Thanks, Emma."

"Feeling better?"

"Yeah, I feel better."

"Let's go take that swim."

"Okay." Laurel nodded briskly. "Okay, let's go drown my pity party."

LATER, STEADIER, SHE SETTLED DOWN IN HER OFFICE. HER paper-work could use some attention, she decided, and since she had some time on her hands, it might as well get it.

She took care of her filing, invoicing, bills, with Bon Jovi for company. Then shifted over to check out some of her suppliers' websites.

She needed more pastry bags, cake boxes, pastry boxes, maybe some new transfer sheets. Liners, she thought, and paper doilies. After dealing with the necessities, she started to study tools and display items she really didn't need—but might be fun to play with.

Icing at Vows' budget could handle a few toys, she decided. Plus she could use some new crimpers, some new chocolate molds, and God, she really wanted that double guitar cutter.

Her practical side made her sit back, stew over the price. But when they finished with her new storage area, she'd have room for the bigger cutter. It would be practical, really. She'd be able to cut twice as many petit fours, chocolates, ganaches as she could now. And it had four frames.

She could put the one she had now, the one she'd bought used, on eBay.

Hell with it. She deserved it. But even as she clicked Add To Cart, she jumped in guilt when Mac said her name.

"God, don't sneak up on me when I'm spending money I really don't need to spend."

"On what? Oh." Mac shrugged when she saw the bakery supply site. "Tools, we all need them. Listen, Laurel . . ."

"Emma told you." Laurel heaved out a breath. "You'd better not be here to apologize for Linda."

"I'm allowed to be sorry." Mac stuffed her hands in her pockets. "My first reaction was to call her and ream her, but that only gives her attention. Which is what she wants most next to money. So I'm going to ignore it, and that way she gets nothing. Which will piss her off. A lot."

"Good."

"Yeah, but since I'm going to ignore it, I have to be sorry—and you have to let me."

"Okay, be sorry." Deliberately Laurel looked at her watch, counted to ten. "Now, be finished being sorry."

"All right. You know what I wish? I wish I didn't have to invite her to the wedding. But I do."

"We'll handle it."

"I know. Maybe a miracle will happen and she'll behave

herself. I know," Mac added with a half laugh when Laurel cast her eyes to the ceiling. "But as a bride I'm allowed the fantasy."

"She'll never understand you, or us. That's her loss."

"It really is." Leaning down, Mac kissed the top of Laurel's head. "I'll see you later."

Whatever crumbs of self-pity remained were swept away as Mac left.

All done with it, Laurel thought, and bought herself a brand-new double guitar cutter.

CHAPTER SIXTEEN

$\mathcal{L}$AUREL WASN'T SURE WHERE THE IMPULSE CAME FROM, but she followed it to Del's law offices. Though she rarely visited there, for personal or legal reasons, she knew the setup.

The front door of the dignified old town house opened, as she deemed it should, to a dignified foyer. That angled into a pretty reception area, with leafy plants in copper pots, antique tables, generous chairs, muted colors warm with the flow of light.

Offices maintained privacy for clients behind thick old doors, lovingly restored, and time-faded rugs highlighted the deep tones of the wide-planked floors.

Del, she knew, appreciated the mix of the dignified and the warmly casual.

She stepped out of the sweltering heat into the cool where Annie, a woman she'd gone to school with, manned the desk and its computer.

Annie shifted, and her professional smile spread to a friendly grin. "Laurel, hi! How are you? Haven't seen you in months."

"They keep me chained to the oven. Hey, you cut your hair. I love it."

Annie tried out a little head toss. "Sassy?"

"Absolutely."

"And best, it takes about two minutes in the morning."

"So, how are you otherwise?"

"I'm great. We should have a drink sometime soon, and catch up."

"I'd like that. I brought something for Del." She lifted the bakery box she carried.

"If it's anything like the cake you made for Dara, I just gained five pounds looking at the box. He's with a client. I can just—"

"Don't interrupt him," Laurel said. "I'll leave it with you."

"I don't know if I can be trusted."

With a laugh, Laurel set the box on the desk. "There's enough to share. I had to come into town, so I just brought these by before I—"

"Hold that thought," Annie told her as her phone rang. "Good morning, Brown and Associates."

Laurel wandered away while Annie handled the call, taking a casual study of the art on the walls. She knew they were originals, and from area artists. The Browns had always been serious patrons of the arts, and involved in local interests.

It occurred to her she'd never given much thought to how Del had set up his practice. After his parents died, she remembered now, and shortly before they'd formed Vows. They'd probably been among his first clients, now that she thought of it.

She'd been working at the Willows, keeping her own finances afloat while Vows took its first events. She'd been too busy, she supposed, and too damn tired to think about how Del must have been juggling his own fledgling practice, the details of his parents' estates, the legalities of Vows as a business and a partnership.

They'd all been scrambling like mad with plans, obligations, test runs, part-time work to fill the coffers. But Del had never seemed rushed, had he? she asked herself.

The Brown cool, she supposed. As well as that seemingly innate Brown confidence that whatever they outlined they'd make work.

They'd grieved together, she remembered. Hard, hard times. But the grief and the hard had acted as another kind of glue, fusing them together.

She'd moved in with Parker, Laurel thought, and had never really, not seriously, looked back. And Del had always been there, handling details that had whizzed right by her. She'd understood it, she thought now, but had she given him credit for it?

She glanced over as someone came in the door. The young couple held hands, looked happy. Looked familiar, Laurel realized.

"Cassie?" She'd made them her Bridal Lace cake in the spring. "Hi. And . . ." Shit, what was the groom's name?

"Laurel? Hello!" Cassie held out a friendly hand. "It's wonderful to see you. Zack and I were just showing our wedding pictures to some friends the other night, and talking about how we're looking forward to Fran and Michael's wedding in a couple months at your place. I can't wait to see what you do for them."

If she'd been Parker, she'd remember precisely who Fran and Michael were, and all the details of the wedding confirmed so far.

Since she wasn't Parker, Laurel just smiled. "I hope they're as happy as you two look."

"I don't know if they could be, because we're flying."

"About to buy our first house," Zack told her.

"Congratulations."

"It's wonderful and scary, and oh, Dara. Everyone's right on time."

Laurel supposed Annie had given Dara the signal, and turned to say her hellos.

"Oh, that cake." With a laugh, Dara gave Laurel a quick hug. "It was so cute —and so delicious."

"How's the baby?"

"Wonderful. I've got several hundred baby pictures I could show you if you don't make a quick escape."

"I'd love to see baby pictures," Cassie said. "I love babies," she added with a wistful look at Zack.

"House first, then baby."

"I can help you with the first part. Come right on back." Dara gave Laurel a wink, then led the clients off.

Laurel heard Annie's phone ring again—busy place—and decided she'd just slip out. Even as she had the thought, she heard Del's voice.

"Try not to worry. You've done everything right, and I'm going to do everything I can to get this resolved quickly."

"I'm so grateful. Mr. Brown, I don't know what I'd do without your help. It's all so . . ." The woman's voice broke.

Though Laurel stepped back, she caught a glimpse of Del and his client, and the way Del put an arm around the woman's shoulders as she struggled with tears.

"I'm sorry. I thought I got all that out in your office."

"Don't be sorry. I want you to go home and try to put this out of your mind."

His hand rubbed up and down the woman's arm. Laurel had seen him use that gesture of comfort and support—or felt it herself—countless times.

"Focus on your family, Carolyn, and leave all this to me. I'll be in touch soon. I promise."

"All right. And thank you, thank you again for everything."

"Just remember what I told you." As he walked his client to the door, he spotted Laurel. Surprise crossed his face briefly, before he turned his attention back to the woman he led out. He murmured something that had the client blinking at tears again before she nodded, and left.

"Well, hi," he said to Laurel.

"I'm so in the way. Sorry. I just dropped off something for you, then a couple people came in for Dara, and I knew them, so . . ."

"Zack and Cassie Reinquist. You did their wedding."

"God, you and Parker have spreadsheets for brains. It's scary. Anyway, I'll clear the field so you can—"

"Come on back. I've got a few minutes before my next appointment. What did you bring me?"

"I'll get it." She walked back to pick up the bakery box.

"Sorry," Annie murmured, tipping the phone away from her mouth. "Floodgates."

Laurel made a "don't worry about it" gesture, and took the box with her.

"You brought me a cake?"

"No." She walked back to his office with him, where the sunlight streamed through tall windows, where more antiques gleamed—and the desk she knew had been his father's, and his father's before—held prominence.

Laurel set the box down, opened the top. "I brought you cupcakes."

"You brought me cupcakes." Obviously puzzled, he looked in the box at the dozen cheerfully iced cakes. "They look good."

"They're happy food."

She studied his face. Just as Emma had claimed about hers, Laurel knew that face. "You look like you could use some happy."

"Do I? Well." He bent to give her an absent kiss. "That makes me happy. How about some coffee to go with the cupcakes?"

She hadn't intended to stay—her own schedule was so damn tight as it was. But, oh, he really did look like he needed a little happy. "Sure. Your client looked pretty distressed," she began as he walked over to the coffee machine on the Hepplewhite buffet. "You probably can't talk about it."

"In general terms. Her mother died recently after a long, difficult illness."

"I'm sorry."

"She was the primary caregiver, and as her mother's condition required more—and it was important to them both that her mother die at home—she took an extended leave of absence from her job so she could care for her mother full-time."

"It takes a lot of love and dedication to do that."

"Yes, it does. She has a brother in California. He came in a few times, helped out some. She has a sister in Oyster Bay—who was apparently too busy to visit or help more than a couple times a month, if that."

He handed Laurel her coffee, leaned back against his desk. He took out one of the cupcakes, studied it.

"Not everyone has a lot of love and dedication."

"No, not everyone," he murmured. "There was insurance, of course, but it doesn't cover everything. What it didn't my client paid for out of pocket until her mother found out, and insisted on putting her daughter's name on her personal checking account."

"Which takes love, and trust."

"Yes." He smiled a little. "It does."

"It sounds like, even though it had to be a terrible thing to go through, they had something special. Your client and her mother."

"Yes, you're right. The leave of absence was a financial burden, but my client and her family dealt with it. Her husband and kids pitched in when they could. Do you know what it must be like to care for a dying parent, one who at the end is essentially bedridden, incontinent, who requires special food, constant care?"

Not just sad, she realized. Angry. Very angry. "I can only imagine. It must be a terrible strain, physically, emotionally."

"Two years, with the last six months all but around the clock. She bathed her, changed her, did her laundry, fed her, took care of her finances, cleaned her house, sat with her, read to her. Her mother changed her will, left the house, its contents—but for some specifics—and the bulk of her estate to her daughter. Now that she's gone, now that the client and her brother from California made all the funeral arrangements, the sister's contesting the will. She's accusing my client of unduly influencing their mother in her favor. She's livid, and has privately accused her of stealing money, jewelry, household items, turning their dying mother against her."

When Laurel said nothing, Del set his own coffee aside. "Initially my client wanted to give it to her, just let her have whatever she wanted. Between the grief and the stress, she didn't think she could handle any more. But her husband and—to his credit—the brother wouldn't have it."

"So they came to you."

"The sister hired a lawyer who fits her like a fucking glove. I'm going to kick their asses."

"My money's on you."

"The sister had a chance. She knew her mother was dying, that there was a finite time left. But she didn't use it to be with her, to say good-bye, to say all the things most people think they have endless time to say. Now she wants her cut, and she's willing to destroy her relationship, such as it is, with her siblings. Add to her sister's grief. For what? For money. I don't understand how . . . Sorry."

"Don't be. It occurs to me I've never thought very much about what you do. I just figured lawyer stuff."

He managed a smile. "I do lawyer stuff. This is lawyer stuff."

"No, I mean, just the lawyer stuff that pretty much annoys the rest of the world. Sign this, file that—and the this and that is so complicated and written in such ridiculous language it's more annoying."

"We lawyer types enjoy our 'whereases.' "

"With or without the stupid 'whereases,' it's about people. Your client's still going to grieve, but her stress is lightened because she knows you're behind her. It matters a lot what you do, and I'd never thought about it."

She lifted her hand to touch his face. "Eat a cupcake."

To please her, she imagined, he took a bite. And this time when he smiled, it reached his eyes. "It's good. It's happy. This one's gotten under my skin. I don't think I realized how much until you were here to dump on."

"Is it what you were working on last night?"

"Primarily."

"And why you're tired today. You hardly ever look tired. I could come over tonight, fix you a meal."

"Don't you have a rehearsal tonight, and an event tomorrow?"

"I can shuffle things around tonight. Tomorrow's tomorrow."

"I should look tired more often. How about I come to you? I've been buried here or at home the last couple of days. Change of scene wouldn't hurt. Neither would being with you. I've missed being with you."

Her heart melted, and she went into his arms for a kiss that was anything but absent. When he rested his cheek on the top of her head, his phone beeped. "Next client," he murmured.

"I'm clearing out. Share the cupcakes."

"Maybe."

"If you eat the dozen, you'll be sick—and entirely too full for that meal. Though you might want to remember I'm a better baker than I am a cook."

"I can pick up a pizza," he called out, and heard her laugh as she walked away.

He took another moment with his coffee and his cupcake, and thoughts of her. He hadn't meant to say all that about the client, and her situation. Hadn't realized, really, how angry he was about that situation. And the client didn't pay him to be angry, but to represent her interests.

Or would pay him, once he'd kicked her sister's lawyer's ass. He'd waived a retainer. He could afford it, and he simply couldn't justify taking one from a woman who'd dealt with all she'd dealt with.

But the main thing had been he hadn't understood just how much it helped to have someone who'd listen to him spew, who'd understand why this particular case hit home with him.

He didn't have to explain to Laurel. She just knew.

An invaluable gift, he mused.

And there'd been something about the way she'd touched his face—just that simple, understanding gesture, that had something inside him shifting. He wasn't sure what it was, what it meant, or what it meant that every time he looked at her now he saw something new, something *else*.

How could you know someone all your life, and still discover something new?

He'd have to think about it, he told himself. Setting the bakery box with its happy food beside his coffeemaker, he walked out to meet his next client.

𝒮HE SHOULD'VE LET HIM BRING PIZZA, LAUREL THOUGHT as she raced around the main kitchen to set up. She still had cakes and other desserts to complete in her kitchen, and the construction noise had picked today to peak.

She couldn't possibly make dinner there.

"I could put it together for you," Mrs. Grady commented.

"And that would be cheating. I can hear what you're not saying."

"You're hearing what you think I'm not saying when what I'm actually not saying is it'd be cheating if you pretended you made dinner."

Laurel paused a moment, actively *yearned* to take that route. She could just tell Del Mrs. G had done the cooking as she'd been too busy to do it herself. He wouldn't care, but . . .

"I said I'd do it. Plus you're going out with your friends tonight." She blew out a breath. "So, field green salad with a nice balsamic vinaigrette, seafood linguine, and the bread. It's fairly simple, right?"

"Simple enough. You're in a dither over it. And him."

"It's food. I know how I am about it, but I can't be otherwise. It has to be perfect, and that includes presentation." Absently, she adjusted the clip holding up her hair. "You know, Mrs. G, if I ever have kids, I'll probably take twenty minutes to perfect the presentation of a PB and J. They'll all need therapy."

"I think you'll do well enough on that score."

"I never really thought about it. Having kids, I mean." She got out the field greens, the grape tomatoes, the carrots she intended to straw, to wash, dry, and chill before she prepared the salad. "There's always been so much to do right now, that I haven't thought much about someday."

"And now you are?" Mrs. G began to dry the greens Laurel washed.

"I guess it's the sort of thing that keeps passing through my mind. Maybe it's a biological clock thing."

"Maybe it's a being in love thing."

"Maybe. But two people have to be in love and thinking about someday. I saw this couple today who'd gotten married here last spring." She glanced out the window as she worked, toward the green and the blue of summer. "They were in Del's office to do some sort of legal stuff for their first house. Dara was handling it, and the baby came up. The bride—well, wife—got sort of dreamy-eyed over the thought of a baby, and he said: House first, baby later . . . or something like that. Which is absolutely sensible."

"Babies don't always come when it's sensible."

"Yeah, tomorrow's bride found that one out. But I just mean it makes sense to plan the steps, to take them in logical order. To be patient."

"Running low on it." Mrs. Grady gave Laurel's back a quick rub.

"Sometimes, a little anyway. I don't need all the fuss, all the details, all the trimmings. All, essentially, that we do here. Emma does, and Parker will, and God knows Mac's gotten into it."

"She has, and I think it's been a surprise to her."

"But I don't. I don't need a ring or a license, or a spectacular white dress. It's not marriage so much, or at all really, that matters. It's the promise. It's the knowing someone wants me to be part of his life. Someone loves me, that I'm the one for him. That's not just enough, it's everything."

"Who do you think Del would want to be with tonight other than you?"

Laurel shrugged. "I don't know. I do know he'll be happy to be with me. That may not be everything, but it's enough." The timer she'd set went off. "Crap. I've got to get back to my kitchen. Don't cook anything."

"I'll act as sous chef and no more. I'll just finish washing these, and get them dried and put away for you. That wouldn't be cheating."

"You're right. Thanks."

As Laurel raced away to the next task, Mrs. Grady wondered why the girl didn't consider maybe Del wanted some of that everything, too.

"Love," she murmured as she washed. "Nobody inside it knows how the hell to handle it."

NATURALLY, THE ONE TIME, THE *ONE* TIME, LAUREL NEEDED a rehearsal to run smoothly, move quickly, it turned into a circus showcasing a weepy bride—hormones, probably—a MOG woozy in the heat, and a groomsman woozy from a little too much prerehearsal celebration. Added to it were the flower girl and ring bearer—brother and sister—who picked the event to display their sibling loathing.

With two kids running and screaming, the bride indulging in a crying jag in her mother's arms, and the MOG fanning herself in the shade, Laurel couldn't duck out as she'd planned.

Parker handled it—they all handled it, but Parker seemed to be everywhere at once. Urging water on the MOG, iced coffee on the groomsman, herding the kids, and distracting the worried groom.

The MOH—and the mother of the battling siblings—did her best to restore order. But, Laurel thought as she passed out iced tea, the woman was outnumbered.

"Where's the father?" she muttered to Emma.

"Business trip. Plane was delayed. He's on his way. I'm going to take the girl, see if I can interest her in making up a quick little nosegay. Maybe you could take the boy—"

"Carter's the teacher. Carter should do it."

"He's got his hands full with the not-quite-drunk grooms-man. I think the MOH could use a little break, and maybe she can help the MOB pull the bride together. Mac and Parker can handle the rest."

"Okay, fine." Leaving Emma to smooth it over with the mother, Laurel set the iced tea and glasses on the table, then approached the boy. "Come with me."

"Why?"

"Because."

It seemed to be an answer he understood, though his brow knit in mutinous lines. He trudged with her, shooting looks that promised revenge at his little sister.

"I don't wanna wear a tuxshedo."

"Me, either."

He snorted, derisively. "Girls don't wear tuxshedos."

"They can if they want." Laurel glanced down at him. About five, she figured, and pretty cute. Or he would be if he wasn't overtired, wound up, and sulking. "But tomorrow all the men in the wedding party get to wear them. Wait. Maybe you're not old enough to wear one."

"I am, too!" Insult radiated. "I'm five."

"Whew. That's a relief," she said as she walked him down toward the pond. "Because it would really mess everything up if we had to find another ring bearer by tomorrow. They can't get married without the rings."

"Why?"

"They just can't. So if we had to find somebody else, it would really be hard. You've got a really important job."

"More than Tissy?"

Tissy, Laurel interpreted, was the little sister. "Her job's really important, too. She has a girl job, but you have a guy job. She doesn't get to wear a tuxedo."

"Not even if she wants to?"

"Nope, not even. Check it out," she told him, and pointed at the lily pads. Near the edge one of them served as a float for a fat green frog.

When Del arrived he spotted her down at the pond, near the sweeping fronds of the willow, with her hand in the hand of a little boy with hair as bright and sunny as her own.

It gave him a quick start, a little jump in the belly. He'd seen her with kids before, he reminded himself. Weddings usually included a few. But . . . There was something odd, maybe a little dreamy, about the picture they made, beside the pond, too far away for him to clearly see their faces. Just that sun-washed hair, and the joined hands.

As he watched they started back, the boy looking up at her, Laurel looking down at him.

"Hey, Del."

He pulled himself out of that odd, dreamy picture and turned to Carter. "Hi. How's it going?"

"Okay now, I'd say. Ten minutes ago, it was touch and go. We're about to get started. Again."

"One of those."

"Oh yeah. I think Laurel . . . There she is."

Laurel stopped by a woman with a little girl on her hip, shared a quick word, an easy laugh with her. Then bent to the boy and murmured in his ear. He grinned as if she'd promised him a lifetime supply of cookies.

Del walked over to meet her halfway. "Make a new friend?"

"Looks like. We're running behind."

"So I hear."

"Parker'll get it back on track," she said even as Parker called for everyone to take their places.

Del stepped out of the way with Carter as Parker called out instructions, and the other three women guided and aligned.

It looked smooth as silk to him, with everyone smiling. He saw the boy and Laurel exchange a quick grin as he walked toward the pergola.

Moments later, she signaled to Del and slipped into the house.

CHAPTER SEVENTEEN

$\mathcal{H}$E FOUND HER IN THE MAIN KITCHEN, MOVING FAST.

"I'm a little behind," she began. "It's not like a Parker schedule, but—"

He stopped her by getting in her way, moving in, drawing her into a long, warm, indulgent kiss. And when he felt her go under, just a little, just enough, he eased back.

"Hi."

"Well, hi. Was I saying something before all my brain cells went gooey?"

"Something about schedules."

"Oh, yeah. That. Okay. I have a nice sauvignon blanc chilling. Why don't you open it so we can try it out while I get things going."

"I like when my main chore is opening the wine. What was the problem with the rehearsal?" he asked as he moved to oblige.

"What wasn't, is more like it." She shot him a look over her shoulder with those bluebell eyes. "The bride learned just this week she's pregnant."

"Uh-oh."

"They're good with it. In fact, they've turned the unexpected expecting into a surprise instead of a problem."

"That's good for everybody."

"Yeah, but it's added some stress—and she's more emotional and a whole lot tired. She's crying, then the two kids are trying to murder each other, the MOG worked herself up, plus the heat got to her. Probably because she was worked up. Add in a groomsman who started celebrating a bit early. Just another day on the job."

Laurel put water on for the pasta, added olive oil to a skillet, then moved past Del to retrieve the salad makings she'd prepared with Mrs. Grady's help. "It's a good thing I did most of this ahead, because I'd hoped to duck out of the rehearsal, but no dice. Thanks," she added when he handed her a glass.

After sipping it, she began to peel and dice garlic.

"I should feel guilty about you cooking after you've put in a full day. Want me to chop something? I'm a reasonably experienced chopper."

"No, we're under control."

Content to do nothing, he watched her add the garlic and some red pepper flakes to the oil. "This is new."

"Hmm?"

"Seeing you cook. This kind of cooking, that is."

"Oh, I dip my hand in every once in a while. I picked up some of it from Mrs. G, and some from working in restaurants. It's an interesting change of pace. When it works."

"You always look in charge in the kitchen. That was supposed to be a compliment," he said when she frowned at him.

"I guess it is, as long as it doesn't put me in the same camp as Julio."

"Completely different camp. A different camp in a different country."

She added some butter to the oil, got out the shrimp. "Good. Because I don't often have—or want—company when I'm in the kitchen, but I rarely throw knives." She added the shrimp to the oil, then pasta to the boiling water.

"Do you just keep everything that goes in, when and how, in your head?"

"Sometimes. Do you want a lesson?"

"I absolutely don't. Real men grill."

She laughed, and with spoon in one hand, pasta fork in the other, stirred skillet and pot at the same time. "Hand me the wine, will you?"

"Lush." But he held it out.

She set down the pasta fork, then dumped a good cup of wine on the shrimp. Del visibly winced.

"It's really good wine."

"So it's really good wine for cooking, too."

"No question." Her hands, he thought, were so quick, so competent. Had he ever noticed that before? "What are we having?"

"For the main? Seafood linguini." She paused, took a sip from her glass. "Field green salad, some herb bread I baked for dipping. Vanilla bean crème brûlée for dessert."

He lowered his glass to stare at her—his Laurel, with her hair clipped up as always when she worked, her quick, competent hands busy. "You're kidding."

"I know you're partial to crème brûlée." She lifted one shoulder in an easy shrug as the kitchen filled with scent. "If I'm going to cook, I might as well cook what you like."

It occurred to him he should have brought her flowers or wine or . . . something. And realized it hadn't occurred to him because he was so used to coming here, coming home, to seeing her in his home.

Next time he wouldn't forget.

When the wine came to a boil, she lowered the heat, covered it. Then tested the pasta, deemed it done, drained it.

She got a dish of olives out of the fridge. "To hold you off," she said, then turned her attention to the salad.

"You know what I said about being in charge when you're in the kitchen?"

"Uh-huh."

"Something about being in charge makes you just stunning."

She looked up, blinked in such obvious surprise he regretted not thinking of flowers even more.

"You're already getting crème brûlée," she managed.

"You're beautiful. You've always been beautiful." Had he never told her that before, in just that way? "Cooking just spotlights it, the way dancing spotlights a dancer, or a sport spotlights an athlete. It just never struck me until now, I think because I've gotten used to seeing you at some stage or other of baking. It's a kind of taking for granted. I need to be careful not to do that with you."

"We don't have to be careful with each other."

"I think we do. Even more because we're so used to each other."

Maybe taking care was more accurate, he thought. Wasn't she doing just that now? Taking care by making him a meal she knew he'd like particularly, and doing it because she knew he'd had a difficult day? This *newness* between them wasn't just about dating or sex. Or it shouldn't be.

He didn't know, couldn't know, where they were going, but he could start paying more attention to how they got there.

"Do you want me to set the table?" he asked her.

"It's done." The fact that she was a little flustered, and it showed, delighted him. "In the dining room. I thought, since—"

"That's nice. Parker?"

"Is doing what any good friend does and making herself scarce tonight."

"Very nice."

She walked over, checked her skillet, then added more butter, some scallops before briskly zesting a lemon into the mix.

"That smells amazing."

"Not bad." She added some fresh herbs, salt, pepper, stirred. "Couple minutes to cook through, then we'll let it sit for a few more. Fairly easy-peasy."

"Not from where I'm standing."

"I probably couldn't write a brief—especially since I'm

not sure exactly what one is. I guess we both picked careers with job security." Her eyes met his as she tossed the salad. "People are always going to need to eat, and they're always going to need lawyers."

"Whether they want to or not on the lawyer front."

She laughed. "I didn't say that." She took a lighter out of a drawer. "For the candles," she told him. "You can take the salad in, and take care of that."

She'd fussed, he noted, when he carried the bowl into the dining room. She probably didn't think of it that way, he mused as he studied the pretty plates, the candles in slim holders, the bright-faced sunflowers in a blue glass vase. The women in his life had a talent and a vocation, he supposed, for making things pretty and comfortable, for seeing to tiny details that always melded together into a perfect picture.

That made him a lucky man.

Very lucky, he thought moments later when they sat with the salad, the warmed bread, the wine.

"When we get to the beach—" He broke off when she groaned. "What?"

"Sorry, I always have a little orgasm when I think of vacation."

"Really?" Amused he watched her eyes sparkle as she took a bite of salad. "I'll mention it more often. Anyway, when we're there, I'm going to grill you such a steak. In fact, my pact now is for the men to put on a serious meal— just the guys. All you have to do is eat."

"I'm in. I actually have a calendar going in my office where I mark off the days until. Like I did when I was a kid for the end of the school year. I feel like that. Like a kid coming up on summer."

"Most kids don't get orgasms when they think of summer vacation. Not in my experience anyway."

"You liked school more than I did." When he laughed, she sipped her wine. "I like my work a lot more than I did school, and still, I'm really ready to step away from it for a couple weeks. I want to sleep until the sun's actually up, and stretch out and read a book without thinking I really should be doing something else. No suit, no heels, no meetings. How about you?"

"The last part's a match—except for the heels. Not having to make a decision about more than whether to have a beer or a nap. That'll be good."

"Naps." She sighed and closed her eyes.

"Another orgasm?"

"No, just a quiet little tingle. I can't wait. The rest of us were so surprised—and happy—when Parker told us the two of you bought the place. Is it wonderful?"

"I like it. She's taken it on faith, as she's never seen it except in pictures. It's a good investment, especially considering the economy right now. We got a good deal."

"That's the lawyer speaking. Is it wonderful?"

"You can hear the ocean from the bedrooms, see it from every window that faces oceanside. There's a pond and a wonderful sense of seclusion."

"Okay, no more. I can't take it." She shivered, then rose to remove the salad plates. "Be right back."

"I can—"

"No, I'll take care of it. In charge, remember?"

He topped off her wine, and had sat back with his own when she came in with the main. She'd garnished the pasta with sprigs of rosemary and basil.

"Laurel, that looks seriously amazing."

"Never underestimate the power of presentation." She served him, then herself.

"Wow," he said after the first bite. "It's great. And impossible to feel guilty now. Maybe a little since Parker's missing out."

"I left her a serving in the kitchen. She's sneaking down for it."

"Guilt assuaged." He took another bite. "Of course, now you've done it, and I'm going to want to do this more often."

"We might be able to work a deal, if you fire up the grill now and then."

"Works for me."

"You know, I nearly called you last night. I was in the mood for a cookout, then I had the run-in with Linda and—"

"What run-in?"

"Oh, Parker had just left for a meeting, and I was done for the day and walking down to Emma's to see if she wanted a swim. And there's Linda at Mac's door. Going in, too, even though they weren't home. Pissed me off."

His eyes narrowed, heated. "Parker told her not to come here again."

"Yeah, and Linda listens so well. Anyway, after an ugly scene I ran her off."

"What kind of a scene?" He saw her start to speak, then catch herself and shrug.

"A Linda sort of scene. I won, which is the important thing."

"What did she say to you?"

"That I didn't have the authority to run her off, that sort of thing. I'm always amazed someone like her could've had any part in creating someone like Mac. I don't know if she'll ever understand that Mac's not going to drop everything and do her bidding anymore."

She wasn't changing the subject so much as shifting it, Del thought. He laid a hand over hers as if to hold her in place. "She upset you."

"Sure, she's Linda. She upsets just by existing. Hey, can we get a restraining order? On the basis that she's a major pain in the ass?"

"Why didn't you call me?"

"For what? I got her gone."

"Not before she upset you."

"Del, if I called you every time somebody upset me, we'd never be off the phone. She went, and Emma and I took a swim. She did spoil my mood for a cookout though. Let's not let her spoil the linguine."

"She couldn't. But if she comes back, I want to know about it."

"Fine."

"No, promise me. I'll deal with her if she comes back here, but I have to know about it to deal with her."

"No problem. I promise. You really can't get a restraining order just because she's a pain in the ass?"

"There are other ways to deal with Linda. Mac didn't want me to before. Things are different now."

"Legal question? If, since she was technically trespassing, I'd knocked her on her ass, could she have me charged with assault?"

He grinned because she so obviously wanted him to. "Gray area. Plus, I'd get you off."

"Good to know, because next time I might not be so polite. Now for something much more cheerful. I met with Sherry Maguire and her guy for a tasting and design approval. It was such fun."

They passed the rest of the meal talking about casual things, mutual friends. And in the back of his mind he continued to wonder just what Linda had said or done to upset Laurel.

They opted for a walk after dinner—and after a laugh over the note Parker left in the kitchen.

My compliments to the chef.
As payment for the meal, I'll do the dishes.
So don't.

P.

Summer stretched the days so they walked the gardens in the soft, settling light. The close, sticky heat of the day lifted, just enough, and still warmed the flowers so their scents seemed stronger, more vital.

Stars winked on as she took him down to the pond to show him the frog. When he crouched for a closer look, she shook her head.

"You're just as thrilled and fascinated as Kent—the boy from the wedding party."

"A man never outgrows a good frog. It's a whopper. I could probably catch it, and chase you. Like I used to."

"You could try, but I'm faster these days. Besides, you usually caught Emma."

"She was more girl than the rest of you, and squealed more. Those were the days." He sat back on his heels, scanned the grounds, the green, the cool shadows. "I liked coming down to the pond before dark in the summer, just sitting here." He did so now. "Thinking long thoughts with my dog, watching the lights go on in the house. See, there's Parker's room. Now, anyway. It used to be there."

He pointed.

"I remember. I spent a lot of happy hours in that room." She sat beside him. "The Bride's Suite now. So, I guess, it's still a happy room, full of female. Yours is the same. I remember when you moved up to the third floor. To get some privacy."

"I was stunned when they said okay. They trusted me. Then, of course, I *had* to move up there, even though it was a little scary. I had to bribe the dog to sleep up there with me. I miss my dog."

"Aww." She tipped her head to his shoulder. "He was a great dog."

"Yeah, he was. I think about getting a dog, but then I remember I'm really not home enough, and it doesn't seem fair."

"Two dogs."

He ducked his head to look at her. "Two?"

"They'd keep each other company when you weren't there. They'd be pals, hang out, talk about you when you were gone."

The idea tickled him. "That's a thought."

He turned, slipped an arm around her, rubbed his lips over hers. "When I got a little older, sometimes I'd bring girls down here to neck."

"I know. We used to spy on you."

"You did not."

"Of course we did." She snorted out a laugh because he looked both stunned and deeply disconcerted. "It was entertaining and educational. It helped give us a heads-up on what to expect when it was our turn."

"Jesus."

"You got to second base here with Serena Willcott."

"Okay, that's it. Memory Lane's closed."

"You had smooth moves, even then. I bet you could get to second base with me here, too." She took his hand, slid it up her body, pressed it lightly to her breast. "See? You've still got it."

"I've worked some new ones in since Serena Willcott."

"Is that so? Why don't you try them out on me?"

He leaned in again, a brush of lips, a rub, a gentle nip while he used just his fingertips.

"Okay, yeah, that's a good one."

"If that worked, I might try this." He slid his finger down her throat to the top button of her shirt, flicked it open. "Not too fast," he murmured against her mouth, "not too slow." He opened the second button, then the third, pausing between to glide his fingertips over newly exposed skin.

"Yeah, you've probably improved." Her heart was already skipping. She made a sound of approval as his lips trailed along her throat, then one of surprise when his hand circled around to unhook her bra.

"Well done," she managed. "We should take this inside."

"No." Still kissing her, still touching her, he laid her back. "Right here."

"But—"

"I don't think four little girls are spying on us tonight. And I want you. I want you here, by the water, under the starlight, on the grass, in the air."

His tongue swept under the loosened cup of her bra, over her nipple, and sent a shiver of need along her skin.

He made her weak; made her want to be. He made her want to give herself over to him and what he stirred in her.

The warm grass, the warm air, the easy play of his hands, his lips, left her wanting nothing more than what was here and now. So she entrusted herself to the moment and to him, while to her dazzled eyes the stars seemed to burst to life in the sky.

The scent of her, seductive as the summer night, allured. The taste of her, so irresistible, stirred. He let his hands wander, to tease and to pleasure while the night deepened around them, cloaked them. Over the hum of the summer evening, an owl began its two-note call.

Moonlight danced on the surface of the pond, and on her body as he undressed her.

She started to sit up to unbutton his shirt, but he pressed her back.

"Not yet, not yet." His gaze swept over her, the hunger in it bringing another shiver over her skin. "You can't know how you look. You can't know."

He needed, craved, the touch, the taste, now. All of her, all his. He took, let the greed come so her cries and moans only sharpened his arousal. Her nails dug, her body bucked, and still he drove her on.

Now those stars exploded, blinding her. She couldn't find her breath as sensations pummeled her. It felt wicked, wonderful, to lie there, near to helpless, naked, crazed, while he did what he chose. His shirt brushed her breast, and she moaned again.

She wanted his flesh against hers, desperately, and yet knowing he was dressed and she exposed heightened the excitement toward a delirious panic. And even that burst.

"Now. Inside me. Oh God! Del."

She tugged at his shirt, his belt until together they managed to strip him.

She rolled. Straddled him. Took him.

Pleasure swamped her, and spurred her. Her head fell back as she steeped herself in it. He laid his hands on her breasts, then glided them down her body. Then gripped hers.

The storm rose, wildly, and they rode it out together.

* * *

𝒮HE'D MEANT TO TEASE HIM A LITTLE, TEMPT HIM A little—some groundwork for what she'd expected to follow in her bedroom. Now, she thought, she lay naked, stunned, and exhausted by the pond where the fat frog croaked in what might have been approval.

She'd just had wild outdoor sex with Del by the pond where they'd often played as children.

She wasn't quite sure if that was weird or wonderful.

"Second base?" He ran a hand down her back, over her ass, and back again. "Baby, that was a grand slam."

She had to laugh, it was a little wheezy, but she had to. "Good God, Del, we're naked and sticky. What if Mac and Carter, or Emma and Jack had decided to take a walk down this way?"

"They didn't."

"But what if—?"

"They didn't," he repeated, his voice as lazy as the hand that continued to stroke. "Besides, they'd've heard you making sex noises before they got close enough to see anything—then they'd've politely taken another direction while they sighed in envy."

"I didn't make sex noises."

"Oh yeah, lots of them. Grade-A porn sex noises. You could have a fallback career there."

"I most certainly do not—"

He rolled on top of her, slid down and found her breast with his mouth. She couldn't quite bite back the gasp and groan.

"Hear that? Wasn't me."

Because he just nuzzled in, she found her breath again. "Okay, well, it's good to know if Vows goes under I can make a living doing porn moan-overs."

"You'd be a star."

"Maybe you should gag me." When he lifted his head and grinned, she felt heat wash over her. "Not really. I don't think."

"We'll keep it as an option." He lowered his head again, but eased over to take his weight off her. "If we'd thought to pitch a tent we could just stay here all night."

The idea made her snort. "When's the last time you went camping?"

"I think I was twelve."

"Yeah, not your thing. Or mine. I guess we need to get dressed and get up to the house."

"We're naked and sticky. But I can fix part of that." He wrapped around her, rolled, rolled.

Her brain engaged, too late, but soon enough to understand what he had in mind. "No, Del! You can't—"

They hit the cool water of the pond tangled together. She didn't swallow much, and wiggled and kicked her way to the surface to sputter it out. While she did, he laughed like a lunatic.

"Shit! Shit! You maniac! There are frogs in here. And fish. Fish!" She squealed it as something fluttered against her leg. She struck out for the bank, but he nabbed her.

"It feels great."

"Fish." She shoved at him. "Frogs."

"You and me. I'm naked in the pond with Laurel McBanc. And she's all slippery. Oops," he said when his hand slid between her legs, when he cupped her.

"Del." Breathless now, clinging. "We'll drown."

"Let's find out."

They didn't drown, but she barely had the strength to pull herself out and onto the grass where she lay gasping for air.

"We never, *never* saw anything like that through the binoculars."

He reared up in shock. "You had binoculars?"

"Of course we did. We couldn't get close enough to see anything without binoculars. But the frog? He didn't need them, and he's seen entirely too much."

"He'll keep quiet about it if he wants to keep his legs."

She managed to turn her head, meet Del's eyes. "Now we're naked and wet."

"But happy."

She smiled. "I can't argue with that. But how are we going to get into the house?"

"I'm a Brown. I have a plan."

In the end, she wore his shirt, he wore the pants, and they balled up the rest. Still damp, and trying not to laugh, they snuck in the side door to make the dash to her room.

"I think we pulled it off," she said and dumped her load the minute the door was closed. "Now I'm freezing. I need a hot shower."

"Yeah, you probably do. You look like somebody who just had sex in the pond."

He put his arm around her to warm her as they walked toward the shower.

"Del? Remind me to do some extra training the next time I make you dinner."

SHE SLEPT LIKE A WOMAN IN A COMA, AND SURFACED JUST as groggy and disoriented when her alarm sounded.

"No, it's a mistake. It can't be morning." She opened one eye, read the time display on her clock—and with a resigned slap, turned off the alarm.

Beside her Del murmured something, and tried to draw her back.

"I have to get up. You should just go back to sleep, stay in bed."

"Good idea." He rolled over.

She scowled at him, then got up to dress in the dark.

Down in her kitchen she brewed coffee, and drank the first cup hot and black while she scanned her day's schedule. It might as well have been written in Greek.

To clear the cobwebs, she poured a second cup, added a generous spoonful of sugar, then got a muffin out of her tin. She took the coffee and the muffin outside, into the air, into what was arguably her favorite time of day.

Just before dawn, just before the light beat back the dark. Before anyone or anything stirred and the world—her favorite place in the world—was all hers.

Maybe she was tired, maybe another couple hours' sleep would've been blissful, but it was hard to beat the view, the feel of that hushed early morning.

She nibbled on the muffin, sipped the coffee, felt her brain start to clear as the sky turned pink and pale in the east.

Her eyes scanned the horizon, and back over the roll of green, skipped over the gardens, the terraces, the pergola Emma and her crew would be busy dressing before long.

And she saw the light shimmer over the water of the pond, the vague shadow of the willow swimming on it.

She thought of the night, of Del sleeping in her bed. And smiled.

It was going to be a beautiful day.

CHAPTER EIGHTEEN

*V*ACATION. LAUREL COULD SCENT IT, NEARLY TOUCH IT. SHE would be on it if this damn event would ever *end*.

Sunday afternoon events tended toward smaller affairs. Sophisticated or casual, fussy or freewheeling, weddings or anniversary parties booked on a Sunday afternoon leaned toward a pretty brunch or an elegant tea, most often ending early enough for guests to go home, maybe catch a ball game or a movie.

But not this one. Not the last event before the glories and raptures of vacation began. At four on Sunday afternoon, the Ballroom rocked. Champagne flowed. The bride and groom—second-time-arounders in their early forties, danced to the oldies the DJ spun like a couple of teenagers on spring break.

"Why don't they want to go home and have sex?" Laurel muttered to Emma.

"They've been together for three years—over a year of that living together. They probably have sex whenever they want."

"But it's Wedding Day sex, and they can only have

Wedding Day sex today. At midnight, that ship has sailed.
They should want it. Maybe we need to mention it."

Emma patted Laurel's shoulder. "Tempting—boy, tempting. But we have to stick it out until five." She snuck a
glance at her watch.

"You have a Tinker Bell Band-Aid on your finger."

"Isn't she cute? It almost makes up for daydreaming
about vacation and nicking myself a good one. Anyway,
forty-nine more minutes by my clock. Then it's two weeks,
Laurel. Fourteen beachy days."

"It makes my eyes sting when I think of it. But if I start
crying, people will just think I'm touched by the wedding,
so that's okay." She had to order herself not to shift impatiently from foot to foot. "We're all packed." She narrowed
her eyes at Emma.

"I'm packed. I'm packed."

"Okay then. So in forty-nine minutes we load up the
cars. I figure you have to allow twenty minutes for load-up
because of the beach gear and the arguing. That's sixty-nine
minutes. Another ten for Parker to check and recheck her
lists. Seventy-nine minutes and we're on the road. Vacation
begins the minute you're on the road."

"It does." Emma smiled at a small group of guests on
their way to the bar. "Seventy-eight now. And a couple
hours later, we're drinking frozen margaritas on the beach.
Del's going to have margaritas ready, right?"

"He'd better, seeing as he's already on the beach."

"Well, somebody had to go up, open the house, get supplies, make sure everything's set up."

"Yeah. He's probably kicked back with a beer now, but
I'm trying not to resent that. It's okay because in a hundred
and ninety-eight minutes, give or take a few, we'll be there,
too. Damn, we have to change—add twenty more minutes.
Two hundred and eighteen—"

"Seventeen," Emma interrupted. "Not that we're watching the clock or anything."

"We'll be sipping those margaritas, and our biggest

worry will be what to have for dinner." She gave Parker's arm a pinch when Parker walked over.

"Ow."

"Just making sure none of us are dreaming. We're having a private countdown. Two hundred and seventeen minutes till margaritas on the beach."

"Two hundred and seventy-seven. They just asked for the extra hour."

Emma's big brown eyes went sad as a hungry puppy's. "Oh, Parker."

"I know, I know. But it's their option, their money, and we can't say no."

"There could be a bomb threat by an anonymous caller. Just a suggestion," Laurel said when Parker gave her a bland stare. "I'm going to start transferring the gifts to the limo. It'll pass the time. If you need me, beep me."

It kept her busy, supervising the transfer, carting gifts out herself. Afterward, she made a trip up to the Bride's and Groom's suites to make sure they'd been put to rights, then headed down to her kitchen for the boxes needed for leftover cake and desserts.

"Two hundred and twenty-nine minutes," she told herself.

At six sharp, she stood with her partners, with Jack and Carter, waving off the newlyweds and the stragglers.

"Go away now," she said under her breath. "Bye-bye. Keep driving."

"Somebody out there might read lips," Jack commented.

"Don't care." But she gripped his arm and angled herself slightly behind him. "Go home. Go away. Okay, there's the last ones. Why are they standing there talking? They've had hours to talk already. Yes, yes, hug, hug, kiss, kiss, *go*, for pity's sake."

"They're getting in their cars," Mac said from behind her. "It's happening. Starting the cars, backing out. And they're driving, they're driving." She clamped her hands on Laurel's shoulders. "Almost to the road, almost there, nearly clear, and . . . Yes!"

"Vacation!" Laurel shouted. "Everybody scatter, get your stuff." She dashed inside and up the stairs.

Within fifteen minutes, dressed in cropped pants, a tank, a straw hat on her head and sandals on her feet, she dragged her bags downstairs. Then frowned at Parker.

"How could you be faster than me? How could you? I was like the wind. I was a freaking tornado of speed and efficiency."

"My talents are many. I'll bring the car around."

Mrs. Grady wandered out while they loaded up, and put an insulated bag in the car. "Road supplies," she said. "Cold water, some fruit, cheese, and crackers."

"You're the best." Laurel turned to give her a squeeze. "Change your mind, come with us."

"Not on your life. Two weeks of quiet right here will suit me." With her arm slung around Laurel's shoulders, she studied Parker. "Don't the pair of you look ready? Pretty as they come, too."

"Beach girls of Southampton," Parker said and did a stylish turn. "We'll miss you."

"You won't." Mrs. Grady smiled as Parker kissed her cheek. "But you'll be glad to see me when you get back. Here comes the next group." She jutted her chin as Mac and Carter pulled up behind Parker's car. "You see she doesn't forget to slather on plenty of sunscreen," she told Carter. "Our redhead fries like an egg."

"We're stocked."

She handed him an insulated bag. "Road food."

"Thanks."

"Emma's late, naturally." Parker checked her watch. "Carter, you're in the middle of the convoy so you don't fall behind."

"Aye, Captain."

"You have the directions on your GPS, in case?"

"We're good. We're ready." Mac adjusted the brim of her ball cap. "We're set."

"It's about a two hour and ten minute drive," Parker began. Laurel tuned her out and stared in the direction of

Emma's house as if to will her friend to hurry with the power of her mind.

"It worked! Here she comes. Bye, Mrs. G. If you get lonely, drive over."

"Not likely."

"No wild parties." Sober-faced, Parker put her hands on Mrs. G's shoulders. "No boys sleeping over. No drugs. No drinking."

"That doesn't leave me much, does it?" With a laugh, Mrs. Grady gave her a last farewell hug, and muttered in her ear. "Don't be such a good girl. Have fun."

"Fun is the first item on my list."

Laurel climbed in the car as Mrs. Grady passed the last bag of road food to Emma, as more hugs were exchanged. Laurel indulged in a quick bounce on the seat when Parker got behind the wheel.

"This is it."

"This, my friend, is it." Parker started the car, engaged the GPS. "Roll 'em out."

Laurel let out a *yee-haw* as they headed up the drive. "I can already feel the sand in my shoes, the salty breeze in my hair. You must be dying to get there. You own the place, and you haven't seen it yet."

"Co-own. I've seen plenty of pictures, from the Realtor and some that Del took."

"I can't believe you, of all people, furnished the place by phone and online."

"No other way to do it. No time to go there. Anyway, it's an efficient way to shop, especially for what's primarily an investment. We bought some of the furnishings already in place as the previous owners didn't want to move most of it. Lots of fussy stuff to see to yet. It'll be fun to pick up little things, or decide to have something repainted."

"What do you want to do, first thing, when you wake up tomorrow morning?"

"Try out the gym, then take a walk on the beach with a huge cup of coffee. Or, depending, skip the gym for a run on the beach. Run. On. The. Beach."

"And without your BlackBerry."

"I don't know if I'd go that far. I could go into withdrawal. What about you? First thing."

"That's the beauty. I don't know. I have no idea what I want to do, or what I will do. Mac will start taking pictures. Emma's going to plop herself on the beach and stare at the water while she makes happy noises. And you, admit it, will make sure to check your laptop and phone for messages right after the workout and the walk. Or after the run."

Parker lifted her shoulders then dropped them. "Probably, but then I plan to do a lot of staring and making happy noises."

"And start a list of what you want to change or add to the house."

"We all vacate in our own way."

"Yeah, we do. And thanks in advance."

"For what?"

"For the two weeks in a beach house in Southampton. Yes, partners and pals, but you could've said you wanted a couple weeks to yourself."

"What would I do without you?"

"There's a question we've never had to answer." She opened the bag, took out the bottled water. She uncapped them both, set Parker's in the drink cup, tapped it with her bottle. "To us. Beach girls of Southampton."

"Absolutely."

"Tunes?"

"Unquestionably."

Laurel switched on the radio.

Everything changed when they cut east of New York and started across the skinny island. She lowered the window, leaned out. "I think I can smell the water. Sort of."

"More than halfway there." Parker bit into an apple slice. "You should call Del, give him our ETA."

"Good idea, because I'm going to be starving when we finally get there, and jonesing for a margarita. Should I tell him to fire up the grill? Is there a grill?"

"Del co-owns the house, Laurel."

"Of course there's a grill. Burgers, chicken, or steak?"

"You know what, first night of vacation. A really big, fat steak."

"I'll put in the order." She took out her phone, hit Del's number.

"Hi. Where are you?"

She looked at the GPS screen, gave him their location.

"Hit some traffic?"

"No, work. We put on such a good event, they added an hour. But we're making good time. Parker made Carter drive in the middle so he's squeezed between us and Jack and has to keep up. We'd like to place an order for many frozen margaritas and big fat steaks."

"We're happy to serve you. Hey, listen."

In a moment she heard the whooshing sound. "It's the ocean! Parker, listen." She held the phone to her friend's ear. "It's *our* ocean. Are you on the beach?" she demanded when she had Del back.

"Just walked down."

"Have fun, but not too much fun until we get there."

"I'll pace myself. Oh, hey, do you know if Mal got off?"

"No. Is he coming in tonight?"

"He wasn't sure. I'll give him a call. See you soon."

"Can't wait." She closed the phone. "Mal might be coming in tonight."

"Lovely."

"He's okay, Parker."

"I didn't say he wasn't. I haven't adjusted to the change in our group dynamic."

"Plus, he's got that kind of look in his eye that says: How about it, sister?"

"Yes!" Parker took her hand off the wheel to point at Laurel. "Exactly. I don't like it. It's a kind of sexual swagger."

"Yeah, but it's honest. Remember that guy you went out with a couple times. Geoffrey—spelled the Brit way—wine baron or something."

"He had an interest in a few vineyards."

"And spoke fluent French and Italian, knew about

cinema as opposed to movies, skied in San Moritz. He turned out to be a complete sleaze, total sexist asshole under all that culture and polish."

"God, he really did." The memory had Parker shaking her head and sighing. "I can usually spot them, but he slipped right under the radar. Look."

Laurel turned her head and got the first glimpse of the ocean. "There it is," she murmured. "It's real. We're so damn lucky, Parker."

She thought the same thing again, with a whip of stupefaction when she got her first glimpse of the house.

"That?"

"Mmm-hmm."

"That's your beach house? It's a beach mansion, Parker."

"It's big, but there are a lot of us."

"It's gorgeous. It looks like it's been there forever, perfect for the spot, and still kinda sleek and new."

"It is gorgeous," Parker agreed. "I hoped it would be, that it wasn't just the pictures. And it's so private. Oh, and look at the sand and the water, and the pond and everything!"

Together they studied the rooflines, the long span of windows, the charm of decks, the fancy of the cupolas.

She spotted a tennis court, a swimming pool as Parker followed the private drive to the front of the house.

Laurel realized it was moments like this that reminded her Del and Parker weren't rich. They were wealthy.

"I love the angles of it," Laurel said. "You'll be able to see the water—ocean or pond—from any room."

"It's partially on a preserve. Del and I wanted to be a part of that. Keeping it pristine, protecting it. He found it, and it's just exactly right."

"I can't wait to see the rest." Even as she spoke, Del stepped out on the front deck, and started down. And for that moment, she forgot the rest.

He looked so relaxed—khakis, tee, bare feet. The sunglasses couldn't disguise the pleasure on his face.

She got out first, and he held out a hand for hers as he

walked to her. "There you are," he said and gave her an easy greeting kiss.

"Nice little beach shack."

"I thought so."

Parker stepped out, took a long look at the house, turned, took another at the water, the views. Nodded. "Good job."

He lifted his arm, so she went over to slide under it, and for a moment the three of them stood, the breeze wafting and the house spread out before them.

"I think it'll do," Del decided.

The others arrived, and with them noise, movement, choruses of approval and curiosity as they started unloading the cars and hauling luggage and supplies.

The impressions came fast—sun and space, glossy wood, soft colors. Out of every window stretched water and sand, solitude and sanctuary, the offer of a spot to sit or a path to wander.

High ceilings and the easy, open flow from one room to the next added an appealing touch of the casual to the simple elegance of furnishings. A place, Laurel thought, you'd be comfortable with your feet up, or sipping champagne in formal wear.

The Browns, she admitted, simply had a way.

The kitchen brought her an instant surge of pleasure with its acres of straw-colored counters. The textured glass cabinet doors showcased cheerful Fiestaware in a celebration of mixed colors and the sparkle of stemware. Opening the pot drawers she hummed her approval of the selection of pots and pans. Surrounding the sinks, the tall, bowing windows opened the room to the beach and the crash of waves.

Even as she took stock she heard Jack let out a crow.

"Pinball!"

Which meant there was likely a game room somewhere, but at the moment, she was more interested in the kitchen, the airy dining area, the proximity to the deck for outdoor eating.

Del passed her an icy margarita. "As promised."

"Oh boy." She took the first frosty sip. "It's officially vacation."

"I staked out a bedroom. Do you want to see it?"

"Absolutely. Del, this place is . . . a lot more than I had in my head."

"In a good way?"

"In an 'I'm stupefied' way."

She peered into rooms as they passed. Sunroom, what she supposed was a morning room, living room, powder rooms. Then up the bare wood steps to the second floor into a bedroom with a wall of windows facing the ocean. She instantly imagined herself lazily lounging in the iron bed with its open canopy and crisp white bedding. Gauzy curtains fluttered in the breeze in the doors he'd opened to the deck.

"It's beautiful. Just beautiful. And listen." She closed her eyes and let the rolling whoosh of the ocean wash over her.

"Check this out."

He gestured, and she walked into the bath.

"Okay." She laid a hand on his arm, patted it several times. "Okay. I may live right here. I may never come out of this room."

The huge tub reigned in front of another wall of windows and on tiles the color of golden sand. Through clear glass she admired the shower with its multiple heads and body jets, its marble bench.

"Steam shower," he told her, and she nearly whimpered.

Generous bowls the color and shape of scallop shells served as sinks. The wall at the foot of the tub boasted a little gas fireplace and a flat screen TV so her imagination shifted from lazy lounging in the bed to lazy lounging in bubbling water.

Mirrored cabinets reflected the tile, the shine of the fixtures, the expanse of counters, the pretty watercolors arranged on the walls.

"This bathroom's bigger than my first apartment."

Mac rushed in, wild-eyed, arms waving. "The bathroom,

the bathroom. It's . . . Wow, look at this one. Never mind. The bathroom!" she said again and rushed out as she'd rushed in.

"I think you have a solid hit," Laurel told Del.

Within the hour, the grill smoked and the entire group gathered on the deck. Or Laurel assumed the entire group until she glanced around.

"Where's Parker?"

"Taking a solo tour." Emma sighed, sipped her slushy drink. "Making notes."

"I wouldn't change a thing." Behind her enormous sunglasses and wide-brimmed hat, Mac wiggled bare toes. "Not one thing. I wouldn't move from this spot for the next two weeks except there are so many other incredibly cool spots I need to be lazy in."

"We need to check out the beach." Jack took Emma's hand to kiss.

"We definitely do."

"It's a great area for bird-watching," Carter said. "I spotted a Cory's Shearwater when I walked down earlier. And . . ." He trailed off, flushed a little. "Geek alert."

"I like birds," Emma said, and reached over to pat his hand. "I'm going to give you some help with dinner any minute now, Del."

"I've got it." Laurel pushed herself up. "That way, one of the pair of you takes it next time we want dinner in. I'll go throw something together to go with the steaks."

Besides, she wanted to play in the kitchen.

Parker came in as Laurel tossed chunks of steamed new potatoes in butter, garlic, and dill.

"Need a hand?"

"Under control. Del must've hit a farmer's market on the way in. Pretty smart of him."

"He's pretty smart." Parker did another scan as she spoke. "I'm already in love with this place."

"God, me, too. The views, the air, the sounds. And the house itself—it's incredible. How much will you change?"

"Not much. Tweak more than change." She walked to a

window. Voices and laughter floated in on the breeze. "That's a good sound. I bet it's beautiful here, even in the winter."

"You read my mind. I was thinking how we almost always have that slow period, a week or so after the holidays."

"Yeah, I had that thought. Maybe. Del looks so happy. Part of that's you."

Laurel's hands stilled. "Do you think?"

"Yes, I do. And I'm standing here watching him man the grill while you put things together in here. It's nice." She glanced back. "It makes me happy, Laurel, the same way hearing the voices carry inside makes me happy."

"I feel the same way."

"Good. It's good from someone who loves you both. So." She turned back from the window. "Are we eating in or out?"

"An evening like this? Out, definitely."

"I'll start setting the table."

Later, they walked off the meal along the beach, wading in the surf, watching the lights of faraway ships that cruised through the night. As the air cooled, Laurel gave some thought to a long bath in the flicker of the fireplace.

But the challenge went out; the game room called. The quiet flipped into the arcade cacophony of pings and whistles.

Jack and Del battled in what looked like a pinball death match when she decided she had to throw in the towel. She left them to it to wander back to the bedroom, and indulged in that long soak. When she'd slipped on a nightshirt to step out on the deck, she realized she hadn't looked at her watch in hours.

Now that was vacation.

"I wondered where you'd gone off to."

She glanced back at Del. "I have to get in some serious practice before I take on you or Jack. I had the most incredible bath, in firelight while I looked out at the ocean. I feel like the heroine of my own novel."

"If I'd known, I'd have taken one with you, and we'd have written a love scene." He put his arms around her so her head rested on his shoulder. "Good day?"

"Pretty much the best. This place, these views, this air, good friends."

"As soon as I saw it, I knew. This is what we need."

Not *I* need, she noted. Not Del. Del was wired for *we*.

"I never asked Parker, but I always wondered why the two of you sold the house in East Hampton."

"We could never sell the house in Greenwich—our house. It's home. But the other . . . We both knew we could never unwind there or enjoy it. Remembering Mom and Dad at home, that's . . . important and there's some comfort in it. But the place we had at the beach? We just couldn't go there anymore. This place is new, and we'll make other memories here."

"And you needed to wait to do it. A little time and space first."

"I guess we did. This is a good place, and it feels like the right time."

"She loves it already. I know that matters to you. She told me, but even if she hadn't, I could see it. We all do. So thanks for finding the right place and the right time."

"You're welcome." He pressed his lips to the side of her neck. "You smell really good," he murmured.

"I feel really good, too." She smiled when his hand stroked down her back. "See?" She tipped up her face, brushed her lips over his. "I think we should write that love scene."

"Good idea." With a flourish, he swept her up into his arms. "I think we should open it like this."

"It's a classic for a reason."

THERE MIGHT HAVE BEEN A MORE PERFECT SPOT AND A more perfect time and a more perfect mood, but Laurel couldn't imagine it. Her stubborn internal clock woke her before dawn, but she snuggled into the luxury of knowing she didn't have to roll out, but could stay just as she was, curled up with Del with the sound of the sea serenading.

She drifted in and out for a time, and even that was perfect. As was the sunrise over the water to the east. She thought it spread its pinks and gold just for her as she stood on the deck with the filmy curtains fluttering behind her.

Inspired, she tugged on a tank and shorts, then jogged down the outside steps. Parker stood at the base, in a tank and shorts, her deep brown hair caught back in a long tail under a sassy white cap.

"You're up, too."

"Oh, yeah."

Laurel lifted her hands. "What's wrong with us?"

"Not a thing. Everyone else is sleeping through vacation. We're wringing every drop out of it."

"Damn right. That beach calls for a run, as previously discussed."

"My thoughts exactly."

They warmed up on the walkway, then set off at an easy pace on the sand. They didn't need to talk, but simply matched gaits, followed the shoreline with the surf foaming beside them.

Birds took wing or strutted in the foam. Carter would likely know what they were, Laurel thought, but it was enough just to have them there, soaring, calling, pecking while the rising sun sparkled on the water.

When they turned back, they kept up the same steady pace until the house came into view again. Laurel reached over to touch Parker's arm as she slowed.

"Just look at it. That's where we're going."

"Don't hate me, but it makes me think, wow, what a fabulous place for casual beach weddings."

"I may have to hurt you."

"I can't help it. It *is* a fabulous place."

"How many calls have you taken since we got here?"

"Only two. Okay three, but all easily handled. And I got a sunrise run on the beach and am now seriously jonesing for coffee. In fact . . . last one there makes it."

She took off in a sprint. Laurel was quick off the mark, but she already knew she'd be making the coffee. Parker ran like a damn cheetah.

Once she made the deck, she leaned over, hands on knees to catch her breath. "I was going to make the coffee anyway."

"Uh-huh."

"I hate that you're barely winded, but I'll still make the coffee, and egg-white omelettes."

"Seriously?"

"I'm in the mood."

The others wandered down, probably lured by the scent of coffee and the music Parker turned on low.

Del leaned on the counter, shoving fingers through his sleep-tousled hair. "Why aren't you still in bed with me?"

"Because I've already had a three-mile run on the beach, and my first cup of coffee." She handed him one. "Shortly I'm having breakfast, which you can benefit by as I'm feeling generous."

He gulped down coffee. "Okay," he said and walked out onto the deck to flop into a chaise.

Emma stopped slicing fruit to roll her eyes in a look that clearly said: *men.*

"He gets away with it today because I'm in a very good mood." She paused at the sound of an engine, shifted closer to the window. "Who could that be?"

Outside, Parker set a pitcher of juice on the table then glanced down to see Malcolm Kavanaugh remove his helmet. He gave his hair a shake as he swung off the motorcycle. "Nice little place you've got here," he called up to Del, then headed up the stairs. He shot Parker a quick grin. "How's it going, Legs? Looks like I'm in time for breakfast."

He slid into the group, Laurel thought later. Parker might find him a little irritating, but he did slide in. By midmorning, they'd staked their territory on the beach with folding chairs, blankets, umbrellas, coolers. The air smelled of sea and sunscreen.

She'd nearly dozed off over her book, when Del plucked her bodily out of her chair.

"What? Cut it out."

"Time for a dip."

"If I want a dip, I'll use the pool. Stop it!"

"Can't come to the seashore without getting in the sea." He waded right in with her over his shoulder, then tossed her.

She managed one short curse, then held her breath.

The cool water closed over her head, and she felt sand swim in every-damn-where as she pushed herself up. When she blinked the salt water out of her eyes, she saw him standing about waist high and grinning.

"Damn it, Del. It's cold."

"Refreshing," he corrected, and dived under an oncoming wave. She, of course, didn't see it coming. Knocked down, breathless, carrying yet more sand, she started to push up again, as he wrapped his arms around her waist.

"You're so pushy, Brown."

"Got you in, didn't I?"

"I like to look at the ocean, swim in a pool."

"We don't have an ocean at home," he pointed out. "Here comes another one."

At least she was prepared this time, rolled with the wave—and had the satisfaction of shoving him under. He only surfaced laughing. Since she was wet, sandy, and covered with salt, she struck off to swim past the breakers. As her skin and muscles warmed, she had to admit Del had a point.

They didn't have an ocean at home.

She dived under again, just for the pleasure of it. And once more, his hands closed around her waist.

"That's far enough out."

"Pushy," she said again.

"Maybe." But he wrapped around her so they bobbed. She felt him take a few strong kicks to bring them closer to shore. What the hell, she decided, and, relaxing against him, let him do the work.

She watched her friends, on shore and sea, listened to the sounds of voices, of surf, of music.

"I could get myself back to the beach," she told him. "Like I could've gotten myself in the water in the first place if I'd wanted to."

"Yeah, but then I couldn't do this." He shifted her, took her mouth as the water rocked them.

Once again she was forced to admit he had a point.

CHAPTER NINETEEN

$\mathscr{S}$HE WANTED TO BAKE. MAYBE IT WAS THE LIGHT PITTER-patter of morning rain outside the windows that turned the beach into a pearly watercolor—or just several days running without doing much more in the kitchen than making coffee or nuking some popcorn.

Laurel supposed it was the same as Parker sneaking off for a couple of hours every day to huddle over her laptop, or Mac with her camera. And hadn't Emma hunted up a flower shop so she could buy armloads to arrange around the house?

After a few days of sleeping in, lazing around, after the long walks and nightly game fests, she just wanted to get her hands in some dough.

She'd already checked out the pantry, noting that Del knew her well enough to stock the basics, and with some surprise realized he paid enough attention to what she kept in her own pantry to shelve more specifics toward professional baking.

But he didn't know everything, she thought, because she was in the mood for pies.

She made a mental list, knowing it depended on what she found once she got to the market.

She left a note for Parker.

Gone to market. Borrowed your car.
L.

And grabbing the keys and her purse, set out on what she thought of as a little adventure.

In the gym, Parker watched the rain as she finished up her cardio session. She hadn't turned on the news as was her habit—a concession to the holiday. Whatever was going on in the world just had to wait until she got back home.

With the exception of her brides. But really, she thought, it hadn't been too bad. A scatter of calls, a handful of problems and concerns she'd been able to handle long-distance.

In fact, it was satisfying to know she could be away and still deal with what needed to be done.

She smiled as she spotted Mac, her shock of red hair covered in a ball cap, her windbreaker a bright blue flash as she headed down to the rain-washed beach with her camera.

They could get away from home, Parker thought, but not from what they were.

She watched a moment longer, then walked over to switch the music to something less driving for the rest of her workout.

It was such a treat to take as much time as she wanted, not to watch the clock, not to adjust her routine to meet an appointment or dig into a chore.

She opted to make use of the barre, started off with some pliés.

When Mal walked in she had her foot on the barre and her nose to her knee.

"Bendy," he commented, then lifted his eyebrows when she stared at him. "Do you have a problem with me getting some time in?"

"No, of course not." It irritated her that she caught herself, too often, stiff and ungracious around him. So she made a deliberate effort to be friendly. "Help yourself. You can change the music if you want. It won't bother me." She refused to be bothered.

He only shrugged, and headed over to the weights to set up for bench presses. "I didn't know anyone else was up until I heard the long-hair."

"Mac's already down at the beach with her camera." No reason not to be civil, Parker told herself.

"In the rain?"

"We can't seem to help ourselves." She turned to face him with a smile—but mostly because she suspected he'd stare at her ass if she didn't.

"Whatever works for you. I've seen some of her shots. You ought to put some up around here."

It surprised her as she'd already planned to do so. "Yes, we should. So . . . What do you press?"

"I keep it about one-fifty. You've got good arms," he said after one of his long surveys. "How about you?"

"One-ten, maybe one-twenty if I'm in the mood for it."

"Not bad."

She watched him out of the corner of her eye as she stretched. There was no denying the man had *arms* on him. Muscles bunched but didn't bulge as he lifted and lowered the weights. High on his sleek right biceps rode a tattoo in the shape of a Celtic manhood knot.

She'd only Googled the design out of curiosity.

She respected a man who stayed in shape. As she'd seen Mal stripped down for the ocean—not that she'd paid particular attention—she knew he did.

She moved on to crunches, and he to curls. She added in some Pilates, and he switched to flies. He was unobtrusive, so she nearly forgot he was there and ended her workout with a few minutes of yoga to stretch everything out again.

She turned to get a bottle of water and nearly walked into him.

"Sorry."

"No problem. You're seriously ripped there, Ms. Brown."

"Toned," she corrected. "I'd pass the ripped to you, Mr. Kavanaugh."

He got two bottles of water out of the cooler, handed her one. Then he moved in until her back was against the cooler, his hands on her hips, and his mouth taking easy possession of hers.

She told herself it was the stunned surprise—where had *this* come from?—that prolonged the moment, the kiss, the slow, sultry rise of heat. She shoved him back a half a step, gulped in air.

"Wait a minute. Wait a minute."

"Okay."

She stared him down, but he seemed unaffected by the look that withered most. Still, he didn't move in on her again, but only stood watching her with those sharp green eyes.

Cat to mouse, she thought. That's how it made her feel. And she was nobody's mouse.

"Listen, if you've got the idea I'm . . . that because everyone's paired up and we're . . ."

"No. That was you. Fourth of July. I remember it really well."

"That was just—nothing."

"I liked it. But no, I don't have the idea. I just like your mouth and thought I'd see if my memory was accurate. It was."

"Now that we've established that." She elbowed him aside, and stalked out.

On a sound that combined amusement and pleasure, Mal stepped over to change the music. He preferred his long-hair with guitar and drums.

WITH VERY WARM FEELINGS TOWARD THE LOCAL MARKET, Laurel unloaded her bags. She might've gone just a little overboard, but since it made her happy, she didn't see anything wrong with that. She had enough to bake her pies, some bread, a coffee cake—and whatever else struck her fancy.

"I think it's clearing up."

She turned to see Mac, windbreaker shiny with rain, crossing over from the beach steps. "Oh yeah, I can see that."

"No, really. See? Look over there." Mac pointed to the eastern sky. "Little patches of blue. I'm optimistic."

"And wet."

"Got some great shots." She reached in for another bag. "Dramatic, dreamy, moody. Jeez, this is heavy. What did you get?"

"Stuff."

Mac peeked in, then sent Laurel a smug smile. "You're going to bake. Just can't take the Betty out of the Crocker."

"You should talk since you haven't dug Annie out of the Leibovitz."

"Emma's making noises about putting in a beach garden. Pampas grass and . . . well, who knows. It doesn't make us workaholics."

"No. It makes us productive."

"Much better," Mac agreed as they hauled the load up the steps. "I'm having the best time, and now I can't wait to upload the digitals and see what I've got. I took some film, too. I wonder what it would take to talk Parker and Del into putting in a darkroom."

"Parker thinks the place would be perfect for casual beach weddings."

Mac pursed her lips in thought. "That may be going too far. Except, shit, it really would."

"Don't encourage her," Laurel ordered and shifted her bags to open the door.

Before she could, Del pulled it open. "There you are." He took a bag from each of them. "Did we need supplies?"

"I did."

He set them on the counter, leaned down to give her a quick kiss. "Good morning. Hey, Macadamia, you're all wet."

"It's clearing up," she insisted. "I'm going to grab some coffee. Have you seen Carter?"

"Briefly. He had a book about this thick." Del stretched his thumb and forefinger out.

"That'll keep him occupied." She poured the coffee and gave them a salute on her way out.

"Missed you in bed this morning," Del said to Laurel. "I woke up to the sound of the rain and the surf, and thought, now this is the perfect place to be. But you weren't there, so it wasn't."

"I went on a mission."

"So I see." He reached in a bag, pulled out one of several lemons. "Lemonade?"

"Lemon meringue pie, and a deep-dish cherry pie, I think. And I want to bake some bread, maybe a coffee cake. Rainy mornings are great for baking."

"Boy, our minds went in different directions on rainy morning."

She laughed as she unpacked the bags. "If you'd woken up sooner, we could've had both. No, let me unpack. I know where I want everything."

He shrugged and left her to it. "I guess I'll hit the gym then, especially since pies are in my future. If you've got the receipt or remember what you spent, I'll pay you back."

She stopped. "Why?"

"You shouldn't have to buy the supplies," he said absently as he pulled a bottle of Gatorade out of the fridge.

"And you should?" She couldn't stop the line of heat that rode up her spine.

"Well, it's—"

"Your house?" she finished.

"Yes. But I was going to say it's more . . . equitable since you're doing the work."

"Nobody did any work last night when we all went out to dinner and you picked up the check."

"That was just . . . What's the problem? Somebody else will get it next time."

"Do you think I care about your money? Do you think I'm with you because you can pick up dinner checks and have a place like this?"

He lowered the bottle. "Jesus, Laurel, where did that come from?"

"I don't want to be paid back. I don't want to be taken care of, and you can screw *equitable* because that's never going to happen. But I can pay my own way, and I can buy my own damn supplies when I want to make some pies."

"Okay. I'm a little puzzled why offering to pay you back for a bunch of lemons pisses you off, but since it does, offer rescinded."

"You don't get it," she muttered as Linda's jeering *hired help* echoed in her mind. "Why would you?"

"Why don't you explain it to me?"

She shook her head. "I'm going to bake. Baking makes me happy." She reached for the remote, turned on music at random. "So, go work out."

"That's the plan." But he set down the bottle to take her face in his hands, study it. "Be happy," he said. Kissed her, grabbed the bottle again, and left.

"I was," she murmured. "Will be again." Determined, she began arranging her supplies and ingredients as suited her.

Mal walked in while she cut shortening into her flour mixture for the pastry dough.

"I love seeing a woman who knows what she's doing in the kitchen."

"Glad to oblige."

He went to the coffeepot, judged the remainder stale, tossed it. "I'm going to make a fresh pot. You want?"

"No, I've had enough."

"So, what's on the menu?"

"Pies." She heard the edge in her voice, made the effort to dull it. "Lemon meringue and cherry."

"I've got a weakness for a good piece of cherry pie." Once he'd set the coffee to brew, he stepped over to her counter, scanned it. "You use actual lemons for the lemon meringue?"

"Well, they were out of mangoes." She glanced at him as she added ice water. "What else?"

"You know that little box with a picture of a slice of pie."

She unbent enough to laugh. "Not in my kitchen, friend. Juice and rind from actual lemons."

"How about that?" He poured the coffee, then poked in a cupboard. "Hey, Pop-Tarts. Is it going to bother you if I watch?"

Stumped, she stopped what she was doing to stare at him. "You want to watch me make pies?"

"I like seeing how things work, but I can take off if I'm in your way."

"Just don't touch anything."

"Deal." He took a seat on a stool on the other side of the counter.

"Do you cook at all?"

He ripped open the Pop-Tart package as he spoke. "When I first took off for L.A., it was learn to put food together or starve. I learned. I make a damn good red sauce. Maybe I'll put that together tonight, especially if the rain keeps up."

"Mac claims it's clearing."

Mal glanced out at the thin, steady rain. "Uh-huh."

"That's what I said." She picked up the rolling pin—a good marble one she knew Del had bought with her in mind. It made her feel small about jumping down his throat.

A sigh escaped as she flour-dusted her board.

"It's hard to be rich."

She looked up, stared again. "What?"

"Harder to be poor," he said in the same easy tone. "I've been both—relatively—and poor's tougher. But rich has some baggage with it. I was doing okay in L.A. Steady work. I built up a rep, and I had a decent cushion when I got hurt doing that gag. That put the brakes on the work, but they ended up dumping a shitpile of money on me for my trouble."

"How bad were you hurt?"

"Broke a few things I hadn't broken before, and a few more I already had." He shrugged it off as he bit into the Pop-Tart. "Point is, by my standards anyway, I was rolling in it. A lot of other people figured the same, and that they could do some rolling, too. Mice come out of the wood-work looking for a nice bite of the cheese, then they get nasty if you don't share, or share enough to their way of thinking. Gave me a whole new perspective on who and what mattered, and who and what didn't."

"Yeah, I guess it would."

"Del's always had the rolling in it, so it's some different for him."

She stopped rolling. "You were listening?"

"I was walking by, heard what I figure was the last of it. I didn't plug my ears and whistle a tune. But maybe you don't want my take."

"Why would I?"

Her frigid tone didn't seem to chill him in the least. "Because I get it. I know what it is to need to prove you can handle yourself, make your own. I don't come from where you do, but it's not all that far off. My mother talks," he added. "I let her. So I've got some of the backstory."

She shrugged. "It's not a secret."

"Pisser though, being gossip fodder, especially when it's ancient history, and not really about you since it's about your parents."

"I guess I should quid pro quo and tell you I know you lost your father, and your mother moved back here to work for your uncle. And that didn't work so well for you."

"He's a fucker. Always was." He picked up his coffee, gestured with the mug. "How do you do that? The crust deal? Get it almost perfectly round?"

"Practice."

"Yeah, most everything takes it." He watched in silence

as she folded it, placed it in the first pie plate, unfolded. "Applause. So anyway, my take—"

"If I'm going to get your take, you can be useful and pit the cherries."

"How?"

She handed him a hairpin, took another. "Like this." She demonstrated, plunging the pin into the base of the cherry. The pit popped out the top.

His eyes, very green, lit with interest. "That's freaking ingenious. Let me try that."

He did so with considerable more skill than she'd expected, so she pushed two bowls toward him.

"Pits in here, fruit in here."

"Got it." He got to work. "Del doesn't think about money like most of us do. He's nobody's fool, that's for damn sure. He's generous by nature—nurture, too, if what I hear about his parents is even half true."

"They were amazing people. Incredible people."

"That's the word on the street." Mal's hands worked quickly, deftly—impressing her—with pin and pit. "He's compassionate and fair. Not a pushover, but believes in using money not just for his comfort and pleasure, but to build, to make a mark, to change lives. He's a hell of a guy."

"He really is."

"Plus he's not an asshole, which counts a lot. Hey. You're not going to water up or anything, are you?" Mal asked cautiously.

"No. I don't water up easily."

"Good. So what I'm saying is he buys this place—or he and Legs buy it."

"Are you really going to call Parker 'Legs'?"

"She's sure got them. An investment, sure. And a getaway for them. But he—they—open it up. Seems to me they could've said, 'Okay, vacation time. See you in a couple weeks.' But that's not what they did."

"No, they didn't." Her opinion of him rose several notches. He understood, and he appreciated.

"So we've got this houseful of people. I felt a little weird about tagging along, but that's on me. For Del, it's, 'We've got this place, let's use it.' No weight, no strings."

"You're right. Damn it."

Those sharp green eyes met hers again, with an understanding that nearly made her "water up."

"But he doesn't get we bring our own weight, our own strings. He doesn't feel them or see them. If he did—"

"He'd be irritated or insulted," she finished.

"Yeah. But sometimes a girl needs to buy her own lemons, so he's got to deal with the irritation and insult."

She finished the other piecrust, placed it in the second pan. "I should be able to explain it to him. I guess that's on me."

"I guess it is."

"Just when I was starting to like you," she said, but smiled.

When Emma wandered in, Laurel was demonstrating the proper way to create meringue.

"Tournament in the game room, in about an hour."

"Poker?" Mal asked, brightening up.

"It's being discussed. Jack and Del are putting together some sort of game decathlon, and poker is an element. They're arguing point system. Ooh, pie."

"I have to finish this, then I'm going to start some bread while Mal makes red sauce."

"You cook?"

"I'd rather play poker."

"Oh, well, I could—"

"Uh-uh." Laurel pointed a finger at Mal. "We have an arrangement."

"Fine. But the tournament doesn't start until I'm done here. And I don't do dishes."

"Reasonable," Laurel allowed. "We need ninety minutes," she told Emma. "If the rest of the entrants want to eat tonight, they'll wait for us."

Laurel brought a timer with her, set for the end of the

bread's second rising. Her pies cooled on their racks, and Mal's sauce simmered low on the range.

It seemed a damn good deal for a rainy day.

When she stepped into the game room, she realized Del and Jack had made their version of pie out of lemons.

They'd set up stations, even had them numbered. The poker table, the Xbox, the mat for Dance Dance Revolution, the dreaded foosball.

She sucked at foosball.

Any number of people had been in and out of the kitchen in the last hour, grabbing snacks, drinks. The bar held bowls of chips, salsa, cheese, fruit, crackers.

Sometime over the last hour or so, they'd fashioned a scoreboard, listed the names.

"This looks pretty serious."

"Competition's not for sissies," Del told her. "Parker tried to ban cigars from the poker rounds. She's been over-ruled. I hear Mal's handling dinner."

"Yeah. We've got that end of things under control. We'll require a couple of time-outs to check on things."

"Fair enough."

Yes, he was, she thought, fair enough. Generous by nature, as Mal had said. He'd gone to considerable trouble here—for his own benefit, sure. The man loved to play. But also to make sure everyone had a good time.

She crooked her finger to gesture him over to a more private spot as Mac argued with Jack over the choices of video games.

"I'm not going to apologize for the content, but for the delivery."

"All right."

"I don't want either of us to feel, ever, your wallet has to be open."

Frustration flickered over his face. "I don't. You don't. It's not—"

"That's what counts then." She rose to her toes to touch her lips to his. "Let's forget about it. You're going to have enough to deal with when I kick your ass in this tournament."

"Not a chance. The trophy for the First Annual Brown Beach Tourney is as good as mine."

"There's a trophy?"

"Of course there's a trophy. Jack and Parker made it."

She followed the direction of his finger. On top of the mantel stood what might have been a piece of driftwood or salvage with shells placed strategically to emulate a primitive bikini. Dried kelp covered the "head." They'd drawn on a face with a fierce and toothy grin.

She burst out laughing, and went over for a closer look.

Better, Del thought. She'd brushed off whatever pinched at her. But brushing it off didn't mean it wasn't lurking in the corners waiting to pinch again.

He'd had time to think about it, and believed he had an idea what some of it, at least, was about—and where it might've come from.

He also believed he knew how to find out.

He glanced over to where Emma manned the bar.

He just needed to bide his time, and use the right approach.

"Let the games begin," Jack called out, and held up a hat. "Everyone picks a number for the first round."

SHE REALLY DID SUCK AT FOOSBALL. SO GREAT WAS HER failure even Carter beat her. Now *that*, she thought, was humiliating.

Still, she'd killed at pinball with a run of luck and skill that had put her slightly ahead of both Jack and Del in that field of play. Much to *their* chagrin.

And that was satisfying.

She felt she'd hold her own at poker. But currently Mal and Parker were ripping it at competitive DDR. She'd have to ace her run to have even a fighting chance for the trophy.

She sipped wine as Parker and Mal hit double A's at the end of their second of three rounds.

Shit, she was probably doomed.

It was probably unfair to think having Mal there balanced things out—but it did. Parker was perfectly capable of getting her own man if she wanted one, but it just added a nice touch.

Plus, they looked really good together.

Really good.

And maybe she should switch back to water if she was heading toward even around the borders of matchmaking.

She shrugged, took another sip, then prepared for her round with the Xbox.

She entered the final round tied with Mac for fifth after scorching Jack at DDR.

"Damn the Wii," he muttered. "It killed my standings."

"You're in fourth." Emma poked his belly. "I'm dead last. Something's wrong with that pinball machine. And my Xbox controller was faulty." She plucked the cigar out of his hand. "For luck," she decided and took a puff. "Ugh, can't be worth it."

Forty minutes into Texas Hold 'Em, Laurel went all in on a pretty heart flush. The pot would put her on top, and potentially eliminate Emma, Mac, and possibly Carter.

As the bet rounded the table, she felt a buzz as her opponents folded one by one. Until Carter.

He considered, weighed—endlessly, she thought. Then called.

"Ace high heart flush." She spread her cards.

"Very nice," Del told her.

"Oh." Carter adjusted his glasses, looked sorrowful. "Full house. Queens over sevens. Sorry."

"Woo!"

At Mac's cheer, Laurel scowled.

"Sorry, I have to cheer. We're getting married."

"Maybe you could check the sauce," Mal said.

"Yeah, I can do that." She pushed away from the table. "It was the stupid foosball."

She took her time, stirred the sauce, then wandered over to step onto the deck.

Mac's prediction had finally come true. It had cleared up. Maybe it had waited all day to do it, but the skies bloomed blue again. There'd be a moon out later, and the stars. Lovely night for a walk on the beach.

She went up to see Emma at the bar pouring a Diet Coke.

"You out?"

"I'm out."

"Yay. I won't come in last."

"I could hate you for that, but I'm magnanimous. Jack's down to his last chips. Our love did not soar us on wings of skill and luck this day. But, hell, it was fun. Oops, there goes my man. I guess I should commiserate."

It took another thirty minutes for the eliminations, and a few more for the tallying.

In the end, Del turned from the board to reach for the trophy. "Ladies and gentlemen, we have a tie. Parker Brown and Malcolm Kavanaugh each end with one hundred and thirty-four points."

Mal grinned at Parker. "Looks like we share the spoils, Legs."

"We could have a tiebreaker, but I'm too damn tired." She held out her hand for a shake. "We share."

CHAPTER TWENTY

$\mathcal{D}$EL FOUND HIS OPPORTUNITY TO TALK TO EMMA ALONE for a good stretch the next day when he suggested the two of them drive to the local nursery to see what sort of plantings she'd like to put in.

She jumped on the idea so quickly and enthusiastically, he felt just a little guilty. He'd make up for it, he decided, by letting her pick whatever she wanted, even if it meant hiring a local landscaping crew to maintain it.

She cut that sop to his conscience the minute she hopped in the car with him.

"Low maintenance is key," she began. "I'd love to do whole rivers of color and texture, but you don't live here. No point in having all that, then needing to hire people to deal with it when you're only here off and on through the year."

"Right." Anything she wanted, he told himself again. Anything.

"Next key is sticking to plants and grasses indicative of the beach, and going for a natural look. It's going to be fun!"

"You bet."

"It will." She laughed and poked him. "I'm going to enjoy this a lot, plus it goes in as my own little payback for the vacation. It's such a beautiful place, Del. We're all so happy to be here."

"Payback? Come on, Emma."

"It feels good to do something to show appreciation. You're not taking that away from me, so don't even think about it. Boy, it's a gorgeous day. I can't wait to get started on this."

"It's nice to get away, relax. It's good for everybody."

"No argument from me."

"Dump the stress. We've all got it. Not just work, but outside sources bring it, too. Laurel going head-to-head with Linda added plenty for her."

"Oh, she told you about that. I wasn't sure she would." Emma sat back as anger shifted over her face.

"It's lucky she caught Linda before she strolled right in Mac and Carter's place, but I don't like knowing she had to take Linda on alone."

"She handled it, sent Linda off with a bug in her ear. But, I know what you mean. She didn't have any backup when Linda went after her. She was so upset. That woman knows exactly where to slip the knife."

"Nothing Linda says means a damn."

"No, but words hurt, and she knows which ones to use. She's . . . She's a predator, that's what she is, and she goes for the weak spots. She really piled it on with Laurel. First her father, then you. Stab, stab, claw."

"Fathers, or parents, are weak spots with a lot of people. What Laurel's made of herself, in a lot of ways despite them, is something to be proud of."

"I completely agree, but it's easier for you and me because we didn't have to deal with despite. We always had love and support. And knowing your father was weak enough—and just had the extremely bad taste—to have an affair with Linda's a tough one to swallow. And while Laurel's choking that down, Linda bitch slaps her with how everyone's talking and laughing at her about you, about her *delusions* that you'd ever be serious about someone like her, and *insults* her with all that 'everyone knows she's after the Brown money and status anyway because look where and what she comes from.'"

She paused a moment, just to seethe, and Del let the silence ride as he turned it all over in his mind.

"Which tied it up in a big ugly bow," Emma continued, "making her the pathetic gold digger and you the slime who's just banging his sister's friend because he can. And because that's exactly the way Linda thinks, she pushes that knife in with authority. It made Laurel cry, and you have to practically beat her with sticks to make her cry. If Linda hadn't been gone when I got there, I'd have . . . And oh shit, *shit*, Laurel didn't tell you about this."

"She told me about Linda and running her off. But she left out several salient points."

"Damn it, Del, *damn it*! You maneuvered me into telling you the rest."

"Maybe I did, but don't I have a right to know?"

"You may have the right to know, but I didn't have the right to tell you. You set me up so I'd betray a friend."

"You didn't betray anyone." He pulled into the nursery lot, parked, then turned to her. "Listen, how can I fix it if I don't know?"

"If Laurel wanted you to fix it—"

"Apparently Laurel gets pissed at the idea of my fixing anything. But leave that out for a minute. Linda's a problem, and she's a problem for all of us. But in this specific incident, she went after Laurel. She hurt her. Weren't you going to say you'd have taken her on over it yourself if you'd known at the time?"

"Yes, but—"

"Do you think I'm with Laurel just because I can be? That I'm sleeping with her because she's available?"

"No, of course not."

"But there's part of her that thinks so."

"That's not for me to answer, and it's not fair for you to ask me."

"Okay, I'll rephrase the question."

She yanked off her sunglasses so she could glare at him. "Don't pull the lawyer crap on me, Delaney. I'm so mad at you right now."

"I needed to know. She won't let me in this area. Part's pride, I think, but another's half believing it. And maybe that's my fault, or some of it's my fault. I got the idea it might be something along these lines yesterday, but I needed confirmation."

"Good for you." She started to wrench open her door. He laid a hand on her arm.

"Emma, by not knowing, not dealing with it or acting on it, I'm hurting her. I don't want to hurt her."

"You should've asked her directly."

"She wouldn't tell me. You know she wouldn't, not unless I have a way to push her into a corner over it. Now I do. Damn it, I hurt her yesterday by offering to pay for a bunch of groceries, because I just didn't get it. It's not about Linda, though I'd already intended to deal with her, and will. It's about me and Laurel."

"You've got that part right." She heaved out a sigh. "But you've put me in a hell of a spot, Del."

"I'm sorry, and I'm going to keep you there by asking you not to say anything to her about this. Not until I can talk to her. If she doesn't believe, all the way, in what we have, it's never going to work. It's never going to fit. And if I'm responsible for that, even part of the way, I have to make it right. So I'm asking for you to give me a chance to make it right."

"God, you're good. How am I supposed to say no to that?"

"I mean it. She and I need to strip away some of the armor, and some of the cushion, and see what's under it. I want you to give me a chance to do that."

"I love you both, and I want both of you happy. So, believe me, Del, you'd better figure it out. Screw it up, or let her screw it up, and I'm blaming you."

"That's fair. Are you going to stay mad at me?"

"I'll let you know after you talk to her."

"Emma." He leaned over, kissed her cheek.

"Oh." This time she heaved out a breath. "Let's go buy some plants."

He struggled to be patient as the scanning, scouting, selection took endless amounts of time. Plus whenever he so much as thought about nudging her along, Emma simply shot him a steely stare.

In the end, they loaded what they could in the car and arranged for the rest—and there was plenty of *rest*—to be delivered.

"Take her down to the beach," Emma said on the drive back. "Away from the rest of us. Don't try to talk to her about this in or around the house. Too many possibilities of interruption. If you're interrupted, she'll have a chance to regroup or evade."

"That's a good point. Thanks."

"Don't thank me. I may not be doing it for you. I may be doing it only for her."

"Either way."

"A long walk, and believe me, if she comes back from it upset, I'm kicking your ass. Or I'll have Jack do it."

"I'm not sure he could kick my ass. But you could."

"Keep that in mind, and don't screw this up." She paused a moment. "Do you love her?"

"Of course I do."

She turned to him. "That's a stupid answer. A stupid thing to say. I really ought to kick your ass."

"Why—?"

"No." She shook her head and stared straight ahead. "No more pointers. You have to deal with this yourself or it's not real. I'm going to stay out of the way. I'm going to start right in on these plants, so I'll be out of the way. That's the best thing I can do for both of you." She bit her lip. "But don't say 'of course,' you idiot."

"Okay."

When he pulled up at the house, Emma was true to her word. She unloaded the tools they'd bought and dug, literally, right in.

But plans to lure Laurel off for that long walk had to be postponed.

"Laurel went off with Parker. Shopping," Jack told him. "Parker wanted some stuff for the house. She had a list. And there was talk about earrings. Mac's in the pool, Carter's down at the beach with one of his books, Mal's somewhere. I'm about to head down there."

"Did they say when they'd be back? Laurel and Parker?"

"Dude, they went shopping. It could be an hour or three or four days."

"Right."

"Problem?"

"No. No. Just wondering."

Jack slid on his sunglasses. "Beach?"

"Yeah. I'll come down in a bit."

"I guess I have to see if Emma wants some help before I go down—thanks a lot for that."

"Wait until the rest of it gets here. We didn't have room for most of it."

"Great."

When they didn't come back in an hour, he fought off the first prickles of irritation. He paced the deck, going over various possible scenarios in his head, as he would before going into court.

He heard Emma's voice, Jack's, Carter's, Mac's, Mal's— come and go. He spotted them on the beach, in the water, on the walkway. When he heard the group of them come in—probably digging up lunch—he went out for a solitary swim and more thinking.

As the afternoon wore on, he considered calling Laurel's cell. He nearly gave in and did so when he finally saw Parker's car turn in the drive.

He headed down while the two of them unloaded a mountain of shopping bags and giggled like a couple of kids with both hands in the cookie jar.

He had no excuse for it, but it annoyed the hell out of him.

"Oh, Emma, that looks fabulous!" Parker called out.

"It absolutely does, and I'm not nearly done."

"Take a break. Come see what we got. We had the best time. Hey." Laurel stopped to shoot a grin at Del. "Just in time to help haul all this stuff. And God, it's way past time to start up the blender, because shopping's made us thirsty for beach margaritas."

"I was starting to get worried." He heard the tone of his own voice, nearly winced.

"Oh, don't fuss, Daddy. Haul." She pushed bags at him. "Em, we found the most amazing gift shop. We have to go back!"

"You mean they have something left?" Mal wandered over to take some bags.

"I think we hit every shop within fifty miles, but we left a few things behind. Don't look so put out." Laurel laughed at Del. "I bought you something."

With no choice, he carried bags upstairs. And had to stand back while the women tore into them to show off their scores.

"Why don't we take a walk on the beach?" he asked Laurel.

"Are you kidding? I've walked a half a million miles. Must have margarita. Who's in charge of the blender?" she called out.

"Got that covered." Mal headed off to the kitchen.

Del shot Emma a look, hopeful for a little help. She merely shrugged and went back to admiring the take.

Payback, he thought.

"Here." Laurel offered him a box. "A memento."

Since he couldn't beat them, Del settled down.

"A sun catcher," she told him when he opened it.

"Recycled beach glass." She reached out to finger one of the smooth, colored shards. "I thought you might like to hang it in your place—to bring back good times."

"It's great." He tapped a piece so several danced and clicked together. "It really is. Thanks."

"I got a smaller one for my sitting room. Couldn't resist."

They drank margaritas, talked about dinner. He couldn't budge her.

Patience, he reminded himself.

He managed to take his own advice until nearly sunset.

"Walk. Beach. You and me." He grabbed her hand, pulled her toward the door.

"But we're going to—"

"Later."

"Pushy," she said, but linked her fingers with his. "And God, it does feel great out here. Look at the sky. I guess I owe the beach a visit since I spent most of the day shopping." She flicked a finger at her newest earrings. "But now I have such pretty things to remind me of these two weeks. When we're socked in next winter, I'll be able to look around and say, summer's coming back."

"I want you to be happy."

"Right now, your wish, my command. I am happy."

"I need to talk to you, to ask you something."

"Sure." She turned, walking backward to look up at the house. "Emma was right about the plants, the grasses."

"Laurel, I need you to pay attention."

She stopped. "All right. What's wrong?"

"I'm not entirely sure. I need you to tell me."

"Then nothing's wrong."

"Laurel." He took both her hands. "You didn't tell me that Linda came at you about me. About you and me." He felt her hands go rigid in his.

"I told you I dealt with Linda. Emma had no right to—"

"Not her fault. I maneuvered it out of her. She thought you'd told me the whole story. And you should have. More, Laurel, much more, you should've told me you felt any part of what she said might be true. If I've done or said anything to make you think that way—"

"You haven't. Let's forget it."

"No." He tightened his grip when she would've pulled her hands free. "She hurt you, and indirectly so did I. I can't forget I had any part in hurting you."

"Forget it, Del. Absolved. I don't want to talk about Linda."

"We're not. We're talking you and me. Damn it, Laurel, can't you be straight with me? Can't we be straight with each other?"

"I am. I said it's nothing."

"It's not. It's damn well not when you get so twisted up when I offer to pay for some damn groceries. Or a cake I've asked you to bake. It's not about that either, but what's under it."

"And I said, clearly, you don't need to pull out your wallet. I won't have you *hiring* me—"

"Laurel." His tone, utterly reasonable, stopped her. "I never intended that. Never. And you should know. You've said this has to be equal ground, but it can't be if you don't tell me what you want, what you need, what you're feeling."

"How can you not know?" she demanded.

"Because you don't tell me."

"Tell you? All this time. You can look at me, touch me, be with me, and not know?"

She whirled away, spun back. "All right, all right. I'm responsible for my own feelings, and clearly it's stupid for me to wait and wait and hope you might *see*. You need me to tell you, I'll tell you. Equal ground? It's never going to be equal ground when you care about me and I'm so hopelessly in love with you. I've always been hopelessly in love with you, and you've never seen it."

"Wait—"

"No, you want it straight? You'll get it straight. You're the one. You've always been the one. Nothing, *nothing* I've ever done changed it. Moving to New York, working to find my way, making myself into *something* I could be proud of. But it was still there. Del's the one, and whatever I do, whatever I accomplish, I'm still missing that. Trying to feel something real and important for other men? Temporary stopgaps, or failures. Because none of them were you."

She yanked the hair out of her face as the wind blew it into her eyes. "I couldn't harden it out or reason it out of me, no matter how hurtful or humiliating or just plain infuriating. I dealt with it, then I changed it. I changed it, Del."

"You're right." He reached out to brush the tears she rarely shed from her cheeks. "Listen—"

"I'm not *finished*. I changed things, but you're still trying, you always will try, to take *care* of things. Of me. I don't want to be your responsibility. Your obligation. Your pet. I won't have it."

"For God's sake, I don't think of you that way. I don't feel that way. I love you."

"Yes, you love me. You love all of us, and you had to step to the front of the line when your parents died. I know that, Del, I understand, and I *feel* for you and what you had to take on. Being with you, I understand more, and I feel more."

"It's not about that."

"In some ways, it's always about that. But it's different now, with us. Or it should be. I'm okay with the way things are—or I was. Didn't I just tell you I was happy? What I need and want? If I have to tell you, give you a damn list, then it's *not* what I need and want. I'm not asking you for declarations. I'm not asking for promises. I can live in the moment, and be happy in the moment. I'm entitled to be hurt and upset when someone like Linda scrapes me raw. And I'm entitled to keep it to myself until I grow fresh skin. I don't need you taking care of it. I don't need or want you to make it all better. I don't need you pushing at me about my feelings when I never push at you."

"No," he murmured, "you don't. Why don't you?"

"Maybe I don't want to hear the answers. No, I don't want to hear them," she said before he could speak. "I don't

want to hear what you have to say when I've ripped myself
open and I feel like a fool. You can't expect me to. I need to
walk this off. I need to pull myself together. You need to let
me. You need to go away."

He watched her run down the beach. He could go after
her, he thought. He could catch her, and he could make her
listen. And if he did, she wouldn't hear him.

He let her go.

She needed more than words, he realized. And he wanted
to give her more. She might have ripped herself open, he
thought, but by doing so she'd shown him, very clearly,
what was inside him.

SHE RAN IT OFF, WALKED IT OFF, SETTLED HERSELF. THE
truth was, she'd come to understand, that moment on the
beach would have happened at some time, at some place.
She couldn't have coasted forever. Neither of them could or
would. Better it happened sooner than later.

If it ended things with Del, she'd heal. She knew how to
tend her own wounds, accept her own scars.

He'd be kind; she'd hate it. Then they'd move on. Somehow.

She went up to her room by the outside stairs, hoping to
avoid everyone until morning.

But her three friends waited for her.

Emma rose. "I'm sorry. I'm so sorry I said anything to
him about Linda."

"It's not your fault, and it doesn't matter."

"It is, and it does. I'm sorry."

"It's my mother who set off the bomb," Mac said. "I'm
sorry."

"He's my brother." Parker held out a hand. "I'm sorry."

"Well, we're a really sorry group." Laurel sat on the bed.
"Nobody's to blame, really. It just is what it is. But I think
I'll skip the fun and games tonight. You can make an excuse, right? Headache, shopping fatigue, one too many
margaritas."

"Sure, but . . ." Mac trailed off, looked at Parker and Emma.

"What? What now?"

"Del's gone." Parker sat beside her.

"Gone? What do you mean *gone*?"

"He said he'd be back in the morning. That he had to go take care of something. He made it sound like work, but . . ."

"Nobody bought that." Laurel put her head in her hands. "Great. Just great. I told him to go away. Since when does he listen? Now everything's screwed up. I should've gone away. For God's sake, it's his house."

"He'll be back." Emma stepped over to rub Laurel's back. "He probably just wanted to give you a little space. You'll make up, honey."

"It's not about making up. The things I said . . . "

"Everybody says rotten things when they're mad or upset," Mac told her.

"I told him I loved him, always had. That there'd never been anyone else. Basically, I ripped out my own heart and threw it at him."

"What did he say?" Parker demanded.

"That's about the time I told him I didn't want to hear it, and to go away. And I stalked off. Okay, I ran off."

"He didn't come after you?" Emma huffed. "Idiot."

"No, really. He knows enough to be sure I meant it. I didn't expect him to actually leave. You can know someone all your life, and they can still surprise you. Let's just try not to have this spoil everything. I think I'd be literally sick if it did. I just want to go to bed."

"We'll stay with you," Emma murmured.

"No, really. I'm going to bed, and you can all do me a favor by going out there and fostering the pretense that everything's fine. Situation normal. I'd really appreciate it."

"Okay," Parker said before Emma could protest. "If you need company or anything else, you just have to knock on my door."

"I know. I'll be all right, and I'll be better in the morning."

"If you're not, and you want to go home, we'll go." Parker pulled her in for a hug.

"Or we'll kick the men out and stay," Mac told her.

"Best friends ever. I'll be fine."

She stayed where she was when they left her, but knowing one of them would come back to check on her in an hour, she made herself get up, get ready for bed.

She'd had her summer, she reminded herself. No one could ever take that away from her. She'd had the love of her life for a season. Not everyone could say the same.

She'd survive. And because, even if they couldn't be lovers, they would always be family, she and Del would find a way to heal the rift.

She lay in the dark and ached. Ached and ached. And she tried to comfort herself that it would get better with time. Then she turned her face into the pillow and wept a little, because she didn't believe it.

The sea breeze whispered over her cheek like a kiss. Sweet and soft. She sighed with it, wanting to cling to sleep, to cling to the numbness that came with it.

"You need to wake up."

She opened her eyes and stared into Del's. "What?"

"Wake up, get up. Come with me."

"What?" She pushed at him, struggled to think. The light was the quiet dull silver of predawn. "What are you doing? Where did you go? What are you doing back?"

"Up."

She tried to snag the sheet when he pulled it off, but missed. "You walked out on your friends. You left when—"

"Oh, just shut up. I listened to you, now you'll listen to me. Let's go."

"Where?"

"Down to the beach to finish this."

"I'm not going down to the beach with you. We had our scene, now it's done."

"You are a contrary woman, Laurel. You can walk or I

can drag you, but we're going to the damn beach. If you ask me why, I swear, the dragging begins."

"I need to get dressed."

He studied her tank and boxers. "You're covered. Don't test me, McBane. I haven't had any sleep, and I've had a long drive. I'm not in the mood."

"You're not in the mood. Isn't that something?" She swung her legs off the bed, planted her feet on the floor. "All right, we'll do this at the beach since that's so important to you."

She slapped his hand away when he reached for hers. "I didn't have the best night either, and I haven't had coffee. Don't *you* test *me*."

She stalked out onto the deck, down the stairs.

"You might as well settle down," he advised. "There's no point being pissed."

"I see points."

"You usually do. Lucky, I'm more even-tempered."

"My ass. Who threatened to drag who out of bed in the middle of the night?"

"Nearly sunrise. That's pretty good timing, actually. I like it. New day dawning and all that." He kicked off his shoes at the base of the beach steps. "We didn't get much farther than this last night. Geographically. I think we can do better in other areas. Here's a start."

He spun her around, yanked her into a hot and possessive kiss. She shoved against him, met a solid and immovable wall. He let her go when she went stiff.

"Don't," she said, quietly now.

"You need to look at me, and listen to me, and Laurel, you need to hear me." He took her by the shoulders, but gently. "Maybe you're right, and I don't see, but goddamn it, you don't hear. So, I'm looking, and I'm seeing. You listen, and you hear."

"All right. All right. There's no point in us being angry over this. It's just—"

"You can't hear if you don't shut up."

"Tell me to shut up again," she invited, with a dare in her eyes.

He simply laid his hand over her mouth. "I'm going to fix this. Fixing things is what I do, who I am. If you love me, you're going to have to accept that."

He dropped his hand. "I can fight with you. I've got no problem with that."

"Lucky for you."

"But I hate that I hurt you by being careless on one hand and too careful on the other. It's a Brown trait, I guess, trying to keep the balance."

"I'm responsible—"

"For your own feelings, yeah, yeah, yeah. I don't know if you were always the one. I got used to looking at you and thinking about you another way. So I just don't know."

"I understand that, Del. I do. I—"

"Be quiet, and *listen*. You changed what was between us. You took the step, and I didn't see it coming. I can't be sorry for that when I'm so damn grateful for it. I don't know if you were always the one," he said again. "But I know you're the one now, and I know you're going to be the one tomorrow, and next month, next year. And you're going to be the one for the rest of my life."

"What?"

"You heard me. Need it simpler? It's you."

She looked at him, the face she knew so well. And saw. And in that moment, her heart simply flew.

"I've loved you all your life, and that was easy. I don't know, not for certain, how long I've been in love with you, but I know it's not so easy. But it's right and it's real, and I don't want easy. I want you."

"I think . . ." She laughed a little. "I can't think."

"Good. Don't think. Just listen, listen and stop, for once, trying to project what I think and feel. I thought the logical thing was to take it slow, to give us both time to adjust to what happened between us. To what happened in me."

He took her hand, pressed it to his heart.

"I thought you needed to catch up, so you were right about that. I didn't see. I should have. But you didn't see either. You didn't see how much I love you, how much I want you, how much I need you. I'll buy those two dogs if I want pets, and I already have a sister. That's not how I think of you, and it's sure as hell not how I want you to think of me. That makes us even. Even ground, Laurel, that's where we're standing."

"You mean it."

"How long have you known me?"

Her eyes blurred, but she blinked them clear. "A really long time."

"Then you know I mean it."

"I love you so much. I told myself I'd get over you, and it was such a lie. I never would."

"I'm not finished." He reached in his pocket, watched her eyes go huge when he pulled out the box, opened it. "It was my mother's."

"I know. I . . . Oh God. Del."

"I took it out of the vault a couple weeks ago."

"Weeks ago," she managed.

"It was after the night at the pond. Everything had already changed direction, but after that night—really after that day when you came to my office, I knew where we were—or where I wanted us to go. I had it resized for you. That was probably a little arrogant, but you'll have to live with it."

"Del." She couldn't get her breath. "You can't— Your mother's ring. Parker."

"I woke her before I woke you. She's good with it. She said to tell you don't be stupid. Our parents loved you."

"Oh, damn it." The tears simply flooded her face. "I don't want to cry. I can't help it."

"You're the only one I've ever thought about asking to wear this. The only one I want to wear it. I've just driven all the way to Greenwich and back to get it for you. To give it to you because you're the only one. Marry me, Laurel."

"I won't be stupid. Kiss me again first, when I'm not wishing I didn't love you."

She felt the sea breeze on her skin, in her hair as their lips met, and the strong, steady beat of his heart against hers. And heard the whistles and cheers.

Turning her head so her cheek rested on his, she saw the group gathered on the deck of the house above. "Parker woke everyone up."

"Well, ours has always been a family affair." He drew back. "Ready?"

"Yes. I'm absolutely and completely ready."

The ring he slid on her finger sparkled in the first beams of the sun while the eastern sky blossomed like a rose. A moment, she thought, to savor, then sealed their moment with another kiss.

"This is the right time," she told him. "This is a good place. Tell me one more time I'm the one."

"You're the one." He cupped her face again. "The only one."

The one, she thought, on this fresh new day. And the one through all the days after.

Hand in hand, they started back up the steps to share the next moments with family.